The Last Chopper Out

A JIM McGILL NOVEL

Joseph Flynn

Stray Dog Press, Inc.
Springfield, IL
2017

PRAISE FOR JOSEPH FLYNN AND HIS NOVELS

"Flynn is an excellent storyteller." — *Booklist*

"Flynn propels his plot with potent but flexible force."
— *Publishers Weekly*

The President's Henchman
"Marvelously entertaining." — *ForeWord Magazine*

Digger
"A mystery cloaked as cleverly as (and perhaps better than) any John Grisham work." — *Denver Post*

"Surefooted, suspenseful and in its breathless final moments unexpectedly heartbreaking." — *Booklist*

The Next President
"*The Next President* bears favorable comparison to such classics as *The Best Man, Advise and Consent* and *The Manchurian Candidate.*"
— *Booklist*

"A thriller fast enough to read in one sitting."
— *Rocky Mountain News*

BY JOSEPH FLYNN

The Jim McGill Series

The President's Henchman, A Jim McGill Novel [#1]
The Hangman's Companion, A JimMcGill Novel [#2]
The K Street Killer A JimMcGill Novel [#3]
Part 1: The Last Ballot Cast, A JimMcGill Novel [#4 Part 1]
Part 2: The Last Ballot Cast, A JimMcGill Novel [#5 Part 2]
The Devil on the Doorstep, A Jim McGill Novel [#6]
The Good Guy with a Gun, A Jim McGill Novel [#7]
The Echo of the Whip, A Jim McGill Novel [#8]
The Daddy's Girl Decoy, A Jim McGill Novel [#9]
The Last Chopper Out, A Jim McGill Novel [#10]

McGill's Short Cases 1-3

The Ron Ketchum Mystery Series

Nailed, A Ron Ketchum Mystery [#1]
Defiled, A Ron Ketchum Mystery Featuring John Tall Wolf [#2]
Impaled, A Ron Ketchum Mystery [#3]

The John Tall Wolf Series

Tall Man in Ray-Bans, A John Tall Wolf Novel [#1]
War Party, A John Tall Wolf Novel [#2]
Super Chief, A John Tall Wolf Novel [#3]
Smoke Signals, A John Tall Wolf Novel [#4]

The Zeke Edison Series

Kill Me Twice, A Zeke Edison Novel [#1]

Stand Alone Novels

The Concrete Inquisition
Digger
The Next President
Hot Type
Farewell Performance
Gasoline, Texas
Round Robin, A Love Story of Epic Proportions
One False Step
Blood Street Punx
Still Coming
Still Coming Expanded Edition
Hangman — A Western Novella
Pointy Teeth, Twelve Bite-Size Stories

Published by Stray Dog Press, Inc.
Springfield, IL 62704, U.S.A.

Visit the author's web site: *www.josephflynn.com*

Flynn, Joseph
The Last Chopper Out / Joseph Flynn
452 p.
ISBN 978-0-9974500-2-6
ISBN eBook 978-0-9974500-1-9

Printed in the United States of America

PUBLISHER'S NOTE
This is a work of fiction. Names, characters, places, and incidents are either the product of the author's imagination or are used fictitiously; any resemblance to actual persons, living or dead, events, or locales is entirely coincidental.

Book design by Aha! Designs
Cover photo courtesy of adobe.com

DEDICATION

To C.R. Flynn, one of the two great loves of my life

ACKNOWLEDGEMENTS

Catherine, Cat, Anne, Susan and Meghan do their level best to catch all my typos and other mistakes, but I usually outwit them. For this book, I've added the efforts of my Advance Reading Team. I thank them for their input and interest. Please be kind, if one or two tiny errors remain. David Fitzgerald, formerly of the United States Navy submarine service, provided info on how those incredible boats work. If there are any errors on this subject, the fault is mine alone

CHARACTER LIST

[in alphabetical order by last name]

Eugene Beck, investigator for McGill Investigations
Abra Benjamin, Special Agent, FBI
Gawayne Blessing, White House head butler
Ellie Booker, independent news producer
Rebecca Bramley, investigator for McGill Investigations
Rockelle Bullard, Metro Police captain
Edwina Byington, the President's personal secretary
Gabbi Casale, partner in McGill Investigations
Celsus Crogher, retired Secret Service SAC
Layla Dart, Senator Oren Worth's campaign manager
Father Inigo de Loyola, Jesuit priest, former guerrilla
Byron DeWitt, Deputy Director of the FBI
Deirdre "Didi" DiMarco, WWN news show host
Carolyn [McGill] Enquist, first wife of Jim McGill
Patricia Darden Grant, President of the United States, second wife of Jim McGill
Giles Henry, British tabloid reporter
Michael Jaworsky, United States Attorney General
SAC Elspeth Kendry, head of the Presidential Protection Detail
Monty Kipp, broadcast reporter for Satellite News America
Ron Ketchum, partner in McGill Investigations
Donald "Deke" Ky, Jim McGill's personal Secret Service bodyguard
Brad Lewis, partner in McGill Investigations
Auric Ludwig, imprisoned gun lobbyist
Leo Levy, Jim McGill's personal driver
Dorie McBride, Patti Grant's former talent agent
Jim McGill, the President's husband, aka The President's Henchman
Abbie McGill, eldest child of Jim McGill and Carolyn Enquist
Ken McGill, middle child of Jim McGill and Carolyn Enquist
Caitie McGill, youngest child of Jim McGill and Carolyn Enquist
Marvin Meeker, Metro Police detective
Galia Mindel, White House chief of staff
Corona Moe, homicide wholesaler
Frank Morrissey, White House assistant chief of staff
Jean Morrissey, Vice President of the U.S.
Jerry Nerón, imprisoned killer and master tailor
Maj Olson, investigator for McGill Investigations

Randall Pennyman, fugitive and former U.S. Senator
Keely Powell, investigator for McGill Investigations
Yves Pruet, partner in McGill Investigations
Odo Sacripant, partner in McGill Investigations
Putnam Shady, head lobbyist of ShareAmerica, Sweetie's husband
Margaret "Sweetie" Sweeney, McGill's longtime friend and police partner; Putnam's wife
John Tall Wolf, Director of Justice Services, Bureau of Indian Affairs
Taps, aka Chris Springer, contract assassin
Clare Tracy, New York fundraiser, Jim McGill's former girlfriend
Michael Walker, aka Beemer, Metro Police detective
Oren Worth, U.S. Senate Majority Leader and presidential candidate
Kira Yates, wife of Welborn Yates
Welborn Yates, the President's personal (official) investigator, Air Force general

CHAPTER 1

Monday, September 12, 2016 — Washington, DC

At 6:30 a.m., Leo Levy pulled Jim McGill's armored and supercharged Chevy into the gated underground parking area of the sleek new three-story structure on O Street just off Wisconsin Avenue in Georgetown. Set between the garage entrance and a walk-in door was a brushed nickel sign bearing incised black letters in a sans serif font that read: McGill Investigations International, LLP.

The building was clad in pale gray marble and glazed with one-way black polycarbonate resin windows. The people inside could see out; the people outside could not see in. Neither could the latter group shoot out the windows with anything smaller than a .50 caliber round. If hostile forces brought weapons of that magnitude, there were discreet battlements notched in the roof's parapet from which defenders could return fire.

In times of a perceived high threat, the sliding structural steel gate at the entrance to the parking area could be reinforced by outer and inner rings of bollards — heavyweight vehicle barriers — that rose and retracted upon encrypted radio commands. Anyone trying to use an explosive-packed car or truck to blow up the building from below was going to face serious challenges.

Likewise, all of the building's cyber infrastructure had been designed by the best minds in Silicon Valley and was updated frequently, at irregular intervals. The Silicon Valley tech wizards had been informed that a team of their peers from the NSA had been retained to try to beat their work. It was great fun for the two teams to have at each other, and it was a stream of steady revenue for both parties.

All of these precautions had been the ideas of President Patricia Grant. She'd told McGill, "I'd like at least another 30 good years with you, and I'm prepared to pay to reach that goal."

"Money well spent," McGill had said.

He thought maybe she'd been taking things a step too far with the small, discreet anti-aircraft batteries on the roof, but she reminded him of the computer generated video the Secret Service had made of the two of them being killed by an armed drone at her second inauguration. The President told McGill that drones had come a long way since then, so …

He had ceased to think of such a precaution as foolish. In fact, he wondered how long it would be before there was a countrywide demand for anti-aircraft emplacements. If only to keep creepy neighbors from snooping on bedroom windows.

McGill, Sweetie, Deke and Leo took the stairs from the garage to the first floor. There was an elevator, of course, but adjacent to it was a sign: *Don't neglect your cardio fitness.* They didn't. Waiting for them, behind a reception desk in the lobby, was Dikki Missirian, McGill's former landlord at his old, far more humble business location.

Dikki still owned his properties and was looking to buy more, but he'd turned over responsibility for maintaining those holdings to his newly arrived cousin, Aart, Americanized as Artie. When McGill had offered Dikki the chance to work as his new facility manager, he'd jumped at the opportunity.

He smiled at the new arrivals and asked, "Coffee, cocoa or mineral water?"

There were also beers, wines and spirits available, but McGill had already put out the word that drinking alcohol before the sun had set would be frowned upon unless champagne was offered at a celebratory occasion.

Dikki went to the company kitchen to fetch three coffees and a cocoa as the foursome headed to the boss's office on the third floor, taking the stairs again. Even the staircase was flooded with natural light thanks to the central courtyard around which the building had been constructed. Every room in the building, save the lavatories, utility closets and the garage, had a view of the outside world.

Besides McGill's suite on the third floor, there was an office for Sweetie, a conference room and spaces for visiting partners and additional senior hires.

Upon seeing the building's architectural drawings for the first time, McGill had told Patti, "Sam Spade never had digs like this."

"Yes, well," she'd replied, "private eyes don't wear fedoras anymore, either."

"Or even trench coats, for the most part," McGill agreed. "Still, I'm wondering if we'll be able to generate enough revenue to justify such a palace."

"There's no mortgage, and from what I've seen of life the past eight years there's more than enough wickedness in the world for you to keep the lights on."

McGill couldn't argue with that. He bowed to his wife's superior logic and stole a kiss just to show she was right that scoundrels were thick on the ground. Sometimes they might even be found right under your very nose.

Patti had used the same architectural firm to put up her new headquarters for Committed Capital, her philanthropic venture capital shop. It was also located in Washington but a few miles from McGill's place of business. Each of them had a reasonable amount of elbow room and wouldn't casually drop in and interrupt the other's workday just to say hello. They both subscribed to Kahlil Gibran's wise advice: "Let there be spaces in your togetherness."

Besides the two places of commerce, the President and McGill had also bought a home in the nation's capital. Galia Mindel had found them a house in Dumbarton Oaks, just down the block from where she lived. Too close for McGill's taste until he learned Galia had bought an apartment in Manhattan and intended to spend most of her time in New York. That being the case, McGill liked the new house.

It was big enough to board the kids when they came to visit, but not so large that if he or Patti dropped a fork it would produce an echo. The grounds were gorgeous and the missus said she'd hire people to tend to the plant life so he wouldn't have to bother with a mower or a pair of clippers. He could laze in a lounge chair out back or swim laps in the pool if he started getting soft around the edges.

McGill decided that if he ever felt he was becoming too much of a swell he'd dig up videos of *Burke's Law,* the '60s cop show in which Gene Barry played a millionaire LAPD detective who rode around in a chauffeured Rolls-Royce. If kitsch like that didn't embarrass him, well, he could always count on Sweetie to give him a smack on the back of his head.

Dikki arrived in McGill's office with the coffee, cocoa and a bottle of San Pellegrino for himself. He was a member of the corporate family, after all. Always welcome in casual moments.

McGill and the others adjourned to the conference room to wait for his other new partners to arrive from points around the country and overseas.

South China Sea

United States Navy Destroyer Squadron One, DESRON1, part of Carrier Strike Group One, was en route from Subic Bay in the Philippines to Singapore when two Chinese Air Force Shenyang J-15 fighter aircraft buzzed the three ships in the formation: the USS *Gridley,* the USS *Higgins* and the USS *Russell.*

Buzz, of course, was an understatement. The jet-wash — exhaust — from a fighter plane could knock over a city bus. Sailors on the decks of the American ships risked getting flung into the sea like litter in a tornado. The commander of DESRON1, Captain Reynauld

"Ray" Winston, was not amused.

"If they do that again —" He paused to consider his next words carefully.

Winston's executive officer, Harlan Pine, said, "We've already warned them once. So next time we tell them that's strike two, and after that they're out?"

Winston shook his head. "Fuck that. Nobody's playing baseball here. They've been warned. They come back and we shoot them the hell out of the sky."

"Yes, sir, but shouldn't we get confirmation from Admiral Crocker at the strike group before we respond with … justified defensive measures?"

"You know what I intend to do?" Captain Winston asked.

"What's that, sir?"

"I'm going to vote for Jean Morrissey. Never in my life thought I'd vote for a woman to be president, but did you read what she said at that press conference yesterday? She said, 'Nobody fucks with the United States military.' She came right out in public and said 'fuck,' but it was in the perfect context. I almost burst with pride. I've read she's going to marry some FBI man but, damnit, I wanted to marry her myself when I heard that."

"You're not the only Navy man who feels that way, sir," the XO said with a smile. "For any number of reasons."

The two men shared a laugh.

And then the message came through that the Chinese fighter jets were returning.

The captain said there was no time to consult with anyone now. The safety of DESRON1 and its sailors was his responsibility, and he was sure both the Navy and Vice President Morrissey would back him up.

He'd also bet his life the damn Chinese didn't know his ship's motto: *Ignis ubi paratus.* Fire when ready. The saying came from Admiral Dewey's historic command issued during the battle of Manila Bay in the Spanish-American War: "You may fire when you are ready, *Gridley.*"

That *Gridley,* of course, was the first vessel to bear the proud name.

The captain of its fourth generation successor now gave permission to fire to all three of the ships in his squadron.

Washington, DC

The one step President Patricia Grant hadn't taken in defense of her husband's workplace was to have the city block on which it sat closed off to pedestrian and vehicular traffic. Not that she hadn't thought of doing it. She would have needed to pull strings and offer favors to any number of people in both the District and federal governments to make it happen, but she could have done it. What stopped her was the certain knowledge that Jim would have put his foot down.

He'd been reasonable — a sweetheart, really — about going along with her other precautions, but she knew there were limits to his forbearance. He was used to being the man who made things safe for other people, and he'd done a fine job of it. The fact that he'd even agreed to permit Special Agent Ky and Leo Levy to safeguard him all these years had been a major concession.

His bow to having his new place of business fortified like … well, *almost* like the White House had been another big compromise. Of course, prior to World War Two, the public had been allowed to wander the White House grounds at will. Stories, perhaps fanciful, perhaps not, had it that Eleanor Roosevelt used to chase off cars parked in the White House driveway that held young couples expressing physical affection for each other.

After the bombing of Pearl Harbor, all that ended and the Executive Mansion became an ever more tightly secure site. Bill Clinton had once referred to it as "the crown jewel of the federal prison system." Left unsaid by Clinton and his successors was that the world was becoming a relentlessly more dangerous place. Especially for presidents and their families.

That was why Secret Service protection was extended to former chief executives and their better halves. Only there had never been any spouse like James J. McGill before. So Patricia Grant did as much as she could to protect the man she loved while accepting that there were limits.

The continuing public access to O Street meant there was nobody to stop a tall, lean individual wearing sunglasses and dressed in black from strolling past McGill's fancy new office building. It was the prepossessed individual indeed who didn't spare the structure at least a glance. Many a passerby stopped in his tracks to look at it, most taking note of the name on the plaque next to the door.

The person in black, whose working name was Taps, didn't break stride, didn't stare but did look at McGill's HQ. Taps scanned it side to side, top to bottom. Assessing all there was to see. Even taking note of the circular indentations with black caps forming an arc outside the shiny steel garage door. Bollards obviously.

Add them to the steel door fronting the garage and you had the modern equivalents of a drawbridge and a portcullis. The pedestrian door had to be as sturdy as a bank vault.

There was no reason not to think that many more defensive measures abounded throughout the structure. More than that, Taps thought, there were likely also features on hand to *counterattack* any assault on the building. Still, that was no reason for real concern. Doing a quick reconnaissance of the building was simply an exercise in due diligence, nothing more.

Taps moved on along O Street without looking back.

Scratch McGill's offices as a place to kill him, that being Taps' job.

Paid for in advance, per custom.

The job would get done regardless. Taps soaked up the layout of Georgetown. Pedestrians and motor traffic moved through it in a steady and substantial flow. It seemed to be a fine place to create large-scale havoc, and once you panicked the mob, well, who would notice a particular individual going down?

The longer Taps rambled along Wisconsin Avenue, the better

the place looked.

An idea to catch McGill unaware came to mind. A ploy to subvert the man's own character. Invite him to take part in his own undoing.

A crew would be needed.

Taps found a quiet corner in a restaurant and called Corona Moe.

McGill Investigations International, LLP

The partners of McGill's newly expanded firm met in the third-floor conference room. Pretending a nonchalance that he didn't feel, McGill sat at the head of the table. He would have been more comfortable sitting somewhere in the middle of things, able to keep an eye on anyone he chose without being conspicuous about it. Those days, however, appeared to be over.

He'd have to ask Patti for pointers about how to be the big boss without coming off like a jerk. Maybe she took a charm pill every morning with her multi-vitamin. If it was something more complicated than that, he might be in trouble.

No, he'd be all right. Sweetie was sitting on his right at the conference table, able to give him a kick on the leg if he got too full of himself. She'd also be based with him in Washington, which would be a big help with any investigations done in the city.

Deke sat to his left. He'd resign from the Secret Service when Patti's second term was over at noon on January 20, 2017. He'd also work out of the O Street building. His area of responsibility would be handling investigations from Virginia to Maine.

Seated next to Sweetie was Brad Lewis, McGill's old detective friend from the Chicago Police Department. He'd work out of Chicago and cover the Midwest from Ohio to Colorado. Maj Olson, seated to Deke's left, would be based in Austin, Texas with the yet-to-arrive Gene Beck and handle the South from Miami to Phoenix. Seated to the right of Brad Lewis was Rebecca Bramley,

John Tall Wolf's wife, who would be subbing for Byron DeWitt and work out of Los Angeles, handling California from San Diego to San Francisco. When DeWitt returned, it was likely Rebecca would open an office in Toronto. Ron Ketchum and Keely Powell, seated to the left of Maj Olson, would work the Pacific Northwest and the Mountain West.

Working cases in the European Union were Gabbi Casale, Yves Pruet and Odo Sacripant from the Paris office.

Also present were FBI Deputy Director Abra Benjamin, Secret Service SAC Elspeth Kendry, John Tall Wolf of the BIA and Putnam Shady, the firm's chief legal counsel.

Gene Beck was the last person to enter the room, with good reason. "Sorry for being late, but I went to Aubrey Gadsden's office to invite him to this morning's meeting."

Looking at the other faces in the room, Gene added, "In case some of you don't know the name, Gadsden was Corona Moe's lawyer. He was the guy fronting for the creep trying to kill Mr. McGill here. I thought if Gadsden saw what he was up against, maybe that would convince him now was the time to come clean."

McGill said, "He politely declined your invitation?"

That was when Gene delivered his bombshell news. "Well, he just couldn't make it. Somebody hanged him. Right there in his own office. I called the cops and two homicide detectives showed up. Said their names were Marvin Meeker and Mike Walker, though Meeker called his partner Beemer."

"They excused you from the proceedings?" McGill asked, a bit incredulous.

"I mentioned that I had a meeting with you. You seem to carry a ton or two of weight around this town, Boss."

"For the time being anyway," McGill replied.

"They said their captain, a woman named Rockelle Bullard, would be taking charge and she knows you."

"She does."

SAC Elspeth Kendry decided she should get together with the DC cops and make sure nothing slipped through the cracks between the local and federal investigators. She gave a nod to Deke before she left, making sure he understood that despite the crowd in the room he was still McGill's bullet-catcher in chief.

As Elspeth left the room, McGill told the others, "Losing Gadsden as someone we might pressure has just made our job harder."

Putnam raised a hand and McGill acknowledged him.

"I'd better go to Gadsden's offices, too. Make sure no over-zealous investigator pokes a nose into his case files before we get a judge's permission. After we do, I'd like to be included among those who get to pore through them."

McGill asked, "Did you know Gadsden?"

Putnam shook his head. "Not him personally, but I know other members of the defense bar who might step over ethical and legal lines on their clients' behalf. I might spot something the cops might miss."

McGill nodded. "Use my name with Captain Bullard. That seems to work magic."

"Right."

Once Putnam had left, McGill looked at the others in the room. "Let's get down to working out the firm's organizational needs for the moment, and then we'll turn to the matter of the threat against my life."

Sweetie shook her head. "No, Jim, you come first. Without you, there is no firm, no reason for any of us to be here. We need to focus on keeping you alive."

Everyone in the room agreed.

McGill was touched by the sentiment but kept a straight face.

"Okay," he said, "if that's the way all of you feel about it."

They all did.

The White House

Seated in the Oval Office in front of the President's desk, Galia Mindel asked Patricia Grant, "Can you believe Jean Morrissey used the word 'fuck' in a press conference yesterday?"

"It was only a matter of time before someone did," Patricia Grant said. "Might as well have been Jean. She even got a standing ovation from the press corps. When did that ever happen before?"

"Never happened before," Galia said, and then asked devilishly, "So do you think Oren Worth will use the word in one of the presidential debates?"

The President smiled. "I'm not familiar with all the tenets of the LDS Church, but I believe that they frown on profanity."

Galia replied, "That's true, but if Worth's polling numbers continue to slide, he's going to be sorely tempted."

"What he'll need to do, Galia, as I'm sure you've already figured out, is find exactly the right context to take the social sting off the word while also showing he's a big, strong man."

Galia laughed. "That's exactly what Jean did, co-opting the military as her own license for cursing. Finding a better niche than the armed forces will be a real challenge for Worth."

The president sighed and shook her head. "Politics. I'll be glad to put it all behind me. Won't you, Galia?"

The chief of staff took a moment to reflect. "I need a year or so off. I hope by then I'll be finished with politics … but I wouldn't be surprised if I had a relapse."

Before the discussion of what the future might hold for either of them could continue, the President's phone rang. With a nod from the President, Galia answered it. It took only seconds for the chief of staff's face to go ashen.

Alarmed, the President asked, "What is it? Jim or one of our children?"

Galia shook her head. "It's Secretary of Defense Dempsey, Madam President. He said the navy has just shot down two Chinese fighter aircraft over the South China Sea."

K Street, Washington, DC

"Give it to me one more time," Captain Rockelle Bullard said, rubbing her forehead to ease the discomfort of an approaching headache.

Aubrey Gadsden, Esquire, still dangled a foot above the polished hardwood floor of his private office. A neatly tied hangman's noose circled his neck. The taut rope was secured to a sturdy neo-industrial light fixture set into the 12-foot high ceiling.

A spiderweb of fine cracks in the plaster ceiling above the heads of the three police officials suggested that Gadsden had swung back and forth a bit at the end of his rope before finally coming to rest. The lawyer's hands were tied behind his back. Unlike an official execution, he hadn't been provided with a hood to cover his head, but his mouth was taped shut. He wasn't a pretty sight.

"What's that name again," Captain Bullard asked, "the guy who found this sorry bastard?"

Detective Marvin Meeker looked at his notebook, even though he didn't need to. "Eugene Beck."

"You checked to see if Mr. Beck has his own criminal record?"

Both detectives rolled their eyes. Like they'd ever overlook something that basic. Big Mike Walker, aka Beemer, said, "Yes, ma'am. Nobody with that name showed up on NCIC."

The National Crime Information Center, the official national crime database managed by the FBI.

Rockelle Bullard thought the man's absence of a criminal record might be either good or bad. Good if he was an honest citizen; bad if he was a smart thug who hadn't been nabbed for any of his misdeeds. The other possibility, of course, was he'd used a false name when reporting the dead body.

The fact that Beck had been allowed to leave the premises, after invoking the name of James J. McGill, didn't incline the captain to think the man was a prospective legal client who just happened upon the scene. Then there was the fact that Beck hadn't used 911 and had called the police directly; that said something about his familiarity with encountering corpses. She just hoped he wasn't some bad cop.

She looked at her own two coppers. "You two, being the veteran detectives you are, think our hanging man is, in fact, the lawyer with his name on the door of these fine offices?" the captain asked.

Meeker picked up a framed photo from the large desk in the room. It showed a happy couple, the male a good twenty years older than the peroxide-blonde woman. He held it up in front of the suspended corpse.

"Beemer 'n' me think the guy in the picture is the same one with the purple face," Meeker said.

Beemer nodded. "Never met the man, but the name's on the office door, and he's not gonna have someone else's picture on his desk, is he?"

Rockelle Bullard figured things the same way.

"Let's find out who the woman in the photo is," she said.

Both detectives nodded, having figured that out by themselves.

"I know you told me," the captain said, "but tell me again why Mr. Beck couldn't stay right here until I arrived."

"Said he had an important meeting with James J. McGill," Meeker said.

"We figured he meant the same one who lives at the White House," Beemer added.

Rockelle Bullard sighed. "Yeah, but not for much longer."

Feldman Rehab, Alexandria, Virginia

Byron DeWitt smiled with the right half of his face. After months of therapy, recovering from his stroke, he was still working on getting the remaining muscles of his face to respond properly. At the moment, he thought he looked like someone auditioning for the role of the Joker in a Batman movie. He consoled himself with the fact that he was once again able to eat and drink without either food or water dribbling out of his mouth.

His speech, though still slow, as if every word his mind chose had to be typed before it could be spoken, was becoming increasingly fluid.

"You really said that?" he asked Jean. "Fuck?"

The former deputy director of the FBI sat in an armchair. He no longer needed to return to his bed after either physical or occupational therapy. He extended a hand to his fiancée.

She took it and smiled. "I really did. I didn't plan it. The word just came spontaneously."

"Better that way. Shows authen … ticity." Polysyllables were still an effort.

"Yeah, I thought so, too. Got a great response."

"Will you marry me, Jean Morrissey?"

"I'm pretty sure I've already answered that question."

"I mean soon."

The Vice President's engagement to DeWitt was public knowledge. It gave her one of the unofficial credentials a presidential candidate needed; if elected, she would govern as a married woman. Better yet, much of the electorate saw the way she'd stood by her stricken fiancé as a sign of character. She wouldn't abandon either him or them in a time of need.

"I don't cut and run," was another memorable line Jean had delivered spontaneously.

None of that, though, was what Byron was thinking. His recovery had been steady, but he and his prospective bride had both been advised of what might happen to him: another stroke. Perhaps a fatal one. The doctors were watching him closely but the timing of such a misfortune couldn't be foreseen.

Byron wanted to get married sooner in case he didn't have a later.

"If there's a chaplain on the premises, you want me to send for him?" Jean asked. "I can always get a marriage license for us afterward."

Before he could answer, there was a knock at the door. The head of Jean's Secret Service detail stepped into the room. "Sorry to intrude, Ms. Vice President. The President needs you at the White House immediately … and there are visitors to see the Deputy Director."

Jean looked at Byron, torn that she should be called away at that particular moment.

He gave her his asymmetrical grin.

"Go. Don't think I'm gonna kick off right now." Looking at the Secret Service agent he asked, "Who's here for me?"

"Director Tall Wolf, sir, and Ms. Maj Olson."

Byron looked at Jean. "Old friends. Go help the President."

She did, but only after she firmly kissed her betrothed.

Washington, DC

Majority Leader of the U.S. Senate, Oren Worth, was making the rounds of the morning TV news programs. He was five points down, on average, in the big national political polls. Satellite News America, aka SNAM, had him down only one point but the NBC/*Wall Street Journal* poll had him down eight points.

Some of Jean Morrissey's polling bump at NBC/WSJ undoubtedly came from saying, "Nobody fucks with the United States military." That declaration had drawn both gasps and cheers — and bitter envy from Worth.

In the Majority Leader's first interview that morning, with the conservative suck-ups at SNAM, he was asked for his opinion of the Vice President's bluntly stated position.

He'd answered, "Well, of course they don't. Who'd ever dare do that?"

He thought that should have covered him politically, until he saw his trio of interviewers sitting silently and plainly expecting more. What exactly did they want, he asked himself. That question, he was sure, answered itself.

They wanted him to be profane. If a female candidate could use a four-letter word on television, how could he demur? What kind of a man would that make him? A sissy was what.

Worth then made the mistake of trying to weasel out of his predicament and have things both ways. "In the context of the question put to my opponent, I imagine I would have used the same language to respond."

The three cretins facing him remained mute, waiting for him to use that language.

They wanted someone to say "fuck" on SNAM.

With nowhere else to go, Worth had to oblige them. "You're damn right nobody fucks with our armed forces … or we'll fuck them up but good."

Both halves of the statement sounded forced even to Worth, and on the way to his next interview, this one at CNN, his media person told him the "damn" had been okay, but the second "fuck" had probably been one too many. Worth had to grind his teeth. He hadn't wanted to use the word at all, and now look at what had happened. How the hell was he supposed to know there was a fucking quota on the use of "fuck?"

Jesus Christ … no, no, he couldn't take the Lord's name in vain.

His base would disown him if he did that. His media person told all the other TV networks in advance that the Majority Leader wouldn't be saying "fuck" for them, not even once. They all agreed to the condition, but their questions were really snotty, making him look like a weak-kneed wienie. He almost canceled his last appearance, but it was on PBS, and he figured they'd be both civil in their questioning and wouldn't even raise the notion of using coarse language.

The network's interviewer, Ellie Booker, had promised she wouldn't.

Instead, at the end of a polite discussion in which Worth thought he'd more than held his own, Ellie asked him, "Do you think you could win an arm-wrestling contest with Jean Morrissey?"

Worth blinked and said, "Pardon me?"

"Arm wrestling," Ellie repeated. "You plunk your elbow down on a table, the VP does the same and you go at it. First one to pin the other's hand to the table wins. That simple. Do you think you could beat the Vice President in such a competition?"

Worth was about to ask, "What the hell would that have to do with governing or anything else?"

He caught himself before expressing that sentiment. Part of

the reason he was trailing Jean Morrissey in the polls, he felt sure, was he'd made the mistake of appearing to be weak in the public eye. He'd complained that it would be unfair of Patti Grant to resign and let Jean Morrissey run as the incumbent president. That had made Worth seem far weaker than he really was. Both physically and mentally. By God, it just wasn't true that he was a wimp. He'd made a staggering fortune in the mining business. That was hardly a pantywaist accomplishment.

Worth's temper flared. He had to show the voting public who he *really* was.

"Of course, I can beat her in arm-wrestling," he said in a dismissive tone. Then, as before, he went a step too far. "I'm sure she knows that, too."

Worth instantly realized his mistake. He'd just made a carnival sideshow inevitable.

The devilish mischief he saw in Ellie Booker's eyes told him he had that exactly right.

More than that, he saw that she knew something he didn't.

Not that she was going to tell him, not then anyway. She'd let suspense build and then someday soon reveal … what? Oh, shit, he'd really put his foot in it. He thought he'd better hire a fitness trainer and build the muscles in his right arm as quickly as he could.

Because he was sure that for the amusement of the masses he was going to have a literal arm wrestling match with Jean Morrissey. And if he lost he'd never become president.

That grim fate looked far more likely after Worth saw his media wizard go pale while looking at her iPad on the ride back to his Senate office.

"What?" Worth asked. "What the hell is it now?"

He was beginning to sound more natural using vulgarities anyway.

The damn woman couldn't find her voice to reply. Something really had scared her.

Worth grabbed her iPad and what he saw sent a jolt of fear

racing down his spine, too. A photo showed Jean Morrissey during her college days in Minnesota. She'd just pinned a male opponent in an arm wrestling competition. The accompanying headline read: *Hockey Team Captain, Strongest Woman on Campus, Takes on the Guys and Wins.*

That bitch Ellie Booker, Worth thought. She knew about this all along. There was only one thing for Worth to do. He fired his media advisor for not knowing and warning him.

The White House

Arriving at the Oval Office, having been briefed en route about the destruction of two Chinese Shenyang J-15 fighter aircraft by RIM-162 Evolved SeaSparrow Missiles fired from the USS *Gridley*, the Vice President asked the Commander-in-Chief, "Jesus, did I provoke this? More important than that, what are we doing now? What are the Chinese doing?"

Patricia Grant told her VP, "They've accused us of open warfare in their territorial waters. Repercussions, they say, will be terrible and swift in coming. All the more so if we engage in any further hostile actions."

In an uncharacteristically quiet voice, Jean Morrissey asked, "Did you respond to the threat, Madam President?"

"I did," she said, "shortly before you arrived."

She turned to Galia to provide the details. The chief of staff said, "The president told her Chinese counterpart that neither the United States nor the rest of the world recognizes China's claim to the majority of the South China Sea. She said that the Chinese military in the area had been warned that any hostile approaches to U.S. Navy ships by Chinese military aircraft would be met with appropriate defensive measures. She informed the Chinese president that our navy is now operating under battle conditions and any further hostile acts against our armed forces would result in a similar outcome."

With a straight face, the President added, "I told the man, in the nicest possible way, nobody fucks with the U.S. military."

"So it was my fault," Jean Morrissey responded.

The President shook her head. "No, it was the fault of the military commander on the other side who didn't take you at your word. Both Galia and I think they were testing us."

Jean said, "So now we're hoping they'll take you at your word, Madam President?"

"We fervently hope they will," Galia said.

The President said, "We're also moving all our naval assets at Subic Bay in the Philippines out into the South China Sea — and we've moved to DefCon 4."

One notch up from DefCon 5, the usual state of military readiness, also known as Fade Out. DefCon 4's nickname was Double Take, and stood for increased intelligence watch and strengthened security.

"Did either of the pilots who were shot down survive?" Jean asked.

Galia shook her head.

"You might be taking office during a very tense time, Jean," the President said.

The VP nodded. "I'll be ready."

McGill Investigations International, LLP

In the absence of any specific knowledge as to how McGill might be attacked by unknown assassins, his partners could only offer broad suggestions as to the best way to protect him. Traveling with two armed companions any time he ventured outside the White House was the first suggestion offered.

"I never go anywhere without Deke and Leo these days," McGill pointed out.

Sweetie said, "Leo's a wizard behind the wheel, but you should have two *dedicated* bodyguards. I'm not saying Leo is anything less than committed to you, but I'm talking about someone who doesn't have to concentrate on his driving."

Having been invited into the room for the discussion, Leo said, "Driving is pretty much a natural thing for me. No doubt in my mind I could do it with one hand and shoot with the other. Heck, I could likely drive with my knees and shoot with *both* hands."

McGill said, "We won't put that idea to the test."

"Even taking Deadeye Levy at his word," Sweetie persisted, "there's no question that having another trained professional on hand would increase the odds of having a happy outcome."

"I'll do it," Gene Beck said. "I'll be the fourth guy…or the third, depending on who's counting. If it's all right with the three amigos, that is."

McGill, Deke and Leo all considered the matter and nodded in synchrony.

"What else should we consider?" Sweetie asked the others in the conference room.

Uncomfortable being the focus of this particular exercise, McGill said, "I promise, I won't play cards with anyone named Doc or eat at anyplace called Mom's."

He regularly slept with a woman whose troubles were worse than his own, but that situation would change on Inauguration Day.

Some of the people around the table recognized Nelson Algren's famous warnings; others didn't know the source but caught the gist. The subtext, too. The boss had had his fill of everyone fretting about him.

McGill had his own thoughts on how to find Corona Moe and take the fight to him and any accomplices he might have. Before he could raise the subject, FBI Acting Deputy Director Abra Benjamin, who was present so she might fill in Byron DeWitt on the proceedings, received an official business call. She excused herself from the conference room.

McGill waited until she'd closed the door behind her and then told the others, "I think the first thing we need to do is to put out a team picture."

Odo Sacripant frowned and whispered to Yves Pruet, "*Une*

photo de l'équipe?"

Pruet sensed what McGill was about to suggest and smiled. *"Patience, mon ami."*

McGill continued, "My thinking is if Corona Moe thought going after me is too big a job for him alone, what's he going to do when he sees all the people around this table who will be hunting him? Recruit a small army? There probably aren't enough people he trusts to do that. But he might add a few more guns to his team, and the more he expands his recruiting effort, the better the chances are that someone will talk, and we'll find that weak link."

Pruet said, "Or some of this fellow's current compatriots might decide they no longer have a stomach for the fight."

"That'd be okay, too," McGill said. "If enough of his people fall away, he may have to give up the job."

Deke said, "But we'd still have to get Moe to make our point: Nobody should even think of going after James J. McGill."

Everyone agreed on that point.

Gene Beck entertained a contrarian thought and it showed on his face.

Nobody missed that either.

"What is it, Gene?" McGill asked.

"We've got to get Moe, yeah, but there's still another step to take. We've got to find out who he brought in on the job even if Moe pays their fees and sends them home. And especially if he *doesn't* pay them."

Odo was up to speed now and told the others. "Gene is right. There might be some fellow …" He paused to gesture at the women in the room. "Or *une femme formidable* who might care to establish a reputation of her own that would last for ages."

Ron Ketchum nodded. "Sure, you couldn't beat taking out James J. McGill for criminal career advancement."

Before anyone could add to that, Abra Benjamin returned and told McGill, "We got them, our top three fugitives: Turner Bidwell, Kyle Nance and Axel Bing."

It took McGill a moment to shift gears, but he made the

transition. She wasn't talking about Corona Moe or any of his accomplices. She meant people the FBI had already put on its most-wanted list.

McGill asked, "The kidnappers? The guys who grabbed Special Agent Ramsey in L.A.?"

Everyone in the room knew of the case and when Abra nodded, applause sounded around the table.

Intuitively, McGill said, "Somebody in the militia movement gave them up."

Abra said, "Dr. Peter Nash, the militia's on-call surgeon, in the hope of reducing his own prison time."

"Did you tell Carrie Ramsey and her parents?"

"I'm going to do that right now. I thought you might appreciate knowing first."

McGill thanked Benjamin and turned to the others as she left the room again. "See. If a criminal conspiracy spreads far enough, somebody always gives it up."

"Unless all the conspirators are Corsican," Odo said.

Pruet rolled his eyes.

McGill said, "We'll bear that in mind, but this news makes me feel optimistic."

The White House

Edwina Byington buzzed the President while Vice President Morrissey and Chief of Staff Mindel were still in the Oval Office with her.

"Madam President, His Excellency Han Zhen, Ambassador from the People's Republic of China, is at the East Gate."

Of all the gates people used to visit the White House, the Chinese always chose to arrive from the east, even though their embassy lay to the northwest of the Executive Mansion.

Edwina continued, "He's said it's a matter of extreme urgency, ma'am."

"He's not exaggerating," the President said. "Please tell the

Secret Service to let the ambassador in, Edwina."

Putting the phone down, Patricia Grant said, "Jean, please stand at my right shoulder, just a half-step behind me. If I tap the right arm of my chair, you respond to whatever the ambassador has just said. Galia, please move to the chair to my left. If I tap the left arm of my chair, that's your cue. If I leave my hands in my lap or place them on the desk in front of me, I'll do the talking. If I stand up, we'll trust that the ambassador understands our little talk is over."

"What if he holds his ground, Madam President?" Jean asked.

Galia replied, "I'll go open the door for him. If he still remains obstinate —"

"I'll have the Secret Service escort him out," the President said.

A moment later Edwina opened the door to the Oval Office and said, "Madam President, His Excellency Han Zhen."

The President stood to acknowledge her guest but didn't extend a hand in greeting. "Mr. Ambassador … are you here to apologize for the menacing fly-bys of two Shenyang J-15 fighter aircraft that I am informed came within ten meters of striking the USS *Gridley?*"

The President also didn't offer the ambassador a seat.

Ambassador Han said stiffly, "I was told by my government that our aircraft came no closer than a nautical mile to any of your naval vessels, and I am here to vehemently protest the American aggression that killed two of my country's pilots and destroyed their aircraft."

The president locked her eyes on the man, let him know who the unquestioned power in the room was. "It's regrettable that *your* country's aggressive actions caused any loss of life. I'm told that the jet-wash from your aircraft almost swept three United States sailors aboard the *Gridley* overboard. I'd be calling their families right now with terrible news if not for a bit of good luck that prevented *their* deaths. I've seen video showing that your country's planes were as close to the *Gridley* as I've said, not as distant as you've said. Furthermore, both of your country's aircraft were armed. They could have attacked the *Gridley* or the other two United

States vessels nearby. Our squadron commander was not going to give them another chance to kill any of his people or sink any of his ships. I intend to commend him officially for his actions."

Han's icy voice countered, "Your naval vessels are intruding in Chinese territorial waters."

The President tapped her right arm rest.

Jean cleared her throat and the ambassador glared at her. He'd undoubtedly heard her notorious warning about the dangers of confronting the armed forces of the United States. Now, with Chinese blood in the water, she chose to be less direct but equally pointed in stating the American position.

"Mr. Ambassador, do you know that in 1969 American astronauts landed on the moon?"

Han Zhen immediately understood where she was going but only grimaced in response.

"Those astronauts, Neil Armstrong and Buzz Aldrin, took an American flag with them and planted it in the lunar soil," Jean added.

All three women in the room thought they could hear the ambassador grinding his teeth.

Jean added, "At that point, I suppose, the United States could have claimed the moon as its own territory. I mean, why not? We got there first. Tell me, Mr. Ambassador, do you think your country would have recognized such a claim? Do you think *any* country would have accepted such a brazen assertion? Just because one country says something is so doesn't make it so."

The President subtly tapped the left arm of her chair.

Galia accepted the pass of the verbal baton.

She told the ambassador, "The International Court of Justice at the Hague has ruled there is no legal basis for China's claim to a vast area of international waters. If China continues to pursue that claim, especially if it is supported by reckless military efforts, it undoubtedly will be branded an international outlaw."

The ambassador grimaced and said, "We do not recognize this court nor do we accept its ruling. We demand a full and sincere apology from the United States for causing the deaths of our airmen and the destruction of our aircraft, and we demand a solemn promise that such an unprovoked attack will never again be repeated."

The President nodded and said, "And you shall have everything you want …" Getting to her feet she added, "Just as soon as China officially recognizes the United States' sovereign possession of the moon."

Neither Jean Morrissey nor Galia Mindel laughed, but they both smiled.

Even that was more than Han Zhen could bear. He left without another word.

McGill Investigations International LLP

Having planned ahead, McGill had a photographer Patti had recommended from her modeling days on call and waiting to take the team picture. His name was Victor. Apparently, a surname was superfluous to those who could afford his services. That included McGill, but just barely. Victor brought with him a make-up artist and a hair stylist to make sure everyone looked his or her best.

To McGill's delight, the stylist was Caresse Montaigne, the stylish pixie who'd cut and colored his hair in Paris some years ago. Gabbi Casale had been the one who'd made the introduction. McGill looked at the co-head of his Paris office and saw her shrug.

"Small world," Gabbi said with a mischievous smile.

Standing on tiptoe, Caresse put her hands on McGill's shoulders and bussed his cheeks, making him blush in front of the whole room. Sweetie, in particular, gave the boss an appraising look. Victor saved McGill from further embarrassment by stepping forward and shaking his hand.

"I am pleased to meet you, sir," he said with a Central European accent. "The shoot I did with the President, in her earlier career, was one of the most memorable of my life. Please extend to her my congratulations on leading this country so magnificently."

For just a moment, McGill wondered just why Patti's photo

shoot with Victor had been so noteworthy, and why he'd never heard of it. Then McGill gave himself a mental kick. Patti's modeling days had ended before she'd married Andy Grant. As her *second* husband, McGill certainly wasn't entitled to judge what his wife had done in her days as a young, single woman.

That didn't mean he couldn't be curious, though.

And, jeez, the guy had to have twenty years on him, and McGill had two on Patti. Not that age kept Victor from presenting a dashing figure. The photographer's face was craggy, but he was tall, lean and in possession of a full head of silver hair, tousled just so. Probably Caresse's doing, that hair style, McGill thought.

He thanked Victor for the compliment and said, "I'll be sure to tell her."

With that the photographer got down to business, shooting each member of the team individually; McGill would go last. Then they'd do the group photo. The plan worked perfectly. When McGill had to take a phone call, he did so without ruffling any artistic feathers.

An authoritative female voice told him, "Metro police."

McGill said, "Captain Bullard."

"My name came up on your phone? It's just supposed to say MPD."

"It does. I have a good ear and a memory that hasn't started to fail me yet."

The captain laughed.

"I recognize that sound, too," McGill said.

"Yeah, well, Detectives Meeker, Beemer and I thought we had ourselves something of a whodunnit over here on K Street. A lawyer hanging from his office ceiling, looking like a poster boy for the cruel-and-unusual argument against capital punishment. If that isn't bad enough, we had the head of the Secret Service's Presidential Protection Detail, SAC Elspeth Kendry, drop in on us. On top of that, Mr. Putnam Shady, Esquire, who we remember from an earlier case, also stopped by to say hello, and mentioned you sent him."

"It was his idea," McGill said, "but I thought it was a good one. Told him he could drop my name."

"Just like a Mr. Eugene Beck did earlier today, him being the one who discovered the dangling body of Mr. Aubrey Gadsden, also esquire."

"Gene works for me."

"Your little firm's growing?" Rockelle asked.

"Going national, and we have an office in Paris."

"My, my. Suppose you have to keep busy when you and the President leave town."

"We're staying in DC. Hope to maintain good relations with the MPD."

After a moment's silence, Rockelle said, "So you sent me a little help, the Secret Service and a high-dollar lawyer, to assist me with this case — when what I want to do is talk with Mr. Beck."

"How about I bring Gene by to see you shortly and give you an angle to investigate?"

"Shortly?" Rockelle said.

"An hour, maybe two."

"Any reason you can't come right now?"

"We're having our pictures taken, my new partners and me. It's part of a plan I have in mind."

"Does that plan have anything to do with the dead man hanging in front of me?"

"Most likely," McGill said.

The captain wasn't able to repress a sigh.

"You and I, we're going to be working together, aren't we?" she asked.

"In a mutually cooperative fashion, I'm sure," McGill said.

"Is Colonel Welborn Yates gonna be in on this, too?"

McGill took a moment to consider. "You never know, and he's General Yates these days."

"Of course, he is. Me, I'm stuck in grade."

Yielding to the inevitable, Captain Bullard showed McGill some cooperation.

She texted him copies of the framed photos on the dead lawyer's desk.

Feldman Rehab — Alexandria, Virginia

"Probably be a little while before you want to ride dirt-bikes with Director Tall Wolf and me, huh?" Maj Olson asked Byron DeWitt.

Sitting at his bedside, she'd just told him how she'd wound up going to work for James J. McGill. The book she wrote about her role in helping to find the stolen SuperChief locomotive and keeping John from plunging off a mountain road had resulted in offers of teaching positions from half-a-dozen prestigious universities. John had written a forward to the book praising her heroism and scholarship as being critical to both his survival and solving the case.

"Just trying to be helpful, and show a little gratitude," John said.

"And, believe me, I was grateful," Maj said looking from John to DeWitt. "Thing was, every school that interviewed me was more interested in my momentary celebrity than my long-term potential as a teacher."

"Still, a foot in the door," DeWitt said at his deliberate pace.

"True, and I could have used that entrée to prove my teaching chops, but then I realized I was more interested in catching bad guys than standing in front of a class. That came as a big surprise, but I couldn't deny it. So, being 1/64th Pequot, I went to see Director Tall Wolf and asked if he might use me at the BIA. He thought I might do better with Mr. McGill and set up an interview. I got the job and now I'm Dr. Gumshoe."

"Cool," DeWitt said with a lopsided grin.

John's phone rang. He looked at the caller ID and said, "I better take this."

He stepped out of the room and said, "Good morning, Ms. Vice President."

John could see Maj and DeWitt bantering from where he stood.

So he was able to offer a response to the Vice President's question as to the present condition of her betrothed. "He's not ready to ride a wave yet, but I bet he will be eventually. He seems to be enjoying his conversation with Ms. Olson at the moment. Pardon? Yes, that Ms. Olson. The one who worked the missing-train case with me. She's working for Mr. McGill now."

John listened to the Vice President in silence for a moment and then said, "Of course, Ms. Vice President, I'd be happy to do that. Just a moment and I'll ask him."

He stepped back into the room and covered his phone with one hand. "Byron, Vice President Morrissey would like to know if it would be convenient for you to marry her later today, circumstances permitting."

DeWitt gave John a crooked grin and an upraised thumb.

He told the Vice President. "He's all for the idea. What, there's one more thing?"

John said to Byron, "If it's all right with your doctors, the future Mrs. DeWitt would also like to know if you might help her and the President assess the thinking of the Chinese Politburo."

DeWitt formed a fist and held it as high as he could.

John informed the VP. "He's happy to be of use, Ms. Vice President. Yes, of course, we'll both gladly do that."

He ended the call and told DeWitt, "Your fiancée will be here ASAP with His Eminence Cardinal Sean Fitzroy to do the honors. White House Deputy Chief of Staff Frank Morrissey will give away the bride."

John Tall Wolf seemed unruffled by the sudden turn of events, but Maj Olson was gobsmacked. She gave DeWitt a buss on the forehead and said to John, "We better be on our way, huh?"

John shook his head. "No. You and I, we're here to represent the groom."

DeWitt gave a small nod and another smile. "Stay, please."

Valletta, Malta

The man calling himself Lachlan Williams told Giles Henry, ace scandal reporter for the London tabloid *The Intruder,* "I can kill you right here."

The two men sat across a table on the terrace of Williams' island home.

Henry smiled. He'd had his life threatened by far more dangerous characters. He'd even had a salad fork plunged into his neck by an aging actress in a New York restaurant.

"What?" Henry asked. "Just because I said your phony Aussie accent is bloody awful?"

Henry had followed Williams home from a café and had gained entrance to his home by telling the man that he'd purchased a wine glass — the one from which Williams had been drinking at the café. The glass, Henry said, was on its way to a laboratory to do a DNA analysis.

Williams took a small semi-automatic pistol out of a pocket and pointed it at Henry.

The reporter said, "I followed you in a taxi. Told the driver I was on the trail of a very dangerous character. He thought I was joking, of course. That is, until I gave him a hundred euros and told him if he didn't pick me up tomorrow at my hotel at a certain time he should go to the police and tell them I'd met a bad end at your hands."

Williams blinked, and Henry laughed.

Henry said, "Of course, all that might be just a story I made up here and now. But look at my face. See the blooms of broken blood vessels on my cheeks and nose. Look at my eyes. There's a definite cunning in them, but their gleam is starting to blur. My doctor tells me with what I've done to my liver I can't have more than a year left, if I continue to drink the way I do. And I hope to die with a glass in my hand. That, I assure you, is the truth."

Williams lowered the gun but kept it in hand. "What do you want?"

"I want you to tell me your story, of course. How you went from being a United States senator to a swindler. Or vice versa. I want to know who found you out and set you running, first to Australia and now to Malta. That's what I'd like to know, Senator Randall Pennyman."

The face of the man calling himself Lachlan Williams changed upon hearing his true name. Fear and desperation reshaped his features. He looked like a cornered animal.

Giles Henry airily waved off the gun that Pennyman was now pointing his way again.

"You're not the one I want, Senator. I want the person who put your willie in the wringer. That's where the story is. Give me that name and your current location will be safe with me."

The tabloid reporter leaned back in his chair, hands clasped over his paunchy middle, the picture of a man without a care in the world.

"If you are going to shoot me," he said, "do try to get the job done with your first round … and I really would appreciate it if you'll allow me one last drink. Doesn't matter what it is as long as it has a decent alcohol content."

Henry smiled, a man beyond any fear of death.

Randall Pennyman put his gun away.

He said, "Galia Mindel is who you want."

K Street — Washington, DC

Aubrey Gadsden's neck had begun to stretch, elongated by the weight of his stocky frame and the tug of gravity. His bladder and his bowels had released. The man's suit was expensive and well cut but it didn't conceal the stench or the dribble of human waste dripping from his pants legs.

That was the tableau that greeted McGill, Sweetie, Yves Pruet, Odo Sacripant and Gene Beck when they arrived at the deceased criminal defense attorney's K Street offices. Uniformed MPD coppers had admitted them and kept the public and the press at bay.

McGill told Captain Rockelle Bullard, "You could've bagged the guy, if you wanted, Rockelle. We've all seen people who've died badly. The photos you texted me were enough."

Detective Marvin Meeker said, "Yeah, but ain't nothin' like the real thing, is there?"

McGill didn't argue. He was inserting himself and his associates into a police investigation. Back in his CPD days, he wouldn't have appreciated such an encroachment. Unless, of course, the outsiders contributed to a quick and successful resolution of the case.

"No there isn't," McGill conceded, "but that guy's going to pop his cork pretty soon."

Meaning the corpse's body would pull free from its head.

That would be a mess nobody needed. Rockelle waved a relieved crew from the Medical Examiner's office forward and they went to work freeing Gadsden's remains from the rope while they were still intact. Odo stepped forward to peer at the noose as it was worked free from the corpse's neck.

He didn't let either the stench or the puddles of human waste on the floor bother him. Neither the captain nor her two detectives raised an objection. The Metro cops all came to the same conclusion about the guy's indifference to the stink and the visual horror of the murder.

Rockelle Bullard looked at McGill. "This guy's one of yours and he was a cop at one time, wasn't he?"

"That or an undertaker," Detective Beemer said.

The crack brought a laugh from McGill and a smile from Yves Pruet.

Odo didn't react in the same manner. He leaned in for a closer look as the body was lowered onto a plastic sheet.

"What's funny?" Rockelle asked McGill.

He said, "My two French friends here and I had a memorable set-to with a homicidal giant in Paris. He was called The Undertaker."

Yves Pruet stepped forward, extended a hand to Rockelle and

introduced himself.

"So you were a police official over there in Paris?" she asked.

"An investigating magistrate. Now, I'm one of the partners in *M'sieur* McGill's office in Paris."

"Him, too?" she asked pointing a thumb at Odo.

The Corsican turned his head. *"Oui, moi aussi.* I know the knot on this noose. It is Sicilian."

He stood and shook Rockelle's hand. "Thank you for keeping the body here. I might not have noticed the technique from a photo."

Rockelle looked from Odo to McGill.

"Anything we can do to help," she said. "Is that country-looking guy with you Eugene Beck?"

Gene gave Rockelle a nod and a smile. "Yes, ma'am."

"All right then. Let's everyone get out of the way of the Medical Examiner's people. Mr. Gadsden's suite has a conference room right over there." She pointed to the door of an adjacent room. "SAC Kendry and Mr. Shady are already in there making phone calls. I think there's space for the rest of us, too."

Ever the gentleman, McGill gestured for Rockelle to lead the way.

James S. Brady Press Room — The White House

The President convened a meeting of the White House press corps. She stood at the lectern with Jean Morrissey to her right. Their purpose was to inform the nation of the military action in the South China Sea. China had yet to go public with the news and Patricia Grant decided to get the U.S. story out to the world first. Before the other side could try to spin things their way.

Getting straight to the point, the President said, "Earlier today, the USS *Gridley,* while transiting the South China Sea en route from Subic Bay, Philippines to Singapore, used RIM-162 Evolved Sea Sparrow Missiles to shoot down two Chinese Shenyang J-15 fighter aircraft. This occurred after the Chinese planes had already recklessly and provocatively harassed the ship on a first fly-by that came within 30 feet of the *Gridley.*

"The Chinese aircraft were armed and could have inflicted grave damage to the ship and killed many of our sailors. As it was, the backwash from the engines of the Chinese aircraft almost swept three of our sailors off the deck of the *Gridley*. Rescuing men overboard in the open ocean is an uncertain endeavor at best. The lives of these three service members might well have been lost. The commanding officer of the *Gridley*, Captain Reynauld Winston, warned the Chinese aircraft not to attempt another such aggressive maneuver or they would be fired upon.

"The Chinese pilots chose to disregard this warning and their aircraft were shot down. The Chinese ambassador came to the White House today to lodge a protest. He claimed that none of that nation's aircraft came within a nautical mile of any of our ships. He also asserted that our ships were operating in Chinese territorial waters. I rejected both his claim and his assertion.

"I'll now take your questions."

All the newsies in the room leapt from their seats and yelled at the President to be recognized. She picked the correspondent from the *L.A. Times.* "Linda."

Getting right to the heart of the matter, the reporter asked, "Madam President, could this incident lead to war with China?"

The question had been anticipated in a pre-announcement huddle including the President, VP Morrissey, Chief of Staff Galia Mindel and Press Secretary Aggie Wu. The President had a ready answer, but in the moment decided to improvise.

"Vice President Morrissey pointed out to the Chinese ambassador that as the first nation to put people on the moon, the United States could have claimed that celestial body as our own. We didn't, of course, and no other nation in the world would have recognized such a claim if we had done something so ridiculous.

"But let's look at something more down to earth. The United States is one indivisible country composed of 50 states, including Hawaii. So would it really be too presumptuous of us to claim all of the Pacific waters between Hawaii and, say, Alaska to the north and San Diego to the south?

"That would certainly cause an uproar, wouldn't it? If we actually tried to enforce such a preposterous notion, other nations would surely follow our precedent and also claim vast areas of ocean as their own. If they were able to make good on their claims, what stretch of water would be left open to free, unhindered international navigation?

"Such attempts to claim vast areas of ocean, by the United States or any other nation, would violate the United Nations Convention on the Law of the Sea. China has, regrettably, chosen to ignore the ruling of the Court of Justice at the Hague on this point. The United States does not and will not accept or recognize China's unilateral claim to a great majority of the South China Sea.

"All of that is preface to saying, in answer to Linda's question, the United States has no intention of going to war with China, but we will defend our ships, our country, our allies and the rule of international law. We have proven that today and will do so again as often as is necessary."

The reporter for the *Boston Globe* got in the second question, which was also anticipated.

"Madam President, is there any proof that the Chinese planes came as close to the *Gridley* as we say and were not as distant as the Chinese say?"

"Yes," the President said. "We'll show that to you now."

Two of Press Secretary Aggie Wu's assistants rolled a 50-inch TV monitor into the room, placing it so everyone present would have a clear view. Video taken by cameras aboard the *Gridley* showed the Chinese aircraft zooming frighteningly close to the Navy ship. The roar of their engines quickly drowning out cursing coming from the American crew. Several cameras provided different angles on the Chinese fighter jets as they approached, but each revealed the scant distance between the aircraft and the ship.

One camera, at the level of the *Gridley's* bridge, looked directly into the cockpit of one of the Chinese fighter jets. It zipped past in the blink of an eye but its roar conveyed frightening power and proximity. That was when the President said, "Stop the video, please."

All the newsies turned their attention to her.

"The pilots in the Chinese aircraft were wearing flight helmets so we can't see their faces, but a frame-by-frame inspection of the video taken by the camera on the bridge of the *Gridley* revealed something quite interesting.

"In our country, if we wish to express contempt without saying a word we might raise a middle finger to someone. The Chinese have a slightly different approach. They raise the little finger of one hand. This means, 'You are nothing,' or 'You are no good at what you do.'"

The President nodded to Aggie and at her direction a still image of the pilot that buzzed the bridge of the *Gridley* appeared on the TV screen. His head was facing the camera and he was raising a pinkie to the Americans and their ship.

"I think his message and his feelings were clear," the President said.

Taking a beat, she added, "So was our response."

The *Chicago Sun-Times* reporter beat his colleagues to the next obvious question. Jumping to his feet and speaking bluntly, he asked, "Madam President, do you think Vice President Morrissey's comment that nobody fucks with the U.S. military might have provoked this incident?"

A humorless smile crossed Patricia Grant's face. "No, what happened today was just a matter of time. What I think Jean's comment did was clarify that the United States will not be bullied. Not by anyone."

K Street — Washington, DC

In the conference room of the late Aubrey Gadsden, Esquire, Captain Rockelle Bullard of the Metropolitan Police Department turned her attention to the tough-looking Frenchman who'd told her he was really a Corsican and said, "You want to do what?"

"To be put into your prison with this man Ludwig."

"The architect of the plan to kill Mr. McGill," Pruet, the other Frenchman, said.

"So you like this idea, too?" she asked him.

Yves Pruet said, "I understand its risks. I would not volunteer to do it myself. But I have a deep faith in my compatriot, *M'sieur* Sacripant, and it might lead us to where we need to go."

Detective Meeker addressed Odo directly. "You look mean enough, all right. Probably could handle yourself in a lot of situations. But in any American prison there are *lots* of tough guys."

Detective Beemer clarified: "My man's telling you you're gonna be outnumbered."

Odo nodded. "I understand. It is the same in France. Muscle alone is not enough. Force of will and *savoir-faire* are also required."

Meeker looked at Beemer. "*Savoir.*"

"*Faire,*" Beemer replied with a straight face.

"Knock it off," Rockelle Bullard told her detectives.

She turned to McGill. "We're talking about a federal prison here, so it's not my call anyway. But what do you think?"

McGill sat across the conference table from Pruet and Odo. He'd declined to sit at its head. The visitors from France both looked at him impassively. He was the man in charge of their company, but there were other jobs to be had, if things came to that.

"You have a family," McGill said to Odo.

He nodded. "*Oui.* My wife and children are always close to mind and forever in my heart."

"Good to know," McGill said. "There are a couple of qualities you'll need to succeed that you didn't mention: anticipation and foot-speed."

Odo and Pruet looked at each other. They both understood the first requirement clearly, but Odo seemed perplexed by the second and turned to his old friend for help in understanding.

Pruet said, "*M'sieur* McGill is saying a time might come when you will need to run. To save your life. He hopes you are fleet enough to do so successfully."

Odo looked at McGill wearing a frown. "I can run. I have run many times. *Toward* the danger."

Meeker said, "Yeah, well, in prison you need a good reverse gear, too."

Beemer nodded.

McGill asked Odo, "Would this be the first time you've put yourself in such a situation?"

Odo conceded the point with a minimal nod.

"So for your own safety and the well-being of your family, could you make a timely decision to … live to fight another day?"

Odo sighed. "Yes."

McGill took a long beat to consider Odo's notion. The last time the President had directly used an inmate in the federal prison system as a chess piece, Erna Godfrey had been choked to death. He was deeply reluctant to ask Patti to take such a risk again.

God only knew how the French government would react to losing one of its citizens in such a scheme. Odds were good, though, they wouldn't just shrug and say, "Oh, well, mistakes happen."

On the other hand, Odo *was* tough and smart. Also, being a foreigner, it was less likely Auric Ludwig would think he was a planted informant. He just might … McGill had an idea. He liked it so much, it inclined him to go along with the Corsican's scheme.

Still, he turned to Pruet first, not Odo.

"Yves, am I right in thinking the laws allowing gun ownership in France are much stricter than they are in the U.S.?"

Pruet nodded. "By far."

Looking at Odo now, McGill asked, "Are there people in your native Corsica who wish the gun laws at home weren't so strict?"

The Corsican only laughed and nodded.

"So if we were to say you were arrested, convicted and jailed for trying to smuggle guns out of this country so your people could own weapons of war just like Americans do …"

Rockelle Bullard knew a cue when she heard one. "Old Auric Ludwig, Mr. FirePower America, might sympathize with his comrade-in-arms-sales."

Sweetie saw the next step in McGill's idea. "He might even share the glee of how he plans to get even with Jim for putting him in prison."

SAC Elspeth Kendry played the skeptic. "We know how he plans to get even: killing Holmes." McGill's Secret Service code name. "The question is: does Ludwig even know how his hired thugs plan to get the job done?"

McGill answered that one. "Maybe not, but I think that would be part of the fun for him. Someone would have to bring reports to him from the outside." Turning to Odo, "That would be the guy you'd have to spot first."

Pruet added, looking at his compatriot, "You'd have to be wary of every associate of this Ludwig person before taking any action."

Odo smiled indulgently. "And look for a guard doing him favors? Yes, Yves, that is my thinking also. I will be as smart as I can, and as careful as the situation permits."

McGill asked, "Anybody else have a thought on this matter?"

Gene Beck, who'd done a stint in a federal prison, said to Odo, "If you know how to whistle any tunes from back home, do that, but keep it soft. That'll draw attention to you, most often in a good way."

Odo nodded. He liked the idea. Showing he could handle any prison music critics would also help to establish he was no one to take lightly.

McGill told everyone. "I'll take this matter up with the Attorney General. See if he approves."

Rockelle asked, "You're not going to go to the President?"

"Not with this one," McGill said.

As for everybody else, the Metro cops and the McGill contingent were going to try to identify and interview the woman in the photo on Aubrey Gadsden's desk, and Putnam Shady would seek court permission to review the late criminal defense attorney's files with the help of a special master. The AG would weigh in on that, too, if there was any bureaucratic heel-dragging.

Feldman Rehab — Alexandria, Virginia

John Tall Wolf and Maj Olson, honoring Byron DeWitt's wish, were still on-hand at the rehab facility when the circus came to town. That was the metaphor for how many people in government thought of the arrival of the President and her security entourage. In this case, the crowd was even greater as James J. McGill and Vice President Morrissey were also in the parade of notables. Even the prospective bride's brother, White House Deputy Chief of Staff Frank Morrissey, brought some of his own federal muscle with him.

In deference to Director Tall Wolf, McGill brought the director's wife, Rebecca Bramley, along for the ride, introducing her to the president as they rode in Thing One, the presidential limo.

The celebrant of the nuptials, Cardinal Sean Fitzroy, a Jesuit and a maverick, trusted to God to preserve his time on earth, arrived alone, behind the wheel of his Chevy Volt. The Secret Service, having been alerted to his role in the matter at hand, didn't turn the prince of the church away. They ushered him to DeWitt's room with the Cardinal and the agents talking about Notre Dame's college football season.

Fitzroy shook hands with everyone in the room and kissed Jean Morrissey on the cheek, also putting a brief whispered word into her ear. She smiled and bobbed her head. Fitzroy had told her he'd give her a two-for-the-price-of-one deal, repeating the ceremony in a more formal setting later if she and her groom wished.

Then, under his own power, Byron DeWitt got to his feet to stand next to his bride.

Facing the couple, Cardinal Fitzroy said, "My dear friends, you have come together in this place so that the Lord may seal and strengthen your love in the presence of the Church's minister and this gathering of friends. Christ abundantly blesses this love. Since it is your intention to enter into marriage, join your hands, and declare your consent. Byron, do you take Jean to be your wife, to be true to her in good times and bad, to love and honor her in all the days of your life?"

"I do," he said.

Jean made the same promises to Byron.

Knowing that standing was still a challenge for the groom, Fitzroy had kept things short and cut to the quick. He said, "You have both declared your consent. May the Lord in his goodness strengthen your consent and fill you both with His blessings.

Frank stepped forward and handed a ring to Byron. In a clear, evenly paced voice, the groom put the ring on Jean's finger, saying, "Jean, take this ring as a sign of my love and fidelity."

Frank gave his sister a second ring. She placed it on her groom's finger. "Byron, take this ring as a sign of my love and fidelity."

Fitzroy concluded, "Lord, grant that those who wear these rings may always have a deep faith in each other. May they always live together in peace, good will and love." Beaming now, the Cardinal added, "And as we in the Church are wont to say, 'Amen.' Kiss your beautiful wife, lad."

Byron complied to a polite but heartfelt round of applause. Amid the round of congratulations that followed, Fitzroy took McGill aside for a word in private.

"James, I'm told you know my old friend Father Inigo de Loyola."

"I do, Your Eminence, but I haven't seen him for a while."

"Nor has anyone else I've spoken to about locating him, but unlike the others you are a detective of some renown."

McGill said, "I hold my own. Are you asking me to find Father Inigo?"

"I am, acting in this matter as an emissary for the Holy Father."

That set McGill back a step. "The *Pope* wants to find him?"

"He does. His purpose, I'm afraid, is something he didn't confide in me."

Consternation filled McGill's eyes. Finding and stopping the people who were looking to kill him was a full-time job. He might have asked the Cardinal for a delay in taking up the matter had it been for his own purposes. Suggesting that the Pope cool his heels was something else entirely.

Then McGill had a — possibly divinely inspired — thought.

Put Sweetie on the job. Get her fully back into the game. Sure, he was her old friend and she took the threat to his life as seriously as anyone did, but how often did a good Catholic get a chance to do a favor for the heir of St. Peter? There was no way she could turn down this job.

"Is something wrong, James?" Fitzroy asked, just a touch of the parochial high school headmaster in his voice.

McGill smiled. "Not at all, Your Eminence. McGill Investigations International, LLP will do our best to find Father Inigo."

The Cardinal blessed McGill for his generosity.

The President had left word with the Secret Service before going into the wedding of Jean Morrissey and Byron DeWitt that she was to be disturbed by nothing short of an act of war against the United States. When she exited the room where the wedding ceremony had been held and saw Secretary of State Helen Hargitay and Director of National Intelligence Gregory Ishida waiting for her and looking grim, she wondered if she'd missed hearing of the opening salvo of some vast new global tragedy.

Her first impulse was to summon Vice President Morrissey to join them, but she decided to hear the nature of the bad news before ruining the moment for Jean.

"How bad?" was all she said to the Secretary of State.

As if to provide any moral support the President might need, McGill appeared at her right shoulder. He didn't need to be a private eye to see that something was seriously wrong.

The President's subordinates, though, were hesitant to speak freely in front of the presidential spouse. Patricia Grant understood that immediately and dismissed their concern. "Tell me."

Secretary of State Hargitay said, "Per your orders, ma'am, every U.S. warship at Subic Bay left port and is making way to support operations in the South China Sea. The DOD assures me that these massed forces should be more than sufficient to deter any harassment or worse from the Chinese, at least for the time being. What we didn't foresee was the gambit the Chinese did use."

Knowing that she'd just heard the prelude to whatever bad news was coming, the President wondered if Byron DeWitt might have forewarned her about indirect actions Beijing might take. For that matter, was the recovering deputy director of the FBI anywhere close to playing at the top of his game? She certainly hoped so.

Helen Hargitay turned to Gregory Ishida to provide further information.

His description was blunt. "The Chinese bought Philippine President Rogelio "Rocky" Rojas, lock, stock and barrel. With all our warships out of port, he advised Ambassador Thomas P. Johnson that the United States vessels would not be allowed to return. President Rojas has terminated his country's defense treaty with the United States. All the remaining U.S. support vessels and personnel are to leave Subic Bay within 30 days."

The President knew that bearing such news normally would have been the province of the State Department. The fact that the Director of National Intelligence had carried the water meant that there was a kicker here.

"What else?" she asked.

"The NSA intercepted a communication between Beijing and President Rojas stating that Chinese naval forces will be moving into Subic Bay the day after we evacuate. The message was sent in plain text." Meaning it was not coded. "Both Rojas and Beijing are rubbing our noses in this development."

The President took a moment to think. McGill inched closer, letting her feel physically that he had her back. He thought the U.S. Navy should mine Subic Bay as they departed. Stick Rojas and the Chinese with the chore of cleaning things up. With any luck blowing up some of the bastards.

The President had a more sophisticated take on the matter. "Let's bug the place before we leave, in the most subtle, unguessable ways we can. They'll be looking for listening devices, of course, but let's see if we can outwit them. If so, we might turn this situation into a win."

Then she sighed and added, "Of course, without a base in the Philippines we're at a serious disadvantage in maintaining an effective naval presence in the South China Sea, aren't we?"

Secretary of State Hargitay offered a chill smile. "In addition to everything else, the Vietnamese have penetrated the new Chinese-Filipino relationship. Hanoi has offered our navy the use of Cam Ranh Bay. Under whatever conditions they'll demand, of course."

The president sighed and shook her head. "The irony. Former enemies are now… what?"

"A port in a storm?" McGill suggested.

"Maybe," the President replied. Turning to her colleagues in government, she asked, "What does Hanoi want for the privilege of using their facility?"

"They were about to tell me," Helen Hargitay said, "but I said any discussion would have to take place after I consulted with you."

Patricia Grant said, "Talk to Jean. Assuming she wins the election in November, this will become her burden to bear. In the interim, I'll try to keep Byron DeWitt busy helping me figure out what Beijing might try next."

The presidential decision was no sooner made than an unfamiliar female voice said, "Madam President?"

Everyone present turned and looked at a middle-aged woman none of them knew. All of them thought the same thing: *Who was she and how much had she heard?*

Understanding the situation intuitively, the woman introduced herself, "I'm Angela Possemato, a family friend of Deputy Director DeWitt from California. He knew I was in town; I'm a photographer. He asked me to take a few pictures today. We're all set up. The bride and groom would like to know if you and Mr. McGill could please step inside."

They obliged. One last gesture of normalcy before the world might turn upside down.

Middleburg, Virginia

Whenever the President of the United States went for a ride in an automobile, she took 20 to 30 vehicles along with her. Such was the extent of both her security needs and her resources. Local police cars took the lead in the procession and also brought up the rear. The police, working with the Secret Service, planned the traffic path by which the motorcade would travel and the escape route by which the President's limousine would flee, if required.

Flight was not the only option, though. There was also the choice to fight. If there was an assault on the motorcade, electronic countermeasures could be taken. Should things get more elemental, there was a counter-attack team that could produce a tsunami of lethal projectiles. Both of those responses could be pursued from strongly armored vehicles moving at high speed.

The drivers behind every steering wheel were trained and seasoned professionals.

In an abundance of caution, there was always an armored ambulance on hand, too.

Outside of Hollywood movies, nobody had ever tried to attack a modern-day presidential motorcade. The odds against success were too long. A failed attempt would only make the President look stronger and more heroic while her adversaries appeared more incompetent.

That and hideously dead.

The President's henchman, on the other hand and by his own choice, traveled in but a single automobile. A black Chevrolet sedan. Taps, who'd been watching McGill over the past weeks, had decided that it was armored, had puncture-resistant tires and had advanced communications gear able to summon help quickly.

The name and history of McGill's driver, Leo Levy, was foolishly left openly available on the internet. Levy was a former NASCAR driver who'd won three major races and possibly might have been an all-time great if he hadn't retired early. Finding a wheelman who could keep up with him in a pursuit situation was a quickly discarded idea. Still, the idea of getting to McGill either in his car or as he entered or exited it remained under serious contemplation for Taps.

Attacking him as he arrived at his old office location or departed it had also been a natural consideration. The distance from that building's front door to the curb where his car waited was 15 feet. More than enough room to gun McGill down. But then McGill had moved to his new office structure with its underground parking sheltered by bollards and a steel door.

An attack inside the White House, either overt or stealthy, was a cinema fantasy.

Yes, some fools had managed to jump the White House fence; no one had ever reached the family quarters.

Watching McGill as he went about his travels, Taps looked for the right spot, a favored restaurant, say, where McGill might exit his vehicle and be exposed long enough to meet a swift and violent end. But that kind of opportunity failed to present itself after many days of scouting.

Which left only one thing for Taps to do.

Contrive to lure McGill out of his car at just the right time and place.

CHAPTER 2

Tuesday, September 13, 2016 — Washington, DC

"*The Pope?*" Sweetie asked McGill in disbelief for a third time. He had picked up his old friend at her home on Florida Avenue.

Leo was cruising the neighborhood, everyone in McGill's Chevy knowing that a moving target was always harder to hit than a stationary one. McGill had considered that stopping in at Sweetie's place might put Putnam and Maxi in danger if someone genuinely cunning was tailing him. Hence the mobile meeting.

Over the course of their long friendship, McGill had been known to kid Sweetie. He'd never used the name of the Pope to do so, though. Still, these were strange days, Sweetie thought, and that might be enough to warp anyone's sense of humor.

Sitting next to her in the back of the Chevy, McGill said, "You could ask Cardinal Fitzroy, if you have trouble believing me."

From the front seat, never taking his eyes off the road, Leo asked, "What's he like, Boss?"

"Who?" McGill replied. "The Cardinal?"

"No, the Pope. I've seen him on TV. In his own way, he seems like a good ol' boy."

"I'm sure he is, but I've never had the pleasure."

"Oh. I thought maybe when you and the President had gone

overseas …"

"I'd have mentioned that to you," Deke told Leo.

Deke traveled internationally; Leo worked stateside.

Sweetie still had a moment of doubt, wondering if the three men in the car with her had cooked up some elaborate joke.

Then McGill said, "Margaret, this is a genuine request. His Eminence asked me to find Father Inigo de Loyola because the Pope would like to speak with him. If the plea had come from any lesser figure, I'd have begged off. What with a conspiracy of unknown size trying to kill me."

Once McGill used her given name, Sweetie finally accepted that she wasn't being kidded. That always indicated serious intent. So she sat back and thought about it.

"It would be a great honor to be of service to His Holiness," she said.

McGill replied, "I thought you might like it."

"I see what you're doing, though, Jim."

"Of course, you do."

"You're getting me back into the game, making me an investigator again."

"Only if you want to. Otherwise, you can remain my chief ethics officer."

Deke and Leo, up front, did their best not to crack smiles.

"I want to do that regardless," Sweetie said.

"But you'll still lend the Pope a hand? Who knows, he might even grant you an audience someday."

That idea caught Sweetie by surprise. Imagining the possibility made her smile.

"You could bring Putnam and Maxi along, if he did," McGill added.

Sweetie beamed, momentarily. Then she turned to look at McGill with a cop expression that had made many a bad guy reconsider his misdeeds. "You can stop selling me on the job, Jim. I'll do it." Then she addressed Deke and Leo. "You two had better not let anything bad happen to my friend back here while I'm away."

"Yes, ma'am," Leo said.

Deke nodded.

They dropped Sweetie off at home so she could get started on finding the missing priest.

After that, McGill, Deke and Leo headed to the United States Penitentiary in Hazelton, West Virginia. McGill wanted to talk with Jeronimo "Jerry" Nerón, the custom tailor cum hitman who'd killed Jordan Gilford.

Gilford had just hired on with the Inspector General's office at the Department of Defense. He'd earned a reputation for ferreting out corruption. The corrupt politicians in the Senate and House of Representatives who'd been looting the DOD's budget had feared they'd be exposed and spend the rest of their lives in prison. So they'd hired Jerry Nerón to kill Gilford.

Jerry had sworn he didn't know who had hired him. So he'd been unable to help convict the corrupt pols on a murder charge, but they soon fell to ratting each other out on matters of stealing from Uncle Sam.

McGill's experience was that convicts came to know others of their kind in prison. Felonious birds of a feather and all that. Jerry Nerón was doing life for his crime and McGill thought that was entirely appropriate. He wouldn't ever try to cut that sentence to a finite number of years, but he could see seeking to improve Nerón's quality of life behind bars.

In return, the killer would have to work the prison grapevine to see if any of the cons knew someone who might take a serious run at the President's Henchman. McGill even had a name to help Jerry Nerón start his search: Corona Moe.

Hong Kong

Shortly before midnight, two police officials arrived at a penthouse residence in the Central District of Hong Kong. They found the owner no longer able to appreciate what was surely one of its top selling points: a commanding view of the city lights. The man's severed head sat plainly visible in a plastic wrapper in the middle of a king size bed that was covered with a golden silk duvet. The wrapper was tied off with a white ribbon.

Senior Inspector Liu "Charles" Chao of the Hong Kong Police Force and his colleague Wong "Geoffrey" Guo looked at each other. Decapitated or not, they recognized the victim.

The color of the ribbon binding the wrapper was apt. In Chinese culture, white could substitute for gold and symbolize wealth and fulfillment. However, it was also the color of mourning and was associated, aptly, with death and contracting energy. Lights out.

The man had once been rich and powerful and now neither of those things mattered.

"Yang Ju-long," Liu said. "Donald to his Western friends."

Wong only nodded. He spoke as little as possible. He'd learned in childhood that he'd cause himself far less trouble that way, and people tended to listen to him more attentively when he did speak.

"Ju-long," Liu repeated.

The name meant as powerful as a dragon.

"If his head didn't just fall off," Liu added, "maybe St. George killed him."

The English influence still lingered in Hong Kong.

In keeping with his personality, Wong didn't laugh but he did smile.

"Look how tidy everything is," Liu said. "Not a drop of blood anywhere, and the remainder of the slain dragon, I'll wager, is nowhere on the premises."

The head had been found by Yang's middle-aged housekeeper, the only person besides Yang himself who was known to have the electronic password to enter the premises. She was far too old at fifty-four to be of carnal interest to Yang. So a fatal lovers' argument could be ruled out. She'd claimed to have passed out upon seeing the severed head, and the broken nose and bruised cheek she'd incurred supported that claim. When she'd regained consciousness, less than an hour ago, she'd crawled out of the room and done the right thing by calling the police.

Now, Liu and Wong were stuck with the head.

Well, they would have been if the head had once belonged to almost anyone else. Donald Yang, it was well known to the police, was closely tied to Hu Dai, a sitting and fearsome member of the Politburo in Beijing. Yang was thought to be untouchable, until somebody had decapitated him.

Given the situation, the only thing for the senior inspector to do was find out whether the commissioner — the overall boss — of the police force in Hong Kong wanted the news of the dragon's death investigated or quietly pushed into a shadow and never mentioned again.

The two detectives stepped out of the bedroom so Liu could call the commissioner in a less gruesome setting and receive his instructions. Wong excused himself to use the bathroom — and to call Niles Sutton, his contact with MI-6, the United Kingdom's Secret Intelligence Service. The Brits may have ceded sovereignty of Hong Kong to China in 1997, but they had never stopped paying close attention to the place.

The Oval Office — The White House

"FBI Deputy Director Byron DeWitt to see you, Madam President," Edwina Byington told the Chief Executive via intercom, adding dryly, "Along with the new Mrs. DeWitt."

Inside the Oval Office, the President and Galia Mindel heard chuckles, via the intercom, at the currently apt description of Vice President Jean Morrissey.

"Please send the happy couple in," Patricia Grant said.

The President's personal secretary opened the door to the Oval Office and DeWitt stepped inside, one deliberate, crutches-assisted step at a time. Jean followed behind, watching her mate with the attentiveness of the mother of a toddler taking his first steps. No falls would be permitted.

The deputy director made it all the way to the President's desk, carefully disengaged his right arm from its support and shook the chief executive's hand, asking, "Madam President, may I sit?"

"Please do."

The Chief of Staff moved a second chair to let the Vice President sit proximate to her husband.

"How are you feeling today, Byron?" the President asked.

"Not yet ready to hang ten, but maybe I can dip a toe in the water."

"Water sports aside for the moment, are you up to giving me counsel on dealing with the Chinese?"

DeWitt was quiet and then cracked a sly smile.

His new better half asked, "What are you thinking?"

He said, "After my brain was re-plumbed in the operating room, all my thoughts were jumbled and swirling. English and Mandarin were mixing in my mind. I didn't know which language to use. When I tried to form thoughts and sentences the two tongues clashed. I got scared I'd never be able to express myself clearly in either one. Then things settled down and having seniority, English took precedence, but Chinese crowded it."

Jean said, "That wasn't why you were smiling just now."

DeWitt grinned again. "No, I thought I might just start out speaking only Chinese and weird everyone out, but I didn't want Madam President to think I was a fair-haired Asian spy." He rubbed the stubble on his scarred pate. "I guess I'll be fair-haired again someday."

Returning to the topic at hand, he told the President, "I can give you my analysis on matters Chinese, ma'am, but I recommend you check them with Hiram Chen. He knows more than I ever will, even on my best day, which this is not."

The President had read DeWitt's FBI personnel file. She knew of his relationship with the man who'd introduced him to the language and culture of China. Second father and son.

"Mr. Chen doesn't have a security clearance," she said.

DeWitt was silent for a long moment before nodding and saying. "He would make a fine sleeper agent for Beijing. Never thought of that before. Damn, that would break my heart."

Jean took one of his hands and squeezed it gently.

DeWitt said to the President, "Talk to him anyway. Phrase your questions generally. Try to get the right feel from his replies."

"I'll consider that," Patricia Grant said. Then she told him about the military action in the South China Sea, the loss of the naval base at Subic Bay and the outreach by Vietnam. "My first question is, Byron, do you think the Chinese will try any military retaliation at sea or anywhere else?"

DeWitt was momentarily quiet again. "Possible. Not likely head on. That would not be Sun Tzu at all. More probable, a trick to get our people shooting at each other. Computer hacking to do that maybe. Cyber-stuff not my area. Something indirect. But … Beijing will be … very direct with Manila. Money, people, facilities. All things, everything, to become indispensable fast."

"And the Vietnamese?" Galia asked. DeWitt seemed to be losing steam. Getting an answer, if possible, would be helpful — possibly the difference between success and failure.

DeWitt nodded as if agreeing with a thought that had just occurred to him. "Far more pragmatic … sophisticated people than Filipinos. Useful only as long as mutual interests remain intact. After that …"

DeWitt really started to fade now. Jean exchanged a concerned look with the President. Patricia Grant nodded in agreement. It was time to let the man rest.

"Thank you, Byron," she said. "You've been a great help. Would you like to use a wheelchair on the way out?"

"Yes, ma'am. Thank you."

He followed that with something muttered in Mandarin.

Then he managed another grin and translated. "Mama raised me tougher than this."

That got a laugh from everyone and buoyed his spirits. Edwina, quick as a wink, brought in a wheelchair and Jean rolled him out of the Oval Office.

Edwina also used the moment to give Galia a message.

"Madam Chief of Staff, an Englishman named Giles Henry

says he urgently needs to speak with you. Somehow he managed to get your private White House phone number."

United States Penitentiary — Hazelton, West Virgina

The warden of USP Hazelton turned out to be a lifelong Republican named Howard Meacham who had never liked Patricia Grant even when she'd been in the GOP. He told McGill as much when he called from the road on his way to the prison. That being the case, Meacham wasn't happy when Attorney General Michael Jaworsky called the warden and told him to take the meeting with McGill and do whatever he could to help the President's husband.

So McGill had no trouble reaching the man's office, and to make his appearance just a bit less high-handed, he'd left Deke in the Chevy with Leo.

Even so, Meacham still tried to stonewall McGill, telling him, "The inmate you're talking about, sir, can't just take time out from his routine obligations to have tea with a guest from Washington. Nor can the corrections officers needed to attend to such an inmate abandon their regular duties at a visitor's whim, and certainly without proper notice."

McGill sighed.

He said, "Let me guess, Warden: You not only didn't vote for the President either time she ran for national office, you also don't plan to vote for Jean Morrissey."

"I did not and I do not."

"You prefer Oren Worth."

"I preferred General Warren Altman. I was Air Force, too. But he's no longer an option." The man sounded bitter about that, and since he wasn't going to be cooperative anyway, McGill said, "Really? You liked the guy who's accused of killing his wife? The man who slept with subordinate officers? Hell, if he hadn't left the service, he would have faced a court martial."

"You son of a —" The warden bit off his last word regarding McGill's parentage. Instead, he asked, "Where did *you* serve?"

"The streets of Chicago," McGill said. "It wasn't Omaha Beach, but it was a lot more lively than a rear echelon Air Force man's career."

McGill had only guessed the warden hadn't been a combat pilot, but the look on the warden's face told him he'd been right.

Resentment only made the man more foolish. "I will not allow you to see the inmate you requested or anyone else in my facility without a proper request made in advance. Do I make myself clear?"

"Warden Meacham?" McGill said.

"What?"

"USP Hazelton isn't *your* facility. It belongs to the American people. If a phone call from the Attorney General isn't enough to make you see reason, there's only one other person I can call to make you understand that the hole you're digging is where your career will be buried."

McGill didn't want to get Patti directly involved in this little pissing match. He had Galia Mindel on speed-dial, and she answered on the first ring. Saving the chief of staff's life had turned out to be a useful thing. He explained the situation to Galia and then handed his phone to Warden Meacham.

He opened his mouth to get in the first word, but good luck with that. Whatever Galia told him turned his face red and then white. His eyes went wide as if he was actually seeing whatever awful fate Galia was telling him would come his way if he didn't start cooperating quickly and completely.

That was only McGill's speculation, of course, but he'd bet good money it was pretty close to what was happening.

As if to confirm his point of view, Meacham concluded his call with a subservient, "Yes, ma'am." He returned McGill's phone to him.

With his eyes downcast, he picked up his desk phone and asked the person on the other end of the line to give him the location and status of the inmate he specified with a multi-digit number. McGill took it for granted he was asking about Jerry Nerón. In short order, the warden had his reply, but it didn't seem to make him happy.

He put down the phone and raised his eyes, but only to the level of McGill's chest.

"Inmate Nerón is in the infirmary. Not as a result of violence or serious injury. He has an infection. He's being tested for influenza. If the test is positive, he'll be isolated so he doesn't infect anyone else in the inmate population or the staff. If it's not the flu or something else highly contagious, he'll be returned to his normal routine. You can see him now, but that will be at your own risk."

"When will you have the results of the flu test?" McGill asked.

"Tomorrow morning."

"I'll be back then. Nine a.m. will be good?"

"Should be, yeah."

"Sorry we couldn't work things out amicably," McGill said.

But he regretted even more the coming time when he would no longer be able to bring the hammer down on recalcitrant jerks like Howard Meacham. McGill left the prison. He, Deke and Leo got a couple of rooms at a nearby Microtel Inn.

Deke made McGill leave the connecting door open, just in case.

CHAPTER 3

Hazelton, West Virginia — Wednesday, September 14, 2016

Attorney General Michael Jaworsky's call reached McGill at 5:45 a.m.

"Did I wake you, Mr. McGill?" he asked.

The AG was a two-termer with the President. McGill knew his voice.

"No, but only because my bladder beat you to it by a minute."

A moment of silence was followed by a laugh. "I guess my timing is good then. I get up to go to early Mass with my mother."

"I did that, too, a long time ago, but my mom had to drag me out of bed."

"Mine still does."

This time McGill laughed.

Jaworsky added, "I don't mind, though. Who knows how long we'll have each other? I enjoy the time we spend together, and anything I can do to get on the good side of the Almighty is fine by me, especially these days."

"My sentiment exactly," McGill said.

"I had a call from Ms. Mindel yesterday. I was dismayed to learn that she had to backstop my call to the warden at Hazelton. Perhaps I was too polite when I spoke with him. That made me think of my dad. He was a foreman at a steel plant. When he got going he could scorch the ears off a long-haul trucker. He used to tell me, 'Mikey, don't you ever talk like me … unless you're a grown man at the time and have a damn good reason.' Believe me, Mr. McGill, if you get any guff from that warden again, that'll be reason enough. Please don't bother Galia again, just call me. If I'm in a meeting, I'll take your call anyway."

"Thank you, Mr. Attorney General. I'm here at Hazelton to see Jerry Nerón. You remember him, I take it."

"Of course."

"I want to see if Nerón might have heard of a killer named Corona Moe, either in his travels or since he's been locked up."

"This is in addition to my arranging to allow a foreign national to be placed inside the FCI holding Auric Ludwig?"

FCI meant Federal Correctional Institution.

"Yes. I'm trying to place as many bets as I can. I'm truly tired of people threatening my family and me. I want to put an end to it. Legally, of course."

"That is the best way," the AG said. "You don't intend to promise Mr. Nerón any sort of clemency, do you? Because that's farther than I can go."

McGill said, "It's not that at all. I wouldn't ask you for that, and I won't lie to Nerón."

"What then?"

"I had it in mind to promise improved conditions, within reason."

Jaworsky considered that for a moment and asked, "Can you give me an example?"

McGill said, "I started by thinking about the basics: better food and drink, extra time for exercise, but then I also thought what might really get him to help us is a needle, thread and a bolt of cloth. Nerón was a custom tailor. People paid thousands of dollars for one of his suits. So, if he cooperates, let's give him the opportunity to practice his craft again. Have him make custom tailored suits for men and women who complete their prison sentences with good behavior records. When those people re-enter society, let them do it looking good. If that works, maybe he could even teach other inmates his art. That way the decent part of Nerón's legacy wouldn't die with him. I think he might appreciate that."

"You just happened to come up with this plan?" Jaworsky asked.

McGill said, "One of the things I pray for regularly is inspiration."

"Well, you must be closer to the Divine than I am. In any case, I can work with your idea. Let's hope Mr. Nerón might be of use."

"I pray for that, too," McGill said.

The White House — Washington, DC

White House Chief of Staff Galia Mindel read the *Washington Post, New York Times, Chicago Tribune* and *Los Angeles Times* daily. Not in full, of course. That wouldn't have left her time to do anything else. But she read political, economic and crime coverage along with selected op-ed columnists. If there was anything important that she might have missed, her staff highlighted the stories for her.

For all that, she'd never once read so much as a headline from *The Intruder,* a tabloid out of London, featured at finer supermarket racks everywhere. Having been alerted by Edwina Byington that a reporter named Giles Henry had somehow gotten her private White House phone number and wanted to talk with her, Galia knew she'd have to do some research on the rag.

She was grateful that Edwina had already started the process, providing her with a photo of Henry, a capsule biography of the man and a brief history of *The Intruder.* It was a particularly nasty scandal sheet that looked at paying defamation of character judgments as part of the cost of doing business. There were also photos of bare-breasted women sprinkled throughout its pages, but Galia felt sure that Henry didn't want her to do a cheesecake layout for him.

Thinking it was the best place to turn for help, she put in a call to Sir Robert Reed, the father of General Welborn Yates, former personal secretary to the Queen of England and a one-time spy for MI6. Galia and Sir Robert had become friends on a state visit the President had made to the UK. Now, he lived in the Virginia countryside with his wife and former lover, Welborn's mother.

"My God, Galia," he said upon answering her call, "it's good to hear from you. Have you made plans for how you'll pass the time after leaving the White House? If not, I have a lovely little place down in Virgin Gorda. You'd be welcome to stay and unwind for as long as you like."

"A good place to get away from it all, Sir Robert?"

He laughed. "A nice place to do anything that doesn't involve winter sports. And by the way, everyone here in Virginia calls me Bob. We've named our cat Sir Robert."

Galia told him, "You'll forgive me if I don't join the crowd. I could never think of you as Bob."

"As you like. Tell your old chum Sir Robert how he might be of service to you."

"You don't think I just called to chat?"

"Come now, Galia."

"You're right, but it is good to hear your voice again. What I'd like to know is anything you can find out about a tabloid reporter named Giles Henry."

"Find out? I *know* the sod. I broke his nose once when he had the nerve to ask me an impertinent question about Her Majesty."

Galia laughed, wishing she could have seen that. "After that, of course, you had him checked out down to the calluses on his feet."

"Inside as well as out. The blighter is bent on destroying his liver; otherwise, he remains intact. Aside from the S-curve I planted on his beak."

"Good. I'd like to know everything you can tell me that won't either embarrass or jeopardize the monarchy."

Sir Robert said, "And you'll tell me as much as you can about whatever your plan is for Giles Henry?"

"Deal," Galia said.

He gave Galia all the dirt he had on the man, and there was a lot of it.

Then she returned the tabloid reporter's call.

USP — Hazelton, West Virginia

McGill saw Jerry Nerón approaching from the opposite direction as the two of them neared an interview room at the penitentiary that was normally used by inmates and their lawyers. Two corrections officers escorted the prisoner, each grasping an arm. Nerón was handcuffed and wearing leg irons. McGill was unencumbered by any restraints and had but one officer as his escort.

To McGill's eye, Nerón wasn't doing well in prison. He'd gone from slim to gaunt. Neither his face nor his hands showed any signs of trauma, but his eyes continuously darted back and forth as if he'd become accustomed to anticipating danger from any direction. When he first met McGill's gaze and recognized who he was, he stopped dead in his tracks. Not from alarm but in surprise.

Obviously, he hadn't been told who had come to see him.

His minders jerked him forward. They plainly hadn't been told to be on their best behavior in front of the visitor from the White House. Nerón made it unnecessary for the officers to tug at him again. He picked up his step. That was when McGill spotted the man walking behind Nerón and his escorts.

He wore a suit and a crew-cut, neither of which looked particularly well done. His eyes were close-set and his mouth was compressed to a razor's stroke. At a guess, McGill pegged him as Warden Meacham's second-in-command. He stepped in front of Nerón and his minders, but he didn't offer McGill his name or his hand.

He simply told McGill, "You'll have 15 minutes with this inmate. When the time's up —"

McGill shook his head. "I'm Jim McGill. What's your name?"

The guy hadn't liked being interrupted, and he wasn't used to being rebutted, not in the prison and not in front of his staff and an inmate. McGill saw that Nerón kept his eyes on the floor and his shoulders hunched as if he might catch a beating just for being in the wrong place at the wrong time.

"Forgot your own name?" McGill asked.

He saw it then. The guy wanted to take a run at him. It was unclear whether he had the nerve to do it in front of his men or whether he'd expect them to jump in and help in the effort. McGill decided not to let things come to a head, not in the present circumstances.

He said, "Didn't the warden tell you he talked with the White House chief of staff yesterday? No? Well, I spoke with Attorney General Michael Jaworsky, the chief law enforcement officer of the United States this morning. He and I are working together on something here."

That got everyone's attention. Even Nerón looked up.

"It just might take more than 15 minutes. In fact, it'll take as long as necessary."

The tough guy who'd been left in charge was trying to decide if McGill was lying.

"How about answering this?" McGill asked. "When things get difficult around here, does the warden leave it to you to do the heavy lifting?"

Bingo. That grievance lit a fire in the tough guy's beady little eyes. He threw open the door to the interview room and said, "In there."

No mention of a time-limit was repeated, and none was necessary. The stink of urine and vomit hit McGill where he stood. Anyone with a functional sense of smell wouldn't last two minutes in that stench. He reached out, closed the door and shook his head.

"What else you got?"

"That's the only space available."

"What, in a place this big? I was a cop for twenty-five years. I know you don't give a damn what I think, but that's bullshit — *you don't have anywhere else* — and we both know it. Listen, you shouldn't have to take a big hit on your personnel record because your boss put you in a bad spot, but that's exactly what will happen if I don't get a little cooperation."

Gritting his teeth, the deputy warden asked, "What do you want?"

The guy was still acting like he was in command, but McGill sensed a degree of relief that the heavyweight from Washington wasn't going to put all the blame on him if things went bad.

"You've got a big job to do here today, right?" McGill asked. "A lot more to worry about than my little interview with one of your inmates."

"Yeah, I do."

"So, it'd be wrong of me to ask to use your office."

Just the effrontery of the idea set the guy back on his heels.

That didn't stop McGill. He said, "My money says the warden took the day off so he wouldn't have to look at me."

The guy couldn't keep himself from nodding.

So McGill told him. "That'd make his office available, and I promise neither Jerry nor I will pee on his carpet. Isn't that right, Jerry?"

Keeping his eyes down, Nerón said, "Yes, sir. We won't do that."

The corrections officers were all grinning. They'd have a story to tell all their buddies The deputy warden remained poker-faced, though.

He only said, "Okay, let's go."

Chief of Staff's Office — The White House

"I know where Senator Randall Pennyman is living," the English-accented voice on the phone told White House Chief of Staff Galia Mindel.

Ignoring that assertion, Galia asked, "Is this Giles Henry?"

The tabloid pest had called back before she could complete her research on him.

"The one and only," Henry confirmed.

"You shouldn't have my White House phone number, Mr.

Henry." Galia, of course, was recording the call.

"And yet I do, dear lady, yet I do."

"Mr. Henry, are you familiar with the U.S. Code?"

"What's that, something that lets you lot communicate without the Russians listening in?"

"No, not that kind of code. I was referring to the official compilation and codification of the permanent federal statutes of the United States. The body of laws governing this country."

The tabloid reporter gave a phlegmy chuckle. "My, my, have I put a foot wrong?"

"You should not have my White House phone number, Mr. Henry. The fact that you've used it twice now tells me someone gave it to you. Under Article 26, Section 7213 of the U.S. Code, regarding the unauthorized disclosure of information, the person who gave my phone number to you can lose her job, be fined $5,000 and be sentenced to five years in a federal prison."

"That sounds a bit harsh, now, doesn't it?"

"The same fine and prison sentence also apply to you, sir. If you either paid for or extorted the information you received, other charges might also be brought."

"Well, bugger me. Good thing I'm not over there in the colonies with you."

"The United States has a global reach, Mr. Henry."

"Don't I know it?" Henry said. "You lot shot those two Chinamen out of the sky, didn't you? Thing is, m'lady, I don't intend to put myself within the reach of your laws or your naval missiles. I've found your missing senator, but you won't find me."

"Is that so?" Galia asked. "Perhaps I should mention I have friends in MI6. I think an Anglo-American effort might turn you up sooner rather than later."

That stung the man. Galia heard a muttered, "Bitch," not spoken directly into the phone.

Then Henry told her clearly. "You haven't even asked me what I want, you gorgon."

"I don't need to ask," Galia replied.

If the man had indeed found Randall Pennyman, and Galia felt he wasn't bluffing, then Pennyman had told Henry how she'd threatened him, told him he'd better vote against convicting the President after she'd been impeached, and how Pennyman's refusal to go along had resulted in his criminal acts being revealed. Not only that but how Pennyman felt sure Galia had a similar stranglehold on most of the pols in Washington.

With the suicide of Thomas Winston Rangel, Galia had hoped she'd be able to leave Washington with all of her dirty secrets safely tucked away, and now this cretin had to raise his ugly head out of the swamp he normally inhabited.

Henry said with a sneer in his voice, "You don't need to ask because you know everyone's nasty, wicked ways, don't you? I'd wager you can quote any part of that code of yours that applies to them, too. Well, maybe you can catch me, m'lady, but it won't be in time. Not before I tell the whole world your story."

Having the last word, the bastard ended the call.

Leaving Galia to think: I don't need this shit. Not now. Not with one foot out the door.

USP — Hazelton, West Virginia

Jerry Nerón told McGill, "They're trying to kill me in here."

The two men were seated at opposite ends of a sofa in the warden's office. McGill had chosen not to sit behind the warden's desk, thinking a smear of viral stupidity might be lurking there. Wouldn't want to catch that. Besides, he wanted Nerón to feel as relaxed as possible. Incline him to feel cooperative.

"Who's trying to kill you?" McGill asked.

The last thing he wanted was for a possible source of help to be murdered.

"Could be almost anyone," the inmate said, "or maybe everyone. At least one con and one guard, that's for sure."

"How do you know that?"

"The con came at me with a shank. The guard turned a blind

eye."

"Was this in a shower room or something?" McGill asked.

Nerón shook his head. "No, in the chapel."

That took McGill by surprise. "During a service? In front of other people?"

"Unh-uh. I was just in there alone, kneeling down, looking up at Jesus on his cross, wondering how I was ever going to get right with him? I even came right out and asked Him, was that even possible? I know he's supposed to forgive our sins, but mine … hey, *I'd* send me to hell."

McGill said, "Who was the corrections officer on hand? What's his name? A place like this doesn't let a guy like you wander around unattended."

"You got that right. The guy's name is Kovack. Haven't seen him around since that con came at me."

"Tell me why you were in the chapel alone," McGill said.

"What I did was ask, could I please go to services with the other cons? Told them it didn't have to be Catholic. Protestant would do. Even evangelical if that was all they had here in West Virginia. At first, they told me no. Pray in my cell if I wanted; that was the best I could get. Then, last week, they changed their minds. Still couldn't go to services, but I could have fifteen minutes a week by myself in the chapel. I'd have a CO with me, but I could say any prayers I wanted."

"You didn't suspect something was up?" McGill asked.

Nerón shook his head. "In here, something good comes your way, you grab it — before someone else can take it away from you."

"So what happened?"

"I'm down on my knees in the front pew, got my hands folded and my head bowed and my eyes closed. I'm praying, telling the Lord how sorry I am. I know I've been evil, but maybe He can see something good in me that I can't see. Then I hear footsteps coming my way. I think I've maybe been praying five minutes. No way it's been fifteen. I open my eyes and look over my shoulder."

McGill said, "It wasn't the guard; it was the inmate with the knife. Kovack was nowhere to be seen, right?"

Nerón nodded. "Yeah. The con saw I'd spotted him and he charges me like he's going to plunge his blade down right in the middle of my skull. I didn't try to jump up to my feet. I raised up just enough to slide my ass back on the pew's bench. The guy's momentum took him past me to where I'd been a moment ago. I stuck him in the eye as he went by."

"You had a knife, too?" McGill asked.

"Unh-uh. You know what I did on the outside, right? When I wasn't killing Jordan Gilford, I mean. I was a master tailor. So, in here, I found a chip of the right kind of wood, and made a needle of it. Pretty damn good copy: hard, sharp and easy to hide. Got the guy who came at me *three* times in that eye. Would have gone for the other one, too, if I had the chance. Only now Kovack was finally back. That fucker clubbed my head."

So much for Nerón seeking Divine forgiveness, McGill thought. He was just glad the guy was still alive.

He asked, "Did anyone find your wooden needle?"

"Don't think so. I must have dropped it when I got clubbed. Nobody's said anything about it. Might still be in the chapel for all I know."

McGill considered that. "The surface of your weapon is probably too small to take enough of a fingerprint to identify you. But maybe some of your blood or skin is on it, enough for a DNA match."

Nerón said, "Who knows? What I've been thinking is I've got a lot more explaining to do to the Lord. He didn't send you here to me, did He?"

The question surprised McGill. He certainly didn't think his plan to seek Nerón's help was part of a larger design. But this side of heaven who could say for sure?

What he did was tell Nerón what his plan had been coming into USP Hazelton.

The inmate took the news that clemency was off the table with a shrug, accepting the inevitable, but he beamed at the idea of being able to practice his craft again and to pass it on to others.

"So what you want me to do for you," he said to McGill, "is to see if I can find out anything about a contract killer called Corona Moe and pass the word to you."

McGill said, "Yeah. I thought maybe having been in the same line of work you'd be a natural to talk to other inmates about the guy. See if anyone in here knows about him. It was also pointed out to me that corona is a Spanish word as well as an English one. I thought that might be something to consider."

"Could be," Nerón agreed, "and I'd jump on this deal, only I don't know how much longer I've got to live."

"You'd really help me?" McGill asked. "Try your damnedest to find out what I need to know?"

"For what you're offering me, yeah. I can't promise I'd succeed. I can tell you right now I'd give it my best shot."

McGill took out his phone and starting tapping out a number.

"Who're you calling?" Nerón asked.

"This is a federal facility. Someone tried to kill you here. That's a federal crime. I'm calling the FBI. We'll get an investigation started. Buy you some time here to do your work for me, and then get you a transfer."

"Damn," Nerón said. Smiling, he pointed upward. "Maybe He does have a plan for me."

McGill didn't know about that. He began to speak into his phone.

Highway US 70 Eastbound

On the drive back to DC, McGill called Yves Pruet. He thought having Jerry Nerón work the inside-prison angle would be sufficient. There was no need to risk Odo Sacripant's health or life by doing the same thing.

Once McGill had explained himself to Pruet he heard a sigh.

"What's the matter, Yves?" McGill asked.

"You are a bit tardy, *mon ami.* Odo is already inside your

government's prison in Virginia, FCI Petersburg Medium Security, I am told, where *M'sieur* Ludwig is being held."

"I didn't think that was going to happen so fast."

"Yes, well, your attorney general made it so, and Corsicans can be an impatient people."

"Damn," McGill said.

Pruet told McGill, "I have my own doubts about the wisdom of this plan, but I am certain of Odo's ability to defend himself. He will come through this … perhaps not unscathed but in one piece."

McGill still had doubts but didn't voice them.

Pruet understood the content of the silence and said, "Remember, my friend, Odo survived the battle with Etienne Burel."

McGill clearly recalled the epic battle under the Pont d'Iéna in Paris.

"I remember," he said. "Let's hope there are no monsters like that lurking in Virginia."

The idea of that even being a possibility left Pruet speechless. For a moment anyway.

"Yes, of course, one must always hope for the best."

"Did you and Odo work out a fail-safe plan for him?" McGill asked.

"Qu'est-ce que c'est?" French for: What's that?

Pruet hadn't understood the question.

McGill's rudimentary command of French had allowed him to understand Pruet's inquiry.

"A way for Odo to get *out* of prison if something goes wrong," he explained.

The embarrassed silence told McGill they hadn't.

Pruet only said, "Odo might have considered such a precaution to be an insult."

Now, McGill was the one stuck for a reply.

Yanking Odo out of the prison might cause a fuss that would alert Ludwig to the moves being made against his plan to kill McGill. All things considered, Odo would have to stay locked up. At least for a little while.

Georgetown — Washington, DC

With his usual motoring skills and a military grade radar detector, Leo made the three-hour return trip to the capital in just over two hours. The ride had been mostly silent, each man biding his own thoughts. Until they got to town.

Then as McGill's Chevy rolled down Wisconsin Avenue on the way to the White House, Leo said, "Boss."

McGill said, "Yes?"

"You see that guy up ahead on the corner to our right?"

McGill had no problem spotting the man. He had the height to play basketball in the NBA. Maybe small forward: six-five or six-six. He had olive skin and was otherwise a study in black: hair, sunglasses, jacket, gloves, pants and shoes.

"Got him," McGill said.

Deke picked up on the guy, too, and asked, "What about him?"

"I've seen him two or three times in the past week."

None of the men in the car gave themselves away by staring at the man. They cruised by, faces forward as if he was nobody special. Leo and Deke, though, checked him out in the rear view and passenger side mirrors, and Leo said, "I've got all the video cams, fore and aft, up and running."

Keeping his eyes on the road ahead, McGill asked, "Is he looking our way or doing anything suspicious?"

Leo gave a tight shake of his head. "No. He's just crossing to the other side of the street. Not giving any sign he even saw us."

"So why'd you notice him?" Deke asked. "Just because he's big?"

Leo said, "*Tall.* He's not a bruiser, though."

McGill nodded. "That was my impression, too. The guy's lean."

"Okay," Deke said, "He's tall, slim and does the Johnny Cash thing, dressing all in black. He didn't look to me like he's carrying a firearm or an explosive of any size."

Federal agents, the ones who protected people, were taught to look for posture adjustments, shifts in shoulder, hand and hip placements that people made to accommodate carrying firearms or explosive vests. Gait and arm-swing were also altered from those of a normal stride to provide quick access to a weapon or a bomb trigger.

Many armed people weren't even aware they were making these not-so-subtle changes.

Then again, stance analysis was a relatively recent tool in crime fighting.

Of course, it wasn't perfect. Carrying a knife, even up a sleeve, didn't create a perceptible shift in either posture or movement. If you weren't keeping your eyes open, a blade could do grave damage in a matter of seconds.

"I didn't see any sign of a weapon either," Leo replied.

McGill said, "So what caught your eye?"

"The guy's gloves. Today and the other two times I saw him, he's been wearing gloves when it wasn't even chilly much less cold."

McGill looked at the outside temperature reading on the Chevy's dashboard: 58° Fahrenheit.

Leo was right about the gloves, unless … McGill said, "I think there are some medical conditions that make people feel unusually cold."

Deke said, "There are, and some drugs can do it, too. My uncle was getting chemotherapy and he was cold all the time, even though it was summer. But you've seen this guy three times now, Leo? Today was the first time for me."

Leo nodded and the Secret Service special agent grimaced. He didn't like the idea he was losing his edge.

McGill took some of the sting off when he said, "I didn't spot him either. Maybe he's nobody special. But way to stay alert, Leo."

"Sure thing, Boss."

Still displeased with himself, Deke told Leo, "If we see this guy again, pull over. I'll have a talk with him."

"Couldn't hurt," McGill agreed. "We can all check the video when we get back to the office."

"You buying the popcorn, Boss?"

McGill said, “Sure, butter included.”

Ever practical and focused, Deke added, “We can see if we get any matches from the facial recognition software.”

Rock Creek Park — Washington, DC

Strolling through the park, the killer known as Taps was a deeply troubled individual. Some people saw themselves in an indistinct middle ground of the male-female spectrum. A number of those people used the pronouns they, them and theirs for self-reference. Taps felt this was a clumsy misappropriation, and didn’t have any difficulty with gender-specific pronouns.

Plural pronouns should be left to groups of people, as they were originally intended.

Well, a reasonable exception could be made for schizophrenics, but that was all.

The answer to the problem, Taps felt, was to come up with new words to use as neutral pronouns, not steal and distort existing language. This was an oddly conservative point of view for someone who had no regard for the injunction against *killing* other people.

Then again, Taps had what might be called tribal license in matters of gender confusion. There were times when, with perfect justification, Taps might use either masculine or feminine self-reference. While out stalking or putting down a victim, the choice was usually masculine. After all, men were by far the more prolific killers.

Still, there had been times when seduction and cold-blooded betrayal had been called for to make a hit. In those instances, Taps usually chose and used a feminine persona and frame of reference.

Taps hated what nature and Mom and Dad had made of him, or her, but there were also times when he or she appreciated the versatility. Right now, for instance, the public persona he was using was misleading in height, hair and skin color and predominant gender appearance. The tall man in black was an illusion, and it was much harder to catch and convict a person who didn't really exist.

Taps hadn't set out specifically to look for McGill and his car. He was simply cruising the area between McGill's new office and the White House, walking one likely route or another, hoping to see where happenstance might let him intersect with the Chevrolet carrying the husband of the President. He'd spotted the man and his ride going past him on Wisconsin Avenue four times now, twice in the same place, at very nearly the same time.

There would be no point in stepping out in front of the car and firing at it, of course. Even if he made it stop, then what? None of the rounds from a handgun would penetrate either the windshield or the body work. As soon as he ran through his first magazine, the Secret Service man in the car would pop out and take him down with his Uzi.

From what he'd read in his research, even a shoulder-launched multipurpose rocket might not penetrate the vehicle's exterior. Now, a Hellfire air-to-surface missile that was designed to be an anti-armor weapon, sure, that would get the job done, but what he'd been told by his sources was that even making an inquiry about obtaining a weapon of that sort was all but certain to end in arrest and a life term in a federal prison.

On top of that, acquiring a drone capable of delivering a Hellfire would be another all but impossible exercise.

Where a purely physical assault was likely to fail, though, Taps thought that a psychological ploy might just be the key to success. If he could determine a location that McGill passed routinely at a given time, and there were passers-by on hand, one of Taps' minions might seize an innocent victim and thrust him or her directly in front of McGill's oncoming car.

Based on all his research, Taps couldn't see McGill telling his driver to leave someone his vehicle had struck lying on the street and speed off. Neither would McGill be content to simply let his Secret Service agent aid someone his car had hit. Consciously or not, McGill thought of himself as a hero. He would feel compelled to take part in any effort to provide aid and comfort.

In a moment of inspiration, Taps thought there was a far more subtle way to entice McGill to spring from his car. One that wouldn't induce the President's husband and his underlings to immediately take a defensive attitude. Well, maybe the Secret Service agent would be on guard, that being the nature of his job, but McGill and his driver likely wouldn't. That increased the odds in favor of Taps' attack force.

Taps smiled, warming to the idea.

Both sides of his/her sexual identity liked it.

Federal Correctional Institution — Petersburg, Virginia

When master conman Bernie Madoff was convicted of perpetrating the largest financial fraud in U.S. history, bilking thousands of investors out of billions of dollars, he was sentenced to 150 years in prison, the maximum allowed by law. That meant he was certain to die behind bars. Even so, the authorities preferred him to expire of natural causes.

So the Federal Bureau of Prisons gave Madoff five tips on how not to come to a premature end while in its custody. One: Stay within sight of corrections officers; Two: Avoid confrontation with other inmates; Three: Be polite and respectful; Four: Don't borrow money from other inmates; Five: If threatened, request protective custody.

Auric Ludwig received a sentence only twenty percent as long as Madoff's, but that was time enough for Ludwig to die in confinement — unless his sentence was severely reduced or the verdict against him overturned entirely. As with anyone in his circumstances, Ludwig's mind roiled with regret and self-criticism. That and a burning desire to wreak vengeance on James J. McGill, the architect of his downfall, as he saw things.

Ludwig had been evaluated as being only a moderate threat to himself or others within the penal system and was shipped off to an FCI, a medium security facility. He was told if he conformed to prison regulations and discipline he'd be considered for transfer to the nearby low-security facility where housing and disciplinary conditions were more relaxed.

As with Bernie Madoff, Ludwig was similarly instructed on how not to come to a bad end. He was warned that you didn't have to be placed in a high security or super-max prison to face physical danger. He took the warning to heart but he couldn't help being who he was, a take-charge guy. At least as far as his fellow convicts were concerned.

Well, that had been the first step anyway. Subverting certain staff members came next.

Ludwig's plan was to hew closely to four of the five tips he'd been given: He always made sure there was a guard nearby; he never got in any other con's face; he kept a civil tongue in his head; he'd demand protective custody if anybody ever got ugly with him. But he felt sure the way to acquire power in his captive environment was to play a twist on the remaining rule.

He didn't borrow money from other inmates. He lent it to them, interest free. His largesse was made possible by the fact that the 2nd Amendment faithful, particularly the card-carrying members of FirePower America had raised millions of dollars for his legal defense fund and they continued to donate steadily two years after he'd been incarcerated.

So Auric Ludwig put out the word to the prison's general population shortly after arriving at FCI Petersburg: If you have a relative or friend who's in a bad way as a result of your being locked up, let me know. Maybe I can help. He warned that he would not aid any criminal endeavor, but if somebody needed help making the rent, paying a medical bill or just buying some groceries, let him know. He might be able to provide aid.

In amounts ranging from hundreds of dollars to a few thousand — car repairs costing what they did — he'd assisted over a hundred needy prisoners. He simply called his lawyer's office, had them forward the promised funds to his fellow inmates' families and friends. The only request made of the recipients was that they inform their incarcerated loved ones that the money had been received.

There was nothing at all illegal about the process. Nobody even tried to keep it secret. Ludwig *wanted* the prison administration to know about it. Within a short time, his fellow cons came to love Ludwig and the staff knew better than to mess with him unless they had a damn good reason.

Ludwig never gave them one. He was always polite and respectful. Followed any order he received without objection. Never violated any rules. In other words, he made himself completely approachable. He never offered a loan to any of the guards; that wouldn't have looked good. What he did was wait for them to come to him.

Only three of them did, but that was enough. They did small favors for him in return. Like delivering mail to his lawyer without it passing through the usual channels.

In a relatively short time, Auric Ludwig became a power among the convicts at FCI Petersburg … and not long afterward was when the big, tough-looking Frenchman arrived.

At least, Ludwig thought French was the language he heard the man mutter when the new inmate was brought in and they gave him a cell only five cages down the tier from his own, a fairly nice location as far as prison real estate went. Ludwig thought there had to be a reason for the new guy's placement; he had to have some kind of pull.

So he set about learning all he could about the Frenchman before the two of them would have any direct contact. *What's My Crime* was a favorite guessing game among the convicts. Asking directly, though, could be a risky proposition. The guy being queried might suspect you were a snitch looking for something that might incriminate him further while lessening your own sentence or at least improving your living conditions.

Ludwig had been warned that asking the wrong questions could get you killed. It was better to wait and let a guy tell his story when he felt like it, if ever. After that, the prison grapevine would make it public knowledge. Only the way most guys told their stories they were "half bragging and three-quarters bullshit," a math-challenged inmate had explained to Ludwig.

Besides the possibility of dubious veracity, Ludwig didn't want to wait to learn the Frenchman's story. So he turned to one of his friendly guards, who had been short on the funds needed to cosmetically improve his girlfriend's smile. Ludwig felt sure there would be other esthetic upgrades to come, but he didn't say anything critical yet. Like she's going to take you for all she can and then decide she's too good looking to be a prison guard's girlfriend.

He'd try to time that warning precisely, when he saw the guy getting nervous about losing his honey, and then offer a diplomatic warning. *No offense but …* If he managed things right, the guard would have two reasons to be in his debt.

At that moment, though, what he asked the guard was, "Mr. Kilgore, is there anything I should know about the new inmate down the tier? I like to keep all my relationships here amicable."

"Well, I thought he was French," Kilgore said.

"He isn't?" Ludwig felt sure that French was the language he'd overheard.

"You heard him talking?" Kilgore asked.

"Yes, sir." Guards ate up *sirs* like dogs ate Milk-Bones, quick as a wink and insatiably.

"Well, he does speak French. English and Spanish, too. I think part of his job's going to be translating for Latino inmates who don't have any English. That and maybe teaching one of his foreign languages to anyone who cares to learn."

Guards got detailed descriptions of the people they were expected to keep orderly and confined. That was for their own well-being as much as anything else.

"But he's not French?" Ludwig asked.

"Corsican," Kilgore said. "Had to look that one up. It's an island sorta between France and Italy; France owns it."

The geography lesson had been unnecessary for Ludwig but he

didn't mention it.

Kilgore added, "The other thing is, Corsicans have a reputation for being badasses over there in Europe. Got their own mafia or something like it." The guard gave his prison financier a look of warning. "You be careful around him, okay?"

Kilgore was definitely going to hit him up for another loan, Ludwig knew.

"May I ask, sir, why he's here with us?"

Inmates were not supposed to be told just how much the staff knew, but when you were caught between a demanding woman and a con with cash …

Kilgore dropped his voice to a whisper. "Well, he's innocent, of course, just like everyone else here. But he was convicted of illegally trying to ship a boatload of handguns and semi-auto carbines back home. You know, weapons he bought here. He said he thought he was sending agricultural equipment to Corsican farmers, but somehow the judge and jury didn't believe him. Even so, his courtroom manners were polite, I hear, and he had no priors, so he got sent here instead of a high-security facility. Just between us, the correctional officers are a bit edgy about him. If you happen to overhear that he might act up, let us know and we'll put in a good word for you. Get you sent to low-security where you'll like it much better."

It also wouldn't hurt Kilgore's professional standing if he were the corrections officer who came up with a tip of impending danger, Ludwig knew. Get him sent to low security, too. That was the way things worked. The market exchange of goods and services operated behind bars just like anywhere else.

"Do you know what the Corsican's sentence is?" Ludwig asked.

"Twenty years."

Ten years less than what Ludwig had received. That stung.

"Is he appealing his case?" Ludwig asked.

Kilgore nodded. "Just like you."

"One more thing, sir. What's the Corsican's name?"

"Odo Sacripant." Kilgore shook his head. "Where *do* these foreigners get their damn names?"

From their parents like anyone else, Ludwig thought. But Kilgore didn't expect an answer and having spent too much time talking to one inmate already, he shuffled off.

That was fine by Ludwig. His mind had moved on to another thought.

He was suddenly intrigued by the idea of getting Congress to pass a law making it legal to sell firearms by the ton to any foreign national with the resources to buy and ship them out of the country. Wasn't that within the scope of the 2nd Amendment? If not, it should be.

He should be the one to expand the gun market globally. Explaining it as a broadening of American liberty, of course. The money-making potential of the idea would force America's gun companies to do whatever it took to secure his release from prison.

Ludwig decided to give the Corsican a day or two to settle in and then he'd make his approach. See what practical applications he could devise to advance his plan in the meanwhile.

Then there was another matter he might bring up with the fellow, the Corsican badass.

Ludwig had come to think recently that, despite his popularity within the general prison population and among the corrections officers, it just might be a good thing to have a personal bodyguard. So nobody tried to *extort* money from him.

The White House — Washington, DC

The First Couple was enjoying lunch together in the Family Dining Room at the White House: a green salad, roasted fingerling potatoes seasoned with sage, wild salmon and a Chardonnay that was way too good for a beer-drinker like McGill. As a bow to blood pressure control, McGill went easy on the salt. A cursory check-up with White House physician, Dr. Artemis Nicolaides, had shown McGill's BP was edging up to the point of being a medical concern.

"Having a mob of unknown assassins gunning for you can

make things a little tense," McGill had said upon hearing the news.

He was unwilling to concede that advancing age was a factor.

Diplomatically, Nick didn't bring that up either. He only said, "So go a little easier on the salt. Do some more cardio exercise; intervals are especially good. Find a bit more personal time with the President."

McGill was willing to go along with those prescriptions, even the diminished salt. He told the missus what Nick had advised. She was the one who suggested they eat meals together as often as possible.

"Who knows?" she said. "Some days maybe we'll just have a light snack for lunch and find time for other diversions."

McGill was all for that, too, but this wasn't one of those times.

"Do you think we should have made more time for each other from the start?" he asked, sipping his wine and thinking maybe there was more to life than cold draft beer.

"You mean from Inauguration Day 2009 onward?"

"Yeah."

"And how do you think we might have done that?"

"Let Galia run the government."

"And let Sweetie operate McGill Investigations, Inc?"

"Sure, why not? You and I could have been figureheads, had all the time in the world to ourselves."

"All right, let's say we pulled off a gigantic deception on the American people in general and your clients in particular, and didn't think twice about it. Would you feel the same way about misleading our children?"

McGill shook his head. "There has to be some limit on moral failings."

"One would hope. But even if we were depraved enough to set bad examples for the rising generation, are you and I creatures of indolence, interested only in satisfying idle whims and base pleasures?"

McGill waggled his eyebrows. "The pleasure part doesn't sound bad, but you're right. Our parents had to go and instill work ethics in us. Now, we're stuck with them." He sighed. "But does it always have to be that way?"

Patti said, "From what I see and hear, personal industry declines along with everything else as we age."

"Great. We finally get to take our noses away from the grindstone only to find out everything else is worn down to a nub, too."

Patti reached out and put a hand over one of McGill's, gave him a come-hither look.

He grinned and said, "Well maybe not everything. Some things might stay a step ahead of others."

And they might have proved that very notion if Blessing, the White House head butler, hadn't knocked on the door and interrupted them with news that couldn't wait.

Because it was still technically the lunch hour, and the President could redefine her schedule any time she wanted, she brought McGill along with her to the Oval Office. Galia was already waiting, and by the chief of staff's design, she had Vice President Morrissey, Director of National Intelligence Gregory Ishida, and Deputy Chief of Staff Frank Morrissey also on hand to join the President.

Doubtless other pillars of the Administration were en route to join the party within minutes. Patricia Grant's stomach tightened as she anticipated what had to be bad news. She was glad that she'd brought Jim along with her, even if he didn't contribute a word to whatever discussion was about to begin.

She honestly didn't think she was getting too old to do her job but, Lord, she had gotten tired of it. That didn't keep her from nodding to all those already assembled and taking her seat behind her desk. Jim stood behind her at her right shoulder. Providing all the emotional support she could want.

"All right," the President said, "tell me what waking nightmare we're looking at now."

Galia had a manila folder with the presidential seal on it

pressed against her bosom. It was clear from her expression and those of the others in the room that they'd already seen whatever was inside. The chief of staff stepped forward and told the President, "Mr. McGill's former landlord and current building manager, Mr. Dikram Missirian, was approached approximately 30 minutes ago by Ms. Ellie Booker. She was upset to learn that Mr. McGill wasn't in his office. She asked if Mr. Missirian could take an envelope to Mr. McGill at the White House. If he wasn't in, Mr. Missirian should attempt to get it to you, Madam President.

"Being diligent and determined, Mr. Missirian presented himself to the uniformed officers at the West Gate. He identified himself, told his story and it worked its way up the food chain to me. I had him brought here, thanked him and took possession of the manila envelope he had with him. Since it was directed to you, Madam President, as well as to Mr. McGill, I made the decision to open it."

Galia handed the folder to the President. She and McGill, looking over her shoulder, saw what was inside: a crime-scene photograph of a severed head. Just the thing to make the wine in their stomachs go sour.

"Donald Yang, multi-billionaire Hong Kong businessman, wired directly into the Politburo in Beijing," Galia said.

Patricia Grant closed the folder and placed it on her desk. She looked to her husband — her henchman — to see if he had something to say while she gave the matter further thought.

McGill asked Galia, "Did Dikki have any idea why Ellie Booker didn't bring the picture to the White House herself?"

"I asked," Galia said. "Mr. Missirian said Ms. Booker told him she had a lead to run down."

"On the matter of Mr. Yang losing his head?"

"She didn't specify, according to Mr. Missirian. But he was savvy enough to ask where she got whatever it was he was supposed to deliver. I asked him if he looked at what he'd been given. He said no, and even though he was keyed up, I got the impression he was being truthful. He also said the item came from London, according to Ms. Booker."

"But Ellie didn't say where she'd gone to run down her lead?" McGill asked.

Galia said, "I wanted to know that, too, but Mr. Missirian denied knowing."

McGill thought for a moment. "My guess is that photo is a copy. Ellie has the original and she's making plans about what to do with it."

That shook everyone in the room except McGill.

"We really don't want this going public, Jim," the President said. "Not immediately anyway."

Implying broad dissemination might serve a useful purpose eventually.

He said, "I'll track down Ellie and talk with her."

McGill was tempted to deliver a farewell kiss to his wife, but given the context of the moment and all the government nabobs in the room he decided not to, leaving with only a nod to the woman he loved.

St. Aloysius Rectory — Washington, DC

Sweetie had decidedly mixed feelings as she rang the doorbell of the rectory at St. Aloysius parish. The church's pastor, Reverend Desmond Nkrumah, SJ, was her confessor and her friend. She'd told Father Dez her most personal failings and sought God's forgiveness for her sins through his intermediation. She did whatever penance he prescribed twice over.

But for the past year she'd kept one important secret from Father Dez: her inability to completely renounce her past as a cop. She'd told him that she would turn her energy and ambition to becoming a public servant, a politician. An honest one to be sure. Progressive as well. Not doctrinaire in any way, except to follow the social justice teachings of the church.

Only that ambition had proved unrealistic. Even dipping a toe into the waters of running for elective office had shown her that compromise was the only way to work with other pols, if you wanted to get anything done. Some of the concessions you'd have to make would advance the goals of others, outcomes to which she'd never let herself be a party. On the other hand if she stayed true to herself, she'd never get anywhere. Democracy demanded collaboration and morality could get compromised in the process, if it wasn't abandoned altogether.

Despite the intrinsic faults of partisan politics, she couldn't think of a better way to govern. Leaving her to think that the idea to take her life in a new direction was nothing more than a false start. That had come as a bitter realization.

Jim McGill, bless him, had been gracious enough to indulge her idea of working for him as a chief ethics officer — as if she was fit to tell anyone else how to behave. Well, maybe she was slightly qualified. A bit less driven by personal ambition, slightly more generous in spirit.

Sweetie was lost in thought when the rectory door opened, not by Mrs. Woodrow, the housekeeper, but by Father Dez himself. In his usual fashion, he got straight to the point. "Is something troubling you, Margaret? Is everything well at home?"

The church had a fixed schedule for parishioners to go to confession, but Father Dez had made it clear from his first day at St. Al's that if anyone felt an intense need to cleanse his or her soul the pastor would be available at any hour.

It was the rare day that someone didn't come to the rectory to seek an urgent return to grace. Either that or phone in a plea for the priest to make a house call. In either case, Father Dez almost always responded affirmatively.

Sweetie smiled. "Putnam and Maxi are fine, Father."

"And you, my daughter?"

"I … I might have experienced a revelation."

The priest extended a hand to Sweetie, drawing her into the rectory. "Enlightenment is always a benefit, even when it sometimes feels painful. Come in and we'll have some tea."

Mrs. Woodrow, the pastor explained, was visiting her sister in

North Carolina. Sweetie would have to make do with his efforts to boil water, find the tea bags and honey and set a proper kitchen table. When everything was accomplished to his satisfaction, he took a sip of tea, pronounced it good and asked how he might help Sweetie.

Before answering, she sampled her cup and offered a compliment.

Then she asked, "Father, do you believe God gives us signs in life?"

The pastor gave the question serious consideration and didn't respond with a platitude. Instead he replied, "I think God is more often subtle than obvious in how he communicates with us. He provides us with nudges rather than billboards."

Sweetie liked that. "Good one, Father."

"Do you think you've been nudged, Margaret?"

"I do." She told him of her failure to engage in the political sphere and, on the other hand, how Jim McGill had been agreeable to the position she sought with his company.

Father Nkrumah smiled. "A chief ethics officer? That is a wonderful idea. It should be spread far and wide."

"Don't you think it's just a bit self-aggrandizing, too, Father? Who's to say I'm any more moral than anyone else."

The priest raised his hand. "Me. I do not wish to embarrass you, my child, but when I sometimes face difficult moments, I ask, 'What would Margaret Sweeney advise me here?'"

Sweetie's jaw dropped. "Come on, Father. You're kidding me."

He shook his head.

"But you've never called me to talk about any problem you have," she said.

"I did not wish to add to your own burdens." Then he smiled slyly. "But now that I know you have taken on such duties as part of your job …"

"Anytime, Father," Sweetie said. "Feel free to call on me day or night."

"Thank you. I will remember. Now, back to your nudge from

Our Lord."

Sweetie told him that Cardinal Fitzroy had made a request of Jim McGill and he'd delegated it to her. "It would mean going back to being an investigator, Father."

"In service to His Holiness, our blessed brother, Francesco, if I can believe my ears."

"I had trouble giving credence, too, at first," Sweetie said. "But Jim wasn't joking; this is something real."

The priest started to speak but then held his tongue.

"What is it, Father?" Sweetie asked.

"I can't tell you that you must help His Holiness, my daughter, even though I'm sorely tempted to do so. That must be your choice."

"Do you think I'm being nudged here, Father?"

The priest laughed. "Margaret, I think this instance may indeed qualify as a billboard."

Sweetie laughed. "Yeah, I think so too."

"But do you wish to take up this task? Do you feel at peace with doing so?"

"Father, I'm *eager* to do it."

"Then you've forgiven yourself for a death that was never your fault?"

It took a moment, but Sweetie said, "My fault or not, I think I've done my penance for what happened to Erna Godfrey."

"So do I. Now, if it's permissible, may I know what the Pope wishes you to do?"

"Father, do you know a fellow Jesuit named Inigo de Loyola?"

Desmond Nkrumah smiled and nodded. "We are old friends."

"Good. The Pope wants to find him. That's my job now. So where should I start to look?"

McGill Investigations International, LLP — Washington, DC

McGill made phone calls from his office to Ellie Booker's cell phone, home phone, PBS office phone and even her old World-Wide News phone. The first three numbers sent him to voicemail;

the fourth was no longer in service. He left messages for Ellie to call him and decided to let his subconscious work on the problem of finding her for the moment.

In the meantime, he reconvened the gang, as he called his new business partners and associates, at the conference room in his new office suite. Leo Levy was also there, and Elspeth Kendry joined them. Their purpose was to review the video Leo had shot of the tall man in black clothing, the guy McGill's driver suspected was shadowing them. Before that exercise got underway, though, McGill first had a question for Yves Pruet.

"Did Odo get safely placed in the prison at Petersburg?"

"Yes. The warden let me know he was assigned a cell close, but not too close, to this man Ludwig. The corrections officers were also warned that Odo could be a most dangerous fellow if anyone irritated him. This was meant both for the prison officers' benefit and to filter down to the inmates. Also, if there was any …" Pruet searched for an English word. *"Mêlée?"*

"Melée," McGill agreed, "though most Americans would probably say riot."

"Yes, riot, exactly," Pruet said. "In that case, Odo is to be taken swiftly to the warden's office."

"Good," McGill said.

He was about to have the video of the guy in black screened on a 50-inch flat screen when SAC Elspeth Kendry cleared her throat.

"Yes, Elspeth?" McGill asked.

"Per the President's order, three Secret Service agents have been placed at FCI Petersburg working undercover in rotating shifts around the clock, to provide Mr. Sacripant an extra measure of security. The President doesn't want anything bad to happen to him. Perhaps Mr. Pruet can pass the word in French, so the native cons won't understand, to Mr. Sacripant so he'll know what's up."

Pruet brightened at the news. "That is wonderful, most kind of *Madame la Présidente.* Yes, of course, I will inform my dear friend with the utmost discretion."

McGill gave Elspeth a look. He knew she had ratted out the

plan to place Odo in the prison to Patti. But he could understand why: Nobody wanted another tragedy like Erna Godfrey's death to happen again.

So McGill only asked, "Are the undercover agents posing as guards or prisoners?"

Elspeth clearly didn't want to reply in front of a roomful of civilians, but she appreciated the fact that McGill could have chewed her out in front of them but hadn't done so.

She said, "Two cons, one guard."

McGill understood the division of labor. "The cons for when Odo might be moving about the facility; the guard for when he's locked in his cell. He's covered around the clock."

Elspeth nodded.

Pruet said, "*Bon!* I am greatly relieved. Odo will say, of course, he needs no such help, but he will be touched by the President's concern."

McGill bowed to the inevitable and said, "All right, let's look at some video."

K Street — Washington, DC

Putnam Shady was intent on gleaning information the old-fashioned way: reading. He and a special master, Caryn Osborne, appointed by the Honorable Geryl Cerney, Chief Judge of the United States District Court for the District of Columbia, were handling the task of reviewing the case files of the late Aubrey Gadsden, Esquire. Ms. Osborne had been given specific guidelines: Mr. Shady would be permitted to read the files of those clients of Mr. Gadsden who had faced prosecution for taking the life of another person or had committed great bodily harm that might have resulted in the victim's death.

Clients who had committed other types of criminal acts would be out of bounds.

Also present were Captain Rockelle Bullard and Detectives Meeker and Beemer of the Metropolitan Police Department.

Captain Bullard was the first one to object to Chief Judge Cerney's guidelines. "Seems like that scope of inquiry is a bit narrow, Ms. Osborne."

Putnam Shady had been going to make the same point, but was content to let the police captain play the bad cop, if that was the role she wanted.

Caryn Osborne, who was cute as a button and looked barely old enough to go to a sock-hop, frowned. Which only made her look even more precious. "What do you mean, Captain?"

Rockelle Bullard gestured to her detectives.

Meeker said, "Well, you never know, Counselor."

Osborne was an attorney, not that you had to have a law license to be a special master.

Beemer, earlier, had asked her if she'd graduated from an Ivy League law school.

"University of California at Irvine Law School," she said proudly.

The local cops were underwhelmed. They'd been expecting Georgetown at a minimum. Putnam knew better. UC Irvine had an up and coming law school.

"What might I never know, Detective Meeker?" Caryn asked.

"Well, it's on record in the annals of police work that killers oftentimes have accomplices," he said.

"Say, a getaway driver," Beemer explained.

"Or an arsonist to destroy the crime scene," Meeker added.

The special master turned to Captain Bullard.

"If I let them," Rockelle said, meaning the detectives, "they could go on for an hour."

"Somebody, maybe even a kid, to ditch the murder weapon," Beemer added by way of example.

"How could a child afford a criminal defense lawyer like Mr. Gadsden?" Caryn asked.

Putnam couldn't resist jumping in. "If the kid's a part of the plan, he could have, let's say, a benefactor."

All three of the Metro cops grinned, liking that one — a

benefactor.

Putnam didn't want the young special master to feel she was being ganged up on. Having her take an adversarial attitude would only slow things down.

He told Caryn, "I spoke at the UC Irvine Law School, delivered a speech on the law evolving to keep pace with technological change. The faculty and the students there knocked me out. If you like, I could join you on a conference call with Chief Judge Cerney and see if we can work out a reasonable approach to our problem."

Behind Caryn Osborne's back, Meeker silently moved his lips to shape the word, "Smooth."

The captain and Beemer nodded.

The look Caryn gave Putnam said that she knew she was being massaged but appreciated the gesture nonetheless. "Thank you, Mr. Shady. That would be helpful. At least I hope so. The chief judge tends to be wedded to her initial opinions."

Putnam nodded. "I remember that from our study groups back in the old days."

Caryn's jaw dropped, and the Metro cops couldn't keep from chuckling.

Picking up the framed photo of the woman from Gadsden's desk, Rockelle Bullard said, "Now, all we need is to find out who this sweetheart is."

Caryn glanced over her shoulder. "Oh, you don't know her? That's Zoë Tinker. We play tennis at the same club. She's a terrible flirt, but she has a very strong backhand."

Putnam and the three Metro cops beamed at each other.

Catching a break early was always a great feeling.

McGill Investigations International, LLP — Washington, DC

The crew at McGill's conference room was taking a second look at the videos Leo had shot of the tall man in black. The first time through, everyone agreed that the guy hadn't been obvious enough to stare at McGill's armored Chevy as it drove past him.

There were other pedestrians who did. Over the objections of the Secret Service, and overruled by the First Amendment, an online celebrity news site, NeverBlinks.com, had done a feature on McGill's ride.

The President's Henchman, himself, hadn't objected. The windows on the car were both tinted and bulletproof. Leo Levy also remained unconcerned. He felt sure he could evade any trap and outrun any pursuers, saying, "With me at the wheel we could leave Judgment Day behind."

McGill foresaw another measure of security that would be soon in coming. When the story about his car went viral, Chevy experienced a boom in the sales of black sedans like his. Tinted windows became standard equipment. Few of the other features in McGill's ride could be matched, but with the increasing number of lookalike vehicles on the road in DC and across the country, telling which one had James J. McGill inside became more of a problem.

"Until we roll into the White House grounds," Deke had said. "Then all anybody needs to do is write down our license plate number and — bang — they've got us."

"Good point," McGill conceded. "The *bang* is well taken, too."

So McGill's car went into the government shop that serviced it for a modification, an update of the old James Bond rotating license plates trick, electronic plates. The pixels forming the letters and numerals on the car's plates changed every time the ignition was switched on or when Leo hit a button on his steering wheel.

The strategy wasn't perfect because, as Deke had noted, McGill's Chevy still rolled into or out of the White House grounds. That was a definite giveaway. It could have been countered by exiting or entering the security perimeter of the Executive Mansion without McGill inside, but that would mean using Leo not just as a driver but also as a decoy target.

After what had happened with Caitie recently, McGill vetoed that idea.

At the moment, everyone in the room was concentrating on

the tall man in black on the TV screen. John Tall Wolf, who stood a bit over six-four himself, spotted the first anomaly. He said, "That guy's arms are too short."

McGill froze the image of the man in mid-stride as he walked down Wisconsin Avenue.

"Too short for what?" McGill asked.

"I see it, too, now," Rebecca Bramley added. "His torso is also too short."

"What, we're talking body proportions here?" McGill asked.

Both Tall Wolf and Bramley nodded.

McGill and everyone else turned to look at the image.

Tall Wolf said, "I'd say that guy is about an inch taller than me, but look at where his hands reach on his legs as he walks. With most people, as you swing your arms, your hands come to mid-thigh. This guy reaches barely beyond his hips."

Bramley added, "His other proportions are off, too. Look at how short his torso is in comparison to his legs."

The artist in the room, Gabbi Casale, smiled and said, "You're right. I can see that now. The guy is wearing lifts of some sort, big ones."

"How big?" McGill asked.

"Just a second," Gabbi said.

She focused on the video image of the man's head and used her right thumb and index finger to bracket it. Keeping the distance between thumb and finger consistent, she worked her way down the body of the image. Then she turned to McGill.

"An average person is seven-and-a half heads tall, including the person's head. If an artist wants to convey a sense of nobility, power or grace in a subject, she paints that person as eight heads tall. This guy, he's eight-and-a-half."

"So how much should we deduct from his height?" McGill asked.

Gabbi said, "Average head length is somewhere between eight and nine inches."

"So if John's right about how tall the guy looks in the video, say six-five," McGill said, "his real height might be five feet eight inches or five-nine."

"Yes," Gabbi said.

Ron Ketchum said, "A little guy pretending to be a big man. That tells us something about his personality right there."

Heads around the table nodded, but Maj Olson said, "Can we take another look at him walking, please?"

"Sure," McGill said. He found two sequences of the man walking along Wisconsin Avenue, one shot from behind, one from in front.

"I don't see anything unusual," McGill said.

Maj nodded. "Exactly. When I ran track in college, I studied other runners' strides to see if I could make mine more efficient. This guy is so smooth he flows, never puts a foot wrong. He's an athlete."

Gene Beck added a thought. "He's probably walked in those lifts a lot, too."

"Lifts or high heels," McGill said. "The next time we see him he might be wearing a wig and a dress."

Gabbi Casale nodded. "I think you may be right about our target wearing a dress. That very tall man in black might be a relatively tall woman. I'm going to pull some stills from the video, see if I think the facial features are more feminine than masculine. I'll make some sketches of what I think the face might look like without the sunglasses, as a man or a woman. See which one rings truer."

"Good idea," McGill said. Then a question came to mind. "When you painted that official portrait of me, did you give me any extra height? You know, for nobility."

Gabbi held her thumb and finger a whisker apart. "Just a smidge."

Before Elspeth Kendry left the meeting, she privately offered a pertinent thought to McGill.

"Leo Levy was really on the ball here, getting video of this person."

"Leo's more than just a pretty face," McGill agreed. "He's sharp and I've never seen anyone drive like him."

Elspeth nodded. "I've heard as much from several of my people. That's why the thought occurred to me that you can't afford to lose him."

"Lose him? Why would I —"

Then it hit McGill. Elspeth wasn't saying he would let Leo go; she meant someone could target him. That would be an enormous loss, a good friend as well as an invaluable employee.

What concerned Elspeth first and foremost, though, was the loss of Leo would make McGill more vulnerable. She was trained and paid to think that way.

"I can't force you to take on additional Secret Service protection," she said. "I also can't be your bodyguard because Holly G. is my primary responsibility."

McGill agreed: Patti came first.

Elspeth continued, "What I'm thinking is this. Special Agent Ky is also a friend of Leo's, right?"

McGill nodded.

"So we'll have him stay close to Leo. Meanwhile —"

"Gene Beck has already volunteered to be the fourth man in my car," McGill said.

Gene had volunteered even though his fiancée was pregnant, McGill thought uneasily.

Well, hell, he'd just have to assume Gene had already thought of that.

"We'll all be extra careful," McGill told Elspeth.

McGill's new office was three times the size of his old one. The lighting was recessed in the ceiling and provided by LEDs conserving both electricity and the environment. Following that theme, the heating, cooling and electricity were provided by geothermal and photovoltaic technologies. The floors were polished oak, salvaged from another building. The color scheme, aptly, was earth tones done in a subtle gradient, lighter and airier up top, darker and grounded at the bottom.

Patti had picked out the Persian rugs, all of them woven prior to the ayatollahs' takeover in Iran. McGill had set the keynote for the furnishings: the long leather sofa in his White House Hideaway. He'd had a duplicate made and let the interior designers, under the President's guidance, go from there.

The original sofa would go into the new house in Dumbarton Oaks.

The walls of the office were adorned with tastefully placed and spaced Gabbi Casale original oils. In addition to the paintings, there hung one framed front page from the *Chicago Tribune* trumpeting the Chicago White Sox 2005 World Series victory. McGill wasn't sure he'd live long enough to see another such triumph.

When McGill had been allowed into the completed office for the first time all he could do was smile and wonder how he'd come so far in life. Now, he sat behind his new desk and tried to reach Ellie Booker again on her personal cell phone. This time he remembered to use the numeric code she'd given him to bypass the slush pile.

"For VIP contacts or an urgent call from Mom," Ellie had told him.

As far as McGill knew, Ellie was an orphan.

In any case, she answered the call. "Mr. McGill? The President saw the photo I sent?"

"She did. So did I. We both have the same question: How did you come by it?"

"A source sent it to me electronically."

McGill said, "A source you'd prefer to remain confidential, no doubt."

A pause followed, long enough to make McGill wonder if the connection had been broken. Then Ellie said, "I told you I might have been targeted for my investigation into Congressman Philip Brock's death."

"You also said you're licensed to carry a concealed weapon and know how to use it," McGill reminded her.

"That's true, and I'm not bad for an amateur. Going up against a pro, though, especially if there's more than one, I don't like my chances. Shit, I have to tell you I'm really nervous about all this."

McGill said, "I know that going to the FBI for protection didn't work out. Want me to try the U.S. Marshals Service? Put you in witness protection?"

"No. I don't think that would work either. Truth is, I can be a pain in the ass." When McGill didn't object to the notion, Ellie laughed. "See, even you feel that way."

McGill felt sorry for the young woman, almost as if she were his own wayward child, someone with a lot of talent and reckless courage who'd gotten herself into a very tight spot.

"What can I do to help, Ellie?"

"I don't know."

"How about this? Tell me what you know. I won't share it with the media, but I will take it to the appropriate federal authorities. Maybe their involvement will head off anyone who might be coming after you."

"You don't want to handle things personally?" she asked.

"I have my own problems right now. When I clear them up, then, yeah, I'll help personally."

Whatever the dangers of her own situation, McGill sensed Ellie yearned to ask what his predicament was. To her credit, she refrained.

She decompressed with a sigh and said, "Okay, I was shocked when I saw the photo my source sent me: a severed head. I did an image search online and found out he was Donald Yang, Hong Kong billionaire businessman with reputed ties to the big boys in Beijing. My first thought was: Who's going to kill a guy like him except his bosses?"

"A reasonable assumption," McGill said without explicitly confirming it.

"Okay, but here's where things get touchy. I also saw a copy of what happened to Congressman Philip Brock, his severed head sitting between the two pig heads."

McGill knew how that had to happen, too. A source — someone in government who should have known better — had shown it to her. There was no point in asking who that someone was.

All he said was, "My guess is you did side-by-side comparison of the two decapitations."

"Yes. It looks to me as if they were done by the same person. One very clean cut about an inch below the chin. The flesh at the sides of the neck even curls up the same way in both victims. A lab could do a tool-mark analysis to make a closer comparison."

McGill said, "Good idea, but why would the same person want to kill both men?"

Ellie told him, "I don't know. You could look for a motivational tie or — and this is what really scares me — it could be one killer, a guy who specializes in decapitation, was hired by two clients who didn't even know each other."

That idea was enough to give McGill a chill. "So what are you going to do now, Ellie?"

"I'm already doing it. I'm going into hiding. I don't know for how long. And I'm getting rid of this phone."

She apparently did just that, not even saying goodbye to McGill.

FCI Petersburg — Prince George County, Virginia

Odo Sacripant took his *déjeuner* — lunch — at FCI Petersburg alone. It was the first time he'd set foot out of his cell since being escorted there that day. He'd skipped breakfast that morning, using the time to get a feel for the place. Listening to its sounds, sniffing its odors, watching the movement of the guards and memorizing their faces. Most inmates, the ones not being treated for illness or being punished in an isolation cell, were obliged to follow routines, eat their meals and do their work at specified times and places.

Fitting in with the others, being nothing more than another prisoner, would have been one approach to his task. That way, though, would have been a longer trek. With who knew how many men looking to kill *M'sieur* McGill, Odo thought speed was of the essence. Also, how long would someone used to eating French cuisine be able to tolerate American prison cooking?

So *Madame la Présidente's* people had spoken with the prison administrators and persuaded them to give Odo an unusual degree of leeway in varying his movements from an inmate's normal routine. The purpose of this was to make him a figure of intrigue. Draw the attention of some minions of this fellow named Ludwig, and then meet the man himself.

The warden had warned Odo, "That might not be the only kind of attention you get. This is a medium security facility, but there are some hardened individuals here. They might express physical resentment of your getting special treatment."

"I will defend myself," Odo said, "but only to the extent necessary."

The warden nodded. "Yeah, restraint would be appreciated. It wouldn't look good if you broke someone's neck, and we had to let you go."

Odo gave a small bow. "Discretion in all things."

The prison allowed all inmates, not being penalized for infractions of the rules or engaged in a work detail, to have what it called controlled movement. That was, for the first five minutes before a daytime hour until five minutes after the hour they were free to move from Point A to Point B. Once at Point B, they had to remain in place for the next fifty minutes.

Everyone had to be back in his cell before lights-out. Inmate counts were done each night and every morning.

Odo had been briefed on all this. What he expected — hoped — would happen was that one of Ludwig's lackeys would appear at his cell for a brief look-see, try to assess for the boss what kind of man had arrived in his fief, another peasant or someone who might challenge him for power. The minion would speak to Odo briefly, get a reading on him and scurry back to his overlord to report while the controlled movement period was still in effect.

The fact that Ludwig was a figure of dominance in the prison had been made clear once the warden had told Odo that Ludwig lent money to the families and friends of other inmates without charging interest. There was nothing illegal about it; nothing the authorities could do to stop it. When Odo asked the source of Ludwig's funds, he was told it came from donations made by gun-nuts across the country. Again, perfectly legal.

Odo had to admire Ludwig's cunning if nothing else.

After eating his abominable lunch, he was surprised when he got back to his cell. No gang of cons sought to find out how tough he really was. No bootlicker was there to wheedle secrets out of him. Ludwig himself sat on Odo's bed and smiled at him.

He said, "I'm told you like to smuggle arms. I've got a proposition or two for you."

The White House — Washington, DC

McGill had Leo and Deke take him back to the White House. The remainder of his colleagues remained at the office throwing ideas at the wall to come up with a way to identify Corona Moe. McGill had decided from the start that he wasn't going to be a micromanager when his expanded business rolled out.

He'd given his people only two initial guidelines for how to go about their business. Don't break any laws and don't do anything you wouldn't want your mother to read in her weekly church bulletin. He figured if you weren't embarrassed either legally or personally, you'd be in the clear.

On the way to 1600 Pennsylvania Avenue, McGill informed Leo and Deke about Elspeth's speculation that Leo could be in danger. The former NASCAR driver laughed and said, "They'd have to catch me first."

McGill replied, "You sleep in your house, don't you, Leo?"

"You've got a point, Boss. Maybe I'd better sleep in the car."

"What about me?" Deke asked.

"Elspeth didn't fret about you," McGill told him. "Either she thinks you can hold off a small army or your skill-set is more easily replaced."

Leo grinned but didn't say anything. Deke sulked in silence.

As they pulled up at the White House, McGill added, "You could sleep in the car, too, Deke. That way, any bad guys who make a move will have to deal with both of you, and you can tell yourself they want you as badly as they do Leo."

McGill exited the Chevy before any response could be made, possibly one questioning his heritage. He made his way to the Oval Office and stopped at the desk of the President's secretary, Edwina Byington. He inclined his head toward the door to the President's lair and raised his eyebrows inquisitively.

"Just the chief of staff," Edwina said. "Deputy Director DeWitt is on his way, but you should have five minutes, if that's all you need."

"That's all I need. Should I knock or will you announce me?"

"Let's go with the announcement. Makes you seem more important that way."

McGill grinned. He wondered if there'd be a place for Edwina at his company after he and Patti moved out of the White House. Or if she'd even be interested if he could find something. He'd miss the old girl if they went their separate ways.

"Your henchman is here, Madam President," Edwina said on the intercom line. "I told him he might have five minutes, if that's all right with you."

She looked at McGill and gave him a nod. He entered without delay. Just in time to see Galia exit through the side door to her own office.

"Galia didn't have to leave on my account," McGill told his wife.

"Byron DeWitt is coming back here today. Our meeting with him might go on for a while. We both thought a brief trip to the loo might be in order before it starts."

"Oh, right. I'll make it quick then."

He told her about the tall man in black Leo had spotted and the suspicions arising therefrom.

The President nodded. "Very alert of Leo. I'm glad you have such good people working for you. So you and the gang are looking for someone who might be a very tall man or a somewhat less tall woman. Is there some way you think I might be of help?"

"Maj Olson thinks this person, whatever the gender, is probably an athlete, based on the way he or she moves. I came up with another possibility: a dancer."

"An entirely reasonable guess," the President said, "but where do I come in?"

"Well, I asked myself who might have knowledge of a tall, cross-dressing, possibly transgender dancer with homicidal tendencies. My first guess was I'd have to seek someone with a show-biz background."

"And you thought of me. Well, I did know some dancers back in my film days, Jim, but that was a long time ago. How old did this person appear to be?"

McGill said, "Hard to tell looking at a video of someone wearing sunglasses and maybe makeup. But I wasn't thinking of you as my primary resource, dear lady."

"No, then who?"

"Your former talent agent, Dorie McBride. Doesn't she know everyone who's trod the boards since Ol' Will was busy writing his dramas and comedies?"

The President nodded. "Pretty much, yes, she does. But you know what she'll say when I call her."

"That she has the *perfect* script for you? Now that you're about to retire from politics and all, you should jump at the chance." McGill sighed. "Oh, well, it was just an idea."

Patricia Grant stepped over to McGill and embraced him. "You know I'll make the call. Anything to keep you from harm."

McGill kissed his wife. "Exactly how I feel about you, too."

Then he quickly recapitulated his conversation with Ellie Booker and got out of there without further ado. Didn't want to back up his wife's schedule.

DuPont Circle — Washington, DC

Senator Oren Worth had his DC presidential campaign offices on two floors of a commercial building at one of the capital's best addresses. Clerical personnel worked on the ground floor and gladly accepted small donations — anything less than $10,000 — and handed out bumper stickers and yard signs: ELECT WORTH. In a penthouse suite, senior management and sometimes even the candidate himself met with big-money donors.

People who expected more than knick-knacks in return for their money.

Worth's latest presidential campaign manager — his third — had just come aboard. She was a woman named Layla Dart. She'd gotten her start in politics as a fund-raiser. The word on Layla in those days was she could suck money out of a fat-cat donor faster than Dracula could drain his blood. Of course, she had a big edge in sex appeal over Bela Lugosi or any of his successors.

Besides physical attractiveness, she possessed a predator's cunning. Spotted vulnerabilities at a glance and knew exactly how to exploit them. More than that, she left her victims begging for more. The chumps inevitably thought they'd learned a thing or two from the first go-round with her and would do better, in a personal sense, the next time. They never did.

Worth was Layla's first presidential candidate. Her biggest wins up until now were bagging the governorships of Florida and Texas for a pair of twin brothers who came from big oil money. In an uncharacteristic flash of regret she'd almost felt sorry for what she'd done to the tens of millions of Americans living in those two states, inflicting those two clowns on them.

Then she remembered that she preferred to winter in St. Barts and summer in the Hamptons, where she'd never have to lay eyes on any of those gullible good ol' southern boys and gals, and any sense of guilt vanished.

She watched as her newest, biggest and richest client yet worried himself sick, and thought if she put this guy into the White House she might have to move out of the country year-round. She understood how big-time, big-money business tycoons might think they could take the next step and run the most powerful country in the world. It was just a matter of letting themselves imagine they were cut from the same cloth as Washington, Lincoln and Roosevelt.

A simple exercise in narcissism for most of them.

Their unvarying mantra was, "I can do *anything*."

When they got close to the goal, though, winning a major party nomination to be President, things got a whole lot scarier. If they had half a brain, that was. From what she could see, Oren Worth was smart in a gender-specific way. He knew how to deal with all sorts of men from Harvard MBAs to the hard-hats who operated monster mining machines. Pit him against any of them, he'd come out on top.

Where he fell short was dealing with a strong, smart woman. Worth had been married twice, the first time for five years. No kids. His ex-wife had a Ph.D. in economics. Worked out of the London office of a Japanese bank. Never had a public word to say about her marriage to Worth. What she did have was a pair of well-tailored bruisers who kept the paparazzi and the hoi polloi at bay.

Layla had no doubt the former Mrs. Worth had been well paid, and most likely still was collecting dividends, to be discreet. That was only fair. Her marriage to Worth continued to provide him with an air of respectable heterosexuality. For a number of years, he'd added to that image by occasionally "dating" other photogenic women. Not models or actresses but women who'd achieved significant status on their own, either in business or philanthropy.

Those liaisons never lasted more than a few months and the partings were always amicable, creating whispers that none of the pairings had ever involved intimate physical contact.

His second marriage was to a woman who was age appropriate to the 60-year-old senator. Her name was Marjorie. The infrequently published photos of her showed she came with a pleasant if not stunning appearance. She appeared in public less frequently than a cloistered nun. A joke told in the Senate, though never in Worth's presence, was that the senator and his wife got together for lunch at least every other year to see if it was still too soon to consummate their marriage. After Worth's customary five-year period, they, too, divorced.

One Washington wag assessed Worth's style as: "Love 'em and leave 'em well off."

Nonetheless, Worth's history of relations with the fair sex put up a sufficiently good front that nobody had ever found the least hint that he lived in a closet.

So he'd navigated the social waters of both business and politics successfully.

Until he decided to run for president and found himself matched against Jean Morrissey. He was looking at a front-page *Washington Post* photograph of her right now. The Vice President had just married her FBI hero in a rehabilitation facility. The happy couple was sharing their first kiss as husband and wife.

Layla doubted there existed any photograph remotely like it featuring Worth and either of his exes.

He looked at Layla, shook the newspaper at her and asked, "How the hell am I supposed to compete with this?"

She said, "Go to Vegas, discover a Keno girl who's your true soulmate and get married by Elvis, all within 48 hours. Remembering, of course, to have a photographer on hand for the nuptials."

For the blink of an eye Worth seemed to give the idea consideration, until he realized he was being mocked.

"I didn't pay you a small fortune to give me shit," he said.

He had paid her, in full. Layla always got her money up front. Win or lose, politicians were apt to delay payment or stiff you entirely once an election was over. She'd heard such horror stories many times. Her check from Worth had been deposited, cleared and wired to her offshore bank account before she showed up to work.

She told Worth "Here's what you really do, Senator. You make a public show of good manners. You congratulate the Vice President, wish the Deputy Director a speedy and full recovery, and hope the happy couple has many wonderful years together."

"Out of government," Worth muttered.

"Yes, of course. That's understood, doesn't need to be said. Senator, you have everything you need to win the White House except for one thing."

Worth recognized Layla's verbal snare, but he put his foot in it anyway.

After all, he knew his check had cleared, too.

"What?"

"Charm. You need to work on your charm. Men with charm, especially in politics, are all but extinct. I want you to watch a handful of Cary Grant movies I'll select for you. He played opposite many strong female characters. He was their fervent antagonist but he brought off his rivalry with élan. Charm, if you don't prefer the French."

"I don't, and I'm not Cary Grant."

"That's all right, neither was he."

"What?" The senator's expression told Layla not to toy with him.

"He started life as Archie Leach; he *became* Cary Grant," she said.

Worth shook his head. "It's too late for that. I have no acting talent."

Layla shook her head. "If that were true, you'd never have gotten this far in politics."

Worth's face turned red. "All right, I don't *want* to be charming, goddamnit. I think there's no way I'll be able to avoid arm-wrestling Jean Morrissey, and I *have* to win or I'm sunk."

"Okay," Layla said, "let me ask you this: Who do you think is physically stronger, the Vice President or me?"

Senator Worth eyed his third campaign manager. Layla Dart was toned head to toe. She had a nice tight round backside, but the rest of her was long and sleek. She could probably do yoga poses that would break him in two, but she didn't look like she had any brute strength.

"Her," he said.

The word was no sooner out of his mouth than he felt he'd stepped in another trap

"What's that got to do with anything?" he added defensively.

Layla said, "Let's handle the matter this way. You and I will arm-wrestle right here, right now. No one will ever know. If you win, you take on Jean Morrissey. If I win, you see how close you can come to becoming Cary Grant. Deal?"

He stared at her once more, up and down, in a way that would have been completely rude in any other circumstances.

Worth asked, "You're not going to eat a can of spinach first, are you?"

Layla laughed and beamed at him. "A Popeye joke. That's very good. You might have some charm after all."

Worth sat at a card table and positioned his right arm to wrestle. Layla sat opposite him. Positioned her arm and clasped his hand.

The senator didn't wait for either of them to say, "Go!" He tried to win immediately.

Cheating didn't help. Layla had anticipated the move and her arm didn't budge. She waited just long enough to look Worth in the eye and smile. Then she pinned him in nothing flat.

Leaving Worth with only one alternative: performance enhancing drugs.

When he shared that thought with Layla, she shook her head and said, "Don't you know? Those things can shrink your testicles."

The senator told Layla that no price was too high to pay for the presidency.

But he did agree to watch some Archie Leach movies.

The White House — Washington, DC

Byron DeWitt, feeling stronger than he had the day before, returned to the Oval Office. He entered the room using his crutches more certainly than on his previous visit. Jean Morrissey followed behind him but didn't hover. He shook hands with the

President and took the same seat in front of her desk that he had previously. Jean and Galia Mindel also sat where they had before.

DeWitt said, "I wasn't at my best yesterday, Madam President. I'm feeling a bit closer to my normal self today, and I woke up with new ideas to share with you."

"Please do, Byron, and thank you for coming."

DeWitt nodded.

The President said, "Do you still think the Chinese will strike back? If so, in what manner and how soon?"

DeWitt nodded. "They have to do something. Both domestic and Politburo politics will demand a reprisal. President Li can't afford to look weak or he will be replaced. General Hu Dai is no doubt using proxies right now to suggest a response that's ..." DeWitt searched for the right word. "Disproportionate. Spectacular."

The Deputy Director closed his eyes for a moment.

Opening them again, he said, "An aircraft carrier. That's what came to me this morning."

Galia said, "China has only one carrier, a refitted vessel bought from the old Soviet Union. They can launch planes from it but —"

DeWitt shook his head. "No, no, one of *our* carriers with a full complement of warplanes aboard. That would be General Hu's kind of target. Possibly using anti-ship missiles."

Jean said, "But that would be the start of all-out war. Conventional war at a minimum with a risk of going nuclear."

The Deputy Director nodded in agreement.

Patricia Grant said, "Wouldn't General Hu have to displace President Li before an attack like that could be put into effect?"

DeWitt nodded.

"Is Li likely to step aside without a fight?" the President asked.

DeWitt shook his head.

"What might Li's counter-plan be? For Hu and for us."

"He'd want something on the same scale as a carrier. He's bound to know General Hu's thinking. If he settled for anything less ... he'd lose face, lose his job and probably lose his life."

"So you think war is inevitable?" Galia asked.

"Might be getting close to that. We have to be ready for almost anything on short notice. Only Li won't act in the same way as Hu. The general is brass knuckles to the face; Li is a knife in the back. He'll follow Sun Tzu's dictum that the supreme art of war is to subdue the enemy without fighting."

"How would Li do that?" the Vice President asked.

"Computer hacking is my guess. I don't know how that stuff works, but if he could get one of our military assets to take out another one, say, a bigger, more valuable one, they could rejoice and how could we respond against them?"

None of the three women present, the most powerful people in the United States government, had an answer to that. They also didn't know if such a scenario was even possible, but the idea was enough to chill them all. What the hell good was the best military hardware in the world if its software could be corrupted and redirected by an enemy?

Now that the question had been raised it would need to be answered immediately.

Despite the need to focus on the harrowing new prospect DeWitt had raised, Galia had another question relevant to China to ask DeWitt. "Mr. Deputy Director, what do you make of the murder of Donald Yang?"

That bit of news caught DeWitt by surprise. "Yang is dead?"

Jean told him, "Decapitated."

DeWitt thought about that for a moment.

"Killing Yang had to be President Li's work: a warning to Hu Dai and a show of strength to the others. 'Fear me. If I'm willing to take Yang's head, I can come for yours, too.'"

"Won't Hu and the others fight back?" Jean asked.

DeWitt said, "Only if they think Li isn't ready to pounce on them right now. Otherwise, they could see the killing as a trap."

"Could a coup already be underway in Beijing?" Galia asked.

"It's possible," DeWitt said. "Li, Hu or any number of Politburo members might soon lose their heads."

Patricia Grant understood one possible implication. "If General

Hu emerged victorious, he would have the power to fight a war against us on his terms."

DeWitt said, "It's possible, but I don't think Hu has the edge, at least right now. If he did, Li wouldn't have had Yang killed. Things might change, but I think you have at least a little time, Madam President. To get our forces ready or to make a countermove."

"What kind of countermove?" the President asked.

DeWitt offered a suggestion.

Satellite News America — Washington, DC

Having gone to Patti to ask for help in finding the identity of the tall individual in black, McGill conjured yet another avenue of investigation. He had Leo and Deke take him to the Washington headquarters of Satellite News America. As a measure of enhanced protection, they'd picked up Gene Beck to go with them.

Deke waited outside with Leo, in case McGill's driver truly was a significant target. Gene accompanied McGill inside SNAM's building. The security people in the lobby were armed, this being the United States, but they obliged McGill by calling Monty Kipp's office.

With just a hint of trepidation in his voice, Kipp came on the line. "To what do I owe this honor, sir?"

McGill got a distinct feeling Kipp had a back door out of the building in case someone, maybe even him, gunned down the guards and came storming after the tabloid TV reporter.

"A possible idea for a story, Monty. You said I owed you a favor, remember?"

"I do, but I wasn't expecting to collect."

"Then think of this as a pleasant surprise. Of course, if you're not interested, I could go see Didi DiMarco." Normally, he would have used Ellie Booker's name, but who knew if news of her sudden departure hadn't already reached her TV peers.

A moment of hesitation on Kipp's part followed. There was some area of overlap in story interest between the two media figures, but

Didi usually went with more straight news reports. Still, if it was something big enough …

McGill knew what the Brit was thinking and said, "You'll like this one, Monty."

"You're sure?"

"Positive."

Kipp knew McGill still might be playing him, but he'd hate himself if he turned down a story that might be a true capstone to his career.

"Let me speak to the security blokes, please," he told McGill.

"I have a friend with me, Monty. We're both armed. Tell your security people that's okay."

"Of course, it is. SNAM has several firearms firms amongst its advertisers. Do try not to shoot my secretary when I send her out to meet you, though. I'm sincerely fond of her."

"She's safe with us," McGill said.

Gene added, "Unless she shoots first."

Le Petit Prince Restaurant — Washington, DC

Secretary of State Helen Hargitay and Ambassador Tran Van Danh of the Socialist Republic of Vietnam met for an early dinner at Le Petit Prince, a French restaurant on Wisconsin Avenue in Georgetown. They had a private room in back to themselves and small talk prevailed until their Mushroom Risotto and Grilled Chicken Paillard had been served. Both diplomats passed on a bottle of wine, given the weighty matters they had to discuss, in favor of Badoit sparkling water, a favorite of King Louis XVI.

Once the food and drink were set on the table, the room was theirs alone until closing time and beyond should that be necessary. The restaurant was headed by Paul Legrand, a Cordon Bleu chef, but its operating costs were covered by the NSA. Not a word spoken on the premises, frequented by many foreign dignitaries living in Washington, went unrecorded.

Chef Legrand had lent his name, reputation and culinary gifts to The Little Prince's kitchen because he knew a restaurant that had no overhead expenses would be vastly more profitable to him than one that did. Also, his *grand-père,* Marcel, had fought in the Resistance during World War Two and had his life saved on more than one occasion by operatives of the American OSS.

The *entente cordiale* between the Legrand family and *les États Unis* was now in its third generation. The peaceful relationship between the USA and Vietnam was of a more recent vintage, but both countries had a long-time affection for French cooking. The restaurant setting was also far more discreet than if Secretary Hargitay had flown to Hanoi to discuss an agreement to use Cam Ranh Bay as a base for the U.S. Navy.

Doing that would have been poking a stick in China's eye. Under the right circumstances, both countries would have been happy to do that, but being hasty was never wise.

Ambassador Tran opened the discussion by raising the subject of money. He said, "The United States has been paying $2 billion dollars annually to the Manila government for the American use of the port at Subic Bay. Another $10 billion dollars was invested annually by American companies in the civilian economy of the Philippines. Eighteen percent of the Philippines' exports were to your country, Madam Secretary. For the use of our port at Cam Ranh Bay by the American navy, we will want twice the amount you paid the Philippines for military rent and twice the civilian investment. As to exports from the Socialist Republic of Vietnam, we ask that you absorb only 25% of our exports."

A piddling increase above the current 24% level.

Hargitay replied, "Very gracious of you not to ask for the doubling of that figure, too."

Skilled diplomats always framed their insults politely.

Madam Secretary wasn't done, though. She marshaled economic facts to push back. "Mr. Ambassador, the United States is already the *top* importer from Vietnam. At the same time, my country is not even in the top five countries exporting to Vietnam. Why, I believe the number one exporter to your country is China."

Ambassador Tran hardened his voice in rebuttal. "China is not looking for military facilities in Vietnam."

Hargitay smiled. "I imagine it would cause some sleepless nights in Hanoi if it were."

Tran grimaced. Clearly, things were not going as smoothly as he'd hoped. But the Vietnamese were nothing if not a determined people. "Our port facilities are superior to Subic Bay. Our workforce is more efficient than the Filipinos. And we'll honor any agreement we make down to the final punctuation mark."

Unlike the new president in Manila, he meant.

Hargitay was hardly overwhelmed. "Of course, Mr. Ambassador. The United States will also honor its commitments, but issues of dollars and cents are not to be haggled over by diplomats at our levels. We'll pass the demands and counter-offers along to the bean counters and see what can be worked out. But I sense you have another card to play. Please show it to me now so we can finish our meals before they get cold."

Tran straightened his tie, sat taller in his chair and said in a flat tone, "If Vietnam allows the United States to establish a naval base at Cam Ranh Bay, it will increase the risk of direct countermeasures by China."

"You mean military attacks, Mr. Ambassador?"

"Yes, that would be a real possibility."

"Beijing might respond only by stopping trade with Hanoi."

"We can ignore economic threats even if they are painful. There are other partners in commerce for us around the world."

"Of course, there are," Hargitay agreed, "but China will always squat atop Vietnam like an elephant above a wasp. You could sting the giant but you'd get crushed in the end. Please specify what kind of insurance you'd like against that unhappy ending, Mr. Ambassador."

Without batting an eye, Tran said, "American troops on our northern border. Five hundred thousand, just like the greatest number in your war against us. That and a commitment to use your nuclear arsenal against China should it invade Vietnam, just as you guarantee the safety of Japan and South Korea."

Helen Hargitay kept a straight face and digested all of the ambassador's demands. Then she said, "So you'd like the United States to make your country both rich and safe. Well, I suppose that's nothing more than the rest of the world wants from us."

Having lost her appetite, the Secretary of State stood. "I'm afraid, though, I can't guarantee all that on my own authority. Thank you for speaking with me, Ambassador Tran. Please enjoy your meal. You should be hearing a response from the White House soon."

Satellite News America — Washington, DC

Esme Thrice, Monty Kipp's secretary, greeted McGill and Gene Beck with a smile worthy of a magazine cover. Pretty much any magazine cover. She shook their hands, provided her name and said, "A pleasure to meet you, gentlemen. Please follow me."

McGill walked alongside her. Gene brought up the rear.

Paying attention as they made several turns to both the left and the right, McGill deduced Monty had snagged a ground floor corner office as far from the main entrance as possible. Anyone who had a serious bone to pick with the scandal reporter would have a hard time finding his lair. The building's security people would have an extended opportunity to stop an aggrieved party in the maze. And most male malefactors would stop dead in their tracks when they saw Ms. Thrice at her desk in the outer office, wondering what might be the best way to ask her for a date before doing something evil to her employer.

She knocked gently on Monty's door, opened it and said, "Your guests are here, Monty."

"Thank you, Esme. Please show them in."

Gene told McGill, "If you feel safe in there, maybe I should keep an eye on things out here."

The easy assumption was Gene wanted to plant his eyes on Ms. Thrice, but McGill had heard from the man that his girlfriend was due to deliver their first child in a matter of weeks and the couple planned to be married next spring. So Gene was thinking professionally not carnally.

"Sure," McGill said. "Monty and I have a non-aggression pact."

Standing behind his desk, the reporter nodded.

Esme offered drinks but both visitors declined with thanks.

As McGill stepped into Monty Kipp's office, though, he heard Gene ask Ms. Thrice, "Will it bother you if I whistle a bit? Softly, I mean. I feel a song coming on."

The door closed, cutting off the reply, but McGill felt sure the answer would be affirmative.

"What's he mean," Kipp asked, "'a song coming on?' You hire tunesmiths now, do you?"

McGill detected a note of jealousy in the aging reporter's voice.

He didn't want to get off on the wrong foot, so he said, "Might be a lullaby. Gene's about to become a new dad. And I look for help from people with all sorts of skills. That's why I'm here, Monty."

McGill took a seat without being offered an invitation to do so.

Kipp continued to look at the door briefly and then took his seat, too.

"She's gay, you know," he told McGill.

"Ms. Thrice?"

"Married to a woman."

"Me, too," McGill said. "I highly recommend it for those so inclined."

Kipp frowned, knowing he was being twitted.

"How may I help you, sir?" he asked. "Or should I say how may we help each other?"

"First off, Monty, we need to agree on some ground rules or this will be a very brief visit."

"What sort of rules?" the reporter asked, suspicion in his voice.

"Delaying any word of what I'm about to tell you and ask of you until the matter is successfully concluded," McGill said.

Kipp raised his eyebrows. "Is there any guarantee of success?"

McGill took a moment to honestly assess. "Ironclad, no. But I have a pretty high batting average."

Still a Brit to his core, Kipp had been in America long enough to understand the baseball metaphor; McGill swung a bat to his advantage more often than not.

"Need I fear your wrath if I fail, through no fault of my own, to live up to any bargain we make?" the reporter asked.

McGill replied with a question of his own. "Come on, Monty, have you ever made an honest mistake?"

Kipp had to laugh. "Not since I was in swaddling cloth. Even then, I've been told, I always tried to put one over on my mum."

"On the other hand," McGill said, "I'd bet you've saved any number of juicy stories for your memoirs, ones certain to shock polite society and titillate your fans."

Kipp's eyes went wide and his mouth fell open … and that's when he realized he'd just confirmed the guess McGill had made. He shook his head in self-disgust and said, "Well, that was an honest mistake, giving away my darkest secret to you just now."

"One you won't make again?" McGill asked.

"Not without putting a gun to my head immediately afterward."

"Don't do that, Monty. I really could use your help."

"And now you'll finally tell me in what capacity?"

McGill nodded. He gave the reporter the name of Corona Moe, told him more than one assassin was engaged in an effort to kill him and handed Monty a glossy print of the tall man/woman in black pulled from the video.

McGill said, "I have a person well placed in the legitimate entertainment industry checking out the possibility of this person having some on-screen or on-stage dance credits."

Kipp smiled and understood where McGill was going. "You'd like me to survey the demimonde of less than respectable entertainment and see if this person has a place in it … when he or she isn't busy assassinating people, I assume."

McGill nodded. "I'm trying to leave no stone unturned. I'm pretty sure my people and I will be able to defend ourselves against an attack, but why take any chances? I'd prefer to take the fight to my opponents."

The reporter nodded. "Catch them unawares. That'd make for a smashing story … which you'd be willing to share with me for broadcast."

"Publication. I'll do print but not video."

"Radio or audio podcast?"

"Okay, that and/or print, but that's all."

"Deal. I'll start making inquiries immediately, but how do I contact you?"

McGill gave the reporter his cell phone number, but told him not to share it.

The two men shook on the deal.

When McGill and Gene got into the backseat of McGill's Chevy, Gene handed him a business card with Esme Thrice's name and title — executive assistant, not secretary — on it.

"What's this for?" McGill asked.

"Ms. Thrice says ol' Monty intends to go back to England before too long. He's asked her to go with him, but she and her wife want to stay Stateside. I told her we might be hiring. There's a Web link on the back of the card where you can find her job history."

McGill pocketed the card and asked, "Did she like your whistling?"

Gene smiled and nodded. "She's pretty good at it herself. Don't know if that's on her résumé, though."

Political Muscle — Washington, DC

With their daughter Maxi doing a rare school night sleepover and study session at a friend's house, Sweetie and Putnam found themselves at liberty to have a night out, an intimate night in or a walk in the park if they wanted to get a head-start at being old fogies. Then Putnam pulled a rabbit out of his hat and said, "I rented Political Muscle for the evening, the whole place."

Sweetie said, "What?"

Political Muscle was an ultra-high-end fitness center in Washington that catered to top Congressional and White House staffers, lobbyists and criminal defense lawyers who specialized in saving politicians who got caught with their hands in the public till. The cost of membership for a single person at Political Muscle amounted to that of a semester at an Ivy League school.

The idea of renting out all three floors and many thousands of square feet of fitness nirvana would approach the amount of money the Pentagon spent for cost overruns on a given day. In other words a fortune and then some. But if Putnam said he had done so …

Sweetie had to ask, "Did Darren Drucker give you signing privileges on one of his checking accounts?"

Drucker was the billionaire stock-picking genius with whom Putnam worked on building the new progressive Cool Blue political party, Jean Morrissey being CB's first presidential candidate.

Putnam shook his head. "This is on my own dime. Well, make that dollars, but not as many as you might think."

"What, you got a deal?"

"Exactly. But nothing that could come back and bite me either criminally or politically. The club sold an ownership stake to a Swiss interest so it could expand. Take things to a new level of self-indulgent luxury. Officially, the place closed for business a half-hour ago, but I made an offer to management to let me and my fair lady have the run of the place until midnight. With the Swiss now involved, and club management knowing how their new European partners don't like so much as a spare franc to pass them by, they said, 'Okey-dokey.'"

"Okay," Sweetie said, "I can buy that, but it probably didn't hurt that everyone in town knows you're tight with one of the world's richest men."

Putnam shrugged. "Things like that never hurt."

Sweetie moved on to the next salient point. "And just maybe you think I'm not quite the physical specimen I used to be."

"Who among us over-40 types is?" Putnam parried.

He was, Sweetie knew. Well, actually, no he wasn't. Her husband had been a verging-on- chubby wise-ass when she'd met him. Now, he more closely resembled the Live Strong physique once exemplified by Lance Armstrong, only without the performance-enhancing drugs.

Meanwhile, Sweetie's crisis of confidence had resulted in the first prolonged period of physical slothfulness in her adult life. No yardstick was required to measure her backside, but her muscle tone, top to bottom, was far from the sculpted curves and planes that once had defined it.

"Okay, I could use a good workout," Sweetie conceded. "What do you have in mind?"

"A little stretching, aerobics and strength work to start. Then for dessert we could do some steam and-or sauna and finish floating nude in a 25-meter pool we'll have all to ourselves."

Sweetie frowned. "Naked?"

Her attitude toward nudity had relaxed considerably since marrying Putnam, but that was in the privacy of their own home. After Maxi was sound asleep. And the bedroom door was locked.

"Wait a minute," she added, "isn't the pool in that place on the top floor with glass walls?"

Putnam nodded. "Exactly right. But we'd have the overhead and wall lights off, and the pool lights dimmed. We'd be two shadows floating in a candle's glow. Outside, we'd have all the lights of the city to look at. It would be magical."

Sweetie thought about that and asked, "How warm is the water?"

"I don't know, but probably cool enough to be refreshing after a workout."

"Is there a hot tub?"

Putnam said, "Big enough for a baker's dozen, but we'd have that to ourselves, too."

Sweetie acquiesced. "Okay, I'll swim a length of the pool, if I feel comfortable about it, and then jump in the hot tub."

Where the bubbles would shield her from any joker with a

telescope.

Turned out Sweetie swam *four* lengths of the pool. The cool water felt so good after a workout that was far more vigorous than either she or Putnam had planned. She had thrown herself into it. Stretched her muscles until they all but melted. Did free-weight reps and cranked out enough chin-ups to feel the burn and then some. Ran two miles on a treadmill, pushing up the speed until the last quarter-mile left her gasping.

When she felt too tired to swim another stroke, she just floated on her back.

Let the water reduce the swelling and ease the lactic acid out of her muscles.

If any creepy peeper was getting his jollies from afar, let him.

When she and Putnam sank into the frothing heaven of the hot-tub she felt relaxed enough to share the news about the investigation Jim McGill had assigned to her, and that she'd agreed to take.

Putnam raised his eyebrows and smiled. "You're going to be working, even if it's indirectly, for the Pope? There must be a God in heaven."

Sweetie socked him on the shoulder, but not too hard.

"Of course there is, and he does seem to move in mysterious ways. What I'm concerned about is that the first few calls I've made trying to locate Father de Loyola have come up empty. I talked to Father Nkrumah at St. Al's and a few other priests, nuns and lay people he suggested but I got zilch."

"Well," Putnam said, "from what I recall you telling me about Father de Loyola, he has one foot in the ecclesiastical world and one foot in the secular. You said he has a history fighting as a guerrilla in Central America."

"That's right. Unfortunately, *I* don't have any background in those conflicts."

"Me neither, but maybe our good friend General Welborn Yates might be able to find someone who does. Coming as your assignment does from James J. McGill, Welborn might be inclined to help out. At least let you know where, south of the border, the padre used to fight godless Communism."

Putnam paused to frown. "De Loyola wasn't on the Communists' side, was he?"

A look of concern formed on Sweetie's face, too. "I don't think so … but whatever his past might be, it's my job to find him now."

"For *Il Papa*," Putnam said.

"Exactly."

"That brings my mind back to the Church. What was the name of that local priest de Loyola teamed up with in the fight for gun control a while back?"

Sweetie's memory found the name in a heartbeat.

"Father Dennehy, pastor of St. Martin de Porres Parish."

Putnam grinned. "That's my girl, still sharp as a tack."

She kissed him and said, "So are you thinking of the connection to Father D."

"It just seemed to me, from what I heard and read, those two are kindred spirits. Maybe one priest knows where the other one has gone."

Sweetie nodded, and then frowned.

"What?" Putnam asked.

"I was just thinking: What if I need to leave the country to find Father de Loyola? You're busy, and we can't leave Maxi alone."

Putnam smiled. "Not a problem. That's why kids have grandparents. Maxi's high elders can come down from Baltimore and stay at our place. I think they'd be good with it for at least a week. You don't think you'd have to be away longer than that, do you?"

"I hope not," Sweetie said. "If I do, maybe we can park Maxi at the White House."

Putnam laughed. "I'm not sure, in an election year, that's a fit environment, but maybe."

"Or I could tell the Pope he's out of luck."

"As if you'd ever do that."

"For Maxi, I would."

Seeing his wife was serious, Putnam leaned over and kissed her.

"Let's not over-worry it. Even a lost soul like me thinks we must have God on our side this time."

Sweetie kissed him back. "Probably true, and without a doubt you redeemed yourself a long time ago. So how's your search of Aubrey Gadsden's legal files going?"

Putnam sighed, sat back and looked up at the glass ceiling.

He said, "It's depressing … seeing how many genuinely bad people there are. That and how too many of them can afford wickedly smart lawyers to defend them."

"Welcome to a cop's world."

"Yeah. The one that really scared me was this guy called Guillermito Tonto."

From her time as a Chicago cop, Sweetie had picked up a smattering of Spanish. "Stupid Willy?"

"Silly Billy from the translation I saw," Putnam said. Twenty-three years old. Suspected of killing a family practice doctor for refusing to treat a local thug's gunshot wound off the record. The doc was no fool. He knew he'd become an after-the-fact accomplice to a crime if he did that. Worse, he'd become the physician who was called on in other such situations. So one night Silly Billy creeps up behind the doctor and, bang, shoots him dead. Poor guy left a wife, two small kids and a developmentally disabled adult sister behind."

Sweetie squeezed Putnam's hand.

"There was no witness with the guts to come forward," he said, "but the police made a strong circumstantial case against the little prick. Then an anonymous party put up a million-dollar bond and Billy got out."

"And somebody took Billy down so he'd never talk," Sweetie said.

Putnam shook his head. "No, and Gadsden didn't have to worry about getting Billy off, just delay his trial for six months and they'd be good."

"How's that?" Sweetie asked.

"Turns out Billy was one of what he called *los muertos.*"

"The dead?" Sweetie asked. "Plural?"

"Yeah. Billy had a terminal illness: cystic fibrosis. No cure and in Billy's case not much time left. All Gadsden had to do for his client was get a couple of continuances and by the time the second one was requested, the bastard was already in intensive care. The judge let him expire on his own tab. The interesting thing was another anonymous donor was paying for the bastard's final days of medical care. No charity ward for Billy."

"Somebody knew his medical condition before hiring him," Sweetie said.

"Yeah, *los muertos,* a really scary new concept in crime."

CHAPTER 4

Thursday, September 15, 2016 — Hazelton, West Virginia

For killing Jordan Gilford, Jerry Nerón's fate in criminal court had been settled with a guilty verdict and a sentence of life in prison without the possibility of parole. The jury hearing Jerry's trial had needed only 90 minutes to return its finding, and most of that time was probably consumed by eating their lunches. In a doubly ironic twist of fate, the federal judge hearing the case acceded to the wish of the victim's wife, Zara Gilford, and gave Jerry a life sentence instead of an execution date.

It was only after the guilty verdict had been returned that Zara made her preference known. The inevitable first question was, "Why did you choose to spare Jerry Nerón's life?"

Rather than invoke Christian charity and forgiveness as her reasons, she said, "I want him to suffer as long as possible, and I dearly hope Mr. Nerón will burn in hell for eternity. Short of that, I pray he has the longest, most dreadful life possible in prison. He deserves far worse than the humane termination we'd give an old, beloved and ailing pet."

The first irony of the situation was that the widow had spared the killer's life; the second was that her bluntly delivered rationale for doing so resonated with a vast majority of the American public. Family members of murder victims around the country took up

Zara's point of view and asked judges to deliver life sentences without hope of parole rather than death penalties to the villains who'd claimed the lives of their loved ones.

At a stroke, Zara Gilford had done more to rescind the death penalty than any state legislature. Social psychologists claimed it was the unfavorable comparison of taking Nerón's life to that of a cherished animal that turned the trick. You put poor Rover out of his misery; you make an evil SOB sweat blood as long as he continues to draw breath.

Jerry had been in court, of course, to hear both Zara Gilford's plea and the judge's sentence. He accepted both with mute decorum, but the truth was he admired Zara. If you couldn't tear your enemy to pieces with your own hands, prolonging and intensifying his suffering was the next best thing. He'd have felt the same way she did.

On the other hand, he did everything he could to make sure his time behind bars was as tolerable as possible. Not a big man, Jerry Nerón still managed to thumb an eye out of a far larger thug while still in the DC metro correctional center awaiting assignment to a high-security federal prison. The attacker had thought he'd make Jerry his bitch, if only for a night or two.

The oversized SOB had expected his smaller target to shrink from his approach, not attack, but the former hitman and custom tailor glided inside his opponent's outstretched arms and hooked his right thumb into the corner of the guy's left eye and popped it out of its socket like a grape. It dangled from connective tissue for a second until Jerry grabbed it in his hand and stepped back.

He showed the orb to its stunned and horrified former owner and asked, "You want me to take the other one, too?"

The guy went into shock and collapsed.

Jerry gave the eye to the corrections officer who came to see what the trouble was.

Video of the attack showed Jerry was only defending himself. He wasn't punished for enucleating the big guy's eye socket, and word of what he'd done circulated through the prison system coast to coast. When he arrived at USP Hazelton, none of the other cons tried any rough stuff or even mouthed off to him. Who the hell knew? Maybe the guy could rip your tongue out, too.

Establishing an immediate reputation that guaranteed his physical safety was a positive step for Jerry. Otherwise, Zara Gilford's plan to make him pay dearly for killing her husband was working out just fine. A stretch of soul-crushing time, long enough to seem eternal, lay ahead of him. For the first time, he thought of taking his own life. Maybe take a running start, lower his head and slam it into a concrete wall.

Only doing that might not do more than paralyze him. Make a bad situation far worse.

Almost as a parlor game, he came up with scenarios for suicide, ones that would get the job done at the cost of only a momentary flash of pain. He soon came to understand that his imagination was more macabre than he ever knew. Despite that, he'd yet to arrive at a way to do himself in that would both meet his criteria and be within his limited means.

That had been his state of mind when James J. McGill came to see him and, sonofabitch, the guy who'd caught him actually provided a measure of real hope for a better life and just maybe eventual freedom. McGill had said if Jerry could help find the guy who was trying to kill McGill he'd see to it that Jerry could do some tailoring in prison, make custom suits for people who'd served their sentences while behaving well and were about to get out. Jerry could send them out into the world looking good.

Damn, he liked that idea.

Work at his craft again and help other people who'd screwed up. Maybe turn their lives around. Wouldn't that be something? Just thinking about it made him smile. That McGill was one wily bastard, finding just the right button to press. The devil couldn't have made a more tempting offer.

Still, a hope raised could become a hope dashed. No way was he ever going to get released while Zara Gilford was still alive. Probably not while his trial judge was drawing breath either.

That *bastard* had yearned to give Jerry the needle. The only thing that persuaded him otherwise was Zara had been so persuasive that letting Jerry rot was the way to go. Working in Jerry's favor, though, both the widow and the judge were almost 30 years older than he was.

Chances were they'd kick off a long time before he did. Once they were out of the way and Jerry had his suits-for-cons gig well established, showing what a hell of a guy he really was, he'd have a much better chance for clemency. With hard work and a trainload of luck, he just might be free again someday.

Of course, he had to come through for McGill first.

Help McGill find this Corona Moe prick who was trying to kill him.

That was a far from certain outcome. But Jerry had one big advantage. While his conviction for killing Jordan Gilford was never in doubt, there was an ongoing legal battle about what would become of Jerry's personal fortune, a not insignificant sum.

As a tactical move, Jerry had agreed to forfeit his fee for killing Gilford. That money undeniably was the proceeds of a criminal act. But the murder of Jordan Gilford was the only crime anyone could pin on him. The FBI and all sorts of Florida cops had looked for more wrongdoing but they'd been unable to find any, *gracias a Dios.* What that left was an eight-figure net worth directly attributable to Jerry's fame and years of work as a custom tailor to the wealthy and powerful. That money had been reported to the IRS and all taxes had been paid in full.

Such precautions hadn't kept government leeches from going after it anyway, but another judge had lifted the hold that the feds and the state had put on his funds. That meant the power-of-attorney that Jerry had given to *mami y papi* would allow his parents to withdraw funds and spend them on his behalf.

The law put a $290 per month limit on what family and friends could deposit into a convict's commissary account. But that didn't mean Jerry's outside money couldn't have been filtered into any number of other inmates' accounts. He could have bought the loyalty of a small army of jailbirds for a pittance.

Unlike Auric Ludwig, though, Jerry didn't do that because he foresaw two possible pitfalls. On a practical level, if you made other inmates dependent on you, some of the ungrateful bastards would inevitably come to think you *owed* them that money. Any failure to meet payroll would cause dissent and hostility, and Jerry knew he could get away with popping only so many eyes out of his fellow inmates' heads.

Even if things went well, Jerry feared if he improved his living conditions too much in prison he'd be thwarting Zara Gilford's wish that he suffer on a daily basis. If she ever got word that he was living it up, relatively speaking … Hell, it was irrational but Jerry feared she and the judge would contrive a way to put a needle in his arm after all.

McGill's visit had dispelled Jerry's paranoia. That guy had the power to waltz right into USP Hazelton and offer him a deal. He had to have more clout than either the widow or the judge to do that. McGill being married to the President, that wasn't surprising. So Jerry moved fast.

He called his attorney and told him to jet up to Hazelton right away.

Jerry also had funds, legal money taxed to the last penny, that he'd moved out of the country just in case. He was going to tell his lawyer how to tap some of it, $50K, payable as a reward to the family or other beneficiary of any inmate in the country for information leading to the capture of Corona Moe.

The news would be put out on the underworld wide web to all federal and state penal facilities, and municipal lockups, too. How could he miss getting results doing that?

Well, maybe he could if Corona Moe had no rap sheet himself.

Then again, McGill had told him more than just one guy was involved in trying to take him down. Any accomplice Moe used would have to be a virgin, too, for the cops not to have an arrest sheet and a prison record on him. The chances of that were slim to none — and slim just got shanked in the shower room.

Jerry felt optimistic about his future.

He'd have to make sure Zara Gilford didn't find out.

Middleburg, Virginia

Taps sat at the head of the table in the pale morning light of the estate house dining room outside Middleburg, Virginia. In its current presentation, Taps' face might have been considered that of a pretty man or a handsome woman wearing a short but not severe haircut. Taps' voice, a well-modulated countertenor, also gave no definitive clue as to sexual specificity.

Neither did a slenderly muscular physique draped in a black suit and matching mock turtleneck sweater, cut for both freedom of movement and to conceal a number of small but deadly weapons.

"We go tomorrow," Taps said to the six people sitting around the table, "assuming Mr. McGill keeps his regular hours. A morning attack when he's on his way to his new offices would be preferable. We'll all be freshest at the start of the day, but if we have to catch him in the evening on his way back to the White House we'll use the hotel rooms we've reserved to rest during the day. So there will be no reason we shouldn't be in good form then, as well."

A thin hand went up. The woman seated closest to Taps on the right had a point to raise. She was well-dressed and coifed but painfully emaciated. Her skin tone, once a radiant almond, was now flattened by a leaden gray undertone. Tomorrow, a gloss of expertly applied makeup would brighten her features. Drops would clear the red from her eyes. Her chic Chanel ensemble would cover the track marks she bore from her collar bone on down.

"Yes, Paulette?" Taps asked.

"I'm gonna do my best, just like I told you, but it's gonna be lots harder for me if I gotta wait all day. I'm gonna be real shaky by then."

A measure of involuntary tremors was a part of the plan.

Inability to move at exactly the right moment was not.

Taps said in a kindly tone, "We'll make sure you get exactly what you need, Paulette, both to feel good and to do your part."

Paulette smiled, revealing a gap-toothed and discolored set of dentition. She'd been warned to keep them hidden while giving her performance. As if remembering her instructions, she pressed her lips together and mumbled, "Feeling good before I go is all I ask."

"That and making sure your sister gets paid," Taps said. "You've done that?"

Paulette nodded.

"Everyone?" Taps said. "Your beneficiaries have all received their money?"

The other five, all men, nodded.

"Good. We'll go over the plan one more time this evening, eat and then get a good night's sleep. Especially you, Paulette. You're the star of the show; everything depends on you getting your part and your timing right."

Paulette said, "I step out in front of Mr. McGill's car, looking like I'm not paying attention, get hit good and solid, making it look like an accident."

"It's probably not necessary to remind you," Taps told her, "but a loud, horrifying scream of pain will be a big help. Pull Mr. McGill out of his car when he sees it has hit a well-dressed old lady of color. And then ..."

Taps went around the table to each man, all of whom would also be well dressed, looking for all the world like the privileged class of the capital. They would open fire from different angles and if necessary, and at the cost of their lives, block any open doors on the car from being closed again so a follow-up man could shoot into the vehicle from close range.

Depending on the proximity or the arrival of any police officers, each shooter had to be prepared to engage them, too. Again, they had to be ready to sacrifice themselves to assure the success of the attack, that being defined as the certain death of James J. McGill.

Ideally, as Taps saw it, all of the principal actors should die.

The attackers were all *muertos,* dying of circumstances that would claim their lives within a year's time. Far better that none of them leave the scene alive to be questioned by the Secret Service or the FBI. McGill, of course, was the point of the whole bloodbath, but taking out whoever was with him would help make it all but impossible to catch up with Taps.

Of course, it was possible the attempt would fail miserably.

That was also acceptable. Taps would be observing from a safe distance and learn from the mistakes, and eliminate them from the next plan. As long as the money flowed so would the hunt for McGill's head.

Paulette and all the shooters had been warned, of course, what would befall their loved ones if they were caught alive and told the authorities what little they knew: Their loved ones wouldn't live to spend the windfalls that had come their way.

After everyone at the table had outlined his or her roles and duties correctly one last time, Taps alerted the kitchen staff, who knew nothing of the business at hand, to bring in everyone's personal choice for breakfast. Lunch and dinner would also be each person's favorite meal.

Small kindnesses for those about to die.

The White House — Washington, DC

"My uncle, Jack Malloy, served in Vietnam," Jean Morrissey told the President, Galia Mindel and Chairman of the Joint Chiefs of Staff General Nicholas Mills as they gathered in the Oval Office. "He was a West Point graduate and a first lieutenant when he got sent over there. He was on leave in Saigon when the Tet Offensive started. He didn't have his M-16 with him, but he did have his sidearm. He wound up helping a South Vietnamese unit trying to stop the Viet Cong who'd seized the national radio station from broadcasting that Saigon had been 'liberated.'"

General Mills nodded. He'd served in Vietnam, too, as an 18-year-old enlisted man.

"They succeeded in that," Mills said. "Our side cut the line between the broadcast studio and its tower. The VC inside the station never got their propaganda message out and when their ammunition was exhausted they blew themselves to pieces with high explosives."

Jean was not comforted by that small victory.

"My uncle died in the fighting that night," she said. "He was 22 years old. His sister, my mom, was 23 at the time, my uncle's Irish twin. His death just about killed her. She never told me that story, though. My dad did, one of the nights when Mom got quiet and tearful and needed time alone. Dad said my birth and my brother Frank's helped bring Mom back, but she never really made it all the way. A part of her died when my uncle did."

With a sigh, the Vice President added, "I must have inherited some of her grief. About the only time I cry with any regularity is when I go to the Vietnam Memorial and see my uncle's name on the wall. I won't be part of any decision to send combat troops back to that country. I can't see anything except another tragedy happening if we return the American military to Vietnam."

It was clear from the President's expression that she'd never heard Jean's story before.

She took a moment to let it sink in and then turned to Mills for his opinion. "General?"

"I agree, Madam President. Our current number of active duty soldiers is 479,000; the Marines would add another 182,000. So, combined, that's 661,000 ground force members. If we put 500,000 on Vietnam's border with China, we'd be unable to meet our treaty obligations to the rest of the world, not to mention all the hot spots where we've already committed special operations forces and their support elements.

"To do what the Vietnamese request, we'd have to return to conscription, and I think the idea of sending draftees to Vietnam would be about as popular as it was in the 1960s. On top of that, the People's Liberation Army has 1.6 million ground forces, the largest standing army in the world. The only way to hold the Chinese back if they massed for an attack on our people — if we sent them to Vietnam — would be to use tactical nuclear weapons. I think that's too high a price to pay for the use of naval facilities at Cam Ranh Bay."

"Galia?" the President asked.

"The Vietnamese demand for parity with Japan and South Korea is a non-starter. We're not going to start a nuclear war to defend a so recent — and successful — former enemy. It's not hard to imagine, if we did send a massive number of troops there, the rest of the world would see it as a provocation to the Chinese and be unsympathetic to us."

Mills added, "Hanoi might be content to see us and the Chinese ravage each other and then sue for peace when they might get the best possible terms. Ones that would make a future Chinese threat remote."

The President steepled her hands and thought for a moment.

Then she said, "So we've lost our naval base in the Philippines and the one in Vietnam comes with a price tag far too high to pay. Meanwhile, Deputy Director DeWitt tells us that China will seek some sort of blood reprisal for our shoot-down of their pilots and planes."

Maintaining her prayerful pose, the President closed her eyes.

The others in the room exchanged glances but said nothing.

When the President opened her eyes, she said, "The first thing we have to do is make it clear who the real bad guys are. Galia, I think it's time to consider having Tyler Busby and Ah-lam give a press conference to make clear the Chinese government's involvement in the attempt to assassinate me."

Keeping a poker face, Galia said, "Beijing would deny it, of course. Call us liars and provocateurs."

"Of course, they would. But they made a mistake in killing Donald Yang. His death will help corroborate what Busby and Ah-lam will say. If they're lying, why is Yang dead?"

Still playing the devil's advocate, Galia said, "If we make the charge stick, shouldn't the United States break relations with

China, if they don't break them first?

"We should." Looking at the Vice President, the President added, "And if things get to the point where we have to play that card we will."

Jean Morrissey nodded, confirming that she'd do the job if it fell to her.

"But we could delay long enough for China to make that choice first. Let them own that decision, too. See how that plays around the world. See how China likes it when their $400 billion trade surplus with the United States disappears."

"Tens of thousands of American jobs will also disappear when that happens, Madam President," Galia said.

Without missing a beat, the President said, "That should make Congress eager to pass a full-employment bill. We have a lot of infrastructure that needs repair and replacement. Better that we and China should be exchanging insults than nuclear missiles."

The president paused and then added, "But we do need a show of force, a multi-national one. General Mills, please start making calls to your counterparts in the United Kingdom, France, Italy, Japan, India and the Republic of Korea."

Mills understood what the President meant: the countries and allies with six of the world's most powerful navies.

Combined with the USN, by far the most powerful navy in the world, they could make quite a statement. Of the remaining three naval powers in the top ten, Taiwan was certain to tend to its own business, and the People's Liberation Navy — China — and the Russian Navy weren't comparable in either size or technology to the U.S. alone, much less an allied armada.

Enemy submarines were always a threat, but America's Navy was also unmatched in the area of attack submarines — sub hunters — too.

"I'll get in touch with the heads of state in those countries," the President said. "We'll see if we can form an international battle group in the South China Sea. Send a message that Beijing will find impossible to miss. Freedom of navigation in international waters will prevail."

Sticking to her role as the devil's advocate, Galia asked, "What about Deputy Director DeWitt's assumption that the Chinese will strike back against us, Madam President? Do you think having other nations' ships with us will deter them?"

"I haven't forgotten about that," the President said. Turning to Mills, she said, "General, please bring me every last detail you can find on the SSN *Thresher* tragedy."

FCI Petersburg — Prince George County, Virginia

The word at FCI Petersburg Medium Security was that the big new foreign guy — Corsican not French — might be on a hunger strike. Some of the wise-asses among the inmates claimed he was taking matters even further, refusing to take a leak or a shit, too. All that and saying not a single word in English. Hell, even the Mexicans in the joint could curse you out like an American.

On top of all that there was the guy's name: Odo.

Inevitably, it became Odd-o to the less imaginatively insulting cons, but not to the guy's face so far because he *was* one mean looking mother. In the interest of preserving the peace, the corrections officers had passed the word that the way you were supposed to say the guy's name was, "Oh-dough." That was pretty funny, too.

Not any funnier than Delbert Roy, Asiq Jameer or Emanuel Maria, according to the captain of the COs. He, in particular, didn't want to see any bad shit happen on his watch. Particularly, not because of something as juvenile as name-calling.

In response to the implicit threat of severe discipline or, worse, transfer to a high-security facility, all the cons started calling each other Joe. José if their native tongue was Spanish. The powers-that-be could live with that. The right kind of humor defused tension, didn't crank it up.

That was the situation when Auric Ludwig stopped by, standing in the open doorway of the Corsican's cell during a ten-minute period of controlled movement. Ludwig had brought with him a paper bag from Dunkin' Donuts containing a croissant and a styrofoam cup of coffee with cream but no sugar. A friend on the corrections staff had obtained the goodies for him.

He extended the bag to Odo and said, "*Bienvenue.*"

Welcome was one-third of Ludwig's French vocabulary.

Odo regarded the bag as if it might hold a venomous snake.

Or a trick that would put him in a bad way with the guards. He'd hurried Ludwig out of his cell on their prior meeting without saying a word. Speech had been unnecessary once Odo had lifted Ludwig off his bed with one hand. But the former chief of FirePower America wasn't a quitter. This time, though, he had thought to bring a peace offering.

Ludwig opened the bag to show Odo what was inside. The aromas of both the coffee and the roll poured out. Should have been more than enough to tempt a hungry man.

All Odo said was, "Who are you?"

Ludwig smiled. "You speak English."

"Of course." Odo let his eyes drift to the contents of the bag, as if tempted by them.

"It's okay," Ludwig told him. "The COs will be pleased to see you're eating. Otherwise, they'll have to take you to the infirmary and feed you intravenously. I have to be back in my cell in a few minutes or I'll have to stay here for fifty minutes, until I can move about again. I'd like to talk with you, but if you want me to leave, I'll go."

He put the bag on the floor in front of Odo.

"Either way, I thought you'd rather eat than be fed through a needle."

The thought of having *any* needle stuck in them was a horror to most inmates.

That was how the federal government executed its condemned prisoners.

"I'll go now," Ludwig said.

He'd turned to leave when Odo asked, "Why do you want to talk to me?"

Ludwig smiled. "I was trying to tell you last time. I think we might do some business."

Odo grabbed the coffee cup, removed the lid and took a sip.

He gave a shrug of approval and told Ludwig, "Stay."

West Wing — The White House

United States Air Force Brigadier General Welborn Yates hadn't worn his military uniform to work at the White House for the past month. It wasn't that he lacked pride in his branch of the armed forces. Just the opposite. While the Army, Navy and Marines all flew their own aircraft, in Welborn's eyes nobody did it like the Air Force. Flying was a secondary role for the other service branches. It was the Air Force's reason for being.

Other than the hand of God, the USAF was the mightiest power in the sky.

Welborn took immense satisfaction in that.

Even so, it was his personal standing in the service — his present rank — that made him feel like a sham. How could he possibly be a general? He was 29 years old and had never served in combat. How could he ever be respected by other officers or enlisted personnel?

He couldn't imagine a credible answer to either question.

His current standing was nothing but a matter of random luck.

Bad luck in that a car crash had killed his three best friends and ended his budding career as a fighter pilot. Good luck in that he got into the training program for the Air Force's Office of Special Investigations. *Preposterously* good luck that he'd been plucked from his desk at Joint Base Andrews before he'd worked his first case, installed in an office at the White House and covertly tutored by James J. McGill.

Who deserved such good fortune?

Then again, what had his dear Kira done to deserve an ectopic pregnancy that almost killed her, caused her to lose the fetus, a boy, and with scarring found in her remaining fallopian tube foreclosed the possibility of bearing any future children? The cause of the tragedy? *Appendicitis.* That's what the doctors said had damaged Kira's tubes. Another preposterous turn of fate.

Who deserved such ill fortune?

Certainly not Kira. Nor the son they would never know.

Welborn and Kira were counseled by their doctor to take comfort in each other and their two wonderful girls, Aria and Callista. The twins certainly were a balm for both Kira and Welborn, but both parents couldn't help but wonder what their son might have been like.

Welborn, alone, bore an irrational but implacable sense of guilt that he was responsible for what had happened. He didn't deserve the rapid rise in military rank that had come with going to work at the White House. He certainly hadn't *earned* that opportunity.

So now fate had rebalanced the ledger.

Knocked him down several pegs.

What tore at Welborn was the sense that *he* should have been the one to suffer directly. If somebody had to take the hit, it should have been him. Where the hell was the justice in Kira being put through the wringer? Why did their unborn *baby* have to suffer for his father being a phony the past eight years?

He knew he should have talked to someone, sought some professional help. Only he and Kira hadn't even told anyone she'd been pregnant. They certainly hadn't shared the awful details of how the pregnancy had ended.

What Welborn did was stop wearing his uniform to work.

In the hope that might stop a malign fate from causing further heartbreak.

Despite the personal agony that never left his thoughts, he forced himself to function. He had to earn his pay at the very least. Kira had inherited money but the family lived on Welborn's salary. If that was ever taken away from him …

He couldn't bear to think what might happen then, so when his phone rang he picked it up. "Welborn Yates."

A woman's voice answered, "Hi, Welborn … are you okay?

Your voice sounded strained."

The concern seemed genuine but he couldn't place the voice immediately. He looked at the caller ID on his phone: Margaret Sweeney. Mr. McGill's partner and dear friend.

"I'm fine, Ms. Sweeney. Haven't been getting all the sleep I need, but other than that …"

He let her imagination fill in the blank.

"Is there something I might do for you?" he asked.

"Yes, if you can spare the time, I'm looking for a priest."

It took Welborn a moment to understand. "Not just any priest, I assume."

Sweetie chuckled politely. The small gesture made Welborn feel a bit less miserable. He was surprised that was even possible.

"No, a particular priest, a Jesuit named Inigo de Loyola," Sweetie said. "He worked among the needy here in DC. He was also a guerrilla in some conflicts in Central America. Jim McGill asked me to find him; Cardinal Fitzroy asked Jim to help; the cardinal was put on the job by the Pope."

After a moment's hesitation, Welborn said, "I'm sorry, did you say the Pope?"

Sweetie told him, "I know, I had the same reaction."

"Okay, but I'm not even Catholic."

"Francesco is widely admired. Loved, even."

"Of course." It was more than that, though. Welborn had the uneasy feeling his life was at another turning point. Once again, he had the disturbing feeling he was being plucked for a job well above his pay-grade. Of course, if the Pope really was involved, maybe this was an opportunity for redemption. "How may I be of help, Ms. Sweeney?"

"Let's start like this. Most of my friends call me Sweetie, but if that's too familiar for you, Margaret will do."

"Certainly, Margaret."

"Well, I've checked with a number of police colleagues in Chicago and New York and none of them has any personal knowledge of Father de Loyola being in their towns. They're going to check with other coppers they know locally and with their respective archdioceses to see if they can find him. If not, they'll make calls to police departments in other major U.S. cities and see if that might turn up something."

Welborn said, "That certainly sounds like a good start."

"I hope so," Sweetie told him. "It would be easier if he's still in our country."

"You think he might be outside the U.S.?"

"Well, he did help Jim with a matter in Costa Rica a while back. Jim and I talked about that a few minutes ago and with Father de Loyola's history we wouldn't be surprised if he went back to Central America for some reason."

Welborn understood the reason for the call now. "You'd like me to see if the Department of Defense has any reason to be aware of Father de Loyola."

"Yes."

Welborn considered what Margaret was asking of him. At the moment, with no task delegated to him by the President, he was at loose ends. Not a good situation for someone busy recriminating himself. He'd be much better off if he had his mind on other things.

"Margaret, do you have any reason to suspect Father de Loyola might currently be engaged in any activities hostile to the United States?"

Sweetie said, "The only thing I personally know about the man is that he worked here in DC to feed and house the poor, find jobs for people when he could. I think he owned only the clothes he wore every day and he slept under a staircase in one of Dikki Missirian's buildings. If he's a threat to the nation, I haven't heard about it."

"Okay. I had to ask because I'll be asked," Welborn explained. "Do you know why the Pope wants to find Father de Loyola?"

"No. My job is simply to find him, tell him, 'Call the Vatican,' and hand him a phone number."

Welborn said, "So it's possible you'll have to leave the country to do your job."

"Yeah, I thought of that. I got a passport for the first time a few years back to go to Europe with Putnam on a delayed honeymoon."

"That's great, the honeymoon, I mean. The passport might come in handy, too."

"So you'll help?"

"Yes, gladly. If everything works out, you can tell the Pope I said hello."

Sweetie laughed. "Hey, who knows, maybe he'd let the two of us and our better halves have a five-minute audience."

Welborn said, "I'd like that."

Two minutes later, Welborn received a call from James J. McGill.

He had no problem recognizing that voice.

"Spare a moment?" McGill asked.

"Yes, sir."

McGill had long ago told Welborn that "sir" was an unnecessary form of address for him, but he didn't bother to correct him this time.

"You probably haven't heard yet, but someone is trying to kill me."

"What?" To Welborn's ear, it didn't sound like McGill was playing a joke.

"Yeah, I know," McGill said. "If it isn't one damn thing, it's another. But we have good reason to think the threat is real."

He went on to explain Auric Ludwig was the likely source of the threat, blaming McGill for his incarceration.

"I've got all the people I've recruited to go to work for me, after the President and I leave the White House, working on it, but I thought you might lend a hand in case the would-be perpetrators have ever shown up in one of the federal government's databases."

Welborn heard every word McGill had said, but a thought occurred to him that forestalled a timely response.

"You still there, Welborn?" McGill asked.

"Yes, sir."

"Thought I lost you for a moment. Everything okay?"

Another pause ensued, though not long enough to prompt McGill to fill it.

Welborn asked, "May I ask, sir, why you never asked if I'd like to work for you?"

This time McGill needed a moment to respond. "It … never occurred to me that you might want to do that. You're a general now. I thought you'd go to work for Jean Morrissey and continue with your military career."

Welborn said, "I've just about completed my eight-year commitment to the Air Force. I haven't heard a word from the Vice President or her brother about staying on, and what if Senator Worth were to win the election?"

For all Welborn knew Worth would not only kick him out of the White House, he might demote him in rank … to a major or a lieutenant colonel, where he'd likely be under normal circumstances.

With a jolt of bitter irony, Welborn realized he wouldn't like to be politically *demoted* any better than having been politically promoted.

"Welborn?" McGill said, "are you still there?"

"Yes, sir. Sorry. Just distracted for a moment."

"I was saying," McGill told him, "I think we can use another good investigator, if that's what you really want to do."

"I might. I very well might. I'll need to discuss it with Kira, of course."

"Sure. Meanwhile, I'd like to send you an image of a person Leo Levy thinks might be bird-dogging me for a possible assassination attempt."

That snapped Welborn into focus. Someone really was trying to kill the President's husband. He hadn't heard a word about that until McGill called.

"Of course, sir. I'll run it through all the government's military databases. If that doesn't turn up anything, I'll send it on to the CIA."

McGill laughed. "I really am going to miss all the perks I have as the President's Henchman."

"Yes, sir," Welborn said. "If I may ask, despite losing any advantage the White House provides, are you ready to move on?"

"I am," McGill said.

Me, too, Welborn thought.

FCI Petersburg — Prince George County, Virginia

"You think your life is being threatened?" Odo asked.

After saying Auric Ludwig might remain in his cell during the 50-minute period inmates were required to stay in place, Odo even extended his courtesy to allow Ludwig to sit on the far end of his bunk. Odo had consumed the coffee and croissant Ludwig had brought him. Hunger had led him to concede that the taste of each wasn't as bad as he'd expected.

"Not yet," Ludwig said, "but looking ahead I think it's a possibility. Everyone in this place knows I have access to quite a lot of money. I can't bring it in here, of course. But I can direct it to where I want it to go on the outside. You see the problem?"

Odo gave a minimal nod. "Of course. At the moment, your money gives you power. Soon enough, though, the threat will come: 'Do as I say or I will wring your neck.' Your money will become someone else's money."

"Exactly," Ludwig said.

With a cold stare, Odo asked, "How do you know *I* will not be the one to make that threat?"

A muscle twitched in Ludwig's right cheek; otherwise he remained calm.

"Under other circumstances, you very well might," he said, "but as I tried to say yesterday, I have an offer to make that could bring you a lot more money."

A smile creased Odo's face.

"What's funny?" Ludwig asked.

Odo said, "Where else but America could a man hope to make his fortune in prison?"

Ludwig laughed and said, "I don't know. I've never been locked up anywhere else."

"Moi non plus," Odo said.

"What?"

"Me, neither."

"You have no criminal record elsewhere?"

Odo's eyes turned to slits and he shook his head.

Reading the potential for violence in the man's face, Ludwig knew he'd overstepped. He had to be careful, just as he would with an American inmate. Asking him for specifics about his résumé might well be a fatal mistake. Still, he felt sure that the Corsican had committed crimes back home or somewhere else. He just hadn't been caught.

Ludwig held up a placatory hand.

"Let me tell you about my idea."

He outlined his plan to allow individual foreign nationals to buy all the American firearms they wanted in the United States and ship them out of the country legally.

"That way individuals such as yourself wouldn't find themselves in American prisons," Ludwig said.

Odo asked, "You can buy enough of your politicians to assure this, to pass such a law?"

Ludwig laughed. "We could make nine out of ten of them dance naked in a chorus line."

Even Odo had to chuckle at the picture that conjured. "But what about at the other end of the line?" he asked. "Landing a boatload of weapons would still be illegal at the far end of the voyage."

Ludwig held his hands out, conceding the point, but adding, "That's where enterprising individuals like you would have to apply some ingenuity. I have the feeling *you'd* be up to it, given all the money you'd make."

Odo nodded thoughtfully. "Quite possibly … if I could get out of this place. My *avocat* says I have a chance, but he makes no promises."

Ludwig understood the Corsican meant his lawyer.

"If your attorney can't do the job, the one I hire to get me out will do the same for you — if you'd care to help keep me safe for whatever time I have left in here."

"How long?" Odo asked.

"A year maybe, eighteen months at most. Once I share my idea with —"

Odo shook his head.

"What?" Ludwig asked.

"The moment you tell your idea to another fellow it will become *his* idea, and you will remain right here. Better to say you have *une idée fantastique* but you won't share it until you are a free man again. You and me, that is."

Ludwig looked humbled and then appreciative.

"You're right." He smiled. "This is like the last scene in that old Bogart movie — the beginning of a beautiful friendship."

Odo shrugged. "I do not go to the cinema."

The White House — Washington, DC

The President, the Vice President, Secretary of Defense Martin Dempsey, Chairman of the Joint Chiefs of Staff General Nicholas Mills, Director of National Intelligence Gregory Ishida, Secretary of the Navy Winton Roy, and Admiral David B. Davidson, Combatant Commander of the United States Pacific Command, just in from Hawaii, met in the White House's John F. Kennedy Conference Room, better known in popular jargon as the Situation Room.

As always, Chief of Staff Galia Mindel sat next to the President.

The better to whisper in the Commander-in-Chief's ear, if necessary.

"Sorry to drag you here all the way from Oahu, Admiral Davidson," the President said.

"Always a pleasure to meet with you, Madam President." A former Top Gun pilot, Davidson had a reputation as a charmer. He was also a combat veteran and a Rhodes Scholar. If he was a bit stuck on himself, he had reason to be.

The President nodded in acknowledgment of the compliment and said, "I'm going to start with what might seem like an odd question, gentlemen. Please indulge me for a moment and then tell me whether what I'd like to do is feasible or just fantasy."

Every man in the room kept a straight face and didn't dare look to see if anyone else knew what was coming.

The President asked, "Have any of you seen the movie *The Sting?*"

DNI Gregory Ishida raised his hand. "Saw it as an undergrad at Cornell, ma'am, and again some years later when I was working at Langley."

The second half of the response drew everyone's attention.

Ishida answered the unvoiced question everyone else had in mind.

Why had the film been screened at CIA headquarters?

"We look for inspiration wherever we can find it," Ishida said. "Most Hollywood plot lines lie beyond credulity, that or the reach of current technology. But there are occasional gems, real insights into psychological triggers that can be used to produce desired results."

Admiral Davidson leaned forward and asked, "Does the government pay royalties on the ideas the intelligence community uses?"

The question produced grins around the table.

When Ishida put a "Keep my secret" index finger to his lips and shook his head, that got laughs.

When the jesting faded, the President asked, "What was the Agency's takeaway from watching *The Sting,* Gregory?"

"Two things, Madam President. One is that the concept of the 'big sting,' as it was used in the movie, is plausible but not certain. Two is that the more self-assured someone is that he can't be fooled the more likely he will be."

"Please explain the reasoning behind that second conclusion," the President said.

"It's very simple really. A closed mind can't admit to possibilities that conflict with a firmly held belief. An open mind, one that concedes its own imperfections, is more likely to double-check anything that seems even slightly suspicious."

"Is there any disagreement with the point of view Gregory has just provided?" the President asked the people seated at the table. "Please feel free to object."

Nobody did.

The President nodded. "Very well. I've been told by FBI Deputy Director Byron DeWitt, a China scholar, that Beijing will hit back for our shoot-down of their planes. He also tells me that the supreme art of war, as seen by the Chinese, is to have an enemy defeat himself."

The men at the table all nodded.

"Can't beat that," General Dempsey said.

"We're going to try," the President rebutted. "If we can, we're going to run a game on Beijing, a big con. What I'd like you gentlemen to figure out, if it's possible, is how to fake the loss of one of our submarines and all hands onboard in the South China Sea, and do it in such a way that it's credible we suspect the Chinese are behind the tragedy — not that we can prove it.

"I have the report of the SSN *Thresher* disaster on hand for all of you to read. That was a true case of national grieving. Perhaps it will inspire us to think creatively here."

"Madam President?" Navy Secretary Roy said.

"Yes?"

"Even by simply claiming we lost a sub due to Chinese actions, won't that scare them enough to go to a war footing? Things might get out of hand from there."

"We're not going to make any such public claim, Mr. Secretary. We'll be dealing with off-the-record leaks from sources who can't be definitively relied upon."

"Disinformation," DNI Ishida said.

The President nodded. "We want them to think in our rush to place our surface ships and submarines in the South China Sea that we somehow screwed up catastrophically and lost a vessel. They'll know that they didn't cause the destruction, but if they learn that we suspect they did —"

The Vice President said, "They'll think we beat ourselves."

"The supreme art of war," DNI Ishida said.

Admiral Davidson understood the kicker. "If China thinks that we think they might have taken out one of our subs, they'll also think we think they might have some kind of fighting disadvantage we don't know about. They could laugh themselves silly about that."

DNI Ishida countered. "Or they might try to push their luck militarily. Get aggressive."

The President said, "That is a possibility, but we're going to give Beijing something else to consider. There's not going to be a happy ending for them. Working through both diplomatic and military channels, we're going to make sure China pays a very high price if its Politburo persists in trying to treat international waters as its personal duck pond."

Admiral Davidson raised his hand, "Ma'am, this is probably a foolish question, but when do you need the Navy to execute this *sting* of yours?"

"ASAP, Admiral," the President said. "ASAP."

DuPont Circle Tennis Club — Washington, DC

Captain Rockelle Bullard and Detectives Meeker and Beemer of the Metropolitan Police Department stood off to one side of the tennis court and watched as Zoë Tinker smacked a ball back and forth with a young guy who didn't look like he was out of his teens. Each swing of a racket brought a sharp *thwok* that sent the person on the other side of the net racing forward or back, to one corner of the court or the other to return the ball.

Several times it seemed as if it would be impossible simply to reach the ball, but a burst of speed and some damn quick hands managed to put a racquet on the ball and send it rocketing back the other way, challenging the other player to be just as quick and dexterous.

In a respectfully quiet voice, Meeker told his colleagues, "They call that rallying, knocking the hell out of the ball back and forth where it looks like it's never gonna end."

Both Captain Bullard and Beemer gave him a look.

"How you know that?" Beemer asked.

"Marvina takes lessons, has since she was four."

The detective was referring to his twelve-year-old niece. Her original name was Shauna, but after her daddy bugged out before his baby's first birthday, and Meeker stepped up providing financial support, love and the role-model of a steadily employed man, Meeker's sister renamed her little girl in his honor.

"Your niece hit the ball as hard as Ms. Tinker?" the captain asked.

"Harder."

"Yeah?" Beemer asked. "She gonna be the next Serena Williams?"

"At least. Probably better. Kids keep getting bigger and stronger, don't they?"

"Maybe if I'm nicer to him," the captain told Beemer, "he'll get me tickets to see Marvina play some day. Sit next to me and explain the finer points of the game."

Without taking his eyes off Zoë Tinker and the young guy still going hard at it, Meeker said, "Don't think I can't. You watch what's about to happen. Age is finally catching up to the lady."

"She don't look that old to me," Beemer said.

"Maybe 30 or so is all," Captain Bullard added.

Meeker told them. "The boy's ten years younger. That matters. So she's gonna outfox him any minute … now."

As if Zoë Tinker had heard a cue, she didn't slam the ball. She swung her racquet almost gently with a subtle downstroke. The ball seemed to float in the direction of the net, not looking certain to clear it. The boy, an open-mouthed expression of surprise on his face, raced forward from the baseline. If the ball did land in his forecourt, it didn't look like he'd get to it in time.

Meeker smiled. "Here comes the pretty part."

The ball did clear the net, just barely, and the kid *would* have gotten there in time … if he hadn't set foot in a puddle of sweat he'd put down earlier, had his legs shoot out from under him and landed on his butt. With a never-say-die attitude, he swiped at the ball but missed.

Zoë hopped over the net without visible effort, helped the boy to his feet and kissed his cheek. Then she turned to the three Metro cops and asked, "So what do you think, good show?"

Led by Meeker, they all politely applauded.

Five minutes later, Zoë and the three cops had introduced themselves and sat at a table in the club's juice bar. The drinks were on Zoë, at her insistence.

"Ain't never arrested anyone who's bought me a drink before," Beemer said.

"Least not until you were sure he wasn't gonna buy you another," Meeker replied.

Zoë laughed. Rockelle Bullard rolled her eyes.

"They're trying to scare you *and* put you at ease," the captain said. "It's part of their act: the bad cop and the funny cop. They alternate roles."

"I like it," she said, toweling off her still dewy forehead and taking a hit of her pomegranate float. "Did I do something wrong? Can I get off with a fine?"

All three cops gave Zoë assessing stares. She held up without whimpering.

The captain turned to her detectives. "She doesn't know."

"Unh-uh," they grunted in unison.

"I'd ask what I don't know," Zoë said, "only that would cover a lot of ground."

"Do you know Aubrey Gadsden?" Captain Bullard asked.

"Yes, he's a client of mine."

"Is that all?" Meeker asked.

"That's all, Detective. That's all there ever is with my patients. You went to the trouble of learning I'm a psychologist, right?"

"Yeah, we did," Beemer said.

"And you know there are ethical standards against having personal relationships with patients, I assume."

"We do know that," Captain Bullard said.

"Okay, so you had to ask, but we're clear on that now," Zoë said. "So what is it I don't know?"

The captain said, "Mr. Gadsden is dead."

Zoë blinked and her mouth fell open but she didn't speak.

"And he had a photo of you on his desk," Meeker said.

Beemer added, "One of those side-by-side frames with him in the other slot."

The psychologist's shoulders slumped. "Poor Aubrey."

"You know how Mr. Gadsden earned his living, don't you?" the captain asked.

"He was a lawyer."

"Criminal defense lawyer," Meeker elaborated.

"Real bad criminals," Beemer added.

Tears in her eyes now, Zoë asked, "How did Aubrey die?"

The captain said, "We found him hanging from his office ceiling fan. Didn't look like suicide to any of us, but we're waiting for the final word on that. Would it violate any of your ethics at this point to tell us if Mr. Gadsden mentioned anyone in particular who wanted him dead?"

The psychologist's face got tight. "You know how this works, I'm sure, Captain. Upon a patient's death, the confidentiality privilege transfers to the legal representative of the deceased. If I receive the appropriate authorization from that person, I'll talk to you. If I don't, I can't."

"Yeah, we know that, too," Captain Bullard admitted. "Still, we thought it'd be worthwhile to meet with you and ask."

"To get a look at me, see how I reacted to you and the news about Aubrey."

Meeker and Beemer nodded. No funny cop now.

Meeker asked, "If it's not against anyone's rules or regulations, you want to tell us where your client got that picture of you?"

"The one he put right out on his desk," Beemer added, "like you were someone special to him."

Zoë held up a finger, asking for a moment to respond. She dug into her tennis bag and pulled out an iPad. Took just a moment to fiddle with it and hand it to Captain Bullard.

"Is that the picture you saw?" Zoë asked.

It was a headshot of the psychologist on the homepage of her website.

All three cops took a look and agreed it was the same likeness Gadsden had on his desk.

"Screen-capture, I guess," Zoë said. "I didn't give it to him."

Nobody said it aloud but it was clear the dead lawyer had feelings for his shrink.

She told the Metro cops, "Bring me a valid waiver and I'll be happy to talk to you. Right now, though, I feel like I could use some therapy."

She got up and headed for the women's locker room.

Captain Bullard asked quietly, "Opinions?"

"Legit," Meeker said. "Maybe."

A more skeptical Beemer asked, "They offer acting classes in shrink school?"

Georgetown — Washington, DC

Didi DiMarco sat in a chair at Senator Oren Worth's Washington condo, a place that occupied the entire top floor of a residential building in Georgetown, though at only fifteen stories off the ground calling it a penthouse was a bit of a reach. Still, its furnishings were all high-end and it provided a fine view of the city over nearby, even less imposing structures. The senator, sitting quietly opposite her, was having his makeup applied for their broadcast interview.

Not trusting anyone but her own cosmetician to make her look good on television, Didi had arrived with her TV mask already in place. She'd be fine, if only she didn't sweat the damn thing through. She wasn't worried about the interview itself. She could hold her own with a pack of starving wolves, metaphorically speaking. Senator Worth would certainly be no problem.

What scared her was the text she'd received an hour earlier from Ellie Booker: *Going into hiding. Maybe you should, too. Could be a matter of life or death.*

That was all. No specific threat was mentioned. There was no indication of when an axe might fall. Coming from anyone else, Didi would have laughed off the message as juvenile bullshit. A prank. Coming from Ellie Booker, Didi reached for the hope that it might be, at most, some kind of strategic ploy to get her off the air.

That had to be it, didn't it? Ellie was the one in a serious bind and … shit, maybe Didi was, too. Earlier that year, Ellie Booker had shared a dangerous secret with Didi: Dr. Hasna Kalil, the sister of the late Dr. Bahir Ben Kalil, might have been responsible for the disappearance of Representative Philip Brock.

Brock wasn't the only one to vanish. The head jailer of the Uruguayan prison where the Congressman had been held — *and the jailer's wife* — had also gone missing. Ellie had interviewed the wife before she went poof, and after that Ellie thought she, herself, might also be in danger.

What had once seemed like the story of a lifetime to Didi now looked like a fatal virus that had been passed from Ellie's lips to her ears. Didi had done some digging of her own and that had only made things even scarier. One of Didi's contacts in the intelligence community had revealed a dark rumor about Dr. Hasna Kalil: The woman used her surgical skills for jihadi groups to extract information from prisoners.

The real kicker, Didi was told, was the rumor that Dr. Kalil had taken Philip Brock's head off. It was also whispered that photographic evidence of that atrocity existed. Didi wanted both to see the picture immediately and never see it at all. Her professional ambition was at war with her personal decency. It was an even bet as to which side would win.

What was beyond question: Didi did *not* want to lose her own head.

And now Ellie had texted her: *Going into hiding. Maybe you should, too. Could be a matter of life or death.*

A hand fell lightly on Didi's shoulder, making her jump.

The producer for the interview with Oren Worth said, "We're

ready, Ms. DiMarco."

Didi blinked and saw Worth looking at her, looking *into* her as if he knew exactly what she was thinking. Behind him a camera pointed her way. Its red light was on.

She silently scolded herself: *Get a grip on yourself, woman.*

Didi DiMarco shifted into TV pro mode and smiled.

"Good afternoon, Mr. Majority Leader. Thank you for talking with us today."

"My pleasure, Ms. DiMarco."

For just a moment, Didi felt unnerved again. She'd never seen so warm a smile from Worth and his voice seemed to have a slight English accent. Where the hell had that come from?

Worth added, "I've long respected your work."

"Thank you, sir."

He'd seemed to dial the accent back a bit, but then Didi noticed his hairstyle had changed. The length and color were the same, but he didn't have his usual shellacked, helmet-hair look. His 'do looked like something you could run your fingers through and enjoy. Not only that, his face wasn't its usual pearlescent pink. There was a hint of tan to it that didn't originate in his makeup. Geez, had the guy had a makeover in the middle of a presidential election campaign?

"If you don't mind, Ms. DiMarco, I'd like to start by making a confession," Worth said.

Keeping a straight face, Didi asked, "What's that, sir?"

"After putting the matter to a practical test, I must now admit that in all likelihood, I'd probably be unable to beat Vice President Morrissey in an arm-wrestling competition."

Worth punctuated the statement with a charmingly sheepish smile.

To her surprise, Didi found herself sympathetically smiling back at him. "And what was the practical test that convinced you of that, sir?"

"I was challenged to arm-wrestle by my new campaign manager, Ms. Layla Dart, and was promptly thrashed."

Didi ran that story through her BS detector but couldn't find a lie.

If anything, Worth seemed at peace revealing his defeat.

"You're not concerned that your admission will lose you some male voters, sir?"

Worth nodded. "It very well might. I'll try to console myself that women vote in greater numbers than men."

The bastard had a sly smile on his face. Damn, she'd never thought of the man as handsome before, but he did have a certain appeal when he was in a good mood. Something he hadn't exactly been known for.

"Is there any video, Mr. Majority Leader, of Ms. Dart vanquishing you?"

Worth laughed. "There *was,* but I'm afraid a small fire destroyed it. Accidentally, to be sure."

He laughed again. Didi did, too, damnit. She told herself not to let the guy play her.

"Turning to more important matters, sir …"

Didi brought up matters of rising tensions with China, the economy and the deep divisions among the voting public. On the question of solving these problems, Worth insisted he was second to none, but he still did it with a new and winning casual charm and … Damn, Didi just noticed something. Worth's teeth were whiter than they used to be. Not garishly so, just enough to hit most casual observers subliminally.

This Layla Dart had to be some kind of a witch, Didi thought, working spells of enchantment. Jean Morrissey was going to have a tougher fight than anyone ever expected. She might well be the one asking for an arm-wrestling match soon.

The White House Residence — Washington, DC

Whenever McGill and Patti were both in Washington for an uninterrupted fortnight, they made a point of getting into bed at the same time twice a week. Some couples had date nights; with their schedules, they skipped the preliminaries. Except for a bit of conversation.

Just enough to keep distracting thoughts from intruding at the wrong moment.

Patti told McGill of her plan to forestall a Chinese military action in the South China Sea, hoping to prevent a far more pervasive and deadly conflict. Hearing Patti speak of a situation that had the possibility of escalating to the brink of a nuclear conflict — and maybe, God help us all, to the radioactive abyss — McGill paid strict attention.

Geopolitics was far from his area of expertise, but he did have a fair grasp of human nature, and cultural differences aside people everywhere wanted the same things: food, shelter, safety, sex and status. Working with those givens in mind, McGill considered what his wife told him.

Then he summed up, "You're going to have our navy contrive the destruction of one of our submarines, and without ever directly saying so imply that an act of war by China was the cause."

"Yes, exactly," Patti agreed.

"But you're not really going to sink one of our boats." McGill's uncle, Chief Petty Officer E.P. McGill, the creator of Dark Alley, had instructed his nephew that a submarine was never referred to as a ship; it was a boat. "Isn't that overdoing things just a bit? I don't know the pecking order of military hardware, but simply from a price-tag point of view, isn't a submarine worth more than two fighter planes?"

"In general, yes," Patti said. "The cost difference is considerable — unless you're talking about an antiquated, decommissioned, diesel boat that as great good luck would have it still functions sufficiently to make one last voyage from nearby Indonesia."

"Indonesia?" McGill asked.

Patti nodded. "Their late President Suharto impressed one of my predecessors in the Oval Office by destroying the Indonesian Communist Party at the cost of several thousand lives. Communist lives, not those of his people so much. As a 'that-a-boy,' our commander-in-chief sent him a World War II submarine. Suharto wanted the boat to be armed and also wanted training for his sailors in how to use it but Congress, in a momentary lapse of good judgment, said no. So Suharto made due with his sub as a status symbol. After all, not just any third-world dictator had one."

"So the Indonesians kept it and maintained it?" McGill asked. "What, as a good luck charm?"

Patti said, "We haven't ascertained their motives. We're just happy that it still functions, and we got it at a good price."

"So some of our highly skilled Navy people are going to blow the old boat to bits of flotsam and jetsam that will float to the surface, along with oil, fuel and other noxious substances. The debris gets picked up by the Chinese and —"

Patti shook her head. "Oh, no. We don't let them get their hands on any of it."

"Why not?" McGill asked. Then the light dawned. "Oh, right. If the Chinese start hauling in pieces of an antique boat, they'll know the whole thing is a hoax."

"We think they might suspect as much anyway, but maintaining an element of uncertainty is critical. Our military thinks what the Chinese might really try is to hack the software of our ships and submarines, especially target acquisition programs. Make us shoot at our own people, if we shoot at all. We're doing our damnedest to make sure that doesn't happen, but if our vintage boat is destroyed, they just might think they've succeeded. Even if they don't believe the fake-out, they can still peddle the rumor that they've bloodied the Americans if there's debris in the water. Their spy satellites will be able to photograph whatever floats to the surface. That will make the hawks in their military and the hate-America crowd around the world feel good."

McGill took a moment to let the whole scheme do a few laps around the old gray matter.

"What if even a faux success gets them so excited they want more?" he asked. "You know, look for other victories at sea."

"That was considered," Patti said. "Our Navy assures me we're more than a match for them and then there are the other countries we've signed on."

"Other countries?" McGill asked.

"The five largest navies in the world, outside of China and Russia, will become part of an armada transiting the South China Sea in the very near future."

McGill smiled. "An allied show of might."

Patti said, "That and more. Every country involved in the armada has also agreed to stop trading with China if it tries to dominate the South China Sea. That happens and the sound of China's economy collapsing will be heard around the world."

"That would have some big financial ripples, wouldn't it?" McGill asked.

"Very sizable indeed, but not nearly so bad as if the United States and China get into a shooting war. Still, a lot of work will have to be done to keep our economy and others afloat — and China's, too, once they give up the strong-arm stuff."

Patti fell silent for a moment to review the plan she'd helped to conceive and which she'd solely approved on behalf of the United States. The damn thing might define her place in history. "You think I've got everything covered, Jim?"

McGill tried to pick it apart, but there were too many things beyond both his expertise and his experience. One idea, probably fanciful, did come to him, though.

He asked Patti, "You think you could round up enough additional ships to haul a mountain or two of sand?"

CHAPTER 5

The White House — Washington, DC — September 16, 2016

Chief of Staff Galia Mindel was both surprised and displeased when the private phone line in her office chimed and she saw another unfamiliar calling number on the ID screen. The first unwanted call had been from that obnoxious Brit, Giles Henry. She might have let this call go to voicemail but in the waning days of Patricia Grant's presidency, Galia was feeling more confrontational and paranoid than ever.

She picked up the phone and said in her most intimidating tone, "This had better be good or whoever you are you're going to do time in prison."

"And a pleasant good morning to you, too, madam," the caller said.

Damn, it was another SOB with an English accent.

"I do hope incarceration won't be necessary," the caller added, "as Mr. James J. McGill provided me with your phone number. Will that be a sufficient introduction? I hope so, as I've called solely for the purpose of giving you a warning. A 'heads-up,' as people in this delightful country might put it."

Hearing that McGill had provided the caller with her number removed any chance of prosecution, but Galia was still rankled and now suspicious. Why would some new Brit be calling her with a warning?

"What's your name?" she asked.

"Oh, my. You don't recognize my voice?"

In no mood to play games, Galia asked, "Why would I?"

"Well, I am on television every week."

Now, the guy sounded pained that she didn't know him.

"Listen, just tell me who you are and why you called."

"Very well, this is Monty Kipp calling."

Indignation filled the guy's voice now. As a tactical maneuver, Galia decided not to tick him off any further. Well, not too much further.

"Oh, yes, Mr. Kipp. Formerly of Fleet Street and WorldWide News. Currently of Satellite News America, more commonly known as SNAM."

Hearing his résumé recited from memory by a White House grandee restored Kipp's sense of self-worth.

Until Galia added, "Sorry I didn't recognize your voice; I have staff monitor your end of the political media spectrum for me."

"Shall I ring off, madam?" Kipp asked, clearly offended now.

With McGill having told the man to call her, Galia thought not.

"Let's get to the purpose of the call, Mr. Kipp. I know I'm busy and I'm sure you are, too."

"Very well, madam. In a nutshell, here is what I've found out, incidental to a task I am undertaking for Mr. McGill. Giles Henry of the *Intruder* has just signed a publishing contract with Grantham House in London to do a book on you. My considered opinion, knowing Mr. Henry's work, is it will not be flattering. Indeed, it may be personally and politically devastating to you and perhaps even to President Grant herself, as rumor has it that completing the work has caused Giles Henry to stop drinking."

"That last part is important?" Galia asked.

"Only if true. What's certain is no one knows of *anything* that has ever caused Giles Henry to stop drinking in the past. Good day to you, madam."

Kipp ended the call. In the olden days of desk phones, he probably would have hung up with a bang. That wasn't important to Galia now. Seeing the President immediately was.

Rushing down the West Wing hallway and past Edwina Byington's desk, Galia asked the President's secretary, "Is she in?"

"Yes, ma'am."

"Anyone with her?"

"No, ma'am."

"No interruptions."

"Yes, ma'am."

Galia closed the door to the Oval Office behind her.

One glance at her chief of staff told Patricia Grant the situation was not good.

"What is it, Galia?" she asked.

"Madam President, I have to resign immediately. I'll put my request in writing and have it on your desk within the hour."

The President saw anxiety verging on terror in the eyes of the toughest political counter-puncher she'd ever known. With a nod she said, "Whatever you think is best, Galia."

"Thank you, ma'am." Taking a deep breath, Galia added, "Madam President, if you think it won't damage your legacy too seriously, I'd also like to request a Full Nixon."

A Full Nixon was a complete presidential pardon for any and all crimes a given individual might have committed from the moment of conception to the present day. That was exactly what President Gerald Ford had provided to Richard Nixon immediately after his resignation from the presidency.

Patricia Grant got up from behind her desk, stepped around it and embraced Galia.

"My legacy be damned, Galia," she said, "you're not going to spend a day in prison."

FCI Petersburg — Prince George County, Virginia

In the course of his duties with the *Police Nationale*, formerly known as the *Sûreté,* Odo Sacripant had, on a number of occasions, visited various security prisons in France. Security in this context meant the inmate was serving a sentence of ten years or more. Some of the prisons still operating in France dated to the mid-19th century. Of these, a handful had been converted from religious premises such as convents and abbeys.

It had always amused Odo that the architecture for purging the stain of sin from a soul and that of shielding society from the menace of criminals could be so compatible. The only difference between the past and present classes of inmates was the former were voluntarily confined while the latter were compulsorily secured.

The newer prisons in France, those built since the beginning of the 21st century, weren't nearly so quaint. An inmate's every movement from his cell was highly restricted and involved passing through several locked checkpoints under the cold gaze of a prison staff trained to meet any show of insubordination with massive retaliation. The extent of a violent inmate's injuries — or the cause of his death — were supposed to be confidential matters, but the gruesome details invariably found their way back to the cell blocks.

Education, even when delivered via a prison grapevine, was deemed to be valuable.

The implicit threats didn't mean that individuals or even gangs of prisoners didn't engage in misbehavior that ranged from insolence to riot. When you put two or three men in a cell intended for one, as many overcrowded French prisons did, trouble was assured. So was the combative response from the staff.

Having seen much of what went on in his homeland's places of confinement, Odo thought the conditions at FCI Petersburg Medium Security were relatively benign. Even the awful quality of the institutional food had been mitigated by regular "care packages" of fast food smuggled to Odo by the minions of Auric Ludwig or even the man himself.

Normally a man given to sipping Cap Corse Mattei, a grape-based liqueur, Odo was quickly becoming partial to Wendy's strawberry milkshakes. He'd have to watch himself or he'd need to explain to Yves Pruet how he'd gone into an American prison lean and muscled and come out fat and diabetic.

Binging on sweet empty calories wasn't Odo's only worry. On his second day after becoming Auric Ludwig's jailhouse neighbor, Odo had noticed that two other inmates and one corrections officer were paying unusual attention to him. At first, he thought the two other cons might soon challenge him physically, either with fists or a homemade blade, and he'd not only have to defend himself but do so without killing the other fellows. What kind of pressure the guard might put on him Odo couldn't discern at first.

Then one night the guard had passed Odo's cell and saw the Corsican was watching him closely. The guard placed a fist against his chest and raised his thumb just for a second. That was long enough. Odo understood that the guard was there to protect him.

And the two watchful convicts?

They observed Odo on separate shifts. More protection.

Hardly invisible though. Others in the prison population also must have noticed. Paying close attention to your surroundings was the first rule of survival in any country's prisons. Someone, possibly *M'sieur* McGill, had thought he was doing Odo a favor, protecting him.

Odo, though, felt he might have been given away, increasing his jeopardy.

In one way, he was right; in the other, he was wrong.

More than one inmate had noticed Odo's informal bodyguards, but they didn't attribute his protective detail to the forces of law and order. Being cons, the inmates who'd taken notice — and spread the word to Auric Ludwig — thought the criminal enterprise for which Odo supposedly worked had hired the convicts and the guard to look out for him.

Instead of becoming a figure of suspicion, Odo quickly became regarded as a man who was either very powerful in his own right or had important people backing him.

In any case, the next time Auric Ludwig stopped by his cell to visit he wore a knowing smile. "You really are something, aren't you?"

Odo shrugged. "Who isn't something … or the other?"

"You know what I mean," Ludwig said. "May I sit?"

There were no guest chairs in a prison cell at FCI Petersburg. Ludwig was asking if he might sit on the end of Odo's bed. Doing so without permission might be an occasion for a fight. Just because Odo had allowed Ludwig to sit before didn't mean he had *carte blanche.*

The Corsican sat at one end of the bed with his feet up and his back against a wall. He gestured to Ludwig to sit on the far end. "You've been quite generous to me."

Speaking quietly, Ludwig asked, "Have you thought about the business proposition I mentioned to you? Is there enough of a market in Europe to make it worthwhile?"

Odo laughed softly. "*Oui.* No doubt there are enough people on the Continent who'd love to have their own automatic rifles. Not just the *élément criminel* but ordinary citizens in the cities and countryside who wish to protect their homes and families against … the new arrivals."

"Foreigners," Ludwig said.

"*Oui.*" Odo was playing to his audience. Yves had explained Ludwig's history to him. Odo had an idea of how the man sitting on his bed must think. As a former police officer, Odo was appalled at the thought of France becoming a trigger-happy country like *les Etats-Unis.* On the other hand, he was a Corsican, not someone inclined to turn the other cheek in any case, and with the terrorists committing outrages in Paris and Nice, it would make many people happy to have a weapon with which to fight back.

Of course, if everyone had a gun as the Americans did, many an angry spouse would likely turn it on a straying husband or wife. Little ones might get their hands on Papa's misplaced pistol with tragic results. Domestic, non-political criminals would certainly find it easier to go about their business if they were armed with handguns or assault rifles.

"You have a lot of undesirable immigrants over there, don't

you?" Ludwig pressed on.

Odo had mixed feelings about that situation. He thought a varied population made things more interesting, but the *number* of those coming was overwhelming. It made even him uneasy.

The look on Odo's face was enough of an answer for Ludwig.

"People here feel the same way," he said. "They take comfort in their gun ownership."

Odo sighed. "This is all very interesting, *mon ami,* but you and I are hardly in any position to profit from the fears of our respective countrymen."

"I talked with my new lawyer this morning," Ludwig said.

"Yes?"

"He thinks I have a very good chance of getting my sentence reduced to the amount of time I've already served. If a conservative candidate is elected president soon, I'll not only get out, I'll have my criminal record expunged."

Odo smiled and raised an imaginary glass. *"Félicitations à tu."*

Ludwig understood the gist of the statement and smiled. "Yeah, thanks. I'm going to have to learn some French. Maybe get a pretty ma'amselle to teach me."

"Always the best way," Odo agreed.

"So when you get out, we go into business, okay?"

"*If* I get out. At home, I would feel more confident. Here …" Odo shrugged again.

Ludwig took a moment to think and then said, "Would you like me to have my new lawyer talk with you about your case?"

Odo asked, "What happened to your old lawyer? He was ineffective?"

"He died, hanged himself."

Odo laughed without a hint of humor. "He didn't shoot himself? How un-American."

Ludwig liked that. "So what do you say? My new guy, should I call him for you?"

Odo took a deep breath and let it out slowly. "Let us get to know each other a little better first. Then we will see."

Ludwig stood and nodded. “Okay, we can do that. I’ve got to get back to my cell now before controlled movement stops. Hey, you want another strawberry milkshake later?”

Odo smiled and said, “Why not?”

Georgetown — Washington, DC

When McGill left the White House to travel to work in the morning, Leo drove him and Deke northwest on Pennsylvania Avenue to Wisconsin Avenue in Georgetown. At that intersection, Leo would turn right on Wisconsin, head for nearby O Street, hang a left there and motor the short distance to the new headquarters of McGill Investigations, Inc.

Some days, McGill would have Leo detour to the campus of Georgetown University’s grad school and have breakfast with his elder daughter Abbie. It always did his heart good to see one of his children. If Abbie was busy with her studies or out of town, he might have Leo stop for coffee and a roll at one of the many eating establishments along the way, put a little money into the local economy, shake a few hands.

When he ate out, he often had to tell people for the umpteenth time, no, he wasn’t going to run for any political office after the President left the White House. Especially not the presidency. Spousal proximity for the past eight years, he informed the curious, had inoculated him against any desire to hold public office. If he ever woke up one morning to discover he’d won the presidency by a landslide write-in vote, he’d flee to Ireland where he was eligible for citizenship by virtue of having two grandparents who had been born on the Emerald Isle.

People always smiled and nodded when he gave this spiel, most seeming happy to know that not everyone who’d made something of a name for himself thought he’d be aces at running the country. “So few are,” McGill assured them.

When he got into his armored Chevy that morning, he asked Leo, “You made sure we’ve got new blades in the windshield wipers?

Wouldn't want any trouble if a rain storm pops up."

"Boss, we're good against anything short of the Rapture."

"What?" McGill said with a laugh. "The three of us haven't lived righteous lives?"

Leo said, "Sure we have. Only you and Deke have been baptized, though. I've had a bar mitzvah."

McGill shook his head. "If I can't have my personal race car driver go to heaven with me, I'm not going."

"Thanks, Boss. Now that I think of it, I believe Jesus had a bar mitzvah, too."

"Exactly," McGill agreed.

Ever the one to stick to business, Deke asked, "We about ready to roll?"

"Let's go," McGill said. "Everybody else is already in place?"

Deke nodded. "Just like we planned, and our car will be shooting video fore, aft and both sides the whole way."

McGill drew a deep breath, let it out silently through his mouth.

No more joking now. They didn't know anything unusual would happen, but it was time to think that it might. Just outside the White House gate, Gene Beck would pick up their tail on a dirt-bike that could go just about anywhere a mountain goat might. Others of McGill's associates would be spaced out along the route to the new offices in cars, on bicycles and on foot. Everyone was connected by a Bluetooth network.

"All right," McGill said, "let's go."

The White House — Washington, DC

Welborn Yates sat in his West Wing office at the White House reviewing the conversation he'd had that morning with his wife, Kira. Each of them had been helping one of their twin girls get some breakfast down: Welborn had Aria; Kira had Callista. The girls looked so much alike that even their parents got them confused. The only definitive way to tell the toddlers apart was Aria loved bananas and Callista despised them. In this regard, each girl was like her father or mother.

Welborn's office door was open and he broke from his reverie momentarily as he saw Jean Morrissey and her brother Frank hurrying toward the Oval Office. The Vice President gave Welborn a brief glance and a quick nod; the new deputy chief of staff just charged straight ahead. Something *big* was up. Welborn had understood that without a word being spoken.

It wasn't unreasonable for him to think his services might be required in some way. He stared at his phone for three minutes, according to the Rolex that Kira had given when he'd gotten the stars on his shoulders. When his phone didn't ring, he thought the problem might be something purely political. No need to get an over-promoted gumshoe involved.

Welborn went back to the review of his dialogue with Kira.

He'd been the one to drop the conversational bomb. "If Oren Worth wins the election, I'm thinking of leaving the Air Force. How would you feel about that?"

The spoon of oatmeal that Kira had been about to deliver to Callista stopped in mid-air.

But only until the child plaintively prompted, "Mommy!"

Delivering the sustenance, Kira asked, "Even if you got the boot from the White House, wouldn't your Air Force career continue to … gain altitude?"

Welborn didn't make the same mistake his wife had. He kept shoveling gruel as he responded. "Everyone knows I'm Patti Grant's pet."

Knowing that the word pet applied to dogs, Aria said "Arf."

Inevitably, Callista responded in kind. They laughed at each other and then got back to the serious business of eating.

Welborn told his wife, "I might be *demoted*, if Worth wanted to thumb his nose at his predecessor. If he wanted to be really nasty, he might demote me and post me to Thule, Greenland."

More than mildly disturbed that something so awful could happen, Kira asked, "The Air Force really has a base in Greenland?"

Welborn nodded. "A mere 947 miles from the North Pole. Much closer to Santa Claus for the girls, if you'd care to look at it that way."

Kira didn't, if her deep frown was any sign.

Still, she asked, "Do you really think Oren Worth can beat Jean Morrissey?"

Welborn shrugged. "With the American electorate, who knows what they'll do? Maybe think that another couple centuries of old white guys in the White House is the way to go."

The very idea lit fires of rage in Kira's eyes. "Nobody could be that —"

Having bitten her tongue, Welborn supplied a tidied-up guess of where his wife had been heading: "Effing stupid?"

Aria grinned at her father and said "Effing."

Callista chimed in, "Stupid."

They both giggled and then got back to chowing down.

With a sigh, Kira said, "I suppose they could. That's enough to make me weep. But I'd rather have us live off my family money than go to Greenland."

Welborn shook his head. "Oh, no. Our girls are going to have a working dad, at least until I'm 60."

"Fifty-five," Kira rebutted. "I want some prime-time with you while you're still in your prime."

A smile lit Welborn's face. "Okay, we can negotiate a time somewhere in that five-year niche. But I am going to work, and I'd like to separate from the service with my stars still in place."

"Yes, I definitely agree with that, but what kind of job do you think you might get?"

"Well, I am a trained and experienced investigator, and I do know someone with a burgeoning investigations empire."

"You'd really go to work for Mr. McGill?"

"He called me on another matter recently, and I raised the possibility of working for him. If I can learn to call him Jim instead of sir, I'm pretty sure he'll give me a chance."

"There's no reason why he shouldn't. You've worked out well

for me."

Welborn smiled, knowing Kira was teasing him.

He wiped off Aria's chin and said, "I always try my best, missus."

She gave him a wink and said in a saucy voice, "And don't I know it."

Aria said, "Missus."

Callista added, "Know it."

The twins giggled some more. Welborn wiped off Callista's face, kissed all three of his girls goodbye and headed out to work.

Seated behind his desk in the White House, Welborn thought it would certainly help make a case for gainful employment with McGill Investigations, LLP if he could come up with a definitive identification of the man/woman whose photos Mr. McGill had sent to him.

No sooner had the thought occurred than a notification bell rang on his computer.

A new email had arrived … and another quickly followed.

Welborn looked at the messages and attached photos, and he beamed.

Bingo. Twice over.

Oval Office — The White House

"Galia is about to resign, effective immediately," the President told Jean and Frank Morrissey.

Frank understood perfectly. "She's been found out. But how?"

"She didn't say and I didn't ask," the President responded. Then she turned to the Vice President. "Jean, I don't know how much you know, but —"

The Vice President held up a forestalling hand. "I don't know whatever secrets Galia might have, but her ability to engineer political momentum in this town is a legend, and everyone knows she didn't move political mountains by dint of her personal charm."

"No, she didn't," the President agreed, "but she almost always got the job done."

Frank was more interested in the future than the past. "Until now."

"Yes," the President agreed. "Monty Kipp of Satellite News America called Galia a few minutes ago to tell her that another English tabloid reporter named Giles Henry has just signed a contract with a British publishing house to do a tell-all biography of Galia. Kipp gave Galia advance notice at Jim's behest."

"Hasn't Kipp become a naturalized U.S. citizen?" Jean asked.

Frank said, "He has, but he's about to retire and go home."

Neither woman asked how he knew that.

Frank was a natural to step into Galia's job, working for his sister as her chief of staff once she was elected president. What neither Jean nor Patricia Grant knew was that Galia had turned over a digital copy of all her blackmail files to Frank, wanting him to keep up the good work for a Morrissey Administration.

From Frank's point of view, he couldn't have asked for a better gift.

He told the President and his sister, "I think what must have happened was this Giles Henry character found a glimmer of something Galia would like to keep hidden, started picking at it and realized he'd struck a motherlode of political secrets. He probably pitched the idea for the book speculatively: 'Look at what I've found already, and I'm sure there's more, much more.' He probably got a token advance with the big money waiting on when he delivers ..."

Frank looked at Patricia Grant. "Delivers something that implicates you in a misdeed, Madam President. Maybe even Mr. McGill as well."

The President laughed. "Paint Jim as a political schemer? He's never done anything of the sort. There's nothing to find on him."

Both Morrisseys noted that the President didn't try to paint herself equally as simon-pure, but neither of them said as much.

What Frank did say was, "Even if your husband can't be touched, that doesn't mean a guy like Giles Henry can't fabricate a conspiracy between you and your chief of staff. Everyone knows how close the two of you have been since you first ran for a seat in Congress, Madam President. All Henry has to do is ask a question: 'Can anyone believe that two women who worked with each other for so long, so closely and so successfully didn't know each other's every secret?'"

Patricia Grant had already thought of exactly that.

Jean Morrissey clearly hadn't. This situation was clearly something that couldn't be resolved by a hockey fight. Or even political pressure.

"We can't lean on this tabloid guy or his publisher," Jean said. "That would only make things worse."

"It would be a dream come true for both of them," Frank said. "It would imply that everything Henry wrote was true, even the stuff he'd contrive from that point on."

"So what do we do, Frank?" Jean asked, the hardening note in her voice carrying the clear message that very little would be off limits.

Before responding, he said, "Madam President, may I speculate a bit here?"

Patricia Grant nodded.

"I suggested Giles Henry is tugging at a loose end. Now, I'm wondering who that string might be. I can come up with a dozen names, but the one I like best is Senator Randall Pennyman. He's still a fugitive, and my guess is Galia outed him for the frauds he committed, doing so after Pennyman refused to pledge his vote to find you innocent in your Senate trial. My guess is that Giles Henry unearthed the senator and Pennyman started telling the reporter about other members of government he either knows or suspects Galia has pressured."

Both the President and Vice President bought that assumption.

"If Pennyman is Giles Henry's starting point," Frank said, "I think the only thing to do is eliminate it." When he saw apprehension in the eyes of both women, he added, "I mean *catch* Pennyman, arrest him. If Henry can find him, assuming the senator is his source, we should be able to do so, too, with a dedicated effort.

We'll publicize Pennyman being taken into custody, discredit him and bring him home to serve a long sentence for his crimes. As a convicted con-man, who would believe a word he said? If we undercut Henry's source, his publisher will be forced to dump the book on Ms. Mindel."

Patricia Grant steepled her hands under her chin. "I promised Galia I'd give her a Full Nixon. That was one more thing I wanted to tell both of you. I won't grant Galia's full pardon until after the election, but even then, Jean, it would make your first year in office a lot harder than it would be otherwise."

Jean paused only a moment before saying, "I'd do the same thing for Frank."

Frank grinned and kissed his sister's cheek.

He'd scared the two most powerful women in the world a minute ago.

Both of them thinking he'd meant to have Pennyman killed.

Now, it occurred to him maybe it would be better if Pennyman *and* Henry just disappeared. There wouldn't be any tell-all book then. Nor would there be any need to pardon Galia Mindel. Frank had long heard people describe him as ruthless. At that moment, he realized how right they all were. But how could *he* find Pennyman, and do it fast?

The President gave him the answer. "I'll assign General Welborn Yates to find Randall Pennyman post haste. I'll make sure he has all the resources he needs."

What she left unsaid was one of those resources might well be her own henchman.

En route to McGill's Office — Washington, DC

McGill knew his hometown of Chicago like a map had been imprinted on his genes. Maybe it had, the North Side and downtown anyway. His mother had taught voice in a private K-12 school opposite the Lincoln Park Zoo. She also gave private lessons in the homes of affluent Gold Coast families on North State Parkway and

Astor Street. She was a powerful walker even when taking McGill along for the ride internally. She often logged 30-40 miles per week.

McGill's father had later told him, "If your mother had ever started sleepwalking, we might have had to look for her anywhere between Wisconsin and Indiana."

Mom had laughed at the idea and claimed a robust heart and lungs, along with a supple diaphragm, were necessities for a singing voice to reach the bargain seats without the benefit of a microphone. Not that she sang at the top of her voice as she marched. She sang softly, she'd told McGill, at a level the baby boy inside her might find pleasing.

Having heard his mother's story, McGill credited her with his own vocal command. He also claimed his awareness of local geography owed to *seeing* the city through his mother's eyes.

During his nearly eight years living in Washington, McGill felt he'd come to know his second hometown nearly as well as his first. Like his mom, he loved to get out and walk the city, experience it firsthand with no intervening barriers. He'd been able to do that more in Patti's first term in office. In the second term, it came to him now as his Chevy left the White House grounds, he'd spent far more time behind armored metal and ballistic glass.

After all, when you'd become a high-profile target, you never knew when someone might take a shot at you. Well, actually, he had at least an approximate idea. Soon. Auric Ludwig wasn't going to pay for a hit that was scheduled ten years out.

Rolling onto Pennsylvania Avenue, Leo asked, "Usual route, boss, or should we outfox any scalawags layin' in wait out there. I can give the rest of our guys and gals any change in course."

McGill shook his head. "Go the same way as always. We're as ready as we'll ever be. Let's see if anything crawls out of the woodwork. You *are* ready, right Deke?"

The soon to be former Secret Service agent only grunted.

It was tough for someone with epicanthic folds to roll his eyes expressively.

"Deke's ready," McGill told Leo.

"I'm not surprised," Leo said

He turned right on 17th Street, heading for K Street where they'd make a left.

McGill watched the road ahead. He glanced at the buildings to his left and right. Following Satchel Paige's advice, he didn't look back. Not because something might be gaining on him. Rather because he was sure both Leo and Deke, using the car's mirrors, had a visual rear guard already mounted.

The thing about crossing any well-traveled route, McGill thought, was you became so familiar with your surroundings you soon stopped noticing most of the details. The low-to-mid rise office buildings strung one next to the other along any given block became beads on a necklace that didn't rate a second glance. Occasionally, there appeared new buildings or old ones of some architectural distinction that called out to both the eye's attention and the mind's appreciation. But these were exceptions and even they might be observed without conscious awareness when your thoughts were preoccupied with other matters.

Leo turned left on K Street, heading toward Georgetown.

A cityscape became a far more menacing place, though, when you considered it to be an infinite number of hiding places from which a professional attempt on your life might be made. The honeycomb of office building windows turned into hives of shooters' blinds. McGill's vehicle was as heavily armored as either of the presidential limos, but he knew there were .50 caliber rounds that claimed the ability to pierce armored limos — or sedans — up to a distance of 1,000 yards.

A Hellfire missile or its equivalent would certainly make short work of his car and everyone inside it.

McGill had to take a fatalistic view of such possibilities. If Auric Ludwig had managed to hire assassins with the weapons and skills of a special forces team, his goose was cooked — assuming the well equipped and trained bad guys weren't having an off day. You never knew. Fate could intervene either way: save you or slay you.

Still, McGill was a firm believer that Providence favored those who knew when to duck or throw the first punch. So he kept a sharp eye and conscious awareness of everything he saw ahead and to either side. The intense engagement with his environment proved to be both interesting and tiring.

Small wonder that people zoned out regularly.

The mind needed rest as much as the body.

K Street turned into the Whitehurst Freeway.

McGill let his vigilance ease momentarily, taking a mental respite. There was nothing to say an attempt on his life might not occur on the higher-speed roadway. Still, there was every reason to believe that nobody behind the wheel of any nearby car could keep up with Leo.

Out of curiosity, McGill had asked Leo once, "You know of any former racing colleague who's gone into executive driving?"

"You mean like what I do for you?"

"Yeah."

"I haven't heard of any of the ol' boys I knew doing that, but now you've got me wondering. I'll check it out."

Leo got back to him a week later. "You know, some of the almost-were's are driving for big shots, but nobody who won three major races like I did. That's not to say the wannabes aren't any good, but some of the Secret Service and FBI boys are real good behind the wheel, too. They're just not as good as me."

"None of them?" McGill asked.

Taking no offense, Leo said, "Not a one."

So McGill felt comfortable closing his eyes for a minute. When he felt his car turn onto Wisconsin Avenue, he opened them again. They were close to his new office building now. It looked like it would be an uneventful commute to the office.

There were small shops on either side of the street now. Most of the businesses had incorporated Georgetown into their names. With the rents they paid in the posh neighborhood, they didn't want anyone to forget where they were for a minute. A lane of traffic flowed in each direction at a casual pace, the better to rubberneck all the shops. Spaces for parking bordered both sides of the street.

Diners and coffee shops did a brisk business. Tourists window-shopped. Truck drivers pushing dollies made deliveries. Commerce and comity thrived. Try as he might, McGill didn't see any hint of villainy in the offing.

Neither Leo nor Deke had any hackles rising from their necks.

And then just before they reached O Street where McGill's office building stood …

An old lady stepped out from behind a parked delivery truck directly into the Chevy's path.

McGill, counter-intuitively, decided it was time to turn and look behind him.

He saw two well-dressed men running down Wisconsin Avenue toward the Chevy with Uzis in hand. They peeled to either side of Gene Beck on his dirt bike. Feeling the Chevy start to swerve, McGill faced forward again. In the process, he saw another guy in a suit with an Uzi on the sidewalk to his right.

Leo had already cleared the old lady, moving left without doing her any damage, but there was traffic in the oncoming lane. Leo avoided a crash only because there was space available in the parking lane on the far side of the street. Without any noticeable effort, Leo eased to the left again, so smoothly nobody so much as bothered to honk at him.

But that brought the Chevy adjacent to a point where another guy with an Uzi stood. He opened up on McGill's car. The weapon fired either 9 mm or .45 caliber rounds. Whichever they were, the projectiles deflected off the Chevy like thrown pebbles.

That didn't mean people out on the street were safe. A ricochet might wound or kill someone who'd made the grave mistake of being in the wrong place at the wrong time. So when McGill saw Gene Beck roar down the sidewalk on his dirt bike, he thought to himself, *Do whatever you need to.*

What Gene did was to streak by to the left of one of the shooters, while extending his right arm like an iron bar. The shooter turned at the last second to see what menace was streaking toward him and Gene's arm caught him smack on the throat. McGill half-expected to see the guy's head pop off. It didn't, but he had no doubt the man's neck had been fatally broken before he hit the ground.

Gene didn't linger over the body. He wheeled his bike around on the sidewalk and drew a handgun from his jacket. Up and down Wisconsin Avenue everyday drivers screeched to a halt and did their best to shelter under their dashboards. Leo, though, kept the Chevy moving.

McGill's new offices were on O Street just off Wisconsin. O was a one-way street emptying onto Wisconsin. Normally, Leo had to drive to P Street and loop around to get to the office. That day he thought a minor traffic violation was the better part of valor and made an illegal left turn.

The former NASCAR driver got all the way to the entry ramp of the garage beneath the new McGill Investigations office building when McGill said, "Stop right here, Leo."

He did, had to. The steel gate hadn't rolled out of the way yet.

The three men in the Chevy heard muffled pops. The car's glass and armor were so dense they blunted most outside noise to inaudibility. McGill said, "Give us some ears, Leo."

Leo activated the microphones that picked up external sounds.

Gunfire built to a crescendo. McGill craned his neck to look out the back window toward Wisconsin Avenue. A guy in a suit with an Uzi turned the corner and took one step toward the Chevy when the crack of a single shot announced itself and the guy fell, exhibiting the boneless release of death.

With that body in the foreground, McGill saw another guy in the same kind of suit, but without an Uzi, race up Wisconsin toward P Street. A heartbeat later, Maj Olson raced after him and McGill thought, damn, that woman sure could run. He only hoped she knew what to do with the guy once she caught him.

That thought made him say to Deke and Leo, "We'd better see if anybody out there needs a hand."

They both looked at him as if he was crazy.

"I'd do the same for both of you," he told them.

Leo and Deke knew the truth when they heard it.

Even so, they tried to dissuade McGill.

"No," Deke told him, "they *want* you out of the car."

"You're a bit up their peckin' order from Deke 'n' me, Boss," Leo said.

"Like hell," McGill said.

He popped open the back door and got out. Anticipating the move, Deke was right there beside McGill. He had his Uzi out even though there was no immediate threat. Leo joined them a second later, and he had a Dirty Harry .44 Magnum in hand.

Not wanting to be entirely foolhardy, McGill took out his Beretta MP9.

Deke told McGill, "No bullshit now. I'm taking point. Leo's walking slack. You don't agree, the two of us are going to tackle you right now and drag your ass inside."

The sounds of gunfire had stopped, replaced by a growing volume of first responders' sirens. McGill said, "Okay."

He thought he could take the two of them, if he wanted to assert himself, but it'd set a bad example if the boss started beating up his employees.

They hadn't gone a step when an old lady turned the corner at Wisconsin Avenue and started to come their way.

The same old lady who'd popped out into traffic at the start of the bloodbath.

Coincidence? All three men looked at one another. No damn way.

When they looked back her way she was taking a handgun out of her purse.

Deke raised his Uzi.

But McGill shot first.

The White House — Washington, DC

General Welborn Yates had James J. McGill's private cell phone number. Other than the President, the VP, the chief of staff, the McGill kids and the man's ex-wife, he was the only one who had it. Well, Margaret Sweeney surely must have it, he thought. And Special Agent Ky and Leo Levy. Still, it was a small and privileged group.

You didn't call the man on a whim.

But when you came up with information that he'd asked for, you didn't hesitate.

McGill came on the phone quickly: "Welborn?"

"Yes, sir." In the background, Welborn heard what sounded like a chorus of sirens from most of the emergency vehicles in the city. Forcing himself to maintain a calm tone, he asked, "Is everything all right?"

"I just shot an old lady," McGill told him.

Welborn offered the only response that made sense to him. "With good reason?"

"She had her own gun out and was about to open up on me. I beat Deke and Leo to the draw. Deke was packing his Uzi; Leo carries a .44 Magnum."

Taking a beat, Welborn asked, "So you shot the old lady to save her?"

"You know that movie cliché where the good guy shoots the gun out of the bad guy's hand?"

"Sure."

"Doesn't work. Not for me anyway. I hit the old girl in the forearm. She lost hold of her gun, all right, but the paramedics who got to her think it's anybody's guess whether she makes it."

"You did what you could, sir. Letting either Special Agent Ky or Mr. Levy shoot would have meant certain death."

McGill sighed. "That's what I keep telling myself right now. Well, at least Maj Olson took one of them alive."

Maintaining self-control became more demanding for Welborn. "One of them" implied two bad actors at a minimum and possibly more. Could such gunplay be the result of anything other than an assassination attempt on Mr. McGill? And who in heaven's name was Maj Olson?

"I'm sorry to bother you at such a difficult time, sir, but I received some information on the person you asked me to investigate. I thought you should know right away."

"The tall drink of water Leo spotted?"

Welborn heard excitement in McGill's voice.

"Yes, sir."

"Man or woman?" McGill asked.

"That remains to be determined, but Leo's instinct that the individual was potentially dangerous was a bull's-eye. This person is suspected of being responsible for several killings around the world."

"How can we not even know a bad guy's gender?" McGill asked.

"Because nobody has ever laid a hand on him or her," Welborn said. "The only things law enforcement has to go on are other photographic images, ones not even as clear as Mr. Levy's videos."

"But still good enough to connect with other crimes?" McGill asked.

"Yes."

"And you got this information from a military or civilian intelligence agency?"

"From MI-6, sir. I asked a favor of my father while waiting for a response from our people. Got the information just moments ago. From what I've seen, the person Mr. Levy spotted works primarily in British Commonwealth countries. Besides that, there was one other assassination in Germany and now he or she is here in the U.S."

After a moment's pause, Welborn asked, "Did you or anyone else see that person this morning?"

McGill was quiet for a beat. "I didn't even think to look for that … person. But I sure as hell would have shot for center mass of the old lady if I thought *she* was behind it all."

Welborn stifled a laugh. "You raise a good point, sir."

Now, McGill was amused. "Yeah? What's that?"

"Well, if the operational executive behind the attempt on your life is a master of disguise and chooses to appear androgynous, that offers a huge advantage in concealment. In most cases, you can eliminate an entire gender, half the world's population, when looking for a suspect. In this situation, you can't do that. The search becomes twice as hard."

"I didn't think of that," McGill said, "maybe because I didn't want to make the problem twice as hard. But you raise a good point, Welborn, and I appreciate the initiative you took reaching out to your father. Please thank Sir Robert for me."

"I will, sir. There's always a chance *our* people might have something on this person when their responses come in."

"I'll keep my fingers crossed," McGill said.

"There is one other bit of news."

"What's that?"

"The CIA says Father Inigo de Loyola was in Costa Rica as of yesterday. He's not engaged in any 'extralegal activities,' as they put it, but he is someone they like to keep tabs on. I'm going to let Margaret Sweeney know as soon as we're done speaking."

"Great. She'll be happy to know where he is. You do good work, Welborn."

"Thank you … Jim."

K Street — Washington, DC

Caryn Osborne, the young special master working with Putnam Shady, said to him, "I've never seen or even heard of Chief Judge Cerney doing such a quick and complete turnaround on the scope of investigative latitude."

Detectives Meeker and Beemer, who were also present, smiled. Putnam kept reading a file that seemed to hold a special interest.

Meeker said, "Investigative latitude, I like that turn of phrase. How about you, Beem?"

"Positively grandiloquent. Sounds lots better than snooping."

Keeping his visual focus on the file, Putnam told Caryn, "They're just showing off."

"Using vocabulary from their word-of-the-day calendar?"

Caryn asked and stuck her tongue out at the cops.

They both laughed.

Still multitasking, Putnam said, "I first met Detectives Meeker and Beemer some years back when a friend of mine got killed."

"Did they think you did it?" Caryn asked.

"Guys?" Putnam said.

"Maybe a little," Beemer replied.

"But only at first," Meeker added.

"Nonetheless," Putnam continued, "I thought it would be wise to learn a little about them."

"*What?*" both cops asked in unison.

"Ha-ha," Caryn said gleefully.

"They're both honors graduates of Howard University," Putnam said.

"Don't be givin' away our secrets," Beemer said.

"In fact," Putnam continued, "Michael Walker, that's Detective Beemer's given name, was his class's salutatorian. The year before that, Marvin Meeker was his class's valedictorian."

Beemer looked at his colleague and said, "He got more nutritional meals than me."

Meeker replied, "He spent more time eating; I spent more time reading."

"So why aren't the two of you running the police department?" Caryn asked.

Using a finger to keep his place in the file, Putnam finally looked up. "I've wondered as much myself. Captain Bullard was another exceptional student, but at the very least you guys should be equal in rank to the captain and crowding her for the next step up the ladder."

"Hate all the politics that high up in the department," Beemer said.

Meeker nodded, "Besides that, we like doing the work, mostly."

Beemer grinned. "Fooling people with our act."

"Might co-author a book about our exploits after we retire next year," Meeker said.

Beemer added, "Bound to be a best-seller, maybe even a major motion picture."

"We'd be too old to play ourselves," Meeker conceded, "but casting prerogatives, that'd be in our contract for sure."

Captain Bullard stepped into the file room, having overheard at least the last part of the conversation and maybe more. She looked at her two detectives. "Books and movies? That's a new one. If I'm mentioned, I hope you'll treat me kindly."

Meeker and Beemer grinned.

"We'd be running for our lives if we didn't, wouldn't we?" Meeker asked.

"Spoil all our time layin' out by the pool if we were that foolish," Beemer told her.

The captain turned to Putnam and Caryn. "We didn't have a stand-up comedy class at Rice University or I'd probably be as bad as them. Now, would you care to tell me, Mr. Shady, what information you've put your finger on in that file? Some interesting point of law or even better the admission of a criminal act?"

Putnam opened the file and took out two glossy four-color brochures.

"Advertising materials. One for a hotel. Another for an adjacent hospice facility. Both of them down in Baja California. Mexico."

"I don't understand," Caryn said, "why a criminal defense attorney would —"

"Guillermito Tonto," Captain Bullard said.

"The guy who killed that doctor locally?" Caryn asked. She read the *Post* daily.

"Yeah, him," Meeker said.

Beemer nodded. "An anonymous source paid his bail and hospital bill."

Putnam said, "But if you were going to scale up that scheme, using dying people as assassins, you'd want to make it cost efficient. Open your own small-scale resort. Get your killers down to a place on the beach in Mexico. Let them see the sunset on the Pacific one last time. Give their families a nice place to say goodbye. What more, besides a pile of money, could a homicidal bastard want?"

Meeker said, "What with Aubrey Gadsden getting himself hung in his own office, he couldn't have been the guy running that show."

"More like middle management," Beemer said.

Captain Bullard asked, "Your take, Mr. Shady?"

Putnam said, "Whoever's running the hacienda down in Baja has to be a front man. Aubrey Gadsden, Esquire, was … a travel agent. He could show the brochures to any dying killer on his client list. Tell him, 'See, *this* is the way you should go out.'"

"Only something had to go wrong," Captain Bullard said. "Gadsden made somebody think he'd become a risk and he got himself strung up."

The three cops in the room exchanged a series of looks and without a word came to the same conclusion.

"What?" Putnam asked.

"Yeah, what?" Caryn added.

"Zoë Tinker," Captain Bullard said. "She's a psychologist."

"Yeah, so?" Caryn asked.

Putnam understood now. He told Caryn. "If you're going to hire a dying person to kill someone, you'd want to make sure your killer is mentally and emotionally strong enough to do the job. Assure yourself that he'd *commit* to carrying it off."

"You'd want to make sure he still had enough muscle to do it, too," Meeker said.

"So there could be more than one kind of doctor involved," Beemer agreed.

Captain Bullard said, "Ms. Tinker said she'd talk to us only if we got a signed release from the late Mr. Gadsden's legal representative. I have the feeling that won't be forthcoming."

"I got the feeling the lady's not waiting around for our next visit either," Beemer said.

"Or even in the country anymore," Meeker added.

That idea gave everyone pause, but just for a moment in Putnam's case.

"Gadsden can't be the only member of the criminal defense bar in on this game," he said.

Caryn wasn't sure about that or where it led if it was true.

The three cops, though, they all smiled.

"Time to circulate a photo of Aubrey Gadsden's last gasp," Captain Bullard said.

McGill Investigations International, LLP — Washington, DC

After two hours spent answering questions from the Metro PD and the Secret Service, it was decided by local and federal law enforcement that McGill and his people had acted within the bounds of the law, had countered the threats against them with proportionate responses and had likely saved an unguessable number of innocent lives.

Two tourists from Ohio had suffered lacerations from flying masonry displaced by gunfire.

Another three visitors, South Koreans, had been hit by shattered glass.

All of the injured had been treated and released. Their emotional trauma was mitigated to some degree when each of them received a personal phone call from the President of the United States. She expressed her best wishes for speedy recoveries and provided complimentary tickets to a performance by the National Symphony Orchestra at the Kennedy Center that night.

The Koreans already had seats but not as good as the ones the White House provided.

After that exercise in public concern, Patricia Grant called her husband to see how he was doing. "I would have called you first," she said, "but I was told you were talking to the police and the Secret Service, and that you'd suffered no harm."

McGill said, "Only to my self-image and sense of good judgment. I shot an old lady. Well, not that old, only 52, I'm told, but the fact that she was at death's door before I met her added another 30 years to her appearance."

"Quite the challenge to appear youthful as the end nears," Patti said. "I was also told that you didn't shoot to kill and because of that there's some chance Ms. Paulette Lacroix might yet provide us with some useful information."

"Really?" McGill asked. "From the look on her face when she was pulling that gun from her purse, I wouldn't have counted on her as being the cooperative type."

"Just between us?" the President said.

"Of course," McGill said.

"SAC Kendry informed Ms. Lacroix that palliative care can vary. Her remaining moments might be pain-free and she could exit this life on a narcotized cloud or she could experience every shrieking nerve ending in the arm you shattered with your gunshot."

The ruthlessness of the choice surprised McGill.

"That was your call?" he asked.

"It was Elspeth's idea, but I approved it."

"I think you've become a much tougher lady these past few years."

"Listen," Patti said, "for you or our kids, I'd put Mother Goose in front of a firing squad."

McGill couldn't keep from laughing. "We'd better take a long weekend soon."

"More like a month or two. Just you and me and a platoon of security people who can disguise themselves to look like hammocks and pool floats."

"Can't wait," McGill said. "January 20th isn't that far away."

With a sudden tremor in her voice, Patti said, "Jim, please don't let me lose you before we can walk away from the White House."

McGill said, "Not then or a long time afterward. After all, we have to see how well we can get along without all the pomp and circumstance."

Reassured, Patti said, "We'll struggle through."

McGill left his private office and entered the conference room where his team — his new partners and associates — waited for him. At the request of Rebecca Bramley and Maj Olson, John Tall Wolf had joined them. With Leo's Chevy securely tucked into the building's underground garage, he was there, too.

"Are we all good?" McGill asked everyone.

He'd asked the same question three times already. Repetition was okay. They all knew that the emotional impact of violent exchanges sometimes came with a time-delayed fuse. You could think you'd made a clean getaway and then —

Maj Olson said, "I keep telling myself I did the right thing running after that guy, but every time I do I get a chill down my spine. My knees get wobbly. A little voice tells me, 'Next time, the scumbag could turn on you with a gun. Shoot the ass right off you, girly.'"

Yves Pruet, his face a mask of compassion, said, "That would be a shame in so many ways, *ma'amselle*." He punctuated his sentiment by pointedly staring at Maj's backside and raising his eyebrows.

After just a beat, Maj guffawed and everyone else joined in the laughter.

Pruet added to the merriment by shrugging and elaborating, "You will have to forgive me, Ms. Olson. I am a lecherous old man, and French as well."

McGill laughed at that along with everyone else, especially after Maj gave Pruet a hug, but he was the one who called the meeting to order. "Okay, people, I believe we have some game tape to review."

Florida Avenue — Washington, DC

Sweetie was at home, just having come through her front door after a long run, when her phone rang. In need of a shower, she was tempted to let the call go to voice-mail. Only there was too much going on to do that — and she was hardly the one to yield to temptation.

That did happen rarely, but leap years occurred more often.

Besides the moral compulsion to attend to her obligations, there was the fact that people were trying to kill her oldest friend.

She also had a job to do for the Pope. And, who knew, Maxi might have skinned a knee.

Sweat dripping off her forehead, she took her cell phone in hand. She saw the White House was calling. Didn't know if it was Jim or someone else but —

"Margaret, this is Welborn Yates. I have some news regarding Father Inigo de Loyola for you."

Before he could tell her what it was, Putnam came through the front door. He saw Sweetie was on the phone and made a show of tiptoeing away so as not to disturb her.

"Have you found him?" Sweetie asked.

Intrigued by the question, Putnam stopped to listen in.

"Broadly speaking, yes," Welborn said. "A contact from the CIA put him in Costa Rica as of yesterday. A friend in the State Department talked to Costa Rican immigration and found out that Father de Loyola entered the country last month and has 63 days left on his 90-day visa, assuming he intends to stay in the country legally or hasn't crossed into Nicaragua or Panama without bothering to let their immigration people know."

Sweetie thought about that. "Is there any reason to think the good father might be acting illegally?"

Welborn said, "Well … I haven't read an in-depth profile of the man, and you had good things to tell me about him, but my friend from State mentioned that back in the day Inigo de Loyola cut quite a swath through Central America, being one of the fiercer advocates of liberation theology. My friend didn't come right out and say he had blood on his hands but the implication was pretty clear."

Sweetie mulled that, too. "What's the U.S. military posture toward that area these days?"

"From what I've read, we're always watchful because of Central America's proximity to us, but it's far from a major worry."

"I thought it was a drug trans-shipment point," Sweetie said.

"There is that. Public information is also available regarding the infiltration into the region by elements of jihadist organizations.

The Chinese are also trying to increase their footprint in South and Central America. Thinking about all that now, maybe Father de Loyola *isn't* south of the border just for a vacation."

Sweetie said, "So, this could get complicated?"

"May I offer a suggestion?" Welborn asked.

"Please."

"As you're working, even if informally, for the Vatican, you might ask for help from Church officials down there to find Father de Loyola. Ask Cardinal Fitzroy, here in Washington, to serve as your introduction to them."

Sweetie beamed. "I like that: two terrific ideas. That should help a lot."

"I'm assuming, of course, that you'll be traveling to Costa Rica," Welborn said.

"Unless you or someone else finds Father de Loyola's phone number for me, I guess I'll have to," Sweetie said. "Hey, do you think you could come along?"

"You'd like me to accompany you?" A note of doubt rang in Welborn's voice.

Sweetie paid his reluctance no attention. "Yeah, why not? From what I've heard, you've got a good head on your shoulders. You certainly helped me out already. You speak Spanish?"

"Sorry, no." Following a pause, Welborn added, "I'd have to clear my absence here with the President, and let Kira know I'd be away, of course."

"Sure. Tell you what: Do what you need to do. Give me a call back if you can make it. No problem if you can't."

Sweetie said goodbye and turned to Putnam. "Welborn Yates, he's come up with a lead for me. Father de Loyola looks to be in Costa Rica."

"That's great."

He went to the small wine, beer and water fridge behind the breakfast bar, grabbed a bottle of San Pellegrino and poured two glasses. He put a lemon wedge on hers and took a slice of lime for himself. The two of them touched glasses and drank.

Sweetie said, “Your day hasn’t been as productive?”

“Can’t say that. I think we’re making progress. It’s just that … sometimes I get to feeling that my old point of view, that the world is a sack of crap, was the right one.”

“So you want to go back to being a plump, cynical bachelor scamming taxpayers for a living?” Sweetie asked.

“Well, if you put it that way …” He leaned over the bar and kissed Sweetie. “Mmm, salty. No, I wouldn’t give up you or Maxi for anything.”

“So what’s giving the man who’s seen everything the blues?”

Putnam told her about the hit-man’s hospice by the sea.

“Really? Dying killers go there to breathe their last in comfort?” Sweetie asked.

“Yeah. How’s that for comprehensive health care?”

“Better than most people in this country have,” Sweetie said. “So what are the Metro cops going to do about it?”

“Well … obviously, they don’t have jurisdiction in Mexico. While I was still nearby, they were trying to decide who to hand it off to in the federal government. The FBI is the obvious choice, but the DEA was raised as a possibility because they might have better contacts. In any case, the obvious question arises: Who the hell can you trust down there not to be paid off?”

“Because it’s inevitable anybody running that place *must* be paying off someone,” Sweetie said.”

“Absolutely, paying off quite a few people, and the dude handing out the cash certainly won’t be the guy manning the front desk.”

Sweetie thought about the problem. Drained her entire glass in the process. Sucked on her slice of lemon. A little tartness didn’t bother her. Maybe the Vitamin C was even inspirational. She began to nod to herself.

“What?” Putnam asked. “You’ve got an idea?”

Sweetie said, “Not answers, but maybe a couple of approaches on how to find them.”

“And those approaches are?”

“Well, if you’re looking at a murder-for-hire organization, it seems like a good idea to scout people who have a history of such things."

"Drug cartels?"

"Could be. They certainly kill lots of people. What I was thinking of, though, was more directly focused on the taking of lives rather as a primary focus, not secondary to pushing drugs. During all the turmoil in Central America back in the 80's, weren't there both armies and guerrilla groups who had death squads whose sole purpose was slaughtering people to terrorize the survivors into submission?"

Putnam nodded. "Yes, there were."

"So what happened to all those barbarians? They settled down and became dentists and accountants? I guess I thought of that because Welborn just told me Father de Loyola was involved in those battles in some fashion. He also told me he'd gotten some of his information from the CIA. Maybe they'd know what happened to some of the butchers from the bad old days down that way."

Putnam smiled and said, "Maybe they would. Might be hard for most people to dig out that information, but with her husband's life in jeopardy, my money says the President can do it. That's a terrific idea, Margaret."

"Thanks, but it's only a guess right now. Since you like it, though, here's another. Whoever killed Aubrey Gadsden in his own office had to be cleaning up for someone else."

Putnam said, "Yeah. The cops and I are thinking Gadsden somehow became unreliable and had to go. Now, the cops feel pretty sure a psychologist named Zoë Tinker is involved."

"That may be, but is Zoë someone who could subdue a man and hang him in his own office?"

Putnam hadn't met the woman, but from the picture he'd seen of her, it didn't seem likely. Sexist though the thought might be, he felt it would take a couple of men to get the job done.

"So do you have any suggestions who the cops might look for?" Putnam asked.

"The actual perps, no. But looking at things from another

angle, who'd benefit big time by having the job done?"

It took Putnam all of five seconds to come up with the answer; his devious side hadn't atrophied entirely. "Someone who'd used Gadsden's walking near-dead to do a job for him. You get rid of the lawyer, there'd be no connection between you and the person you targeted. The killers would likely be no threat against you because their expiration date would arrive soon enough, and might have already passed."

"Right," Sweetie said, "so who do we know who wants to kill Jim McGill and not leave even a hint he was in any way responsible?"

Putnam responded without hesitation. "Auric Ludwig. Damn. Did he hire out a double-hit: James J. McGill *and* the crooked lawyer running the kill squad?"

McGill Investigations International LLP

McGill's people clustered their chairs around one end of the conference table so they could get up-close looks at the high-definition TV screen showing the video angles shot from McGill's Chevy. They watched the oncoming automotive traffic, the parked delivery trucks, the delivery people themselves going about their jobs and the pedestrians, both oncoming and moving in the same direction as McGill's vehicle.

At the outset, the scene might have been a cityscape out of a Norman Rockwell painting, if the artist had done such scenes. Everyone was a picture of an idealized 21st century America. Neat, orderly and pleased to be part of a sunny morning's civic pageant. There was nobody panhandling or walking off last night's bender unshaven and slovenly.

Business people, early rising tourists and the gainfully employed were the archetypes.

Everybody looked like they had well-nourished wallets and plenty of available credit.

Seated among the viewers, Gene Beck softly whistled an unfamiliar tune, perhaps an original composition, that worked as a musical score and no one objected.

But Rebecca Bramley observed. "Nobody even jaywalks here." The tone of her voice indicated surprise.

"Georgetown," McGill said, "at least when I've seen it."

Deke contradicted, "Except…right…now."

McGill paused the video with the control he held. The left foot and lower leg of the old lady, Paulette Lacroix, appeared just beyond the front end of the delivery truck belonging to DC Dairy Products.

Turning to Leo, McGill asked, "Is that when you first saw her, when her lead leg appeared?"

Leo reviewed his memory of the moment. "Believe I caught her *foot* out of the corner of my eye. That's what gave me time to make my move."

Brad Lewis, McGill's old friend from the CPD who'd be heading up the Chicago office, looked at Leo and asked, "You noticed a *foot* out of the corner of your eye while doing, what, 30 miles per hour?"

Leo shrugged. "Average speed in your NASCAR race is 200 miles per hour, 220 in the straightaways. To me, 30 is like … what *crawling* is to most people, I guess. Besides, I know blind spots are always potential hazards, and that's what big objects like parked trucks create. You never know when a kid or a granny might pop out from behind one. Also, I make mental notes about the road ahead long before I get to a particular spot. I saw I had a little room in the oncoming lane and more in the far parking lane."

Lewis turned to McGill, "Can I get me someone like him?"

McGill saw the light go on in other eyes. Everybody wanted a Leo.

He said, "I'll make sure we all have the support people we need."

To cut off any further requests, he put the video back in motion. Leo had the Chevy into the oncoming lane before Paulette Lacroix had her lead hip clear of the truck; he was into the parking lane a millisecond later.

At that point, McGill moved to other views of the street from cameras on the sides and rear of the Chevy. The hit team had timing that was nearly the equal of Leo's. In fact, on the video shot from the driver's side of the Chevy, it looked like Leo was giving the shooter on that side of the street a more immediate target to hit. The muzzle flashes were blinding.

And then a blur of a figure riding a motorbike on the sidewalk knocked the shooter down like a tenpin.

Gene Beck said, "Caught him square with my forearm, made sure I hit him with the meat so I didn't break any bones." He pushed up a sleeve. "Did leave a hell of a bruise, though."

The impact also broke the shooter's neck, killing him instantly.

Nobody in the room regretted that outcome.

But Leo told Gene, "That was a nice piece of driving you did, too."

McGill switched to the Chevy's passenger-side camera. The shooter on that side of the car was hosing down the Chevy with automatic fire until Rebecca Bramley threw a crushing ice hockey-style bodycheck into the man from behind. His knees buckled. He fell forward and his head bounced off a car that had been behind the Chevy and had accelerated to get clear of the free-fire zone.

John Tall Wolf, seeing for the first time the risk his wife had taken, went pale and took her hand. The former Mountie only tightened her jaw and nodded as if to confirm the good form of her hit.

The same side-view camera — as the Chevy turned left onto O Street — caught Ron Ketchum taking down the shooter running down Wisconsin Avenue from the direction of P Street. Ron didn't bother to shout a command for the shooter to drop his weapon.

"Wouldn't have been heard over the gunfire," he explained, as he had earlier to the police and feds, "and I wasn't about to draw automatic weapon fire my way."

He just went down on one knee, drew a bead and fired a single round.

Hit center mass and dropped the shooter in mid-stride.

That left only one of the shooters who'd attacked from behind the Chevy. He dropped his assault weapon and ran. Maj Olson holstered her pistol and took up pursuit. She immediately showed foot-speed her quarry couldn't hope to match. The outcome was certain from the start.

Unless, as Maj had pointed out, the guy had turned and shot her with a handgun.

Even that would have been difficult for him as she and everyone else saw now. By the time he would have turned around, she would have been all over him. As it was, she didn't tackle him or jump on him. She just pushed him forward, forcing him to try to move his feet faster than he possibly could. He did a face-plant in seconds, and then Maj had a knee on his spine.

That left only the little old lady, Paulette Lacroix, and damn if she didn't try to finish the job. So McGill had shot her. One of the Chevy's cameras had caught that, too. Something he could have lived without.

His misgivings remained despite everyone saying he'd only done what he had to do.

And Deke adding, "I was about to splatter her."

"Me, too, Boss," Leo added.

CHAPTER 6

Below the Surface of the South China Sea
Saturday, September 17, 2016

The SSN *Chicago,* a Los Angeles-class attack submarine launched in the mid-1980s, played a special role in the Navy's war strategy in the South China Sea. It pretended to be a patsy, a rube, a mark. That was, it looked to be a fat, easy target. The wackiest sub in the Navy.

It made noise when it was supposed to be silent. It radioed for assistance from other vessels, both surface and submarine, far more often than any well-commanded and optimally functioning vessel ever should. It even gave signs — falsely — that its nuclear reactor might be failing.

A potential adversary, in this case China, was certain to worry about the *Chicago* more in terms of an ecological disaster than in its war-fighting capability. In keeping with its sad-sack profile, sailors aboard the sub regularly visited websites that were guaranteed to infect a visiting computer with malware.

The swabbies on the *Chicago,* it seemed, just couldn't get enough of the naked Swedish, Danish and Dutch girls that came to them, nominally, from European fishing vessels on the far side of the world. In fact, the men on the sub did enjoy the porn, but only through the dedicated and discrete computer system that phished for Chinese hackers and mimicked the actual network that ran the boat.

Any submariner or officer who violated cyber security in *Chicago's* actual atmosphere control, fire control, propulsion, reactor, navigation, communications, intelligence, or weapons systems would no longer have a need for any woman, flesh and blood or photographic. Such an act of treasonous negligence would result in a life sentence from a court martial, if the individual lived that long.

Though the crews of the Navy's submarines didn't get the same publicity as certain other military units, they considered themselves to be an elite force. So did the Pentagon. Nobody was assigned to submarine duty; every man was a volunteer and rigorously trained. Submarine crews got a special pay bonus every time they went to sea.

Unlike its phishing persona, *Chicago* ran like a Swiss watch, with split-second precision and at a cost that might make King Midas go broke. When it wanted to, it moved as quietly as a passing regret.

Captain John Delahanty's voice came through the earbuds of his senior fire control technician in a whisper. "We've been hacked, August James."

Using the FCT's full first and middle names was the sign that this was the computer attack they'd been waiting for. The enemy had hit the ineffective sucker system.

A.J. Latz replied softly, "About time, sir. I was beginning to think the bastards were napping."

"No. They want us to clear our tubes at Three-quarter Mile Island."

Navy slang for the aircraft carrier USS *Ronald Reagan.*

There were 22 Tomahawk missile tubes on *Chicago,* and the Chinese apparently wanted all of them fired at the *Reagan.* Each tube could fire seven missiles.

"Well, shit, sir," the FCT said, "did the assholes ask for a reload, too?"

"Maybe they're waiting to see how the first salvo goes. Pick out other targets after that."

"Or they're testing us to see if this is as half-assed a boat as we make out, sir."

"Yeah, I thought of that, too. Well, we're not going to help any Chinese madmen start World War Three. They get two fish into the *Old Gray Lady* and that's it. Fire when ready, Augie."

The range and bearing for the targeted WWII diesel submarine that had been reclaimed from Indonesia had already been locked into the weapons system computer.

"Both fish away, sir," the FCT said. The fish were Mark-14 torpedoes.

The *Old Gray Lady,* as she'd been christened by Captain Delahanty after her proper name had been lost in the tides of time and the shredding of out-of-date files, was underway with the equivalent of a brick on the gas pedal. No one was aboard, though the *Chicago's* crew had quickly come up with the game of whom they'd put aboard if given a chance.

Chicago deliberately hadn't fired contemporary Mark-48 torpedoes that could be guided from the submarine by wires attached to the weapons or use their own active or passive sensors to execute a programmed target search, acquisition, and attack procedures. The Mark-48 was designed to detonate beneath the keel of its target ship, destroying the vessel's structural integrity. If it missed locating the target on its first approach, it could circle back for another try.

The Mark-14, on the other hand, was a World War II weapon. Its job was to provide a direct impact explosion. It couldn't be guided en route, and it offered no second chances.

The United States Navy had stopped using the Mark-14 decades ago. The Chinese still had a stockpile of them on hand, though recently they'd been selling some off to the Iranians. Quietly, through third parties, the Pentagon had been buying some back from Tehran.

The reason for that was every torpedo left a unique sonar

signature, in much the same way every round fired from a gun leaves one-of-a-kind markings. Sonar signatures were recorded not only by surface and submarine naval vessels but also by low-flying aircraft and even satellites.

When the two Mark-14 torpedoes impacted the *Old Gray Lady* and sent its fragmented remains to the seabed, their identities were recorded by both American and Chinese intelligence as weapons officially held by China but not the United States.

As Byron DeWitt might have said, "Very Sun Tzu."

Less than an hour later news flashes circled the globe.

The United States Navy feared it might have lost a submarine.

The possibility of Chinese involvement in the tragedy would be investigated.

Several news sources noted that to protect themselves all American warships in the area were put on imminent danger status. Any attempted hostility by the Chinese navy or air force would be met with an overwhelming response. That order came from the President of the United States.

McGill Investigations International, LLP

After an overnight break, McGill reconvened his people and asked, "Before, during or after all the gunfire, did anyone notice the tall person in black?"

With no video playing at the moment, everyone had moved his or her chair back around the table. Heads shook and people said, "No, not me, unh-uh."

John Tall Wolf looked like he had an idea to offer, but Ron Ketchum beat him to the punch, "My guess? He was in a window or on a roof looking down at everything."

"That's what I was thinking, too," John said, "and following up on that, this guy or woman probably isn't someone at death's door or he likely would have shot at someone from his high perch."

Keely Powell nodded. "That makes sense."

Deke disagreed, partially. "If the guy in black was watching and had a rifle of some sort, he might have risked a shot, but only if he saw his main target." Deke hooked a thumb at McGill. "Management doesn't risk its ass to pick off small fry."

Pruet nodded. "If your task is to kill the king, you don't settle for courtiers."

"I'm the king?" McGill asked, rolling his eyes.

Leo said, "You are the boss, Boss."

"And you'd left the protection of your car," Deke added, his criticism implicit.

Gene Beck said, "I think if somebody took a rooftop shot at either Mr. McGill or one of us the return fire would have been something fierce, most likely deadly. So, yeah, maybe the shooter would take the risk only for the big prize."

McGill could live with the characterization that he was the focal point.

He said, "The irony here, if this last assumption is right, Ms. Lacroix might have saved my life by coming after me, keeping me from reaching Wisconsin Avenue."

McGill had let Deke and Leo hustle him indoors after he'd shot the woman.

"Or," Tall Wolf said, "the person in black never had any intention of shooting anyone personally. Observing and analyzing might have been the only task at hand. Maybe Ms. Lacroix kept any spotter from seeing that you could, in fact, be drawn out of your car. That had to be their plan all along. Have Leo clip the woman with the car expecting that you'd get out to see how badly hurt she was."

Everyone stared at McGill, Deke and Leo more closely than the others.

"Okay, I admit it," McGill said, "that would have been my first impulse."

Deke said, "Impulse? Short of me shooting you *inside* the car, what could have stopped you from jumping out?"

In a quiet voice, McGill admitted, "Nothing."

He bided a moment staring at the table in front of him.

He raised his head and met every pair of eyes around the table.

"Are all of you sure you want to go to work for me? Maybe I should spend a year or two alone in the wilderness. Trying to get over myself."

"Probably not necessary. You sound suitably humbled to me."

Everyone turned and saw Sweetie had slipped into the room unnoticed.

No mean feat in present company.

"So what'd I miss?" she asked.

La Cruz, Costa Rica

Father Inigo de Loyola thought he couldn't find a nicer place to die than the hacienda in La Cruz Canton in the northwestern corner of Costa Rica. The landscape was an embarrassment of God's grace: the magnificent Pacific with mile after mile of beaches, verdant forested hills teeming with creatures who may have been there since the creation of Eden. Blue sky and a warming sun were the usual orders of the day.

Okay, de Loyola thought, when the ocean breeze died the sun could get downright hot. There were also periods of tropical downpours, and even hurricanes. Occasionally, and you never knew when, an earthquake could hit, sometimes hard. So no place in this world was truly Eden.

That was why you were instructed to lead a good life. So that at the end of your days coping with earthly imperfections you would share the Savior's company in a place beyond even the slightest criticism.

De Loyola never claimed to know the details of what heaven would look like, but he felt sure it must bear some resemblance to this part of Costa Rica. After serving the poor in New York and Washington, DC for many years, it certainly felt like heaven to him. He only hoped that his labors of mercy among the *norteamericanos* had cleansed his soul of some of the sins he'd committed in nearby Central America during his fiery youth.

Well, as a *relatively* young man, anyway. One who'd already taken his vows for the priesthood. Those holy promises included chastity, poverty and obedience to the Pope. These precepts had been laid down by the founder of the Society of Jesus and his own namesake: Saint Inigo de Loyola.

In some circles, though, the Jesuits were also known as God's Marines. Moreover, they were famed as free thinkers — which sometimes clashed with their vow to obey the Pope. Their vow of poverty, though, reinforced their objection to opulent riches, especially when it was concentrated in the hands of a few grandees.

Reviewing the span of his life, now approaching 70 years, and the state of his soul, Father de Loyola thought he'd made good on two of his three vows. He'd never lain with a woman. On the few occasions he had come by more money than required for his immediate needs he'd always distributed the surplus to those who'd had even less than him, even at times when that meant he'd go hungry. It was in the matter of obeying His Holiness where he fell down. More than a few times, he'd simply felt he had to make his own choices.

As to the Commandments laid down by God himself, de Loyola felt he'd kept closely to nine of them. It was number five that tripped him up: Thou shall not kill. He'd violated that stricture more than once. Many times more than once.

A former shortstop on his secondary school baseball team before entering the seminary, de Loyola sometimes tried to kid himself by thinking of his life in terms of the game he'd once played. He was two for three with his vows; a batter who got two hits out of every three times at bat would be in the Hall of Fame. He was nine out of ten with the Commandments; a fielder who made nine out of ten plays without an error was more than respectable.

The comfort provided by his sport rationales was always fleeting.

He felt sure God kept score in his own fashion, not in Abner Doubleday's.

As it was well beyond his power to resurrect any of the men

whose lives he'd taken, de Loyola was sure that he'd have to answer for their deaths. Worse, he'd be forced to say that even now he didn't regret killing them. Well, maybe one or two. If that didn't damn him to hell, he didn't know what would.

That's why he never prayed solely for the Lord's forgiveness, though he surely hoped for it. He always said, "Please give me the strength to bear any fate you so rightfully give to me." Meaning he didn't fear physical pain but mental torment scared him badly.

Until judgment came, de Loyola would work on a new mission, caring for the worn out bodies and tattered souls of the men with whom he'd fought so many years ago. He owed it to them to provide whatever meager comfort he could. This wasn't a task he'd sought; a former junior officer in his guerrilla unit had managed to find him in Washington, DC.

This was a small miracle in itself, but suspecting the Lord might be working subtly here, either to save a group of his lesser creations or to ship them off to perdition wholesale, he felt he could not refuse the request. He would have to find a way to stay in Costa Rica permanently, but he'd get around to that later.

His foremost concern now was that upon arrival in the country the former junior officer had confided, "I have learned a terrible secret. I did not know who else to tell but you."

Only the man hadn't told de Loyola, not yet.

He said first he had to wait for another old comrade of theirs to arrive.

That was the situation when Dr. Josefina Delgado approached him with a satellite phone. Josie, as she called herself when speaking English, had been brought to the U.S. from Guatemala at the age of eighteen months. Neither mother nor child had carried a passport. Josie's rough start in life hadn't kept her from graduating in the top tenth of her classes at both Brown University and The School of Medicine at Johns Hopkins University.

Jean Morrissey had promised to let "The Dreamers" and their parents stay in the country; Oren Worth said a case-by-case review would be done for the young people but their parents would have to leave the country if he were elected president.

Deciding she didn't need the uncertainty and would never be separated from her mother, Josie decided she would take her talents south. She and her mother applied for citizenship in Costa Rica. That country was happy to have them.

While waiting for the paperwork to go through, she had met Father de Loyola working at a free clinic in Washington, DC. Now, she handed him the phone and said, "*Una gringa.*"

An American woman.

Josie had lost all her Spanish until she began studying it as an undergrad.

Father de Loyola couldn't imagine what American woman would be calling him.

By way of a greeting, all he said was, "Yes?"

"Father de Loyola?" she said. "This is Margaret Sweeney. I'm in San Jose and I have a message for you from the Pope."

Inverness, Scotland

Giles Henry took his publishing contract with Grantham House and ran off with it to Scotland. Actually, he didn't run at all, he flew the 406 miles, flight time 83 minutes. For someone born in London, though, as Henry had been, the Highlands of Scotland were the ends of the earth.

By way of comparison, the whole of the Inverness metropolitan area possessed under 60,000 residents. On a single day, December 4, 2015, the London Underground, aka the Tube, had served 4.821 million passengers.

Sixty thousand people were scarcely more than a busy night at the pub in London. Even so, Inverness was ranked as the happiest city in Scotland and the second happiest in the whole U.K. That might have had something to do with the plentiful number of fine drinking establishments in town. Henry, with his advance money in hand, decided he had to celebrate in proper fashion, meaning his fleeting period of work-focused abstinence was over.

Still, he didn't mean to drink as much as was his custom. Galia Mindel had, in fact, put a bit of a fright into him when they'd talked. The Yanks with their multiple spy agencies and their eyes in the sky truly did have global reach, and if they had their lap dogs at MI6 sniffing about for him as well … it sent a chill down his spine. He might be in actual danger.

In a perverse way, though, that sense of menace would lend a compelling element of danger to the narrative of his book: the intrepid writer laboring swiftly against a ticking clock, never knowing when foreign thugs or native traitors might break down his door and spray him with a lethal storm of gunfire. That or drag him off to some secret dungeon.

In the event such dangers became imminent, Henry had made precautionary plans to retreat into the wilderness. The Highlands were one of the least densely populated places on earth with only nine people per square kilometer. That was on average. There were many huge spaces with nary a soul.

Henry had rented a refurbished cottage in one such vacant corner. He'd had it stocked with food, water and alcohol. If the hounds started to close in on him in Inverness, he had a bolt hole where no one would be able to find him. He hoped.

He already had Senator Randall Pennyman's entire story of being blackmailed by Galia Mindel secured on a cloud server. Better yet, Pennyman had provided Henry with a list of other likely blackmail targets the President's chief of staff had under her thumb.

Pennyman, himself, didn't have proof positive of these people's circumstances. What he had, though, was one thief's instinct for recognizing another of his breed. Moreover, Pennyman had provided expert guesses about what kind of crooked games they played. That would be more than enough for Henry to be able to investigate them first in cyberspace and later wedge the truth out of them in person.

In the meantime, he was sampling the highly recommended fare at an Inverness establishment called The Castle Tavern. He'd slipped in during a narrow gap between crowds. Seated at a corner table with his back to a wall, he was having a pint of Hobgoblin draft beer and waiting for his broiled salmon when his mobile phone rang.

He had a burner app on the instrument. It allowed him to use different phone numbers and even area codes as contact points for different callers. This call came from his London publisher, Grantham House. Henry wondered if they'd gone ahead and started the publicity campaign for his book.

He and his editor Susannah Webb-Rogers had discussed the idea of leaking some of the more scandalous bits of the book once he reached the three-quarters mark of the manuscript to build public attention and demand. Get people to knock down their local bookshop doors on the release date.

Henry thought that was a smashing concept, but then it was his idea.

Webb-Rogers had wanted to run with it once he was *half* done.

That would have put too much pressure on him, Henry thought, and give the bloodhounds from Washington and London too much time to sniff out his trail. He insisted on keeping the mark at three-quarters. Webb-Rogers said they could talk about it some more once she'd discussed the matter with senior management.

If the woman was calling now to —

"The deal's off," Susannah Webb-Rogers told him without bothering to say hello.

"What? What deal?" Henry asked. "You mean the start point for the teaser campaign? Oh, no, I'm going to —"

"I mean your publishing deal with Grantham House, Giles. You promised us a manuscript with exclusive scandals of historic proportions. You have failed to deliver already."

Henry almost said, "What?" again but chose to object instead of question.

"That's impossible. No one could have beaten me to this story."

"Galia Mindel did. She's resigned from her White House post and just signed a publishing deal with an American firm for a *tell-all* memoir of her time in American politics with an emphasis on her White House years."

"Bollocks," Henry said, "it'll be a White House whitewash."

"To some extent certainly, but there's bound to be enough spice, confession and regret to take the shine off your book, won't there?"

"My book? You mean our book."

"Your book, Giles. We paid for an exclusive story. Once that exclusivity was gone our deal terminated. We'll expect ninety percent of the advance we paid you to be returned within 30 days. We're allowing a ten-percent write-off, assuming you've already spent that much on a premature celebration of your former good fortune."

"You'll be hearing from my solicitor," Henry said.

"You really don't want to take this to court, Giles."

"Why not?"

"For one thing, Monty Kipp found Senator Randall Pennyman in Malta. The senator was making plans to flee, but Monty not only put an end to that by having the police follow him by an hour, but he also got Pennyman to give him, guess what, an 'exclusive' interview for Satellite News America."

"The bastard," Henry growled. "Always hated that git."

"Apparently with good reason," Webb-Rogers agreed. "He's made you look a fool. Me, too. I might survive in my job. I doubt you will do as well in yours. Send us our money, Giles. Things will only be worse for you if you don't."

"Sod off," Giles Henry said and broke the connection.

His salmon arrived. The waitress even brought an unsolicited beer on the house. She told him he looked like he could use some cheering up.

Henry had the instinct but not the energy to curse her.

He focused his bile on that evil bitch, Galia Mindel. He'd never figured her for doing a sobbing confessional, and he was sure she wouldn't. What she'd do was parse and snip her vile story to make herself and Patricia Grant look heroic. She might step outside the bounds of propriety but not decency, and she certainly wouldn't incriminate herself.

Not once in his lengthy career of sliming his betters had Giles Henry ever thought he was punching above his weight class. He never thought he'd taken on an opponent who was just too smart, tough and vicious for him. Now, he did. He'd been schooled, as the Yanks might put it.

As if to confirm the point, he received a text.

It arrived via the phone number his former publisher had just used to ring him.

But it came from someone else entirely.

All it said was: *Global reach.*

United States Capitol — Washington, DC

Senator Oren Worth continued to follow the script written for him by his new campaign manager, Layla Dart, and made a public statement to the nation and the world on the possible sinking of a United States Navy submarine by the Chinese in the South China Sea. Standing on the West Front of the United States Capitol — where presidential inaugurations were traditionally staged — the senator bit his lower lip for a moment and blinked righteous anger from his eyes as media cameras and citizen cellphones captured the moment.

Then he said, "The allies of the United States, and also our foes, should know that when something like the destruction of a Navy submarine occurs, the American people stand as one. There is never an inch of separation, even between traditionally contending political parties. Our military protects all of us, and all of us support our military.

"Any individual or nation that thinks otherwise is making a terrible mistake, potentially a fatal mistake. I pledge to President Patricia Grant and her administration that the Congress of the United States will stand with her in any action she chooses to take to defend our country and the men and women of our valiant armed forces.

"Moreover, Congress will also support economic measures that are sought to punish aggressors, in the event that military reprisals are not held to be appropriate. Let no adversary make the mistake of ever thinking they can take advantage of a politically divided America. When it comes to defending our nation and its people, we stand together, shoulder to shoulder, every man, woman and child …

"Now and always."

Having expressed himself, Worth took questions from the reporters on hand. Yes, he'd spoken to the Speaker of the House before making his statement. Yes, he'd made sure he had the support of every member of the GOP and True South before he spoke. Yes, he was sure every one of those traditional opponents of a Democratic president would hold fast to his or her promise of unity.

"So when do you think things will get all political again, Senator?" one reporter asked.

Worth smiled thinly. "Just as soon as the world gives us some breathing room."

Moments later, Worth found his campaign manager Layla Dart waiting for him in his Capitol office. She looked up as he entered, seemed to be measuring him in some fashion.

"Too cute?" he asked of his quip.

She smiled and shook her head. "No, that was good. I liked it. Sounded authentic because it was. You're coming right along, Senator."

Worth said, "I'm a quick study."

The White House — Washington, DC

Jean and Frank Morrissey had watched Oren Worth's statement on national unity in the Vice President's West Wing office. Frank clicked off the television and looked at his sister.

"What do you think?" he asked.

Jean said, "Maybe it's just me, but I swear he's starting to put on an English accent. Where the hell is that coming from, and what does he expect to gain from it?"

"He's doing Cary Grant."

"What?"

"You don't remember Cary Grant?"

"I remember the name, and I think I saw a movie where he played a jewel thief, but he must've died when I was a kid."

"Fourteen," Frank told her.

He knew things like that.

"So Worth is channeling an old-time movie star because?" Jean asked.

"Because Cary Grant was Mr. Charm."

"But Worth doesn't look anywhere near as good, as I remember things."

"True, but he's not *bad* looking, and his approval numbers among women are up eight points in the last week, ever since he good-naturedly admitted he couldn't beat you at arm-wrestling."

"You're kidding."

Frank shook his head.

"Are his numbers with men falling?" Jean asked.

"No, they're up two points. Some guys think his honesty is refreshing; others are volunteering to become his workout buddies."

"And you didn't tell me any of this?"

Frank said, "It took me a few days to figure out just who Worth was modeling. I was only 12 when Cary died. Then I needed to do some research on how to counter this move."

"And?" Jean asked.

"I found out that Grant said his favorite leading lady was Grace Kelly. Now, Sis, you've got the blonde hair and fair skin like Kelly, but you've got too much muscle to play her, but we don't want lovey-dovey here anyway. We want male-female confrontation: the kind that will get both women and men rooting and voting for you. So we need you to play Katharine Hepburn, probably for just a moment or two."

Wondering if her brother had lost his mind, Jean reminded him, "I've never done a minute of acting in my life."

Frank rolled his eyes. "Really? Every single baby that's been held up for you to admire has been truly adorable? Every diner sandwich you've choked down has been delicious? Or do you forget all that the moment a political campaign is over?"

Jean nodded. "Pretty much, yeah. It's like shaking the other team's hands after a hockey game. It's just something you do for the sake of good form."

"So you have acted, and successfully, as you've never lost an election."

The Vice President took a deep breath and slowly let it out.

"Okay, you've got me," she said. "But Katharine Hepburn?"

"Yeah, only without the East Coast accent. Here, I've got a brief video clip for you to see." Frank turned on the TV and played a canned short scene from *The Philadelphia Story.*

Cary Grant exits a posh house, suitcase in hand, in a state of high dudgeon. Hepburn follows a moment later with a bag of golf clubs he's forgotten. She hands him the bag, minus one club, presumably his favorite. She breaks it over her leg and storms back toward the house. He catches her at the doorway, looks like he's going to punch her in the nose. Then he changes his mind, plants his hand over her face and shoves her to the floor.

Jean Morrissey looked at her brother as if he was truly crazy.

"You think I could get Oren Worth to physically — publicly — assault me and I'd just take it? That kind of crap might've flown 70 years ago or whenever it was, but nobody, especially not a politician, would do that now. And no woman, especially not me, would take it."

"Exactly," Frank said. "First of all, you'd clock Worth if he even tried. But let's say he caught you looking the other way. A televised physical assault, especially at a presidential debate, would put him out of the race."

"Frank, what the hell are you thinking?" Jean asked.

"You have to really get under his skin at a public forum.

Metaphorically, break his golf club. Then at the end of the evening you extend your hand to him with a look in your eyes that only pisses him off all the more. When he takes your hand, what's he going to do?"

Jean understood the strategy now and smiled. "He'll try to squeeze the hell out of it."

"Indeed he will, and what will you do?"

"Knee him in the balls?"

Frank grinned. "That would be one response. What I'm hoping for, though, is that you'll squeeze his hand even harder. Drop him to his knees in front of God and the American public. Posterize him, as they like to say in pro sports."

"We'll have to work out a sure way to make Worth snap," she told her brother, "but I like the idea. Can I ask one question?"

"Sure."

"I'm thinking I'll have to let Worth up eventually. Can I knee him in the balls then?"

Frank said, "Read the crowd. If everyone's pointing thumbs down …"

McGill Investigations International, LLP

Before the partners' meeting at McGill Investigations, LLP broke up, Yves Pruet took a collect phone call from FCI Petersburg where his best friend and fellow Francophone, Odo Sacripant, was working undercover as a faux arms smuggler.

"News," was all Odo mumbled in heavily Corsican-inflected French.

"But not suitable for a phone call," Pruet replied, swallowing several syllables in the manner of quick-speaking Parisians. Few non-native speakers would have understood him.

"No."

"I am on my way … Will you need fresh clothes?"

Meaning, was Odo opting to exit the prison.

"Oui." Yes.

Pruet ended the call and reported its contents to McGill in a quiet one-on-one.

McGill asked, "Did you get the impression Odo's in any danger?"

Pruet didn't have to think long. "No, not that I've ever heard or seen him express fear. But something has happened to change his mind about staying in your prison. He sees some advantage in leaving it."

McGill took Pruet's word on Odo's fearlessness; he certainly hadn't seen any lack of courage in the time he'd spent with the Corsican.

"Maybe Auric Ludwig has confided something important to Odo," McGill said.

Pruet offered a devilish smile. "Perhaps *M'sieur* Ludwig has even made an offer of employment to Odo."

McGill grinned; he liked that idea. He could imagine the look on Ludwig's face as Odo testified against him in court. "I'll keep my fingers crossed on that one, and I'll ask Dikki Missirian to drive you down to Virginia."

"That would be most kind of you."

"Happy to help. I'll be eager to hear what Odo has to say, but I might be tied up. I haven't heard from the President about this morning's adventures yet, but I expect to any minute now."

Pruet said, "Criticism from a beautiful woman? *Mon ami,* even in your misfortunes, you are the most fortunate man I know."

"I feel the same way," McGill said. "I just hope my good luck holds out."

FCI Petersburg — Prince George County, Virginia

Before calling Pruet, Odo Sacripant had walked down the tier to Auric Ludwig's cell during a period of controlled movement. Earlier that morning, he'd seen a close inmate confederate of Ludwig's heading to the man's cell at the most rapid walking pace he could manage. Even during controlled movement, inmates were not allowed to run. Running implied an attempt to escape, and among a convict population the desire to flee could spread like a flash-flood.

The convict Odo had seen hurry past his cell was gone by the time Odo arrived at Ludwig's cage. The man was there alone, staring at the floor. Odo turned to leave.

Ludwig sensed Odo's presence and stopped him. "Wait. What do you want?"

Odo stopped and looked back. Ludwig seemed to be in a state of near despair. On a hunch, Odo decided the right card to play was to add to Ludwig's misery.

He improvised, "I came only to say *au revoir.* My lawyer is coming for me. He has worked a not so small miracle. He has secured my release pending a trial for me at home in Corsica." Odo smiled. "I feel my chances there will be very good. *Bonne chance,* my friend. Thank you for the milkshakes."

Ludwig thought about Odo's news. Contrary to the Corsican's expectations, Ludwig seemed energized, as if the prospect of Odo's release had lifted his spirits in some way. He gestured to Odo to sit on his bunk, right next to him. That would have been a good place for a man to get shanked, if Ludwig had been up to that sort of thing, and if Odo had been a sucker.

The Corsican wasn't, so he took a seat.

And Ludwig played the trusting party.

In a quiet voice, he told Odo, "I had some bad news this morning."

"Regarding your sentence?"

Ludwig shook his head. He looked closely at Odo. Saw a hard face and cold, dark, unblinking eyes. With a nod, he seemed to approve of what he beheld.

Ludwig said, "You look like a dangerous man. Is that a fair guess?"

Odo didn't react for a moment, and then he smiled broadly. His entire face changed, except for his eyes. They continued to regard the world without a hint of mercy.

Even so, Odo said, "I am a charming fellow. I go to church,

leave money in the poor box and never drink more wine than my wits can accommodate."

All of which was true, and rang out that way.

Ludwig played along. "You can probably sing and dance well, too."

"Reasonably so."

"Still, I bet there are other times. Times when people look at you and decide it's time to run for their lives."

Odo didn't deny it, only shrugged.

Ludwig was about to say something else when Odo held up a hand.

He said, "In my country, and probably yours, certain men are taught to be discreet from an early age. I think we're both such men. If you are about to say something of great importance, first ask yourself if you can really trust me. If you decide you can't, I will take no offense. I will respect your sense of caution."

The two men sat silently for a long moment, trying to see what game, if any, the other might be playing, trying to gauge how far anyone could be trusted. Especially in a place where society said the people were so treacherous they had to be locked up.

The period of controlled movement was about to end, so Odo stood up and clapped Ludwig on the shoulder. "Prudence is usually the course of least regret."

He turned to go but Ludwig caught his wrist.

And the lightning change in Odo's expression showed just how dangerous he could be.

Ludwig quickly let go and said, "I'm sorry. Stay, please. I'd like to make you an offer."

"I must get ready to depart," Odo said.

"Don't worry about going back to your cell. When a lawyer comes, they let you go wherever you need to be."

Odo thought about that and said, "*Bon.*"

He sat back down next to Ludwig.

Dropping his voice to a whisper, Ludwig said, "There's a man I want dead. I was just told that he didn't die this morning, the way

I hoped he would."

Keeping his voice down, Odo said, "I have also had this experience. Some people are quite irritating that way. They refuse to bow out when they should."

Ludwig found Odo's shared complaint intriguing. "What did you do?"

"I persisted."

"That's what I'm thinking, too. Keep going. I even thought of asking if you might be interested in … you know. But finding a way to get this particular guy won't be easy."

Odo smiled again, and this time Ludwig saw warmth in his eyes.

"M'sieur, it would amaze you the people I can reach."

Thing One, Presidential Limo — Washington, DC

The President didn't just call McGill about the shootout, she arrived in Thing One to speak with McGill. When he entered the presidential limo and sat next to his wife, she handed him a flute of champagne. She held another glass of bubbly for herself and tapped it against McGill's.

Not sure he wanted to hear the answer, McGill asked, "What are we toasting?"

"Your victory in the shootout on O Street, of course."

McGill closed his eyes to listen for the soundtrack to *High Noon* to start playing. He wasn't sure how far Patti would go with her staging. As President, she had the resources to make it quite a production. But no theatrics ensued and McGill opened his eyes.

He said, "My hope is Ms. Lacroix has survived and I might question her."

"She hasn't; you can't, but the Metro Police did. All she had to say, I'm told, was, 'Get fucked.'"

Patti gestured with her glass and that was a sufficient signal to set the parade in motion. City cops had Wisconsin Avenue blocked off so her motorcade didn't have to wait for cross-traffic.

With motorcycle and Secret Service SUV escorts fore and aft, the show hit the road.

"May I ask where we're going?" McGill said.

"Dulles. I thought as long as I was out fetching you, I might as well pick up Dorie McBride from the airport."

McGill brightened. "She has news on transgender entertainer-assassins?"

"What she said is she has some people who could be possibilities."

"None of them her clients, I suppose."

Patti shook her head. "I'd have to sign a lifetime contract with her to get something like that. As things stand, I'm sure I'll have to listen to a pitch for some project or other."

McGill pointed out, "Ronald Reagan did *Death Valley Days*."

"That was before he was President or even Governor of California."

Realizing he wasn't going to jolly his wife out of her disapproving mood, McGill said, "The wine's getting warm if you'd care to propose a formal toast."

She looked him in the eye and said, "Here's to my ..." She choked up just a bit. "My *beloved* husband who has lived to fight another day." The fact of his survival didn't stop tears from gliding down her cheeks.

They tapped glasses and drank, sitting back and looking ahead not at each other.

"Deke ratted me out?" McGill asked.

"I'll never tell, but I know what happened."

McGill understood. God was omniscient; the President was a close second.

Often the weight of all that knowledge became a terrible burden to bear.

Patti said, "You didn't have to be out there, Jim. You have a wife, three children, an ex-wife, a mother and a father who'd all mourn your premature passing."

"Sweetie, too."

"Sweetie, too. Possibly one or two others."

They both emptied their glasses. Patti refilled them. She turned and looked at McGill.

"Aren't you going to tell me your people were out there? You had to be with them."

"Why belabor the obvious?" McGill asked. "You know all the stuff like that."

Patti said, "I want you to know I'm not getting to be like Carolyn used to be, afraid for you every time you step out the door."

"Only it seems there *are* more people gunning for me now than there were then," McGill said. "I can understand your being a bit nervous occasionally. I feel the same way about you."

"Do you think I've taken any undue risks with my safety?"

McGill shook his head.

"Would you do it again?" Patti asked. "Jump out of the car on a sucker play?"

"I try to learn from my mistakes. I can't say the impulse wouldn't be there, but … damn, it would be hard just to sit tight."

"So you would do it again."

"No," McGill said. "At least not in the same way. I'd set the bar higher. For personal involvement, I mean. In the future, I'll risk sacrificing my ego before my backside."

Patti leaned in and kissed him. "I'm fond of both, but I can get my hands around only one of them."

McGill laughed. "Good to know what really matters."

"I'm sure you feel the same."

"I do … At the risk of breaking an improving mood, Ms. Lacroix really didn't do anything but curse the cops?"

"Not that I was told," Patti said. "You can pursue the matter personally, if you like. But from what I did hear an idea occurred to me."

"What's that?" McGill asked.

Patti usually didn't play detective, but she had a razor-sharp mind and eight years of studying human nature while doing the world's toughest job. McGill welcomed her help.

"My information," she said, "is you are looking for someone who's possibly a transgender individual."

"Right," McGill said.

He explained how that might double the number of possible suspects to be investigated.

"The number might be even bigger," Patti said.

McGill frowned. "What do you mean?"

"Well, tell me if I'm wrong, but right now you might be looking for someone who exhibits a male, female or indeterminate presentation."

Another revelation from Deke, McGill thought.

"That's right," he said.

"But do you suspect that the male and female possibilities will veer toward the middle of the gender spectrum in appearance?"

McGill hadn't thought of things in those terms, but he started nodding before answering verbally. "Yeah, I guess I do."

"Well, what if that's what the killer wants you to think, and he or she has an actual likeness that's far more traditionally defined: say a guy on a bowling team or a woman who sells cosmetics from a pink Cadillac?"

"Wow. Could anyone be *that* devious?" McGill asked.

"You tell me. You're the detective. I'm just a former actress who read a lot of screenplays back in the day."

"Did any of the scripts have an idea like the one you just shared?"

"Good question. Nothing specific comes to mind, but the idea might have originated from one of *my* previous incarnations. I'll ask Dorie about specific scripts when we pick her up. But now, if you don't mind, I have to make a business call before we get to the airport: Ricardo Alves."

McGill, who skimmed the *Washington Post* daily, knew the name.

Alves was the new secretary-general of the United Nations.

San Jose, Costa Rica

Margaret Sweeney and Welborn Yates met Father Inigo de Loyola on the terrace of the Double Tree Hotel in San José. As far as delivering the message from the Pope — *Call me* — went, they could have turned around and caught the next flight to Miami. But Sweetie had another matter to discuss with the good padre, and he had a question for her as well. They had agreed to meet at the hotel.

At Putnam's urging, Sweetie had dressed up for her trip to Costa Rica. That day, she wore one of her higher-end resort ensembles, a sapphire silk blouse, French vanilla linen slacks and Italian flats that were comfortable for walking and supportive enough for running. Welborn looked like her preppie kid brother, wearing a Panama hat for a bit of dash.

Putnam's stated reason to have Sweetie ditch her usual plain-Jane workaday look was you didn't deliver a message from one of the world's great religious leaders looking like you shopped at a thrift store. Modesty had its place, sure, but so did a bit of glamour for a big occasion. As spiffed up as she was, Sweetie was surprised to be outdone by Father de Loyola's appearance.

He certainly didn't look like a street person anymore.

He wore a black silk suit — and an immaculate white Roman collar — that had custom tailoring written into every stitch. His hair had been styled and his beard had been trimmed by someone who was both meticulous in his craft and had a sense of flair. De Loyola's skin glowed with vitality and his eyes were as clear as tropical water. Beyond all that was the way he carried himself — as if he was a force of nature. Yes, this was clearly a man of the cloth, but a second look told you he was also one of God's Marines.

Perhaps a commanding officer.

De Loyola had a young woman walking with him as he approached the table where Sweetie and Welborn sat. She held his arm and murmured into his ear as tears ran down her cheeks. The two of them stopped 20 feet short of Sweetie and Welborn. Father de Loyola whispered something to the woman.

Sweetie saw his lips move and had no trouble interpreting the Latin: *Ego te absolvo …*

I forgive you.

The priest had just heard a confession, most likely acting on an impromptu request from the young woman. He lightly sketched the Sign of the Cross on her forehead with a thumb. She took his hand in hers and kissed it. Then she turned and walked away.

Sweetie and Welborn stood as de Loyola joined them.

He put his hands on Sweetie's shoulders and kissed her on both cheeks.

Something that had never happened back home. Sweetie rolled with it and introduced Welborn, including his military rank and branch of service.

Shaking Welborn's hand, the priest said, "*Mucho gusto, General.*"

"The pleasure is mine, Father."

A waitress came to take their drink orders, telling them their refreshments would be compliments of the hotel. Welborn was the first to respond, offering a credit card. "Thank you for your kindness. Please buy a round of drinks for the staff on me."

Sweetie put a hundred dollar bill on the table. "And please make a donation to a charity you and all your friends think worthy."

The waitress beamed and took orders for a sparkling water, a ginger ale and a Mexican Coca-Cola.

"They use real sugar in the soft drinks down here," de Loyola told his American friends. "I'm afraid sweet drinks are my … well, I can't say my only vice but one among the many others. You were very generous with the young serving woman."

The n*orteamericanos* nodded politely.

Sweetie said. "I have to say, Father, you clean up very well."

He shrugged and held out his manicured hands. "Before coming here, I paid a visit to the archbishop, the spiritual guide of every Catholic in this country. I felt it would be only polite to … put on the best face I could. Also, I've had difficult times with the hierarchy in the past. I thought I should show, or at least pretend, that I'm more civilized than my reputation paints me to be."

Welborn said, "Top notch job, Father. Somebody pointed you to a high-end tailor and a hair stylist who knows his clippers."

"My sister," de Loyola said, "she told me I might be trim enough to fit into an old suit I'd worn only once before, and our family barber is still a wizard at 92."

The drinks arrived. Everyone took a sip and pronounced them excellent. The waitress beamed, returned Welborn's credit card to him and left.

Sweetie leaned forward and asked, "Your family has its own barber? Is this an uncle or someone like that? Maybe a guy who had his own shop at one time."

"No," de Loyola said. "Jacobo has always worked only for my family. At the moment, he has just four regulars so he was able to fit me in without difficulty."

Sweetie sat back, waiting for an explanation. Welborn followed her lead.

Addressing Sweetie, de Loyola said, "I know you will consider this surprising, but I come from money. Even by American standards, it is no small fortune. I was the black sheep of *mi familia*."

"You're rich?" Sweetie asked.

"I was at one time — and terribly self-indulgent — until I found Our Lord and took my vow of poverty. I must admit that putting this suit on again causes a great deal of conflict within me. It feels both so natural and so alien all at the same time."

"Temptation and the urge to fight it?" Welborn asked.

De Loyola smiled at him. "Exactly, *mi general*." He looked closely at Welborn, who obliged him and pushed the brim of his hat up, affording a better look. The priest said, "You have investigated me. You know something of my history, don't you?"

Welborn nodded.

Sweetie said, "We thought it would help us find you."

De Loyola glanced at her and then turned back to Welborn. "Is your government, your military, still watching me? I wouldn't have thought I deserve the honor."

"You've made quite an impression, Father," Welborn said.

He nodded, agreeing that he'd once been someone to reckon with.

De Loyola turned to Sweetie. "Would you like to know who I was?"

"Only if you want to tell me."

"I can step away," Welborn said.

"No, no. Stay." He looked at the two Americans and nodded to himself. He'd just heard a confession and decided now to make one. "I will give you … what is the word? Oh, yes. A condensed version of my life and times.

"My family arrived in this country in the early 16th century, not long after Cristobal Colón first arrived. My ancestors helped in the slaughter of *los indios.* For their murderous ways, they were rewarded with land on the Pacific Coast of what was then known as the Captaincy of Guatemala, a province of New Spain. A few centuries later, my family helped to fight off some *yanquis* who tried to do to us what we did to *los indios.*"

Welborn sat back and looked at de Loyola.

The priest asked, "You know the story?"

He said, "I read quite a bit of military history at the Air Force Academy. Are you talking about William Walker?"

"Sí," de Loyola said.

"Who was he?" Sweetie asked.

The priest gestured to Welborn to answer.

He said, "Walker was a nineteenth century American out of Tennessee. He was supposed to have been an academic prodigy, graduated from medical school at 19. Back then, in the 1850s and earlier, Central America was an important transit point for relatively quick travel from the eastern United States to our present West Coast. Anyway, Walker got it into his head to take over a big chunk of land down here in Central America, make it an English-speaking country and ally it with the slave-holding states of the American South. With the help of some mercenaries, he even managed to overthrow the government of Nicaragua and hold power for a year."

"And then?" Sweetie asked.

De Loyola picked up the narrative. "Combined armies from Nicaragua, El Salvador and Honduras, along with some volunteers from Costa Rica, defeated Walker and his followers, who included French and German soldiers as well as Americans. My family's land holdings increased for being on the winning side once again."

Welborn added, "And Walker made the mistake of attempting a comeback. He was taken into custody by the English, who had their own plans for Central America, and turned over to the Hondurans. They put him in front of a firing squad and that was that."

"From your point of view," de Loyola said. "I am a direct descendant of a member of that execution team, and family lore has it that my many times great-grandfather was the man who took the first shot — before the order to shoot was given — and had the honor of killing Walker. The others were simply shooting into a corpse."

Sweetie asked de Loyola, "Do you believe that story?"

The priest shrugged. "It depends upon my mood. In any case, war has been a regular visitor to these lands and my family. When it came most recently, I'd already been ordained. As a young man who had known nothing but privilege and plenty, I came to feel an obligation to work among the poor to try to better their circumstances. I was a great admirer of His Eminence, Cardinal Óscar Romero. He was fearless in condemning the social injustices, assassinations and torture being carried out by the government of El Salvador. When he was assassinated while saying Mass …"

A look of pain filled de Loyola's eyes. Then he shrugged.

"I did whatever I felt was necessary to carry on Cardinal Romero's work. Things of which the local governments, the Americans and many in the Church did not approve. There was even a price put on my head for several years. That stigma was eventually removed, with help from my family, I think, but there are still many who are not happy to have me back here."

Sweetie said, "But you've come home, and you're going to stay, aren't you?"

"That is my plan at the moment," de Loyola said, "but I've learned that little in life is certain except for growing older and wishing you'd known more when you were younger. That is why I would like to ask a favor of you, Margaret."

"Sure, Father. Anything."

"Call Francesco for me. I fear he might ask something of me I will be unable to give him. Please ask what he wants."

Sweetie blinked twice and asked, "You want me to call the Pope for you? Talk to him?"

"*Sí.* Francesco is very kind, a far better man than me. You need not be afraid."

Sweetie was still processing that idea when Welborn asked, "You know the Pope personally, Father?"

"Yes. The Society of Jesus is not that large. Ten, maybe 12,000 priests across the whole of the Earth. When you consider only men of a certain age from just one part of the world, the number is much smaller."

"Especially if the men in question have attained a certain status or notoriety," Sweetie said.

De Loyola smiled. "Or even if they cheer for the same football clubs."

Sweetie said, "Okay, Father, I'll make the call, but I want to do it at home. If His Holiness comes to the phone, I'll politely ask him what he wants from you. But I have to say that short of giving up my husband or my daughter, I can't think of *anything* I wouldn't do for him."

"I fear as much for myself, but …" He could only shrug.

"Now, there's something I'd like to ask of you, Father," Sweetie said.

He smiled and said, "I have neither a wife nor a child, so how may I help you?"

Sweetie told de Loyola about the plot to kill Jim McGill using assassins who were already near death's door. "They're called *los muertos,* Father. The man behind them goes by the name of Corona Moe. We think he has a place for the dying killers to spend their final days, after they complete their work, in Baja California. We suspect this man might use people who have a history of killing others."

De Loyola said, "Like many of my old *compañeros*."

"Yes. We think Corona Moe pays relatively well, and if someone was dying and desperate to leave something to his family …"

A look of outrage hardened the priest's face, made it easy to see how he once had been a feared man.

"This is a great evil in many ways," he said, "and I know of such things only too well. I even know —"

Neither Sweetie nor Welborn had any trouble completing the thought. Father de Loyola knew of a man or men who might be susceptible to such temptation.

"I will help you, Margaret," the priest said, "whether or not Francesco chooses to speak with you."

Metro Police Headquarters — Washington, DC

While browsing through the crime scene photos that showed Aubrey Gadsden's body dangling from a rope in his law offices, Captain Rockelle Bullard had a thought: What would the man's mother think if she saw these pictures of her son? Assuming the woman was still alive and inclined to give a damn. A few minutes of computer searching and a phone call ascertained that Constance Gadsden was still breathing and cared enough to allow Rockelle to come and see her.

The captain decided this was an interview best handled by a woman.

She told Detectives Meeker and Beemer, "While I'm out, you two think about what Putnam Shady suggested to us."

To wit: Consider Auric Ludwig as the moving force behind Aubrey Gadsden's death.

Putnam's rationale being: Getting rid of Gadsden would eliminate the only known link between Ludwig and Gadsden. Killing Gadsden, Putnam said, would tidy things up for Ludwig.

By the time Rockelle returned from speaking with Constance Gadsden, Meeker and Beemer had a rebuttal to Putnam Shady's logic. After all, two veteran police detectives didn't want to be one-upped by a civilian. Wouldn't be good for their self-images.

They gave the captain time to use the ladies' room, get a cup of coffee and settle herself comfortably behind her desk. She had her detectives sit in front of her and gestured to them to share their thoughts. As much as the two of them liked to clown around, she'd never worked with better police minds.

"You remember those other two lawyers who came to see us a few months back, Captain?" Meeker asked.

"Nicholas Kingsbury and Murray MacMurray," Beemer clarified.

"I remember," Rockelle said. "Couldn't forget that little visit, now could I?"

Kingsbury and MacMurray had arrived with a note purported to be from Auric Ludwig asking to have James J. McGill killed. Problem was, the note was neither addressed to anyone nor signed by anyone.

Still, Kingsbury said the note had been given to him by Ludwig to be delivered to Gadsden. Kingsbury had been scared shitless. He didn't want to be indicted as an accessory to a murder, but he was also scared that he might face disciplinary action by the bar association for violating attorney-client privilege. Captain Bullard and her detectives felt the death threat was real, but they didn't have any way to proceed.

If the Metro Police went out and arrested Gadsden, solely on Kingsbury's say-so, Gadsden could deny any knowledge of what was going on and sue the department. He might even sue the individual officers involved, meaning herself, Meeker and Beemer. None of the cops thought Kingsbury— who'd already lawyered up himself — would stand up for them if the going got tough, as it certainly would.

So Rockelle punted, put the ball in the Secret Service's hands. Keeping McGill alive and well was their responsibility. Threatening

McGill's life was a federal crime. If the Attorney General wanted to proceed against Gadsden, that would be his call.

If Gadsden wanted to sue the federal government, well, good luck with that.

Now that Gadsden was dead he wouldn't be taking anyone to court, but Rockelle saw where her detectives were going.

"What you're thinking," she said to Meeker and Beemer, "is there's still a link between Auric Ludwig and the scheme to kill James J. McGill: that link being Nicholas Kingsbury."

"Yeah," Meeker said. "That's what me 'n' Beem thought."

Beemer said, "Got us to wondering if there's any connection between Kingsbury and Putnam Shady, too, us detectives being suspicious types."

Rockelle grinned. She knew what was coming next. Her investigators wouldn't have mentioned the possibility unless they had the answer, an affirmative one.

"They were both Boy Scouts together?" she asked.

"Doesn't go back quite that far, but they went to the same college," Meeker said.

"Colleges can be big places, thousands of students. Some of them never cross paths with others." Rockelle was telling them they'd have to do better than that.

Beemer did, handing her a copy of a photo. "They played poker at the same table. Pretty hard to deny you know someone you're taking money from."

Rockelle looked at the image. "That's a young Mr. Shady smiling and raking in a bunch of chips, and that's Mr. Kingsbury frowning with no chips at all left in front of him. Okay, you guys have made your point. Your first one anyway. The others are?"

Meeker said, "Shady suggested to us Gadsden was the only link to Auric Ludwig, and that's why he got lynched. Either Mr. Shady didn't know about Kingsbury's connection to Ludwig or maybe he just forgot to mention the man."

Beemer added, "Mr. Shady doesn't strike either of us as the forgettin' type. What that leaves, in our minds, is he's misdirecting, covering up for Kingsbury."

Rockelle looked at the two of them. "Being thorough in your work, both of you also considered the possibility Mr. Shady, himself, was the killer, didn't you?"

Meeker and Beemer nodded, Meeker saying, "Sure. We liked him for another murder once upon a time, didn't we? But now he's married to Margaret Sweeney, isn't he?"

Beemer said, "We checked her out, too. She was good police both in Chicago and Winnetka. Took a bullet for Mr. McGill. We don't see her either being married to a killer or being fooled by one living under the same roof."

"So Mr. Shady's in the clear even if he didn't mention Mr. Kingsbury?" Rockelle asked.

"Yeah," Meeker said, "but our point is maybe somebody has it in mind to get rid of Kingsbury, hang *him* in his office or house."

"I'll advise Kingsbury and the Secret Service," Rockelle said. "We don't need any extra work right now."

That ordinarily might have been the point at which Meeker and Beemer returned to their own desks to figure out their next move in the Gadsden case. Only they sat tight. Looked at the captain with no sign they were going anywhere.

"What?" she asked. "You want to hear what *I* turned up?"

The two detectives nodded.

"Well, it turns out the late esquire, Aubrey Gadsden, he had a mama."

Meeker and Beemer shared a quizzical look.

Meeker said, "Most of us do, Captain, at least for a little while."

Beemer asked, "You sayin' the lady's still alive?"

Rockelle nodded. "Her name is Constance. Turns out she had a complicated relationship with her son. Loved him but didn't like him too much. Felt he'd make a good decision and right away spoil it with a bad choice. He found a nice girl, but left her for a bad one who left him. Said he even had trouble keeping good secretarial help. He was between temps the day he got strung up. Constance loved her son becoming a lawyer, but hated that he represented criminals. All things considered, she was heartbroken that he died the way he did."

Beemer said, "That's why she agreed to talk to you."

Meeker offered another thought. "Might've been heartbreak or she was just wondering did he leave her any money."

Rockelle smiled. "She did raise the subject of money. Said she spent a lot of it putting her son through school. Also turns out the man didn't have any other blood relatives but her. You two ace detectives see where I'm going here?"

Meeker and Beemer looked at each other and nodded.

Meeker said, "Dr. Zoë Tinker."

Rockelle nodded. "What about her?"

Beemer said, "You came up with the idea first, Captain, about whether a dying person would be strong enough mentally and emotionally to carry off a hit."

Rockelle said, "Right. Got to check out your hitmen. Make sure they're good to go. Before you get to that, though, what's the first useful thing for a shrink to do in a criminal set-up like this ?"

Meeker said, "Gotta make sure the *lawyer* is stable enough to hold up his end,"

Meeker and Beemer looked at each other and laughed. They were having fun now.

Beemer said, "A man pretending his shrink is his honey ain't gonna win any mental health awards."

Meeker added. "A guy like that has gotta be a risk."

Beemer nodded. "So ol' Zoë Tinker, she tells the boys back at the home office that Gadsden was cracking up, had become undependable."

"Couldn't have that," Meeker judged.

Rockelle said, "That would fit right in with Mom saying her boy went for the wrong girls. Okay, taking the next step, we all agree that Dr. Tinker is a fine tennis player, but does she have the muscle to string a man up all by herself?"

Meeker and Beemer shook their heads.

Rockelle asked, "So who did that part?"

"Another damn crooked doctor," Meeker said.

"One who checks out the dying killers," Beemer added. "Makes sure they've got the strength to get the job done."

Rockelle had another idea. "Doesn't have to be a doctor. Maybe just a physical therapist. Somebody with a lesser financial interest in playing things straight."

"So where do we start with all this, Captain?" Beemer asked.

Rockelle took a signed and notarized statement out of her briefcase.

Put it on her desk in front of the detectives.

"Constance Gadsden gave me written permission to access Dr. Zoë Tinker's treatment records for her son. Let's go see what she has to say."

Beemer said, "See if she wants to rat out the guy who actually put the lawyer's head in the noose, too."

"Bust his ass, too," Meeker said.

Rockelle summed up matters. "See if *both* of them want to turn on this Corona Moe asshole. We'll call when we're just outside her office, see if she has time for us."

Damn Zoë Tinker spoiled all their fun. She was out. So the cops left a message.

Beijing, China

Chinese President Li Ho practiced meditation twice a day. Not the sort of thing associated with any religion, of course. He simply cleared his mind and relaxed his body to enhance his performance in leading the country's 1.368 billion people. His meditative state was sometimes so peaceful he snored.

Nobody accused him of napping on the job, though. That wouldn't be a good career move, accusing the man who was the head of government, the boss of the Communist Party and the de facto commander of the People's Liberation Army (and Navy) of giving less than his best 24/7/365.

There were rare occasions, however, when Li's silent —or

dozing — contemplation had to be disturbed. The outside world was not always considerate of even a great man's needs. When events intruded, Li's staff always exercised their best manners and gentlest tones in summoning him back to the hurly-burly world of government, politics and —

General Hu Dai entered the president's personal meditation chamber and bellowed, "The Americans are invading!"

It's no easy thing to fall on your face while sitting in the lotus position, but Li almost managed it. He saved himself from that humiliation by extending his hands in front of him. From there, he was limber enough to get to his feet smoothly, almost as if he'd choreographed the move.

He put on a mask of imperturbable calm. He certainly wasn't going to show Hu any sign of anxiety, weakness or even pique. He simply said, "Explain."

"An enhanced U.S. Navy carrier strike group has entered our territorial waters."

Li understood implicitly that Hu was referring to the South China Sea not, say, Hong Kong Harbor. So he only asked, "How is the formation enhanced?"

"Besides the command ship, the aircraft carrier, USS *Ronald Reagan,* there are four guided missile cruisers, not the usual one or two, for air defense. There are *eight* destroyers, six of which are also armed with missiles. There are twice the usual number of logistics and supply ships. There are usually two attack submarines with such an American strike group. With this formation we can only assume that number is increased. And then there is more bad news."

Just the preliminaries — the U.S. Navy vessels — were enough to strain Li's composure. Unless the Americans had completely lost their minds, however, and were planning to attack China with nuclear missile submarines, the armada Hu had described was insufficient to attack the Chinese mainland. Still, the Americans were clearly asserting their military might in an undeniable way. If Li and the Politburo didn't find some way to counter them, China would be humiliated in front of the entire world.

Clearing his throat, Li asked his top military commander, "What is the additional news?"

"The American Navy is not alone. The British have sent two destroyers to join them."

Li knew that London was peeved with China for its increasing pressure on Hong Kong to conform to Beijing's dictates despite the communist government's promise to allow greater freedom in the former British colony. Added to that, undoubtedly, the long alliance between the Americans and the English also explained London's support.

"We might have expected as much," Li said as calmly as he could manage.

Hu said, "The French have sent a frigate as well. An Indian destroyer is currently anchored in Viet Nam's waters and could join the battle group on short notice. Our spies in Japan and South Korea suspect the naval forces of those countries are making preparations to send at least token representation as well."

France and India didn't worry Li. Even the British support was largely symbolic. But the thought of fighting the Japanese and the Koreans again forced Li to repress a shudder. So did the idea that Hu Dai might be looking to depose him.

"Have the Americans made this military action public?" he asked. "Have they told their people that they might be going to war with us?"

Hu shook his head. "They say they've sent ships to our sea to investigate the cause of the destruction of their submarine."

Both Li and Hu knew the submarine hadn't been lost due to China's efforts. They'd been gunning for the *Reagan.* The idea that they might have succeeded and what the American response to *that* might have been overcame Li's pretense of stoicism. His knees wobbled.

Hu was the one who hid his emotions, a sense of elation at his rival's weakness.

"You are feeling ill, Li Zhûxí?" Hu asked, addressing Li by his title as Chairman of the Communist Party.

In a rare moment of candor, the most powerful man in the world's most populous country shook his head. "I just imagined the entire world as a burning coal."

Hu pictured the possibility in his own mind and didn't shrink from it.

If Beijing didn't dominate the planet, and for an indefinite time, why shouldn't it burn?

Before that subject could be debated, a less senior, more protocol-bound person knocked softly at the door to the meditation chamber that had by now lost all its harmony. No greater proof was needed than Hu attempting to respond to the interruption when that wasn't his place and catching a backhanded slap to the face from Li.

For one suicidal second Hu felt the impulse to strike back, but the merciless gaze from Li, such as Hu had neither seen nor imagined before, stopped him cold. He realized that he might have already overstepped himself to the point where his career or even his life might be over. After all, a man didn't become Zhûxí without being willing to crush his enemies.

In a newly calm voice, Li said, "Enter."

The Chairman's personal secretary stepped into the room. She bowed her head politely and extended a sheet of paper to Li. He read it, thought for a moment and handed the paper back. He said to his secretary, "Thank you, Mei Lin. Summon the Standing Committee. Everyone is to be present within the hour."

The woman nodded and bowed out.

Hu wanted to ask what had happened, and whether he would still have a seat at the meeting, but he knew better that to interrupt the Chairman's thinking. Another offense might be the end of him.

"I've met the woman three times, and I never thought her to be this devious," Li finally said.

Hu couldn't help but ask, "What woman?"

"Patricia Grant, the American president soon to leave office."

"She must be the one who ordered her navy into our waters."

Li nodded and said, "More than that. One of her ships is placing buoys in the sea. Each one flies a flag."

"The American flag?" Hu's face flushed as red as the world on fire he had imagined. "That can mean nothing but war."

Li was tempted to slap Hu again, but he knew it would be wiser to shoot him, if things came to that.

"It is not the American flag," the Chairman said. "It is the flag of the United Nations. And there are tanker ships closely following the international strike group. They are suspected of carrying sand. Do you know what this means, Hu?"

The general, just short of being dumbfounded, did. "The Americans are going to build their own island and use the United Nations as their mask. That and use their island to pretend to look for a submarine they must have sunk."

Li nodded. "They are also telling us if we fight them we will be fighting the whole world."

The two men hated the reality of what was happening, but they couldn't help but wish they had been so devious.

Dulles International Airport — Washington, DC

The President got word of the strike force's arrival at the place where the *Old Gray Lady* had met its end just as her limousine pulled to the curb at Washington Dulles International Airport. The call came from the Secretary of Defense at the Pentagon. After hearing the status report, Patricia Grant said, "Thank you, Martin. I'm happy to hear that. Call me the moment there's any sign of an aggressive movement by the PLA Navy."

The Secret Service and the airport cops had cleared a space for the President's limousine outside the general aviation terminal. Armed men would collect Dorie McBride and any luggage she might have, giving her a story she could dine out on for the rest of her life. They'd bring the Hollywood talent agent to Thing One.

Under happier circumstances, Patricia Grant might have stepped out of the limo and given the airport bystanders a memory to share back home about how they'd met the President. Things being what they were on the world stage and within her own family, she stayed put.

McGill said to his wife, "Do you want to talk about that last phone call or is it something I shouldn't know?"

She looked at him and said, "It's something every American should know, and I'll have to tell the nation sooner rather than later. So there's no harm in telling you right now. We're playing a game of chicken with the Chinese in the South China Sea."

She gave McGill the details. Some of them anyway.

He said, "You just talked with the U.N. Secretary-General on the way to the airport. Our navy must've had those U.N. flags all along. Were you going to put them out on the water even if the Secretary-General didn't go along with the idea? I didn't hear you twisting the man's arm."

The President smiled. "I've talked to Ricardo Alves several times over the years. I backed him to become Secretary-General. I've always been polite and friendly, never tried to coerce him into doing anything that would harm him in either Portugal or Europe in general. I've supported his political positions as often as I could."

"You charmed the guy out of his socks," McGill said.

Patti Grant smiled. "Subtly, but yes. So when I explained what I had the Navy do today he was inclined to go along. I thought you heard that part, too. We are sitting quite close to each other."

McGill said, "I tuned out after the first ten seconds or so. I focus on my own challenges when I think I shouldn't be listening in on yours."

That earned McGill a kiss on the cheek. "You really are such a sweet man — when you're not out on the street shooting old ladies."

McGill laughed with a note of rue in his voice. "You're never going to let me live that down, are you?"

"Not for some time anyway."

"Your passenger is here," McGill said. He slid to his left to make room for Dorie McBride. There was a facing seat in the back of Thing One. Hell, there was room for a pool table, but McGill knew his wife's old talent agent would want to sit hip-to-hip with her one-time most famous client.

The President moved over, too, as a special agent ushered Dorie into the limo.

She gave McGill's leg a gentle squeeze before turning to embrace Dorie.

There were no air-kisses for Ms. McBride. She was old school. She planted a good smack on each of the President's cheeks and then blotted the lipstick she'd left behind with a lace handkerchief. "Oh, I'm sorry, Patricia, I'm such a sentimental old fool. I just couldn't help myself. You look so wonderful. Not exactly as young as when we first met, but close. It's a miracle how well you've kept your looks."

She interrupted her spiel momentarily to lean forward and say to McGill, "You're looking well also, Mr. McGill."

He said, "Thanks, Dorie. We appreciate your help."

She gave McGill a wink, letting both him and the President know there would be quid pro quo. That was enough for Patti to say, "How can we ever thank you for helping us, Dorie?"

The presidential motorcade began to move.

"Well," the talent agent said, "there is this one little thing I'd be ever so happy and grateful if you would consider doing it."

The President said, "No feature films, no TV series."

"Not even on PBS, maybe only four times a year, with only the best people involved?" Dorie named a famous documentary film-maker as an example. "Your part would only be to introduce the program. Two minutes on camera at the most. Ninety seconds if you'd be more comfortable with that and, of course, you'd have complete script control."

Patti kept a straight face and asked, "What's the theme of this show?"

Dorie said, "Unsung American heroes."

That notion caught the President by surprise, actually intrigued her.

"People from all walks of life who stepped up in a big way?" she asked.

"Stepped up when most people never would have thought they could," Dorie said.

"Every storyline would be verified by respected historians?"

Dorie nodded.

"You've seen the first script and it's well written?"

"It was beautiful, made me weep and then cheer."

"Well, that's good," Patti said with a smile, "but can the quality be maintained?"

"Patricia, we have a number of excellent talents edging very close to committing. We could be on the verge of doing something meaningful here. I think it would make the whole country feel good, watching this show. Having your name attached to it would bring in a flood of other commitments."

"How many times have you thought some project would be right for me, Dorie?"

The older woman laughed. "Only every day since you left town." She turned to McGill. "Los Angeles, I mean."

"That was my first guess," he replied.

"Is this the best opportunity you've ever found with me in mind?" Patti asked.

"By far, sweetheart."

"How close is it to a go project?"

Dorie held a thumb and index finger an inch apart.

"And with me?"

Dorie raised her thumb.

Patti turned to McGill and said, "Jim?"

He knew what his better half wanted and said, "What if the President doesn't agree a particular individual is a real hero? What then?"

The talent agent gave McGill a sharp look, as if she hadn't expected such show business acumen from a cop turned private eye.

"Well … then I guess she wouldn't introduce that show."

McGill shook his head. “No, the President would need prior approval of an entire season’s choice of subjects before she committed to doing that season. A now-you-see-me, now-you-don’t schedule of appearances wouldn’t be good for anyone.”

With an expression of grudging acknowledgment, Dorie said, “That’s a smart way of looking at it. Anything else?”

“The President will need the flexibility of shooting her introductions in any major city where she happens to be. She shouldn’t have to fly to Los Angeles, if that’s not convenient.”

That stung Dorie a bit, but she nodded. “Very well. Is that all?”

“One more thing.” McGill turned to his wife. “What would you think of donating your fee for each show to a charity relevant to the subject of that show?”

Patti beamed. “I think that’s a great idea, Jim. How about you, Dorie?”

She nodded, telling Patti, “We could put that in the credits. It could help raise other contributions.”

Looking over at McGill, she said, “If *you* ever get tired of catching crooks, I might have a job for you, too.”

Four Seasons Hotel — Washington, DC

Taps sat in the living room of a suite at the Four Seasons, which wasn’t the place where his *muertos* would have stayed that day had their attempt on James J. McGill’s life been delayed until that afternoon. He was watching the video he’d shot from the second floor of a building on the east side of Wisconsin Avenue near the corner with O Street.

The previous day, a hired contractor, who never saw Taps, had installed one-way mirror window film. Neither Taps nor his three video cameras would be visible from the street below. Later that day, another laborer from a second firm, who also would not see Taps, would remove the film. The windows would be restored to their original appearance, making it unlikely anyone would have noticed the temporary change.

The video sequences of the failed attempt had been uploaded to a server tucked into a very deep corner of the Dark Net. There was no guarantee the server couldn't be found and hacked, but it would have to be suspected to exist before that could happen. For additional safety, the videos would be switched from one server to another at frequent but irregular intervals.

Taps' appearance would also be subject to numerous changes. No exceptionally tall man in black had exited the camera-platform building on Wisconsin Avenue after the shooting had stopped. Rather a somewhat tall auburn-haired woman in a pearl gray Chanel pant suit and matte black flat shoes exited the rear of the building. Her pronouns changed with her appearance. She walked to the Tenleytown Metro Station and took the subway to the Adams Morgan stop and strolled to the National Zoo from there.

After feigning interest in the animals and making sure she wasn't being followed, she walked to the Four Seasons on Pennsylvania Avenue. While checking in, she said her luggage had been misplaced at the airport. She hoped it would be found before she had to go out that night. The concierge recommended several fine stores where she might shop in case her bags didn't arrive in time.

Having established her identity as an upscale and sorely put-upon female guest, she took the elevator, unescorted by a bellman, up to her suite. Once there, she pulled a bottle of San Pellegrino from the fridge, filled a glass and sat in an armchair.

She sipped the sparkling water and reviewed the events of the morning from memory. After she finished examining the mental record, she took an iPad out of her purse to see how closely the video of the attempted assassination of James J. McGill would compare.

The first moments went exactly as planned. All the shooters were perfectly positioned and Paulette Lacroix stepped out from the shelter of the delivery truck at what had seemed to be exactly the right moment. Give the old girl credit for her resolve, too. She hadn't hesitated at all. It should have worked the way Taps had planned, except she hadn't anticipated just how good McGill's driver was.

Yes, in doing her research, she'd read that Leo Levy had once been a professional race car driver on the NASCAR circuit. But the video she'd watched on that type of auto racing, maybe 15 minutes, showed cars roaring endlessly around an oval track. She found it stupefyingly dull.

She'd made a point to watch what happened when one of the cars crashed. The vehicle hit a concrete wall and seemed to explode into pieces large and small. Most of the other drivers exhibited exceptionally quick reflexes dodging around the wreckage to the left or right and kept right on going. The amazing part to her was the driver of the demolished vehicle walked away from the high-speed accident seemingly unhurt.

Still, there were differences from the trap she had planned. All of the cars in the race were moving in the same direction and manned by exceptionally skilled drivers. The wreck occurred in plain sight. It most likely wasn't the first time any of the other drivers had found themselves evading a vehicle crash, and practice always helped. Beyond that, for all she knew, there might have been a professional ethos that every driver knew the life-and-death risks he took, so the possibility of causing another man's death, while not to be disregarded, could be accepted more readily than …

Seeing a little old lady step into the street directly in front of your car.

Only Paulette hadn't gotten squarely in front of McGill's Chevy. She hadn't hesitated in the least, but by the time she reached the point where the near side of the Chevrolet should have been, had it continued in a straight line, Leo Levy had already veered left into the oncoming lane. Even that might have worked out all right, if he'd crashed into the oncoming line of vehicles.

McGill almost certainly would have gotten out of his car to see who had been hurt.

Without the least hesitation, though, Levy moved smoothly into the vacant parking lane. By that time the target car was being fired upon from three directions. The damnably competent driver didn't let that distract him in the least. He made a smooth left, illegal, turn onto O Street and out of camera range.

Taps turned her attention to what surely had to be McGill's people counter-attacking the *muertos*. Those bastards were highly skilled, too. They took down Taps' shooters with a minimum of return fire, neither killing nor wounding bystanders with stray shots.

All but one of Taps' assassins did the right thing and apparently either died fighting or suffered what should be fatal wounds, judging by the amount of blood lost. Only Maxwell had dropped his weapon and tried to run. A youngish woman pounced on him like a cheetah running down a rabbit. With any luck, she broke his neck on impact with the pavement, but Taps had to assume the worst. Maxwell was alive and talking.

Well, he'd been warned what would happen to his beneficiaries if that happened.

Then Paulette, bless her failing heart, gave her last full measure of devotion. With traffic at a standstill and bodies lining the street and sidewalks, she did her best hobbling gait to pursue McGill's car down O Street, pulling her handgun from her purse.

Taps couldn't see where McGill's car was at that point, but she got the impression from the intent attitude in Paulette's shambling stride that McGill must have gotten out of his car. Making the feminine side of Taps proud, Paulette was doing her absolute best to complete the job. Until a shot rang out and knocked the old woman flat on her back.

Paulette had to be dead, Taps felt, or soon would be.

She returned the iPad to her purse. She'd watch the video again in an hour or so. See if she noticed anything new.

Sipping a second bottle of water, Taps replayed the action in her mind. Yes, McGill must have exposed himself. If Leo Levy had driven back to the White House or the garage of his office building, Paulette wouldn't have had anyone to pursue.

Why would McGill have put himself at risk?

For the same reason as if his car had hit Paulette on Wisconsin

Avenue.

He wanted to see if he might be of help. He did that despite all the carnage that had gone on behind Leo Levy's brilliant escape maneuver. That told Taps a lot about the man. So did the fact that he'd enlisted so many of his own people to keep him safe. That wasn't the Secret Service down there doing the dirty work.

McGill had people willing to risk their own lives to protect him.

No doubt they were looking to find her, too.

The smart things to do would be to run and hide.

Only Taps was as given to taking big risks as McGill was.

Maybe the thing to do was to see if she could get next to McGill all by herself. Get him to look the other way and slip a knife between his ribs. See the look of fatal surprise on his face and hold him close until she felt the last beat of his heart. She liked that idea.

Of course, Corona Moe would have to pay additional for that.

She gave him a call to see if he was still interested.

Ritz-Carlton Hotel — Washington, DC

Odo Sacripant showered for close to an hour in the suite he shared with Yves Pruet. The other partners in McGill Investigations International, LLP had their travel and lodging expenses covered by the name partner, but those partners had yet to work a case or generate any income. The Paris office, by contrast, had been in business for over a year. A steady flow of clients had appeared at their door since day one.

James J. McGill was internationally famous and highly regarded by substantial majorities of the populace in both the U.S. and Europe. Beyond that Pruet, Odo and Gabbi Casale had made names for themselves across France after their epic battle, alongside McGill, with the Undertaker under the Pont d'Iéna in Paris.

The story of that encounter soon had spread over the whole of the Continent.

The three partners in the Paris office had to defer work to

travel to America.

Their financial position allowed them to pay their own way and stay someplace well appointed. Lavish even. It was a business expense, after all, and tax deductible. By the time Odo emerged from his ablutions in a white cotton bathrobe, his skin glowed from the pounding of hot water.

"I was thinking of sending in a lifeguard for you," Pruet told him.

Odo shrugged. "The physical stink of prison washed away quickly; the memory of it took longer. I thought I'd wait until the hot water ran out, but it never did."

"Yet another reason to stay at a fine hotel," Pruet said. "May I bring you a drink?"

Odo was tempted to ask for a strawberry milkshake, but that was another thing he wanted to put behind him.

"I don't suppose I might have a measure of Mavela," Odo said.

Pruet stepped behind the living room's bar and produced a bottle of the Corsican whiskey. He poured a shot and took it to Odo, presenting it with a flourish, "An excellent choice, *m'sieur.*"

Odo grinned at his old friend. He raised his glass and said, "À *salute.*" He took a sip and sighed in satisfaction. "The hotel had this on hand?"

Pruet said, "No, but I asked the concierge to find a bottle on the day you went off to your confinement. She produced it almost immediately. I would never live anywhere but France, but America does have its charms."

Odo laughed. "Few if any of them will be found in its prisons, from what I saw."

"You faced no real dangers, I hope," Pruet said.

Odo rolled his eyes. "Am I not as handsome as always? Does it look as if anyone has laid a finger on me?"

The two men hadn't spoken of Odo's time behind bars during the ride back to Washington. Dikki Missirian's manners were too good for him to ask any prying questions. They'd all been content to let Dikki practice his French, which wasn't bad at all even with his Armenian accent.

Arriving at the hotel, Odo had immediately proclaimed the need to cleanse himself.

"You are, as ever, a shining example of Corsican manhood," Pruet said. "I am most sorry if I even implied any American thug might cause you harm. Now, may we get down to business?"

Odo emptied his glass and put it on the coaster Pruet had thoughtfully provided.

"There was a bit of commotion at the prison this morning. An inmate hurried past my cell on his way to see Auric Ludwig. He had a look of grievous concern on his face, such as one might have delivering the news of a death in the family."

"But that was not the problem at all," Pruet said. "Else you would not be back at the Ritz-Carlton."

"No, but I'm not sure how much longer I would have lasted. I don't understand how anyone would risk going to prison a second time. Just walking through such a place should be enough to make everyone live within the law." Odo shrugged. As a former policeman, he knew repeat offenders were the rule rather than the exception. "In any case, Ludwig found me fascinating, and I had several conversations with him. He even came up with a business proposition for me in my guise as a gun smuggler."

Odo told Pruet of Ludwig's idea to flood Europe and the rest of the world with guns in the American fashion.

A longtime agnostic, Pruet nonetheless made the sign of the cross and said, "God forbid."

Odo nodded but said, "Even so, making Ludwig think I was a fellow arms merchant unburdened by a conscience led him to trust me. He confided that his bad news this morning was that a plan of his to kill someone had failed. He was sorely wounded by this revelation."

Pruet leaned forward. "Did he mention *M'sieur* McGill's name?"

Odo shook his head. "And I thought it discreet not to ask who his target was. He'd already confessed to his guilt in planning a person's death. I also decided at that vulnerable moment for him it would be wise to add to his distress by telling him I was about to be released."

Pruet approved with a nod. *"Bon."*

"That was when *M'sieur* Ludwig asked me if *I* might be the man to do a difficult disposal job. I asked how difficult. He said he would pay me a million dollars, but I would have to earn every penny of it."

"Your response was a shrewd one, no doubt," Pruet said.

Odo smiled. "I told him I intended to make several million dollars when I got back to my business … but also I am a man who finds it hard to resist a unique challenge. Something that one can look back at over the years and relish in memory."

"Masterful," Pruet said. "What was your next step?"

"Like any skilled villain, I said I would have to think about his offer. He said if I can agree to take on the job within the next 30 days, I am to text a certain guard at the prison. One hundred thousand dollars will then be wired to any bank of my choosing outside the United States, and I will be told my target's name. When I indicate I am ready to proceed, $400,000 will be wired to my account. The remainder will be paid upon a successful completion of my task."

Pruet applauded. "Bravo, my friend, you could not have done better. You have the identity of the guard acting as Ludwig's intermediary. In return for a lesser sentence, he will inform on Ludwig, implicating him in the plan. The sources of Ludwig's money to pay his hired assassin, will make the same bargain. The federal government of the United States still has the death penalty. I wonder if it would apply to Mr. Ludwig."

"The world would suffer no great loss if it did," Odo replied.

"He's truly a terrible fellow?" Pruet asked.

Odo took a deep breath and slowly released it. "He doesn't rise to the diabolical. He simply has a void where most of us have a conscience."

Odo got up, grabbed his glass and walked over to the bar.

"I'm going to have one more," he said. "Would you care to join me, Yves?"

Pruet said, "*Oui.*"

The White House — Washington, DC

Patti thought her former talent agent, Dorie McBride, would be more comfortable talking in the Family Residence, given that the subject under discussion would be the identity of a killer targeting McGill for death. Dorie, however, said she'd really like to see the Oval Office. She'd visited any number of glam homes in L.A., had one herself, but she'd never seen the democratic world's center of power, not in person.

"Okay, but in that context, I'm the President not Patti Grant."

"Really?"

"Really."

A nod from McGill seconded that reality. "Even with me, that's the way it is."

"All right. I won't pitch any more jobs to you."

"No, don't."

Dorie was introduced to Edwina Byington, the President's personal secretary, just outside the Oval Office. The talent agent smiled and was entirely pleasant and correct with Edwina, but both the President and McGill could see that Dorie was working the data file in her mind for casting possibilities for Edwina, and just might have come up with one.

The President gave Dorie a small shake of her head.

And McGill whispered into her ear, "I've got dibs."

With that situation made clear, McGill opened the door for the two women to enter ahead of him. Looking back at Edwina before he closed the door, he saw her give him a wink. The gesture warmed him. There was no saying Edwina wouldn't retire after leaving the White House, but if she felt like continuing to work, McGill thought he had the inside track.

Dorie, meanwhile, was all but gawking at the Oval Office.

McGill saw that she understood that it wasn't just a glorified work space. This was a place where history got made. Matters of life and death were its stock in trade. Over the years, McGill had sometimes forgotten that.

Seeing Dorie's reaction, oddly enough, gave McGill an idea for a television program. Something probably best done on PBS. Feature a series of critical moments that took place in this very room and how they had affected the future of the country and the world. Make the shows historically accurate, get first class writing and maybe have James Earl Jones to do the voiceover narration. Could be a big hit.

Who knew? A show like that might even make voters think long and hard, more so than they did now, about who they wanted to work in this room.

McGill saw the President was already seated behind her desk and was waiting patiently.

He well knew the President's time was always a precious commodity and he cleared his throat to bring the talent agent out of whatever reverie her fertile imagination was cranking out. She focused with a slight start, and took the cue of McGill holding a chair for her.

She sat and said, "Patricia … Madam President, I'm sorry for ever pestering you with trivial matters. I never understood …" She glanced around again. "Any of this. All the things you must have on your mind every waking minute. Thank you for taking such good care of our country."

The President nodded and said, "You're welcome. You did vote for me, didn't you, Dorie?"

The older woman flushed. "I almost didn't the first time. I selfishly wanted you to come back to Los Angeles … and I'd never voted for a Republican before."

"So after I became a Democrat the second time was easier?"

"Yes, politically and personally. I'd mellowed just a little by then."

McGill wanted to get on with things. "You have something to

show us, Dorie?"

She bobbed her head. "Yes, of course."

She reached into a purse big enough to hold an old-time phone book and took out two iPads. She handed one to McGill and said, "I hope you won't mind sharing with the President."

He smiled. "Not at all."

He got up and stood at his wife's right shoulder and centered the iPad in front of her.

"The four-digit password is 1600," Dorie said. "You can change it later at your convenience. If you tap the icon for photos, you'll see an album of head-shots that's shared with my machine. The first image is the person Mr. McGill's driver so cleverly noticed."

With everything else on her plate at the moment, this was the first time the President saw the likeness. She said, "This person's features are nicely symmetrical, but it really would be a hard call to assign a gender identity."

"Some of that is the unisex hairstyle and gender neutral clothing," Dorie said. "You remember Julie Andrews in *Victor/Victoria?* In her male persona, we all still knew it was her because we've seen her so often, but she looked at least as masculine as Joel Grey did in *Cabaret.*"

McGill thought the individual in question split the difference between masculine and feminine even more finely than that, but what he asked his wife was, "Do you still think this could be either a guy on a bowling team or a woman with a pink Cadillac?"

The President shook her head.

Dorie looked confused, so the President explained.

"Oh, no," the agent said. "I don't think we're looking at *that* kind of act here. My best guess is this person ..." She pointed at the image on their iPads. "This person is what's called gender fluid, someone whose sense of self varies."

McGill said, "This is all kind of new to me. Would it be just a coincidence then that this individual not only has a shifting self-image but also a naturally androgynous appearance? I mean, could the internal component occur with someone who has a shelving brow and a lantern jaw?"

"Your guess would be as good as mine, Jim," the President said. "Do you have any idea about that, Dorie?"

The talent agent didn't have an immediate answer, but she ran McGill's question through her decades of exposure to all sorts of people who longed to work in the spotlight. "Well, look at Frankie Valli, the lead singer of The Four Seasons. He certainly has a masculine face but he rose to fame singing in quite a high voice. The same could be said of Michael Jackson, before his makeover. If that kind of variance could occur naturally, why not another kind?"

The President turned to McGill, "You think that something similar might have happened here, Jim?" She pointed at the image on the iPad. "This person started out with a different face and chose one that was more … in line with a self-image."

McGill nodded. "It was just a hazy idea, until Dorie mentioned Michael Jackson. Now, I think, yeah, it could well be. Dorie, do you know who did Michael's cosmetic surgery?"

She gave McGill the name off the top of her head.

He asked her, "Are there other surgeons in the L.A. area who do similar work?"

Dorie laughed. "Silly boy. Not everyone comes out of the box looking like you or Patri— the President. Many of us need help. Los Angeles probably has more plastic surgeons than any place north of Rio or east of Seoul. They practically grow in orchards."

The President confirmed that with a nod.

"Okay, I wanted to get that straight. It's just a hunch."

"Something that works out regularly for Jim," the President told Dorie.

"Can we look at the other photos you found now?" McGill asked.

They did. Turned out there were only three choices. That should have made things easier, except that three different individuals looked like one and the same person, and close matches to the individual Leo first noticed.

"Brothers and/or sisters?" McGill asked.

Dorie shook her head. "I don't have that information."

"Maybe they all have the same cosmetic surgeon?" the President asked.

"Now that you raise the possibility I wouldn't be surprised," Dorie said. "Imitation runs rampant among cosmetic surgeons, like any other artists."

McGill asked, "Do any of these three people have backgrounds in athletics or dance?"

"Numbers one and two respectively. They'd both hoped to work on-camera. Got work as extras or delivering a single line of dialogue now and then. Number three was interested only in voice-over work for commercials. Actually makes a living at it."

McGill examined the three photos closely.

"What are you looking for, Jim?" the President asked.

"Just wondering whether one of these people came by his or her face naturally and the other two are knock-offs. Any of them might be the person we want, but —"

"What if there are more than just these three?" the President asked.

McGill nodded. "Yeah, what if. Hell, it's L.A. What if it's a cult?"

The United Nations Building — New York City

His Excellency Wang Chao, the People's Republic of China's ambassador to the United Nations, was in anything but a diplomatic mood when he confronted Secretary-General Ricardo Alves in the Secretary-General's office. Accompanying Wang, in a show of anti-American solidarity, was His Excellency Gennady Volkov, the ambassador of Russia.

Alves had anticipated Wang might not appear alone, and to even the odds and provide himself with a witness as to what might occur, he had on hand Assistant Secretary-General Freya Ragnardóttir of Iceland. She was the daughter of two diplomats and a former pentathlete on Iceland's summer Olympic team.

Freya joked that what she wanted to be growing up was a shield-maiden, a female Viking warrior. With that option no longer available, she decided to match muscle and wits in sporting and diplomatic competitions. She remained calm when Wang and Volkov stormed into Alves' office.

For just a moment Wang thought to say that Freya should be expelled from the room. Seeing her unflinching demeanor, though, he knew she would not be dismissed easily, if at all, and if his wish was denied he would be the one to lose face. So with Volkov standing to his right he concentrated on Alves.

"The People's Republic of China demands that the American warships invading its territorial waters leave immediately. We further insist that this body censure the United States for its unauthorized use of the United Nations flag in its attempt to justify its act of aggression."

Volkov said in a deadpan tone, "That is assuming, Mr. Secretary-General, you did not give the Americans your unilateral permission to use the UN flag."

"I did not," Alves said. "I was informed of the matter only after it had taken place."

The fact that English was the only language the four diplomats had in common also angered Wang. The damned Americans, he thought, it was time they learned their place. They should recede to the far shores of history as the British had.

"So you ordered them to remove the flags of the United Nations?" Wang asked.

Alves smiled, barely repressing a laugh. "Mr. Ambassador, would President Li leap to obey any order I directed to him?"

Freya Ragnardóttir kept a straight face, but Gennady Volkov, ironically, couldn't stop a glint of amusement from reaching his eyes.

Wang didn't see any humor. He told Alves, "You border on insolence."

"I'll try not to cross that frontier, Mr. Ambassador," Alves said, "but you understand my point nonetheless. The United Nations operates in the spirit of international cooperation. If nations large or small choose not to cooperate ..." Alves shrugged.

"We can bring a resolution condemning this act of American aggression," Wang said.

Alves gestured to Freya. She said, "The Americans will veto it."

Wang looked as if he might spontaneously combust.

Volkov said, "Mightn't you *request* that the Americans remove the UN flags?"

"I might, but I'm not so inclined."

"Why not?" Wang asked at a volume that was hardly diplomatic.

"Well, because when President Grant informed me about the situation she also told me about some ideas circulating at the highest level of the American government. If the international community were to acquiesce to Chinese claims of sovereignty over the majority of the South China Sea ..." Turning to Volkov, he added, "Or to Russia's annexation of Crimea and parts of Ukraine — then the United States would make its own territorial claims."

Volkov knitted his brow. He hadn't expected to be directly drawn into the fray.

Now, it was Wang's turn to repress a laugh. He did so by asking, "What claims?"

Alves said, "The United States would claim sovereignty to the area of the Pacific Ocean between Hawaii and the American mainland. Further, and more daringly, I must say, the United States would also claim sovereignty over the entirety of the moon as the only nation to set foot and plant its flag there."

Wang and Volkov looked dumbfounded, until they turned to each other and laughed.

"Absurd," Wang said.

"Imbecilic," Volkov added.

Alves said, "Unless they choose to enforce the claims with military power. The moon might take some time, but with what is by far the largest, most powerful navy in the world the claim to the Pacific might start quickly. How would your countries feel about that, gentlemen?"

Plainly, they would not be happy.

Still, Wang argued, "The South China Sea has been China's territory since ancient times."

The Secretary-General said, "I'm afraid the Americans have anticipated that debating point. Their Vice President has the following rebuttal: In so-called ancient times, China was ruled by emperors. Only since 1949 has it been ruled by the Communist Party. If and when another emperor resumes the throne in China, then talks of historical claims might begin. Until that time, the internationally agreed upon Law of the Sea will prevail."

Wang's anger choked off further comment.

Volkov said, "This is a very dangerous path."

Alves leaned forward. "I have no doubt of that, Mr. Ambassador, but speaking personally for just this one moment I see the Americans as reacting to the aggressive expansionism of … other nations."

The representatives of China and Russia turned on their heels and departed in grim silence.

Once the door had closed behind them, Freya said, "I don't think their discussions with Beijing and Moscow are going to be pleasant."

"Not at all," Alves agreed. He ruminated for a moment and then asked his colleague, "Just how cold does Iceland get in the winter? We all might need a place to hide."

CHAPTER 7

New York City, Monday, September 19, 2016

Using a variation of a name from her distant past and the cover of half-a-dozen shell companies, Taps owned an apartment on Central Park that had been purchased for $2 million and was now valued at three times that price. The Bible said, "The wages of sin is death." Until that dying day, however, murder for hire done at the highest level with a unique and ruthless efficiency had paid Taps quite nicely.

She had kept a feminine appearance after leaving Washington but had adopted a different look, less businesslike, more high fashion model. At five-foot-nine, she had the height, especially in heels. She wasn't as emaciated as the current vogue demanded, but she was long-limbed and sleek.

She drew many looks as she stepped out of the hired Town Car in front of her apartment building. Some were sly glances; other appraisals rose to full-on gawking. The platinum blonde wig, the flamboyant makeup and the mid-thigh hemline of her dress all shouted for attention.

Both men and women telegraphed their thoughts as they looked at Taps. They wanted to know what lurked beneath the stunning facade. Fewer than one in a million, though, wouldn't have been shocked to see what was there, she thought.

Even now, in her mid-thirties, there were still times when *she* couldn't believe it.

She tipped Kostas, the Greek immigrant doorman, the customary hundred dollars to see that her luggage was brought upstairs. He was the only person she'd ever met who never gave a hint of thinking she was a freak. His eyes were gentle in their regard and his voice went beyond being merely polite. There was always a kindness to his tone that touched Taps' heart.

No one else had ever made such a connection to her.

She'd overheard whispers in the building that he'd been an Orthodox monk back in the old country. If that was the case, though, what turn of events had brought him to New York? It pleased Taps to think maybe the good and kind Kostas had a few nasty secrets of his own.

The apartment building had twenty-odd floors, but Taps had bought in on the fifth floor. No penthouse for her. She'd done her research on high-rise fires. Ninety-nine percent of fire department ladders didn't extend beyond the seventh floor of a building, lower than that the farther from the building the truck had to park. The statistics also showed, however, that 70% of high rise fires started on the fourth floor or below. Despite that stat, Taps felt the more cretins there were smoking in their beds between her and the ground, the worse her chances were of getting out alive.

Besides the consideration of the building going up in a blaze, she also had to take into account the possibility of going out a window should the cops ever come knocking at her door. The shorter the distance she had to rappel the better. Five floors would be easy for her but maybe it would be too high for some out-of-shape cop who had never contemplated the idea.

The elevation of her apartment was also perfect for its view of Central Park across the street. If she had to flee from an arrest, she would also be able to see which way to run once she reached the closest thing the city had to a woodland. That might be just the edge she needed to make a successful getaway.

With her bags delivered, a drink in hand and her door locked behind her, a completely different problem rose to the top of Taps' mind. It was not an immediately existential concern, but it might evolve to that point. For the first time in her career, she'd failed to make a kill.

James J. McGill was not only alive, but her research had told her that he had resources unlike any other target of hers. It wasn't farfetched to think he might try to find her, maybe even kill her. McGill didn't have a reputation for being bloodthirsty, but he did have two confirmed kills to his name: Damon Todd and John Patrick Granby.

In each case, news accounts declared McGill had been acting in defense of himself or others. Even so, the point was he would not fail to do whatever he felt a situation demanded, including the taking of a life. That was something she could not afford to forget.

The precautionary note to herself made Taps think of another possible warning sign. She'd seen the video of Paulette Lacroix being slammed to the pavement by a single shot. McGill was reported to travel in the company of a single Secret Service special agent as well as Leo Levy. So that meant the old woman might have been shot by any of the three of them.

Still, Secret Service people carried automatic weapons, didn't they? She thought so, but would check to make sure. If that was the case, and the government bodyguard had fired a hail of bullets, that would have splattered poor Paulette. So, tentatively at least, Taps eliminated the Secret Service man as the shooter. What about Leo Levy? Was he as quick with a firearm as he was behind the wheel of a car? Possibly. But she hadn't read anything about the driver being a marksman, too. If he had been, she felt it probably would have been mentioned in one of the three write-ups she'd found on the man.

So who did that leave? McGill. The man who already had a modest body count to his name. He also knew how to fight with his hands and feet. Video of him taking down that militia clown on the National Mall had shown just how quick he could be. Taps settled on the idea that he'd been the one to shoot Paulette.

He'd beaten his companions to the trigger.

Beating Paulette to the draw certainly would have been no challenge.

Even though Taps had been the one to send Paulette on a suicide mission, she felt anger at the idea that McGill had been the one to kill her. Who did the bastard think he was? Remaining seated in his car and letting his bodyguard do the dirty work, that would have been reasonable. Affording himself the visceral satisfaction of shedding blood, well, that was just another point of motivation for Taps to complete the job.

As a point of professionalism, Taps had demanded her entire fee to kill McGill up front.

She'd been paid. So she still had the responsibility of earning her keep. The additional effort, of course, would call for additional compensation. Part of which would now be a touch of revenge for Paulette. She watched the video of Paulette being shot again and then called Corona Moe in Mexico.

The man answered his phone personally.

Taps didn't know exactly where he lived. He'd only told her Mexico, but that didn't necessarily have to be so.

"*¿Sí?*" he said.

The man's Spanish was fluent but his accent was … hard to place.

When he spoke English, also without flaw, she thought there was almost a Middle Eastern note to his voice. With maybe a hint of a Texas twang. How that combination might have occurred Taps couldn't guess.

"You've heard?" she asked.

"Yes, Telemundo has run little else the past 24 hours."

"We have a better understanding of our challenges now. Given what happened, it would be a mistake to use the same type of personnel again."

No more *muertos,* she was telling him.

"Definitely. They will still have their uses at times, but we've clearly seen now they also have their limits."

"I think a solo operation would be best."

Taps took it for granted the client would not want to give up.

"Yes, that's been decided."

"I'll need only a slight bump in my fee. I have an —"

"You won't be needed at all this time."

"What?"

"It wasn't my choice," Moe said. "The client says he's found someone else."

Taps had no doubt there were other contract killers available. In fact, there were too damn many of them. Unlike 99.9% of the others, though … Shit, she was going to say she had a perfect record. Only she didn't. Not anymore.

She told Moe, "It wasn't *my* idea to use the others." Fucking *muertos.*

"I know. That was my call. My mistake."

Taps hissed, "But it's *my* reputation, and you said if anything went wrong I'd be able to get it right the next time."

Corona Moe sighed. "That is exactly what *I* was told, but now the client has changed his mind. He's found another contractor. I told him, of course, I will keep my money and you will keep yours. There's no question about that."

"That's not good enough," Taps said. "My record has been *damaged* here."

With all the hurt she'd endured, damage was the last thing Taps ever wanted to feel.

Moe must have intuited that *he* might well be in peril here. Taps would have to find him first and then get past his defenses, but not even he wanted a motivated killer making him a target. He said, "I truly didn't see any of this coming. I'll give you my fee as well, if you like."

That was the moment Taps realized she'd scared Corona Moe, and that did make her feel better. She told him where to wire the money. What she didn't say was that she would keep right on bleeding him if her business from new clients dried up.

To forestall the possibility of any professional downturn, she made another decision.

She'd target James J. McGill on her own initiative.

Kill him before this other damn contractor could.

The White House — Washington, DC

McGill told Odo Sacripant, "I'm glad to see you did your jail time without incurring any damage."

He, Odo, Yves Pruet and Gabbi Casale were drinking coffee as they sat at the table in the White House Family Dining Room. McGill and Gabbi took their liquid caffeine straight, Pruet and Odo added a splash of brandy. They would reconvene with their other partners later that morning at headquarters. The topic of discussion at that time would be whether the threat against McGill's life had been eliminated or merely postponed until further notice.

Odo told McGill, "And I am happy you survived your morning drive to work. I only wish I had been on hand to help. Well, Yves and me. I am sure he would have led the charge."

"Riding a white stallion, no doubt, and yelling, 'To arms, *mes chevaliers,*'" Pruet said dryly. "Either that or remembering my childhood prayers and beseeching the Almighty for our deliverance."

"Either would work for me," McGill said. "Now, if you'll forgive the intrusion of a little crime detection, I have something to show you." He picked up a manila envelope from an end table and sat in the middle of his long leather sofa. "Gather 'round."

Pruet stood to his right, Odo and Gabbi to his left.

McGill took a sheaf of 8x10 photographic prints out of the envelope.

McGill said, "The photo on top here is a screen capture from the video Leo shot from my car. The following three prints were provided by Dorie McBride, the woman who used to be the President's talent agent when she had her acting career."

He handed the first print to Pruet, who studied it and circulated the photo to Odo and Gabbi. The other pictures followed in the same sequence. Pruet and Odo closely inspected each likeness.

Gabbi, possessing an artist's eye and sensibility, examined the faces even more critically.

Pruet offered the first opinion. "At first, I thought I was seeing just one person, but upon reflection I think there are at least two people here and possibly a third."

"Three," Gabbi confirmed.

Being the last one to receive the photos, she sorted them out. She took the print McGill had said came from his car and matched it with the last image she'd received.

"These two are the same person," she said. "The others are of two additional people."

"She's right," McGill said. "Look at the back of each print."

Gabbi handed all four to Odo; he extended them, one at a time, to Pruet.

Each print was numbered on the back: two 1s, a 2 and a 3.

"*Oui,* now I see," Odo said.

"As do I," Pruet agreed.

"It is pretty damn close," McGill said. "Nobody can say for sure of what the odds are of giving birth to identical triplets but the old expression of 'one in a million' is considered to be as good a guess." He turned to Gabbi and asked. "What differences did you see?"

She said, "In shape and placement of the facial features, basically none."

"Might not that be the work of a talented surgeon?" Pruet asked.

"That was the considered opinion of the President, her former agent and me, at first," McGill said.

"What changed your mind?" Gabbi asked.

"The more I looked at the pictures," he said, "the less I could believe that any doctor, no matter how skilled, could sculpt human flesh and bone so consistently. The only thing that left was an extremely rare but natural occurrence." Turning back to Gabbi, he said, "You must have noticed some discrepancies to sort out these faces accurately."

She nodded. "Size. The distance between brows, the width

of the eyes, the diameter of the nostrils, the breadth of the lips, the density of the chins. These individuals look alike, but within a slight variation you can think of them as small, medium and large. It's like one of them, number 2, got the most nutrition from mom, *in utero,* and the other two each got a bit less."

McGill nodded. He was no doctor but he knew how things worked at most kitchen tables.

Gabbi told McGill, "You must have noticed the same differences I did."

He nodded. "Only it took me a lot longer, and I had to verify the idea with a ruler."

"Our would-be killer, number 1," Odo asked, "he or she is the smallest?"

Gabbi said, "That's right."

Odo said, "What I noticed about this person was not the size of the eyes but the emotion in them. With all three of these people it is hard to say if you are looking at a man or a woman, but if I were to ask you who among them has the greatest complaint against the world, which one would you choose?"

Viewed through that lens, the verdict was unanimous.

Number 1, the guy Leo was the first to spot.

"I should have caught that, too," Gabbi said.

"While I will be happy to hold all of your coats," Pruet added.

"Me, too," McGill said, "except I know how to hire good people."

"You have names for these people, *mon ami?*" Pruet asked.

"Professional names only. Number 2 is Kim Welles."

"Kim?" Odo asked. "This is a woman's name, no?"

"That or an Englishman's name," Gabbi said. "Like Kim Philby."

Pruet and Odo rolled their eyes as if to say, *Les Anglais.*

"Common Korean surname, too," McGill said, "but I don't see Asian features in these faces."

"Possibly a Swedish name also, now that I think of it," Odo allowed, "like their footballer, Kim Källström. He also played in our country for Rennes and Lyons, Yves."

Pruet shrugged. "I am a famous non-football fan, global or

American. But it could be this Kim is simply following a path of ambiguity."

McGill nodded. "Could be. Number 3 used the stage name Pat Rickey."

"Also a unisex name in America," Gabbi explained to the Frenchmen.

"Number 1," McGill said, "the person I think we want, she was called Chris Nevers. Dorie McBride said she couldn't find any recent show biz credits for either Pat or Chris, but Kim Welles does voice-over work in L.A. Gene Beck is on his way there to talk to her right now."

Gabbi frowned. "You know, I've been wondering about Gene. Not that I have anything against him personally, but he told me he did prison time."

"Me, too," Odo said.

"So how does a guy like that get a PI license anywhere in this country?" Gabbi asked.

McGill kept a straight face and bided his silence. Pruet laughed knowingly.

His merriment pulled back the curtain for Gabbi and Odo.

There was only one person in the country who could pardon a convicted person and erase a criminal record at will, though sometimes it was wise to be discreet about it. And tell her husband to do the same.

"Glad we got that cleared up," Gabbi said.

McGill nodded. "So let's hear from Odo how things went with Auric Ludwig."

Medstar Georgetown University Hospital — Washington, DC

"You're the only asshole who chickened out, Lester," Detective Marvin Meeker told the man sitting in the wheelchair with a cast on his left arm and right leg."

His name was Lester Maxwell. He'd been too heavily medicated to face questioning before that morning. Captain Rockelle Bullard looked on as her men had the first go at Lester.

Beemer added, "Even that little old lady tried to go out with her gun blazing. She didn't get a shot off but she sure as hell tried."

"Yeah, and *she* never played in the NFL," Meeker said with contempt.

That was an interesting fact the detectives had learned about their perp.

They'd taken the time to read the guy's stats before confronting him.

"Hell, man," Beemer said. "This guy wasn't a real player. He *punted* for the worst team in the league and got cut halfway through his second season. Had kicks returned for touchdowns in six straight games and he never made a single tackle in his whole pathetic career."

In response to the criticism of his football record, Lester told Beemer, "Hell, man, I'm sick and dyin', probably wasn't right even back in my rookie year. But in college I could kick the damn ball out of the stadium. Hang it high enough even your damn mama could get down the field on punt coverage."

Both Meeker and Beemer admired that bit of bravado, but they didn't let it show.

The memory of his glory years brought tears to Lester Maxwell's eyes. He was right about being deathly ill. He'd been examined by three doctors while his limbs were being set. One of the MDs, a young African-American woman, had charmed his medical history out of him. She even talked him into signing a release of his medical records.

The most relevant diagnosis in his records was sarcoidosis, an inflammatory disease that could affect multiple organs and in Lester's case was eating his lungs like a school of piranha. Among its other devastating effects, the disease could cause mental debilitation, including dementia, depression and psychosis.

There was no cure for sarcoidosis, and it was 16 times more likely to strike African-Americans than white people. The young doctor had made a point of telling that to the three black cops waiting to interrogate her patient.

While Lester was not carrying any government-issued identification — no doubt because somebody had told him they just wanted him to die and to be neither identified nor remembered — in the inside pocket of his suit coat he'd had a farewell letter accurately addressed to his sister, Sharona, and signed with his full name.

The whole of the letter read: *I'm gone by now. You take the money and run. Spend it any way you want. Your baby brother, Lester Maxwell.*

Rockelle Bullard moved her detectives away from Lester with a tilt of her head.

It was her turn to see if she could get anything helpful from the man before his misery came to an end and he went on to … Rockelle didn't know where. She just hoped there was something better waiting for most people. Maybe even this poor soul.

"We tried calling your sister, Lester," Rockelle said.

"I didn't give you no phone number … and I don't have no sister anyway."

"You wrote a letter to her. Told her to take the money and run."

Now, the tears in the man's eyes overflowed. He shook his head. "I don't have no sister."

"We checked the address on your letter." Rockelle held up the envelope. "Sharona Maxwell lives at the Richmond, Virginia street number you put on the envelope. Problem is, the phone number that goes with the address just rings and rings. Nobody answers."

Lester managed to swallow hard, no mean feat judging by the pain it seemed to cause him.

"You think maybe somebody found Sharona before she was able to run?" Rockelle asked.

Lester sobbed and started to shake.

Rockelle glanced at her detectives. Meeker and Beemer moved in close to the suffering man. Meeker said in an even tone, "Listen, man, maybe we had you wrong. Your big sister took care of you, right, and now you want to take care of her. That's steppin' up."

"Damn right," Beemer said. "Listen, you tell us if maybe Sharona's got another phone. We'll call her, let her know she better look out. If she's an upright person, we'll let the Richmond police know where she's at; they'll protect her."

Meeker added, "She has some trouble with the law, well, hell, we'll give her a head-start on everyone she needs to run from."

From some reservoir of character, Lester managed to summon a flash of anger. "Sharona's as upright as a Baptist church choir all by herself … I just don't want her to get killed on account of me."

He started to cry again, his energy for resistance exhausted.

Rockelle Bullard stepped forward. Meeker and Beemer glided away. All three cops knew every step of this situation's choreography.

"We understand your fear, Lester," Rockelle said. "We've seen it before, more times than we can count. What you need to know is right now Sharona's best chance of coming out of this without being laid to rest right next to you is to tell us everything you can, while you *still* can."

As far gone as he was, Lester knew Rockelle wasn't trying to comfort him.

She was just telling him straight how things were.

He started talking.

Both Meeker and Beemer had had their recorders on the whole time.

Now, they started writing down Lester's confession, too.

Florida Avenue — Washington, DC

The Pope answered Sweetie's call. Not that he picked up personally on the first ring or anything. Things were more complicated than that. Sweetie had never called Vatican City before, but she had called Putnam when he was outside the country. So she knew that you began an international call with the 011 prefix. After that, she'd learned from Father Desmond Nkrumah that the dialing code for Vatican City was 379. After that, all she could find was the Pope's fax number: 390669885373.

Making Putnam say, "Does anybody really still use faxes?"

Sweetie had him in their living room with her for moral support.

Then Putnam counseled, "If you want to talk to the Pope, you have to expect to fight his bureaucracy first. So hang in there."

A couple of hours into her quest, Sweetie managed to reach a monsignor who spoke English with a thick Italian accent. He told her, as best she could understand him, that His Holiness would read her fax eventually — if it was deemed important enough to require a moment of his precious time.

Okay, Sweetie thought, Francesco had over a billion communicants in the Church. Even the most outgoing shepherd would have trouble keeping in touch with all those souls, but the monsignor had struck her as a petty bureaucrat with an attitude of condescension. She wasn't going to get anywhere with him.

Having grown up in Chicago, Sweetie had learned that when dealing with any form of government, things went a whole lot better if you knew someone with clout, i.e. influence. So she curbed her exasperation and turned to the man who started the quest to find Father de Loyola, Cardinal Sean Fitzroy. She had to speak to only one secretary and mention Father de Loyola's name to reach him.

Fitzroy was pleased to hear from Sweetie that the papal message had been delivered.

"I'll pass the good news on to His Holiness," the cardinal said.

"You can reach him directly?" Sweetie asked.

After a momentary pause, he said, "Yes, I have that privilege. May I know why you ask?"

"Father de Loyola asked me to speak to His Holiness on his behalf."

Cardinal Fitzroy chuckled. "Well, isn't that just like him?"

"You know Father de Loyola?" Sweetie asked.

The cardinal sighed audibly. "To be honest, as the Ninth Commandment instructs us, Inigo and I had many a fine argument during the year we spent together at the Vatican. The subject was what the Church's role should be when it found itself in the midst of violent upheavals, whether they occurred in Central America or

Northern Ireland."

Sweetie was surprised the cardinal was so forthcoming. "Your Eminence, I can see only two ways for me to go here. You can give me the number for a direct line to His Holiness or I can give you a phone number to Father de Loyola and you can work things out with him."

The cardinal chose not to engage further with his old debating partner.

Sweetie got the phone number, after making a solemn promise never to share it with anyone. The connection was made with almost heavenly speed. Another Italian cleric, this one with much better English, answered. Sweetie introduced herself and gave the reason for her call. The only thing she was asked was, "Is English your only language?"

"Yes."

"Very well. I will speak to His Holiness. One of us will be with you shortly."

Sweetie held on, having enough time to think she'd have to call Father de Loyola and tell him —

"I am told your name is Margaret Sweeney," a gentle voice with a Hispanic accent said, and Sweetie felt a chill run down her spine. She looked at Putnam, her eyes wide, and gave him a nod. "You have spoken with my old friend Inigo and he gave you a message for me?"

Sweetie told him what it was.

The pause on the other end of the line was long enough to make her wonder if the connection was still live. Just before she was about to ask if he was still on the line, the voice asked, "May I count on your discretion, Margaret? What I have to ask of Inigo is the most personal of matters."

Hearing that chilled Sweetie. "Your Holiness, I have to tell you again that Father de Loyola asked me to call because he was afraid you might want something he couldn't do. Not because he wouldn't want to but because he wouldn't be able."

To her surprise, Sweetie heard a soft laugh. "*¡Ay, qué pícaro es Inigo!*"

Sweetie hadn't exactly lied to the cleric who'd answered the phone. She wasn't conversant in Spanish — or any other foreign language — but she had a smattering. She was pretty sure the Pope had just called Father de Loyola a joker.

"Your Holiness?" Sweetie said.

"I will ask you to be so kind as to give Father de Loyola a message from me, but first please tell me a little about yourself, who you are, what you do, how you live your life. If I am being too personal, please just let me know."

Sweetie didn't mind sharing. She gave a capsule version of her life moving along briskly … until her voice caught in her throat and she started to speak of her idea of putting Joan Renshaw into Erna Godfrey's prison cell, causing Erna's death. Then Sweetie broke down in tears.

Putnam started to move toward Sweetie to take her into his arms, but she held up a hand and he reluctantly returned to his chair, watching closely to see if the moment came when she needed to be comforted regardless of any objection.

He leaned forward and listened carefully as Sweetie poured her heart out. Not a Catholic, Putnam had nonetheless learned the norms of going to confession, confidentiality being high among them. Nonetheless, he was sure he was witnessing a sacrament in progress.

Sweetie tearily said her piece and then listened to the warm, understanding voice reaching out across the world to her. In it she found forgiveness, not only from a good and holy man but also from the higher power that spoke through him.

Drying her tears with the cuff of a sleeve, she said, "Yes, of course. I'll tell him and make it clear to him that he should make the next call." Sweetie listened a moment and then laughed. "Absolutely. If it's alright with them, it will be my pleasure."

She said goodbye, put down the phone, stood and beckoned Putnam.

He held her for a long time.

"You're okay now?" he asked.

"Yes, I am."

"No more guilt about Erna Godfrey?"

"None. That's done."

Putnam knew better than to pry, but he couldn't help but ask: "So how does the Pope make a girl laugh?"

Sweetie grinned. "He asked if I might lend a hand, if the Swiss Guard ever needed help with a case."

The White House — Washington, DC

Taking the discussion with his Paris office colleagues to his Hideaway, McGill asked Odo, "Did Auric Ludwig confide in you that he set up the attempt on my life? I can only hope that he did."

Odo shook his head. "Regrettably, he did not."

"Damn."

Odo grinned. "What he did was ask *me* to kill you."

McGill laughed. "I hope you didn't turn him down."

"I …" The Corsican turned to Pruet to ask for help with an American idiom.

Pruet told McGill, "Odo strung him along."

"Oui," Odo said. "I expressed interest but did not yet make a commitment. I thought this to be the subtle approach, the most effective lure."

McGill nodded. "Very well played."

Odo continued, "Ludwig told me to contact him through a guard. So we will seize that fellow, turn him inside out for all he knows and then have him pass the word along to Ludwig that I am interested in committing your murder."

Pruet shook his head. "Have the guard pass the message of your interest first and then question him. We don't want Ludwig to smell anything wrong."

McGill agreed. "If we get Ludwig on conspiracy to commit a homicide, he'll die behind bars, and we can insist on aggressive monitoring of any contact he has with the outside world. We can't ask for more than that."

Pruet said, “There is also the not so small comfort that Odo won’t try to kill you, and we can hope that will be the last of the threats against your life.”

Maybe, McGill thought.

“We still have to get Corona Moe,” Gabbi said, voicing McGill’s thought.

“Can’t forget about Chris Nevers either,” McGill added. “Our mystery man and/or woman.”

The Yates Home — Washington, DC

General Welborn Yates went straight home after returning to Washington from Costa Rica with Margaret Sweeney. He wanted to see all three of his girls, hold them in his arms, individually and en masse. He’d been gone fewer than 72 hours, but he still felt an urgent need to be with his family. Welborn thought he’d have to toughen up on the home front before too long. He couldn’t sit around and weep all day when Aria and Callista went off to college.

A lachrymose demeanor also wasn’t a good look for a general, military investigator and one-time fighter pilot. Even if he left his military career behind, there was a certain code of machismo to be observed as a civilian private investigator. Having adjusted his attitude, Welborn held his emotions in check when he stepped through his front door and found his house empty.

He spotted a note from Kira in the kitchen, fixed to the fridge with a magnet in the shape of an F-22, his old plane. The message was dated as of that morning.

Flyboy,

The girls and I have run off with a polo-playing Argentinian billionaire. In the event his charm wears thin quickly, we’ll ditch him, steal his AMG Mercedes and head for Gymboree, Whole Foods and the new Smurf movie. Hope you’ll be home by the time we get back. Those South American moneybags rarely take no for an answer.

K.

Welborn responded by a more contemporary means: texting.

My beloved, all I've ever wished for is your happiness. If you've lost your heart to another, who am to I stand in your way? I'll even pay for your flamenco lessons. As to living in Argentina, would you rather have our girls grow up to be Evita or Patti Grant?

Yours always, Welborn.

P.S. While you're Smurfing, I'll be at the White House keeping the nation safe.

Enjoying the pleasure of bantering with his wife, even indirectly, lifted Welborn's sense of well being. He showered, changed his clothes and drove to the White House. As he approached the iconic building, he realized he was going to miss the place.

There was the professional cachet of having a job at 1600 Pennsylvania Avenue, of course. What mattered more to Welborn, though, was that if you worked hard under that roof, and had the good fortune of laboring for a President who put the country's needs first, you felt like you'd done your part in keeping the Founders' experiment in democracy going. Even if you didn't rate a footnote in the nation's history, being a mere punctuation mark could still be satisfying.

Welborn had just planted himself behind his desk and was booting up his desktop computer when his cell phone chimed.

Kira said, "Welcome home, flyboy. You didn't make any moves on your older woman traveling companion, did you?"

"None that she either accepted or even noticed."

"Well, I suppose subliminal stuff is okay."

Welborn asked, "No movie for you and the girls?"

"After whirling like dervishes for an hour, shopping and eating at Whole Foods, they'd had enough for one day. I'm thinking about napping myself. Haven't you earned a little time off, too, or is the crisis *du jour* still in progress?"

"I just stepped into my office, but the President wasn't waiting at my desk for my arrival. I suppose I could check in with Frank Morrissey and see if I might take the rest of the day off."

"I'll be warming our bed in case you can make it. Don't wake me, just snuggle up close. We'll see what two people can do in their sleep. Without waking the small fry."

With that picture firmly in mind, Welborn reached out to turn off his computer not bothering to see if anything important was waiting for his attention. His finger stopped just short of the mouse-click. He thought to himself: It wouldn't hurt to take one quick peek, would it? He could handle the demands of both job and family, couldn't he?

Sure, he could.

He opened his email and there it was: a reply from the CIA about the person Mr. McGill — his soon-to-be new boss? — had asked about. The Agency said Interpol unofficially suspected this individual of killing ten people in eight countries around the world. A half-dozen grainy closed circuit street photos of the individual didn't define a specific gender.

Even Welborn's fighter-pilot 20/10 vision and lifelong appreciation of the feminine form couldn't bring the matter to a conclusion. Overall, the new material seemed to reinforce what he'd received from MI-6 and passed along already. Maybe someone with a medical or anthropological background could spot a difference.

Welborn called Edwina Byington — the President's secretary made a point of knowing when Mr. McGill was in the building — and she told him McGill was out as of minutes ago.

Welborn tapped in McGill's cell phone number but his call went to voice-mail.

Damn.

Welborn got the President's secretary back on the line. "Edwina, I have some classified material that Mr. McGill asked for."

"And he's nowhere to be found?"

"Right. I'd take it to him if I knew where he was, but —"

"You'd like to know if the President could hold on to it, reasoning she might be someone he'd contact sooner rather than later."

"Exactly," Welborn said.

"I won't ask if you have other pressing matters of your own."

"Emily Post could take lessons from you, Ms. Byington."

"I believe she passed on quite some time ago, but thank you for the compliment."

"I'll be right by with the material," Welborn said.

He hurried to the Oval Office with the photos and information he had downloaded to a thumb drive. Edwina accepted delivery and said she'd pass the drive along to the President momentarily. Welborn bowed to her and scooted for the nearest exit.

Would it be possible, he wondered, to slip into bed without waking Kira?

And could he fake anything even approaching an Argentinian accent?

Hamilton, Bermuda

The weather in the British Overseas Territory was sunny and a heavenly 74° Fahrenheit. A soft breeze out of the west felt like a lover's caress. At odds with his surroundings, Giles Henry squatted like a poisonous toad at a secluded garden table on the lush grounds of the Royal Palms Hotel. His pallid, jowly, blemished face showed not a hint of ever being touched by solar rays. His eyelids blinked constantly as if sending out a signal-lamp distress call.

His clothing was rumpled, soiled and meant for a far chillier climate.

Henry cared not a whit about the repulsive image he presented to the world. His American Express Centurion Card had carried him in style from Scotland to Bermuda and had been accepted gladly at the Royal Palms. The hotel's manager had offered to have Henry's suit cleaned and pressed while he enjoyed a nice soak in his suite's whirlpool bath and perhaps a massage. If he was interested, a cosmetician and a barber might be sent in for a facial and a haircut. A manicurist was also available and —

Henry would have none of it. He asked only for a table in a sheltered spot on the hotel's grounds and to have a visitor directed to him the moment she arrived. For a disquieting heartbeat, the manager feared Henry and his guest might have some unspeakable *au naturel* act in mind. Centurion Card or not, the hotel had its reputation to safeguard.

Henry read the emotion on the man's face precisely, and it gave him the first laugh he'd had in days. Nonetheless, he set the fellow straight. "My guest is a very important political figure from the United States. We have confidential matters to discuss. Please see to it that no one is seated close enough to us to overhear our conversation."

Greatly relieved, the manager promised both comfort and the utmost privacy.

Henry, once he was ensconced in a hidden garden nook, asked for a glass of ginger ale. Gassy swill, he thought to himself, but his throat was parched and he needed to be able to speak clearly. He had it in mind to take his revenge on Galia Mindel, and that would require clarity of both his voice box and his mind.

The ginger ale was brought quickly by a smiling local girl.

She asked, "Would you like me to stop back to take your guest's order and refresh your drink, sir, or do you wish not to be disturbed at all?"

"Wouldn't be courteous not to offer a guest a drink, would it?"

"No, sir."

"Once that bit of business is out of the way, then leave us undisturbed. But once my guest departs, please return. At that point, I will need another drink."

"Yes, sir."

Henry was barely halfway through choking down his soft drink when a dark-haired woman he estimated to be in her mid-30s appeared at the entrance to his semi-tropical nook. She may not have been everything he desired in a woman — sadly she didn't seem the type whose favors might be purchased — but she came damn close.

Beside her physical appeal, she was properly dressed for a resort hotel.

"Layla Dart," she said by way of introduction — without extending her hand.

"Giles Henry. Please be seated."

"I came a long way, Mr. Henry. I hope you're not going to disappoint me."

The tabloid reporter only shrugged. "I believe I have a story for you that might help Senator Oren Worth win the presidency. Is that worth your time and trouble?"

Layla Dart smiled and took the open seat and crossed her legs, giving Henry a good look at a sleek thigh. That was simply a sign of confidence in herself not an offer of things to come, Henry knew. The damn woman probably had her own Centurion Card.

The waitress appeared with a fresh glass of ginger ale for Henry.

Layla Dart took note of it and declined the offer of a drink for herself.

Once they were alone again, Layla asked, "How bad is it?"

"What?"

"The shakes, the dry mouth, the blurred vision, the wandering mental focus and diminished attention span. Hell, the lack of bladder control. Will we be able to have a conversation without you peeing yourself?"

As Henry searched for a reply, Layla added, "You're a longtime alcoholic trying to be at the top of your game for an important meeting. What you should be doing is having just one drink while keeping things brief enough to finish your pitch before you need a second drink."

Henry choked out a phlegmy laugh. "The interval between drinks would be quite short." He studied the woman's face. "You don't know the problem personally, but you have seen it at close range. You wouldn't tolerate it from a boyfriend or a husband. That leaves only … family."

"Wandering attention," Layla said. "Let's stay on point or I'll chalk this up as a bet that didn't pay off."

Henry took a hit off his fresh soft drink and made a face of disgust.

"Very well," he said. "I found Senator Randall Pennyman and the two of us had quite an interesting chat. He told me things that could determine who gets to be your next president. As you are Senator Worth's latest campaign manager, I thought that might be of interest to you."

Layla's eyes narrowed. "How do I know this isn't just a set-up? Something Galia Mindel cooked up to make my guy look like a fool."

Henry laughed hard enough to bring up a vile gob from his throat, which he spat into the meticulously tended foliage. He was pleased to see that Layla Dart had the mettle — and likely the experience — not to flee in disgust.

He said, "Galia Mindel is exactly the shrew I intend to destroy, along with anyone close to her politically, which I believe would include your candidate's opponent, Vice President Jean Morrissey. Now, have I tickled your interest?"

Layla smiled. "For an old soak of a drunk, you still have a bit of your game left. So getting your revenge on Galia will turn out to be a gift to me. Is that what you're saying?"

"Well, I wouldn't mind a brief tour inside your knickers being part of the negotiations, but I don't think you'd go that far."

She shook her head. "Not even if you were dry-cleaned, pressed and wore a titanium condom."

Henry laughed. "That's quite the picture you paint, but you're right. Truth is, I long ago lost the ability to pleasure either a woman or myself in that fashion."

"So tell your story and then you can have the real drink you're dying for. Hell, for all I know, you could have your dying binge all mapped out. Expire in a nice place like this."

The tabloid reporter shook his head. "Bermuda is the closest British possession to the U.S. Just out of reach of your federal coppers. So you see I was really quite considerate, asking you to come here."

"Great. You're a gentleman when you're not out to screw somebody. I still have a lot to do, so let's get on with it."

"Very well. Senator Pennyman told me his crimes were revealed by Galia Mindel after he dared to say he might vote for the conviction of President Grant after she'd been impeached. The example she'd made of him whipped the others into line because Galia Mindel, like Satan, knows everyone's sins. Most importantly, all the misdeeds of everybody in your government. Pennyman said Ms. Mindel makes J. Edgar Hoover look like a small-time extortionist."

Henry coughed up and disposed of another wad. Then he directed a revolting smile at Layla. "I did a bit of research to understand Pennyman's characterization of his nemesis. I found it to be inadequate. To my mind, Nero was an amateur arsonist compared to Galia Mindel and the firestorm she might cause in Washington. So I pitched the story to a publishing house in London. They jumped at the idea. Offered money unlike anything I'd ever known."

Layla knew there was a catch. "Only?"

"Only my bloody publisher canceled my deal when they were informed Galia Mindel was going to publish her memoirs and tell all."

"She's going to white-wash the story," Layla said.

Henry said, "My guess is she'll admit just enough wickedness to titillate the masses while not incriminating herself to the degree where her arse might land in prison."

Layla could see that. "So she undercut you while writing a book that will probably become a movie, and she'll make a pile of money from both."

"Bright girl," Henry said, "You not her. Well, hell, her, too."

"Yeah." Layla smiled. "You don't have enough time left to expose all her BS, but I do. I start with Pennyman and … hell, I could make up the rest from there, if I wanted. Every denial she made would only make her look worse. Make Patti Grant look worse."

"And?" Henry asked.

Layla knew just where the old soak wanted her to go. "And it's a sure bet Galia Mindel shared enough of her dirt with Frank Morrissey so that he can use it to protect his sister when she's sitting in the Oval Office. Only now both Jean and Frank Morrissey can be tarred with the same brush as Galia Mindel. Damn, Giles Henry, you may have given my guy the presidency."

"You're quite welcome," Henry said.

"Yeah, thanks. So where can I put my hands on Senator Randall Pennyman?"

"All the information you'll need is in an envelope with your name on it at the front desk."

Never one to waste time, Layla got to her feet. "So what do you get out of this? You'll have drunk yourself to death before we get to the good part."

"I get the boundless joy of believing you *will* get to the good part. I did my research on you, too. If you don't mind, though, I would like you to answer one question."

"What?"

"I didn't look into your forebears, so please tell me: Was your father or your mother the falling down drunk in your family?"

Layla didn't flinch. "Both."

She turned and left.

Giles Henry called for a bottle of rum.

Caught up in silent rejoicing over the magnificent gift she'd been given, Layla didn't notice the small man following her back to the airport.

McGill's Chevy motoring — Washington, DC

McGill and Sweetie sat in the back of McGill's Chevy. She was taking Gene Beck's place as the fourth armed individual in the car. At the invitation of Captain Rockelle Bullard of the Metro Police Department, they were on their way to watch the captain and her two senior detectives confront Zoë Tinker, the late Aubrey Gadsden's psychotherapist. The captain had no objections to Sweetie tagging along.

"The more cops the merrier," Rockelle had said. "What we're going for here is a lot of intimidation and a quick 'I give up.'"

On the way to the shrink's office, where an MPD patrol unit had reported her presence, McGill recounted to Sweetie the shootout in Georgetown from his point of view. She listened without interruption. Deke and Leo also paid attention, comparing the boss's recall to their own memories.

When McGill finished, Sweetie briefly placed a hand on Leo's right shoulder and on Deke's left shoulder. "Nice going, guys. I wish I'd been there with you."

Both of the men up front spared her a glance.

"You'd have kept him in the car?" Deke asked.

"Possibly," Sweetie said. "Might've had to sit on his lap to do it."

Leo guffawed; even Deke chuckled.

"Don't think he'd let either of us get away with that," Leo said.

Even McGill laughed now.

He also thought the time was right to change the subject.

He said to Sweetie, "So you found Father de Loyola without too much trouble. Gave him Cardinal Fitzroy's message and —"

"Had a nice little chat with the Pope just before you and the guys stopped by."

"What?" McGill said. "You're kidding, right?"

Sweetie shook her head.

"Father de Loyola asked me to give His Holiness a message. Seems the two of them go way back. I had a heckuva time getting through, but Cardinal Fitzroy fixed it."

"Huh," McGill said. "So is the Pope a lively conversationalist or was it just a quick *grazie* and *arrivederci?*"

Sweetie said, "Well, I gave him Father de Loyola's message and his phone number in Costa Rica so the two of them can speak directly, and then he asked me to tell him about myself. You know, I never met either of my grandfathers, but that's who I felt like I was talking to, one of them. A kind old guy who knew more about life than I could ever guess. I … I told him about Erna Godfrey. After that, without even thinking about it, things got sacramental between us. So I can't really say more, except that I feel better than I have since Erna died. I don't blame myself anymore."

McGill squeezed his old friend's hand.

"I'm happy to hear that."

He was also envious. At the moment, he was the one feeling

guilty for taking Paulette Lacroix's life. The capsule biography he'd been given by the Secret Service described her life as a constant struggle: poverty, drugs, prostitution, rehab, relapse and finally a terminal illness terminated by McGill's gunshot.

He'd yet to make a visit to his confessor, but that would have to come soon.

Still, he couldn't help but wonder what the Pope might have told him had he followed through personally on Cardinal Fitzroy's request. He'd have to be careful from now on about what tasks he delegated to others. Still, he felt good that Sweetie seemed to be her old self again.

Zoë Tinker's Office — Washington, DC

Rockelle Bullard and crew found Zoë Tinker in her office and the captain told her, "What you said to me was: 'The confidentiality privilege transfers to the legal representative of the deceased. If I receive the appropriate authorization from that person, I'll talk to you.' I wrote that down word for word in my notebook, Dr. Tinker. Now, I have not only written permission from Mr. Gadsden's sole surviving blood relative, his mother, to talk with you but also to read any medical records you may have produced referring to her son's treatment."

Sitting behind her desk, the psychologist's darting eyes and white-knuckled grip on the arms of her chair said she knew she was in the midst of a fight-or-flight situation. Only she didn't see a realistic chance of doing either. It would have been hard enough for her to brazen out the situation if Rockelle had been there by herself.

Only the captain wasn't alone. She had her two detectives with her, along with a guy who'd been introduced as a Secret Service special agent, a blonde woman who looked like she could be yet another cop and the President's husband, James J. McGill.

Facing that line-up, there was no way she could keep her cool.

She started to say something, but Rockelle held up an admonitory finger.

"Do *not* lie to me, Doctor," she said. "I'll charge you with hindering an investigation if you do, and Special Agent Ky might throw in a federal charge. That'd tack on another five years to any sentence you might receive. So if you were going to say Mr. Gadsden's records somehow got destroyed or even just misplaced, that story will just bring you a world of grief, and things aren't looking that good for you as it is. You are a suspect in a homicide investigation, and things don't get any more serious than that."

Deke raised a hand. "Captain, if I may."

"Certainly, Special Agent Ky."

Deke leaned forward, giving the shrink a hard stare. "Things, in fact, can get much worse if you aided in the attempt on the life of the President's husband. If you're found guilty of that charge, you'll be put into the deepest, darkest hole in the federal prison system. The sun will burn itself out before you ever get to see it again."

Detectives Meeker and Beemer exchanged a brief glance, each of them thinking the same thing: *Damn, that was a good threat. Gotta remember that one.*

In a small voice, Zoë Tinker said, "All I was going to say is I didn't know Aubrey had a mother. He told me he lost her years ago."

Rockelle chuckled and shook her head. "All your education and you never learned people sometimes speak figuratively."

Beemer said, "I believe people in your line of work call that kinda loss alienation."

Dr. Tinker began to weep.

Meeker leaned in and said, "Let me put this in a metaphor you'll be sure to understand, Doc. The point we've reached right here at this very moment, it's called game, set and match. The competition's over and you lost."

That summed things up, but there was still time for Sweetie to make an observation and ask a question. "You know, Dr. Tinker, up until a few minutes ago, before you went all pale, you had a nice golden glow on your face. You take a little vacation somewhere warm recently?"

"Remember now," Rockelle told Zoë, "not even a fib if you know what's good for you."

And that was when Zoë Tinker finally found an escape route. She passed out.

The Oval Office — Washington, DC

McGill didn't know it. Deke didn't know it. Not even Leo knew it. SAC Elspeth Kendry did and so did the President. In fact, Patricia Grant had given her approval to the idea Elspeth had brought to her.

"Madam President," Elspeth had said, "while discussing the possibility that a catastrophic event might befall Mr. McGill as he's traveling in his government-provided vehicle, the thought was advanced that the Secret Service should know where his vehicle is at all times — the better to provide rapid, perhaps life-saving, assistance."

The President had laughed mirthlessly and said, "I thought Jim's Chevrolet was supposed to be catastrophe-proof."

"The best laid plans of mice and men, Madam President."

"Gang aft a-ley," she replied, using Robert Burns' original language for the poem. "An' lea'e us naught but grief an' pain."

It was a rare thing for the President to show off her fancy education, but Elspeth fastened on the relevancy of the phrase. "Yes, ma'am, it's the grief and pain we want to avoid."

"I won't argue that. I'm just surprised Celsus Crogher didn't come up with this plan, bugging Jim's car, a long time ago."

"He did, ma'am. He was the one with whom I discussed it. He just couldn't bring himself to share it with you."

"But you didn't worry about suffering professionally for mentioning the idea: that I should let you snoop on my husband,"

Elspeth wanted to shrug but restrained herself. "Women can be more practical, can't we, ma'am? If something is really important, damn the consequences."

The President smiled. Playing the sisterhood card was a shrewd move. "Well, some of us are more practical. I don't know that I would apply the rule gender-wide."

Still, Patricia Grant gave the go-ahead, limiting knowledge of the situation to herself, Elspeth and the technician who installed the tracking device, another woman.

So the President knew where Jim's Chevrolet was right now, parked outside a medical office building adjacent to MedStar Georgetown University Hospital. Presumably, her husband was in the immediate vicinity. Reflecting upon the snooping she'd sanctioned, she thought she would wait at least five years to tell Jim about it … and possibly not mention it at all.

What she intended to do in the next minute or two was call him.

The President had closely reviewed the photos and dossier Welborn had received from Interpol via the CIA and passed on to her. The grainy images of the suspected contract killer chilled her. There was nothing disfigured about the facial features, the torso or the limbs. In fact, there was almost a machined quality to the overall appearance.

Symmetrical, smooth and sinister.

Patricia Grant knew from her days in both modeling and acting that *all* of the world's so-called most beautiful people had revised at least one physical flaw. She, herself, had spent two years under an orthodontist's care. Hair, eyes, noses, cheeks and chins were also subject to modification to meet contemporary ideals of beauty. Nobody had the complete head-to-toe package naturally because the criteria changed with the times.

What was in one year was out the next. Notions of physical perfection didn't change as quickly as clothing styles, but the lag time wasn't that much longer. That was what bothered her about the photos she'd examined.

It was as if the suspected killer had honed herself — himself? — down to a nub of the human form. Not quite a stick figure, but a subtly rounded version of one. Where was the room for humanity in such an outline?

With this person it was in the eyes. Shakespeare said, "The eyes are the window to your soul." Scientists hypothesized that patterns in the iris might indicate whether a person was warm and trusting or neurotic and impulsive. Even small children could divine whether their mothers' eyes held boundless love or impatient anger.

Patricia Grant thought she could see two things clearly even in the low-resolution photos she had to work with: boiling anger and profound self-loathing. Each of those sentiments might be a motivation for murder. The combination made her fear that despite the failed attempt on Jim's life he was still in grave danger.

Elspeth, in her fervor for maintaining contact with James J. McGill, had added an app to the President's personal cell phone. It let the President turn on McGill's phone and make it ring even if it was powered off. Short of the loss or physical destruction of Jim's phone, she should always be able to reach him.

Patricia Grant decided she'd waited long enough to speak to her husband and made the call.

McGill's Chevy motoring — Washington, DC

McGill was in his Chevy with Sweetie, Deke and Leo heading back to the office when the call from Patti came through. Captain Bullard had just placed Zoë Tinker under arrest, the charge being suspicion of complicity in the murder of Aubrey Gadsden. A copy of the next of kin's grant of permission to search Dr. Tinker's treatment records for the deceased was forwarded to the U.S. Attorney for the District of Columbia. Unlike any other American city, DC was under the exclusive jurisdiction of the United States Congress.

The locals, both police and residents, often chafed under that circumstance, but the conservatives in Congress were never going to let the liberal city have statehood and its own two senators and a voting member of the House of Representatives. Their position flew in the face of the historical grievance of taxation without representation.

At the moment, it was a political gripe that wasn't McGill's concern.

Even when preoccupied, though, he was happy to speak to his wife.

“Madam President,” he said, “how may I brighten your day?”

“Tell me you’re alive, well and likely to remain so.”

“I am well and in all likelihood will continue in fine fashion. I have Deke, Leo and Sweetie with me and I’m riding in one of the finest automobiles our country has ever produced.”

“Sweetie’s gone back to work?” Patti asked.

Overhearing the question, Sweetie leaned in and said, “Yes, hello.”

Patti replied in kind and continued her conversation with McGill.

“Welborn received a number of photos from Interpol via the CIA. They show a person who’s suspected of a number of murders in the UK, Germany, Australia and New Zealand. From what I’ve seen of the still photos taken from the video Leo shot, it seems to be the same individual who was …” Patti hesitated a moment. “I think stalking would be the right verb, Jim. Stalking you.”

“Yeah, that works,” McGill agreed. “So there was an androgynous appearance to the suspect in the foreign murders? Just like my guy. I use the male reference colloquially.”

Possessed of good hearing, Sweetie had kept up with the President’s end of the conversation and said, “Also, the majority of killers are still men. That’s one measure of equality we don’t need.”

“Indeed,” the President said. “Yes, Jim. I think it’s the same individual.”

“How’d the foreign cops make the connection?” McGill asked.

“According to the summary I read, they used the Big Brother method. They compiled all the images taken by street-view closed circuit cameras within a two-mile radius of where the bodies were found for a period of 48 hours before and 24 hours after the time of death. Then face-matching software looked for matches from one country to the next. Only one person appeared in all the countries where the murders occurred. Moreover, the time-frame was two hours, not seventy-two. This person moves very quickly. The problem is, he or she doesn't appear to exist in any official records, not even a passport photo."

McGill said, "Just off the top of my head, maybe a beard and some bushy eyebrows might be a disguise used for traveling. If this person had the skills to make that kind of a dodge look real, not hokey, how many immigrations and customs people would notice?"

"Laggard that I am," the President said, "I never thought to ask our ICE people about that. Given current circumstances, however, I feel sure they'd be watchful for men sporting untrimmed Middle Eastern-type beards."

"Yeah, that'd be a good bet. But what about a substantial yet well-barbered beard? Maybe Dorie McBride could recommend a make-up artist who could suggest a facial hair style that would work for this individual. Knock off a couple of images and —"

"Run those mock-ups against a database of the passport photos of people entering our country and the other countries where the murders in question occurred," the President said. "I think I'm starting to get the hang of this detective business."

McGill said, "I wouldn't be surprised. This Interpol data matches up pretty well with the MI6 information that Welborn got courtesy of his father. The Brits noticed this killer worked predominantly in their Commonwealth countries. Hearing that for a second time now makes me think there's a prominent member of that club just above our border to the north."

"Canada."

"Right," McGill said. "Maybe that's the bad guy's home. A big wide open place to run and hide if things get dicey. So he doesn't do any damage up there or in our country until recently. You think you might ask their PM for a little help checking their nationals' passport photos once you get the mock-ups of what the bad guy's disguise might look like? If he traveled at the right times to the places where he made hits around the world, that would look seriously interesting."

The President said, "Yes, it would. You are one smart gumshoe, Jim."

"All the girls tell me that, but you're the only one who makes me blush."

"Good. Then please listen to one other thing I noticed. All the Interpol people looking at this series of murders concluded that the killer works alone. That was far from the case with the attempt on your life."

"Right. That was the original word Gene Beck got. This Corona Moe guy was convinced trying to kill me wasn't a one-man job. Gene got that from a sickly ne'erdowell who wisely chose not to participate."

The President said, "It's understandable, wanting to mount a large force against you. However, that wasn't the way our gender-neutral assassin was used to working. Maybe stepping out of his or her comfort zone was what led things to go wrong."

"Let's give a lot of credit to Leo," McGill said.

"Certainly, but what if a plan had been hatched that didn't involve Leo's presence or maybe even Special Agent Ky's? What we know, or suspect, is this Commonwealth killer has struck eight to ten times, apparently alone, and succeeded with appalling efficiency. Maybe if left to his or her own devices ..."

The President didn't wish to verbalize her line of thought's conclusion.

McGill did so. "I might be dead. You think there's going to be a second attempt?"

That notion still ticked off McGill.

The President said, "My job has trained me to look for worst-case scenarios."

"Maybe we should both go somewhere and hide," he said.

"Neither of us works that way."

"So we just have to be real careful?"

"That and keep our friends close. Also, be as smart and well informed as we can. Jim, have you ever heard of the term intersex?"

"No, and I don't even want to make a guess."

"Fair enough. While I was looking at the Interpol photos, I compared them to the pictures Dorie provided us."

"The triplets," McGill said.

"Yes. Doing that, I was reminded of someone else I knew briefly in L.A. while I was acting. This person had done only a few bit parts as far as I know. I later heard the person committed suicide. I thought how awful. Then I heard the backstory and it was even worse."

The President told McGill the tale, letting him know just what intersex meant.

McGill Investigations International, LLP — Washington, DC

Monty Kipp's executive assistant Esme Thrice was waiting for McGill in his outer office when he and Sweetie returned to his new digs. Dikki Missirian was chatting amiably with her and must have let her in. Seeing McGill and Sweetie, Dikki and Esme stood.

Dikki said, "Mr. McGill, this charming young woman would like to speak with you. I told her you were out but —"

"I told Dikki I had no other appointments so I wouldn't mind waiting," she said. "He was kind enough to keep me company."

Smart enough not to let someone he didn't know linger unattended in the building, McGill thought. His other gumshoes weren't due back at headquarters until later. He said, "Dikki's a prince, alright. How may I be of help, Ms. Thrice?"

"Monty asked me to let you know he's turned in his resignation at SNAM. He's on his way back to England. He asked me to express his gratitude to you for not shooting him over the years. He also said not to bother thinking you owe him anything as he was unable to provide the help you requested." Pausing for just a moment, she added, "He also said if anyone else deserved to have me work for him, it's you. If you think that's too pushy of either Monty or me, I apologize."

McGill mulled that idea for a moment and said, "Let me make a quick call."

He stepped into his personal office and closed the door behind him.

Sweetie filled the opening in the conversation by introducing herself to Esme.

Once he had his privacy, McGill speed-dialed Edwina Byington.

The President's personal secretary answered on the first ring. "Hello, Mr. McGill. The President is speaking with her new chief of staff at the moment. May I take a message?"

McGill got right to it. "I'm calling to speak with you, Edwina. I'd like to know if you'd care to work for me after the President leaves the White House."

The reply was just as direct. "I'm sorry, sir, I can't do that. I've already told the President she's the only one I'd continue to serve and …" Edwina fell silent momentarily. "I'm not supposed to tell anyone but she offered me the position of being her executive assistant at Committed Capital. I said yes, but you didn't hear it from me."

McGill smiled. "Mum's the word. Congratulations, Edwina."

He opened his office door and said, "Sweetie, Ms. Thrice, please come in. Have a seat."

He thanked Dikki and gave him a nod, letting him know he'd handled the situation well. McGill closed the door and sat behind his desk. He looked at Esme and asked, "Do you really think Monty will retire?"

"No, sir. I'd say he's going to set up his own platform, anything from a blog to a podcast to a TV show, depending on the level of monetary backing he can get."

"Monty Kipp, unshackled?" McGill asked.

"Something like that. He feels he's in physical decline, might not have much time left."

"Are there medical opinions to back that up?"

"I didn't think it was my place to ask, but I've worked for Monty for three years and I've never scheduled a single doctor's appointment for him. Personally, I think he'll be around to report on the Second Coming."

McGill grinned. "Demanding proof that the Savior can, in fact, turn water into wine."

"Suggesting his favorite vintage, too," Esme said, playing along.

McGill liked that, someone with wit. He asked if she had a résumé he might see. She took an iPad out of her purse, pulled up the document and handed the tablet to him. McGill read the education line and looked up. "You're a DePaul alumna?"

DePaul being McGill's alma mater.

"Yes, sir."

"You're from Chicago?"

"Evanston."

"Huh, I have a house there."

"I know. My parents have pointed it out to me."

"You don't have a Midwestern accent."

"I was an affluent kid. Spent summers all over the country. I think my inflections changed over time. Became sort of newswoman neutral."

McGill said, "For someone from Evanston with family money, it seems Northwestern would have been a more obvious college choice than DePaul."

"I applied to Northwestern and was admitted, but it was too nearby. My parents wanted me to live at home. My dad tried to make my choice easier by saying he'd pay for Northwestern; any other college would be on my tab. I went to DePaul as an emancipated minor, got financial aid but still racked up an impressive student loan debt. Worked like hell to pay it off. Once I got free, my girlfriend and I got married."

Sweetie asked, "Why apply to Northwestern at all if you didn't want to go there?"

Esme said, "I wanted to keep the peace, praying that I wouldn't get in. With my grades, test scores and parental ability to pay full tuition that was a slim hope, but I gave it a shot."

"You're happy now?" McGill asked.

"In my personal life, yes. My marriage is great … and even my parents are starting to come around. I am a little concerned about getting a new job without too big a lapse in time."

"Understandable," McGill said. He glanced back at the résumé. "Monty gives you a great reference. The only problem I have is you seem way overqualified for the job."

"I am, as things stand now, but you're planning on building the business, right?"

"Yes."

"So you'll need administration, communications, human resources, all sorts of things. I'd like to be sitting at the top of that part of the organizational table. Unless you and Ms. Sweeney want to take on all those tasks yourselves."

Esme looked at both of them. McGill and Sweetie looked at each other.

They shook their heads in sync.

"So you don't ever want to go into investigations?" McGill asked Esme.

She shook her head. "Not my thing. I'm pretty strong and I have a fair amount of self-d training, but I like to keep my risk horizon fairly narrow." She grinned. "As far as I know, I'm still cut out of my dad's will."

McGill smiled, but his curiosity was piqued by another point Esme had raised. He asked, "What kind of self-defense training do you have?"

"Wing-chun mostly. Some odds and ends of other things."

McGill and Esme began an animated conversation on the topic of physical confrontation and how to deal with it. Easing out of her chair, Sweetie gave Jim a nod of confirmation. She already knew how he'd cast his vote.

35,000 Feet Above the United States.

Gene Beck caught a flight to L.A. with Dorie McBride, courtesy of a suggestion from the President. McGill had mentioned where Gene was headed and Patricia Grant knew Dorie was going back home to let everyone in Tinseltown know she had just met with the President in the Oval Office and was working on a project for her.

That kind of a coup was worth its weight in A-list clients.

Patricia Grant might be nearing lame-duck status politically, but she was still beloved by the film community. After all, she'd once been a member of the club, and her political positions were shared by nine out of ten Hollywood movers and shakers. The fact that Dorie could bring her back into the game, even in a small way, would give the *grande dame* of talent agents a whole new world of professional appeal.

So when the President had asked if Dorie might give a colleague of Jim's a lift to L.A. Dorie had been only too happy to oblige. Not that the Gulfstream G650 was her personal aircraft; it was a studio plane. Normally, Dorie would have been one of a number of privileged show biz characters catching a ride from one coast to the other. Studios believed in currying favor with those who might help them raise their next tentpole projects. Having snagged Patricia Grant for a project, Dorie could have had the whole plane to herself.

She'd been looking forward to it, in fact. Word of the perk she'd snagged would boost her status even higher. Maybe even signing Meryl would have been within reach.

Oh, well. She was pleasantly surprised by Gene Beck. He was tall and handsome in a country sort of way, had just a hint of cowboy twang to a pleasing baritone voice. He was also well mannered, offered to take a seat "at the back of the bus," as he put it. Stay out of Dorie's way. Wouldn't even snore if he dozed off. She'd barely know he was aboard.

Dorie had sworn off men a long time ago. She hadn't futilely tried to cling to a façade of youth with plastic surgery. The best she could say about her appearance was that she was a well-kept old broad. She took comfort in that and not worrying about trying to appeal to younger men … but every so often someone like Gene Beck would pop up and make her want to be 40 years younger again when her juices still flowed and hot flashes were nothing more than an approaching thunderstorm.

So she did what she allowed herself to do: enjoy a younger man's conversation without making a fool of herself. She insisted that Gene sit up front with her.

"We'll save our lovely cabin attendant a few steps that way," Dorie said.

"Whatever you say," Gene agreed.

After drinks were served, ginger ale for him, San Pellegrino for her, Dorie asked, "Have you been a private investigator for a long time?"

"No, ma'am. I was in the Air Force for several years. I used to jump out of airplanes, after I threw my motorbike out first."

Dories's eyes widened and she smiled. She sensed a story here, a good one. Maybe even something worth a movie pitch.

She asked, "Why on earth would anyone throw a motorbike out of a plane?"

"Well, otherwise you have to walk when you hit the ground."

Dorie laughed.

"Does sound funny, I'll admit," Gene said, "but there are places in the world where you have to move fast the moment you arrive. The locals probably won't be glad to see you. The nickname for guys who did that job was bike chasers."

Dorie squeezed her hands together gleefully. This was great material.

Gene said, "I was on my way to becoming what's formally called a combat controller, a special forces job, but they washed me out at the very last minute."

Dorie's emotions did a flip-flop, another strong story element, and she put a hand on Gene's arm. "Why? What happened?

"I whistled while I worked."

Dorie took her hand back, now thinking she'd been being pranked. "What?"

Gene explained with a straight face. "It's something I've done all my life. I pretty much have a tune running through my head every waking moment. So, normally, I whistle it. The Air Force psychologist I talked to about it didn't know what to make of that.

He'd never heard of it before, couldn't find any relevant diagnosis, but he thought he'd better not take any chances and he washed me out. That was a mighty big disappointment."

"You're being serious about all this, aren't you?" Dorie asked.

"Yes, ma'am."

"Couldn't you have sued or something?" Dorie said.

Gene limited himself to a wistful grin. "The U.S. military has a whole lot more money and lawyers than I do."

"That always makes a difference when you go to court," Dorie acknowledged.

Gene nodded. "Besides that, you're looked at as not being a team player if you push back too hard. There were a lot of guys I respected; I didn't want them to think less of me."

"So you went to work for Mr. McGill."

"With a step or two in between, yes."

Dorie reflected on what she'd learned about Gene so far.

Then she asked, "Are all the songs you hear in your head titles you've heard on the radio or some other medium … or do you come up with your own melodies?"

She was hoping Gene had at least a bit of personal inspiration.

He told her, "It's about two-to-one other people's material to mine."

Dorie put her hand back on Gene's arm.

"How many personal compositions would you say you have?"

Gene thought about it. "Maybe a hundred. I've sold quite a few of them around Austin and Nashville."

Dorie's eyes went wide. "What? Why are you still working for anyone else if you're a successful songwriter?"

"Well, starting out, I sold my songs for a hundred bucks a pop. My price tag's up to five hundred now, but that's still not enough to live on."

The blood drained quickly from Dorie's face; she turned so white, it scared Gene. He was about to call the cabin attendant and ask for an emergency medical kit. A plane this fancy had to have one, he felt sure. But Dorie saw Gene's alarm and forestalled a faux crisis.

"I'm all right. I … I just … Did you sign away your publishing rights when you made these sales?"

Gene shook his head. "Never signed anything, just whistled into a recorder and got paid cash."

Dorie said, "You could make a substantial monetary recovery if anyone saw you being recorded as you whistled your songs. That and if anyone else successfully recorded your songs."

"Yeah?" Gene asked.

"If you can get the witnesses to testify, yes."

"I think I could do that."

He could always threaten to throw people out of a plane without a motorbike or a parachute. That was likely to be persuasive.

"Would you like to sign a contract with me?" Dorie asked.

"For what?"

"I'd represent you as a songwriter. I'd get you vastly more than $500 for your work, assuming it's salable. You'd keep all of your publishing rights. My commission would be ten percent of the gross."

Gene liked the broad outlines of the proposal, but he asked, "How would you know if any of my songs are salable? From your point of view, I mean."

"Whistle a few for me," Dorie said.

By the time they touched down in L.A., Gene Beck was a signed client of Dorie McBride.

As a professional courtesy, she also had the limo that met them at the airport take him to the address he had for Kim Welles.

St. Patrick's Church — Washington, DC

After calling ahead to assure his visit wouldn't be inconvenient, McGill rang the doorbell at the rectory of St. Patrick's Church, a low-rise pile of gray stone that from the outside resembled a fortress as much as place of worship. Nonetheless, it was the oldest Catholic church in Washington. A small three-room apartment in the adjacent rectory served as the official residence of Cardinal Sean Fitzroy.

Cardinal Fitzroy's immediate predecessor, a theological liberal, had been taken to task by church conservatives for living in a penthouse on Embassy Row. Never mind that the "penthouse" sat on the third floor of a building owned by the parish of Our Lady Queen of the Americas. What the former cardinal's residence lacked in elevation it made up for in square footage. It was big enough to cast doubt on the theological legitimacy of the cardinal's views.

At least in the angry eyes of his critics.

Religion, like everything else in the city, was a matter of fierce political debate.

Sean Fitzroy, a man of materialistic humility in the same spirit as the Holy Father, lay beyond reproach when it came to indulgences of the flesh. He rose early every morning to hear the confessions of the faithful who wished to start their workdays with cleansed souls. As often as not, he'd celebrate 7:30 a.m. Mass as well.

He did everything his schedule permitted to keep in personal touch with his flock.

He even opened the door to the rectory himself after hearing McGill's ring.

He shook McGill's hand, pulling him inside as much as greeting him.

"Jim, this is a pleasant surprise. I'm so happy Margaret was able to find Father de Loyola for His Holiness." Shutting the door behind them, he added, "I was surprised she had to go to Costa Rica to find him."

"She's like that," McGill said, "willing to go to great lengths for a good cause."

Fitzroy nodded and took a moment to peek out a curtained window set alongside the door. "You have your Secret Service agent and your driver with you. I'm glad to see that. I thought you might have supplemented your security escort after what happened in Georgetown."

The city, the country and the world had heard of the shootout in Washington by now. There was no end of speculation as to who might have been behind the attempt on the life of the President's husband. Without specifying precisely, Aggie Wu, the President's press secretary, told the media that the currently perceived wisdom was that the motive behind the attack had to do with McGill's professional life and was not a matter of political or religious terrorism.

McGill said, "To be honest, it is a risk. The President, my children and my ex-wife would all be happier if I traveled with a small army around me as the President does. I just can't bring myself to do that, though. It's not who I am."

Fitzroy took a moment to think about that. Then he said, "We'll have the place to ourselves for the next hour or so. How about we go to the kitchen and I brew a pot of tea?"

"Sure thing, Your Eminence."

"Now, now. When it's just the two of us, Sean will do. Helps me to keep from getting above myself."

He led McGill to the kitchen, put a kettle of water on to boil and joined McGill at the room's table. "I trust you didn't drop by just to discuss the weather."

McGill shook his head. "How much coverage of the Georgetown attack have you seen, Sean?"

The cardinal said, "I've read everything the *Post* has printed up to this morning's edition. I've heard similar summaries on the radio. I don't watch much television."

"So you know I killed an old lady?"

"I've read that you shot an elderly woman who later died, yes."

"I'd like to tell you what happened under the seal of confession."

The kettle whistled and the Cardinal got to his feet. "Just a moment, Jim."

He poured the boiling water into a teapot. Set out cups, saucers, spoons, lemon wedges and honey. He asked, "Milk or cream?"

McGill shook his head. "No thanks."

Fitzroy brought the teapot to the table and filled their cups. He took his tea straight. McGill went with the lemon and honey.

"From what I read, Jim, you shot the woman in self-defense.

She was taking a gun of her own from her purse — and, yes, we're speaking sacramentally now."

McGill took a sip of his tea. "She did have a gun, and it looked like she meant to use it."

"You could tell her intent by your experience as a policeman?"

"Yes."

"Even so, is there any chance you might have been wrong?"

McGill thought about that and shook his head. "I don't think so. Once Leo avoided hitting her with my car, she was in no danger from me. There was shooting going on all around her. The safest thing for her to do would have been to find a place of shelter. She didn't do that."

"Maybe she panicked," Fitzroy said. "Ran in what she thought might be a safe direction."

"Okay, that's possible, but there was no reason for her to grab for a gun in her purse."

"Did you or your companions have a weapon on display?"

"Yes, all of us did."

"Might seeing the three of you armed have been justifiable provocation for the woman to reach for her own firearm?"

McGill shook his head. "No. Seeing the three of us pointing weapons at you is reason to put your hands in the air or run and hope our guns jam."

"You know that, but would an old woman without your experience know as much?"

"I can't say, but the way I saw it she was intent on shooting one of us, probably me, and she wasn't going to let anything stop her. By then, Sean, I realized that she'd been the one who'd stepped out in front of my car with the intention of having it hit her. The idea behind that was I would get out of the car to see if I could help. I'd be exposed and the guys lying in wait would kill me."

"Would you have gotten out of your car, if the plan had worked?"

After taking a deep breath and letting it go, McGill nodded.

Fitzroy said, "All right, let's say your instincts were right on the money. The elderly woman was intent on killing you and tried to pull her gun for that purpose. How was it that you shot first? Why not your Secret Service agent or your driver?"

"I reacted first."

"Really? You're that quick?"

"I am, in this instance anyway. I beat them to the trigger."

"Do you look at that strictly on a physical level?"

McGill understood what the cardinal meant. "They may have hesitated. I didn't."

"Why the difference? They didn't perceive the same threat?"

"No. I think we all made the same evaluation. They …" McGill shrugged. "Maybe they thought she'd drop the gun or shoot herself in the foot trying to get it out of her purse."

"That would be wishful thinking as you saw it?"

"Yes."

"What else?"

"I knew she'd come to shoot me, not Deke or Leo. It was my responsibility to take action. In part, I may have shot first so they wouldn't have to. Whatever happened next would be on me not them."

"Did you shoot to kill, Jim?"

Tears formed in McGill's eyes. "No, I tried to shoot her gun hand. Got her arm. The round went right through the arm and into her abdomen. Might not have killed a strong, healthy person, but she wasn't either of those things."

"So where's the sin here, Jim?"

"Thou shall not kill."

"Death was not your intent. You just said so, and I believe you. Furthermore, you say it's possible you took action to spare your friends the pain you're suffering now."

"That excuses what I did? Anything does?"

Fitzroy asked, "What responsibility lies with the woman and her gun?"

"All of it … up to the point I shot her."

"And then all of that responsibility transferred to you?"

"Didn't it?"

"Would you feel the same guilt if your shot had saved the President, your children or even your ex-wife?"

Patti's face flashed in McGill's mind, as did those of Abbie, Ken, Caitie and Carolyn.

McGill shook his head. "No, I wouldn't."

"Do you think any of them should feel guilt if they saved your life in a similar situation?"

"No."

"So how is your situation different from the other two I mentioned? Jim, I'm a big believer in following God's commandments, but I'm not always sure they were transcribed precisely. I sometimes think we got the simplified version. All the nuance was lost."

McGill said, "So that's how I should plead my case on Judgment Day?"

Fitzroy laughed. "By all means, blame me if you like. I'm sure I'll have much to atone for anyway. Tell me, if you've thought of it, how do you see heaven?"

McGill had an answer. "I think Cardinal Joseph Bernardin had it right: Heaven's a place you've never visited but once you're there you immediately feel at home."

Fitzroy smiled. "Joe had some amazing insights. I wouldn't be surprised if he was right. So tell me, do you think you will be harshly judged?"

McGill said, "I don't know. I'm just trying to make sure that when I meet my Maker both of us are smiling."

The cardinal beamed. "Now those are words to live by."

For McGill's peace of mind, and switching to Latin, Fitzroy forgave his sins in God's name. McGill's penance was to beat up on himself with less intensity and regularity.

"One last thing, Jim. Why did you come to me instead of your regular confessor?"

He told the cardinal of Sweetie's conversation with the Pope.

"I didn't think I could get His Holiness on the phone," McGill said.

Los Angeles, California

Kim Welles had just stepped out of a handsome single-family stucco home with a red tile roof in the Mid-City neighborhood of L.A. when a black stretch limo pulled to a stop at the curb. There was no shortage of such vehicles in town. Everyone from movie stars going to awards shows to kids going to the prom used them. But she didn't, never had.

Of course, a friend might have sent the ride for her. She was well known as an eccentric in her professional circle: She took the Metro bus to work instead of driving. A limo might have been a cheeky birthday gift, only that milestone date was six months away.

Then again the stretch monster might have been for someone else. Except the only other person in sight was an elderly Latino doing yardwork at a house on the far corner of the block. Meanwhile, the limo sat idling quietly right in front of her place. Ed McMahon was still dead so she didn't think Publisher's Clearing House had come to give her a pile of money.

The thing to do, Kim thought, was just to stroll over to San Vicente, wait for the bus and get on board. Only who knew if the limo wouldn't follow the bus, maybe get her so wound up her throat got tight. She had a late recording session, and someone who made her living by using her voice couldn't risk that. Even if she got through the job without any problems, who knew if the creep in the limo wouldn't be out front again when she came home after dark?

She hadn't done anything to piss off anyone, but in L.A. you didn't have to be offensive to draw unwanted attention. Maybe someone simply liked — or disliked — the way you looked. That could be enough, and from there things could get crazy.

Kim knew that from experience. She'd been beaten up twice on the street. In the first case, she'd absorbed the entire battering. The second time, after six months of martial arts classes, she'd given as good as she got, but still took some lumps. After that, she'd managed to get a concealed weapon carry permit, and now there was an M60 Ladysmith revolver holstered at her right hip under her sport coat.

She was about to take a confrontational approach when the tinted curbside passenger window eased down. A mid-30s guy with a friendly face looked out at her. He smiled in a way that neither made her skin crawl nor reach for her gun.

In fact, surprising herself, she spoke first. "Something I can do for you?"

He said in a polite tone, "If you're Kim Welles, I'd appreciate it if I could speak with you for a few minutes. Nice voice, by the way. Yours, I mean."

Sonofabitch, she thought. The guy had offered just the right compliment. If he'd praised her looks or her clothes, she could have dismissed him out of hand. Recognizing the timbre of her voice, that resonated.

"Thanks. Yours is nice, too."

"Mine's okay, but my specialty is whistling."

He demonstrated with the opening notes of "Daydream."

Damn, he *was* good, Kim thought. She said, "Lovin' Spoonful."

Just like that, he'd hooked her, she realized. Time to take a step back.

"You're not a cop," she said. "Not in that ride."

"Not a cop. My name's Gene Beck. I'm a private investigator."

Kim didn't see how that job fit with the limo either.

Gene saw her doubt and explained. "I flew into town from Washington, DC. Caught a flight with a talent agent name of Dorie McBride. The limo's hers. She let me use it after I signed a contract with her."

Like everyone in town who read the show biz trade papers, Kim knew Dorie McBride's name. The woman was a legend. She repped a list of stars a mile long.

Only ... Kim had never heard of *any* L.A. agent repping a whistler.

She expressed her curiosity on that point to Gene.

He laughed and said, "She's going to represent me for songwriting not performing."

That she could buy. "Okay, but if you can get a big-time agent as a songwriter why are you still working as a PI?"

"I enjoy it. I like the people I work with, too. Listen, you looked like you were heading somewhere before I got in your way. Can I give you a lift?"

With caution still prevailing, Kim asked, "Why would you want to do that?"

"I'm hoping you can tell me something about Pat Rickey and Chris Nevers."

Kim Welles' shoulders sagged and she said, "Oh, shit."

She got into the limo, saw it had a bar and asked for a shot of vodka, straight.

Gene obliged and grabbed a bottle of Perrier for himself so she wouldn't have to drink alone. Seeing that changed her mind. "I should probably have a water, too. Alcohol can dry out the throat."

Gene gave her his bottle and took her glass.

"Where do you want to go?" he asked.

She replied: the Fox Studio on the West Side. The driver heard and nodded. Gene raised the privacy partition, and they were underway.

"Why do you want to know about Pat and Chris?"

Gene said, "There's a strong suspicion one of them tried to kill my boss."

Tears welled up in Kim's eyes. "Jesus." Then she thought to ask, "Who's your boss?"

"James J. McGill, the President's husband."

The tears overflowed their banks and rolled down Kim's cheeks.

"Well, shit, that's about as bad as it can get."

Gene thought that even choked with emotion Kim's voice sounded pretty damn fine. He thought she should work on camera. Or at least do radio theater. Limiting herself to commercials underserved her talent.

At the moment, though, all he said was, "Pretty close."

In addition to all its other amenities, the limo was stocked with Kleenex. Gene handed one to Kim. She thanked him and put it to use. Then she looked at him.

"How do you know it was Pat or Chris who did it and not me?"

"Could be you, but you've got a job and live right out in the open like most people. Pat and Chris, they might as well be ghosts. Can't even find them online."

"They're out of the country, both of them, I think. Pat, I know, is in New Zealand. Married a big time sheep farmer. He came to town and tried to act. Then his dad died and he decided he'd rather be rich down there than scratching for bit parts up here. He took Pat with him. She loves it. They have a phone, and computers for their business but they don't hang out online. No social media presence at all. What kind of news they get in their papers, I don't know, but it's probably not the same as here."

Gene said, "But you heard about all the drama in Washington the other day, right? I mean, the shooting in Georgetown, not any political BS."

Kim nodded. "Why?"

"Well, if it wasn't you behind the assassination attempt and it wasn't Pat, that'd leave Chris."

Sadness morphed to anger, prominently displayed in Kim's superb voice. "Why does it have to be any of us?"

Gene held up a placatory hand. "I'm going to reach into my coat for a photo. Don't shoot me, okay? When you stepped into the vehicle I noticed you're carrying a weapon."

That caught Kim off guard. Before she could decide how to react, Gene had a photo in hand. "This image was taken by a camera in Mr. McGill's car. Tell me if you recognize this person."

The anger fell away as quickly as it had come, and Kim looked ten years older than she had a moment ago. Verification if he'd ever seen it, Gene thought. He asked, "You think you can tell me about Chris? Might help things work out better in the end."

She looked at him and asked, "Have you ever killed anyone?"

Not wanting to lie completely, Gene shaded the truth. "In the service, yeah."

"Was it awful?"

"The mental process was bloodless — the SOB was the enemy — the end result was anything but. Still, you do wonder why things had to come to that. Do you think or know if Chris has killed someone?"

"Pat and I both suspect that's what happened."

"Who died?"

"Our parents."

"And you think Chris did it, why?"

"Because neither of us could think of anyone else, and we tried real hard."

"Why would she do it?"

"Because Chris hated my parents, hates who she is. Or who he is, depending on the moment."

Gene said, "What do you mean?"

"My mom gave birth to the three of us at the same time: identical triplets. Except it turned out there are some real differences. I'm gay, Pat is straight and Chris is intersex."

Kim saw the look of puzzlement on Gene's face. So she explained.

He did his best to keep a straight face, but she saw the reaction in his eyes.

"Yeah," Kim said, "a lot of people do their best to be openminded these days but some things are still hard to wrap your head around. Pat and I always told Chris the three of us would stick together through anything, but Chris couldn't accept that. Mom wanted to go one way with her; Dad wanted to go the other way. They could never agree and they kept pulling Chris in different directions. Pat and I thought Chris might kill herself, but then one night when we were off at college our family house burned down. Mom and Dad were the ones who didn't make it out, and Chris was nowhere to be found. The fire marshal called it a clear case of arson."

Gene asked, "Did either of you ever see Chris after that?"

She shook her head. “Pat and I both wanted to go into show business. We nibbled around the edges for years. Then I focused on voice work and started to make a living; Pat got married and left the country. Occasionally, we heard that Chris was getting a little work in the off-Broadway theater community in New York, but we didn’t try to get in touch. Not after the fire.”

The limo pulled up to the guard station at the entrance to the Fox lot.

Kim laughed. “I got a job here doing voice-over narration for the offscreen grown-up version of the child character who carries the movie. Only a half-dozen lines, but it was a nice change from my usual ad work. Now, I don’t think I can do it. All I can think is Mom and Dad might be just the first two people Chris has killed. I mean, you don’t start out by trying to kill the President’s husband, do you? You need a lot of practice before you do that.”

Gene couldn’t argue with her.

What he did was call Dorie McBride.

Said he’d met someone with real talent she should see.

USP Hazelton — West Virginia

Jerry Nerón stood alone in his cell making gestures in the air with his right hand. Correction officers and the occasional inmate who passed by took notice. In an environment where people were known to get stabbed with improvised knives, it paid to be alert to what guys were doing with their hands. Once the passersby saw Jerry’s hands were empty, they moved on without worry or comment.

The only guy who said anything was a CO who must have been exposed to at least a touch of high culture. He smirked and asked, “You conducting Beethoven or Mozart?”

Jerry smiled and said, “It’s an original composition.”

“Yeah, right.” The guard moved on.

Jerry had been serious. Not that he was directing an imaginary symphony orchestra. He was sketching in the air the first suit he would make for some convict about to return to freedom. It had to make a strong statement: *Though I failed in the past, I will succeed in the future.*

That was an idealistic goal when you considered the five-year recidivism rate for federal prisoners: 44.7%. Not as bad as the 76.6% for state prisoners but substantial even so. What Jerry hoped was that putting on one of his fine suits would inspire hope, maybe even optimism, in the men who wore them. That would be a first step in beating grim odds.

He was still sketching suits in the air when the deputy warden stopped in front of his cell. The man had two COs with him for safety's sake. The prison hadn't lost a high-ranking official in years but there was no room for carelessness. There were plenty of guys inside the walls — guys like Jerry, actually — who had killed without remorse, and would still be at it if they hadn't been caught.

"Warden wants to see you," the deputy warden said.

Jerry let his sketching hand fall.

"Is Mr. McGill here again?"

The deputy warden shook his head.

Jerry was disappointed. He had a tangential idea he thought might help McGill's plan. He didn't know if he could trust the warden to deliver it.

"Come on, Nerón. Let's go." the deputy warden said.

Jerry fell in behind the man and the guard who walked point for him. The other guard brought up the rear. Any wrong move by Jerry and the guy behind him would bust his head with his baton. Of course, the guy at the tail end of the parade had to listen for anyone coming up from behind him, too.

Nobody did anything stupid and Jerry made it to the warden's office uneventfully.

With only a trace of mockery, Jerry bowed slightly to the prison's chief executive.

He, in turn, made a dismissive gesture to the deputy warden and the correction officers. Like well-trained hounds, they left without objection. Jerry watched them go, wondering what the hell was going on. The warden was a fairly big guy but Jerry had been convicted of one murder and was suspected of several others. Even with a size disadvantage, he was no one to be taken lightly.

Showing no apparent anxiety, the warden took his seat behind his desk and gestured Jerry to a visitor's chair. "Take a load off, Nerón."

Jerry followed the order, at a very deliberate pace. He didn't really think the warden was going to pull a gun, shoot him and then yell for help. When you were locked up with a lot of killers — other than yourself — anything out of the ordinary was a cause for … you couldn't call it paranoia. Justifiable concern was more like it.

Jerry stiffened when the warden opened a desk drawer, but he took out a magazine not a gun. He flipped it across the desk. Jerry waited unmoving until he was told to pick it up.

"You're in there, but you already know that, don't you?" the warden asked.

Jerry nodded. The cover was well known to him, not that he was on it. The magazine's name was *Latitude 25.76,* Miami's latitude. The cover was reserved for young women, tanned or naturally brown, in bikinis, lingerie or minidresses. Blonde hair was allowed and Jerry recognized the fair-haired beauty on the issue with the story about him inside.

She also held his arm on an inside photo.

"You have your fun with that girl, Nerón?" the warden asked.

"It was just a photo shoot. 'Hi, nice to meet you.' Like that."

He had slept with the woman, but he wasn't going to share that with the warden, give the bastard any vicarious thrills. It was bad enough how many women, once his arrest and conviction made the news, had faced the horror of learning they'd shared a bed with a killer. Of course, there had been a couple who found him more attractive for his evil ways.

He hadn't answered the letters they'd addressed to him in prison.

The warden said, "I made the mistake of telling my wife about you and McGill and your plan. You know what she did?"

Of course, Jerry knew, and he spoiled the warden's fun by telling him. "Your wife showed you pictures of my work, told you how much I used to charge and she said you should have me make a suit for you."

Wearing a sour expression, the man nodded.

All able bodied federal prisoners were required to work. Minimum prison wage was 23¢ per hour; maximum was $1.15.

Jerry gave the warden a cursory appraisal and a rough estimate.

"For a man your size, to do something nice, and that's all I do, I'd have to charge you $5,000 for top-grade wool and tailoring. Can't give you a discount or it'd look like something funny was going on."

"I didn't say I want one of your suits," the warden told the inmate.

Jerry put a hand to his chest and lowered his eyes. "My apology."

Grinding his teeth, the warden said, "My *wife* wants me to have one. Said she'd pay for it, no matter what it costs." In a near whisper, he admitted she earned more than he did.

Meeting the man's eyes, Jerry told him, "I could make you look like … like your wife would never forget the moment she first saw you in one of my suits. Like one of these guys."

Latitude 25.76 used professional female models, but it featured older athletes and business executives for their male counterparts. The implicit idea was a classic: For every Midas there was a gold-digger. Jerry opened the magazine to an apt page and slid it back across the desk to the warden.

The warden paid close attention. The irony here would be if Jerry put the warden in a suit paid for by his wife and it wound up wrecking their marriage. Guys in custom-made suits drew a lot of female attention. Well, Jerry thought, he'd done far worse.

The warden readjusted his attitude and asked Jerry, "Would you do it for free?"

"What?"

"I talked to the Bureau of Prisons' ethics office. They said no way can a warden pay an inmate, even indirectly through a relative. But they said you could pick a legitimate charity, not one of your relatives, to accept your fee as a donation and that would be an acceptable way to go."

Jerry thought about that. It went against his every commercial instinct to let a customer set the terms of a deal. Then again, he was no longer a free man. He had no leverage, and it wouldn't hurt to be on the warden's good side. Assuming the prick wasn't going to leave his job soon.

"Can I at least write the donation off of my taxes?" he asked.

The warden grinned. "Yeah, we'll even get H&R Block to do them for you. Just as soon as you meet the threshold for paying income tax."

At $1.15 per hour, that would be never.

"Okay, so I get no money," Jerry said. "But if you and your wife want my best work, and I won't do any other kind, there have to be a few conditions."

"What?" Suspicion filled the warden's voice.

"I have to be released from all other work duties."

"Okay, as long as you're working on the suit."

"Yeah, that's another thing. I want to start that program Mr. McGill brought up whether I'm able to help him or not. It'd be a good thing to let guys get released looking good. Maybe that'd help them to think they can be something more than cons. Might actually cut recidivism."

"I can't just call up the Attorney General and get a nod like McGill can, but I think that's a good idea. I'll try."

"My last condition might help me get the information Mr. McGill needs."

"What is it?"

"Since I'm going to make a suit for you, let me make one for Peter Mancuso, too. Well, not for him personally, but for someone on the outside of his choosing."

Mancuso was a New York crime boss who hadn't been careful enough running his businesses. He'd been tried and convicted on

36 racketeering charges and sentenced to life without parole. He was going to die in prison just like Jerry. But that didn't mean he didn't have more pull than any other con in the joint or wouldn't like to send someone on the outside a nice gift.

The *quid pro quo* would be if any inmate in the prison knew anything about Corona Moe, Mancuso would find out and tell Jerry about it as fast as he could.

Hearing that idea, the warden pushed his desk phone over to Jerry.

"You know what? That kind of stuff is above my pay grade. Why don't you call McGill and see how far you get?"

McGill Investigations International, LLP — Washington, DC

When McGill got a phone call from Jerry Nerón, he said, "How'd you get my number?"

"You didn't give me your number so I called the White House."

"The switchboard people don't know my number, so they didn't give it to you."

Jerry said, "I just told the nice lady who answered that I was a federal inmate you sent to prison for murder. She thought I was pranking her, I could tell. Then I gave her my name. It's nice to know some people out there still remember me. Anyway, she put me through to a guy named Frank Morrissey. He knew my name and my work, my custom tailoring, I mean. Said he'd meant to buy a suit from me, before you put me away and after he saw what I'd done for Mr. Putnam Shady."

By that time, McGill was buying Jerry's story.

"So Frank gave you my number, something he's not supposed to do."

"You'll have to take that up with him. I'm here with the warden in his office. He's letting me use his cell phone. I've got an idea on how I might get the information you want a lot faster than I could on my own."

Jerry gave him a quick summary of his idea, explaining how

if Peter Mancuso put the word out that he wanted to know about Corona Moe, news would get back to him a lot faster than if Jerry had to make careful inquiries one con at a time.

McGill had never met Mancuso, but he'd read about him, and knew similar organized crime thugs from Chicago. The idea of getting help from a mob boss wasn't easy to accept. He told Jerry he'd get back to him shortly.

"Yeah, fine," Jerry said. "I'm not going anywhere."

McGill called Sweetie. "I need the name of a non-profit organization in New York that's dedicated to helping prison inmates lead a better life when they get out of the joint. Something you or I could donate to in good conscience."

Sweetie answered off the top of her head. "PREP, all caps: The Prisoner Reading Encouragement Project. It works to enhance literacy and general education for inmates."

"Thanks, Sweetie."

"Why'd you think I'd know something like that?"

McGill said, "You're my chief ethics officer, aren't you?"

He said goodbye and called Jerry Nerón back.

"Here's the deal, Jerry. You can tell Mancuso he can have his parish church in New York auction off one of your suits. The parish can keep 25% of the winning bid as its auctioneer's commission; the rest goes to the Prisoners Reading Encouragement Program."

McGill's idea was that any prestige Mancuso earned from being the shadow sponsor of the event — even while incarcerated — would be offset by helping inmates who wanted to go straight. He hoped the number of guys leaving a life of crime would exceed that of those being recruited into the underworld.

"One more thing, Jerry," McGill said. "You think twice before you even go to this guy. If you have the feeling he's going to want a walk or even get his sentence reduced for helping with this, don't bother going to him. He's going to stay right where he is."

Jerry replied, "Okay, I understand. You're right, I should check things out first. But, you know, if Mancuso buys into this, he's going to want his goombahs to bid hard. With him involved, this suit has to go for top dollar not a bargain price. It might be the most expensive one I've ever made."

McGill read between the lines. "You're thinking the auction could make news."

"Yeah. The publicity won't hurt me, but —"

"I'll take any heat that comes my way."

"Warden says he'll need the okay from up top before he can let me do any of this."

That made McGill stop and think. "You're going to make a suit for the warden, too, aren't you? That's why he would let you do this. Why he let you use his phone."

Jerry laughed without humor. "If I'd known how smart you are, I'd never have left Miami."

"Try not to underestimate anyone else," McGill told him. "I'll talk to the Attorney General."

Rural Costa Rica

"Inigo, mi hermano," Berto Benavides said with a gap-toothed smile of surprise. "If you've come to save my soul and give me the last rites of your church before I die, you must have forgotten I am a communist and an atheist."

Father Inigo de Loyola, dressed casually but stylishly in layman's clothing, took a seat on the rickety chair next to the sagging cot where his old comrade in arms lay dying. The hilltop shack, sitting on the forested border between Costa Rica and Nicaragua, looked like it was also near a fatal collapse. The former Sandinista guerrilla commander and his hideout, fittingly, would disappear into the soil together.

"I forget very little, *compadre.* It is part of the curse I bear," Inigo said.

Berto gave a rasping laugh. "We're all cursed, are we not? We are born hoping our mothers can suckle us until we are old enough to scrounge and steal food on our own. If we manage to avoid starvation, we can turn our sights on redistributing the holdings of the wealthy so other peasants won't starve. *Hermano,* you are the only son of wealth I've ever known who renounced his fortune to help the *campesinos.* I would bless you for that only we atheists don't do such things. May I buy you a drink instead?"

With an effort that made him wince, Berto reached under his cot and brought out a bottle: Johnny Walker Blue Label Blended Scotch. The seal on the bottle was unbroken but its surface was smudged with a welter of fingerprints. Conflicting signs, Inigo thought.

He said, "My father used to drink that brand. Quite expensive as I recall."

Berto responded with a phlegmy laugh. "You are thinking the capitalists have corrupted me at last?" He shook his head. "I am like Fidel and Che, a revolutionary to my last breath."

Inigo said, "Che died far younger than you are now, and you will never live nearly as long as Fidel did."

All signs of good humor fled Berto's ravaged face. "You know, Inigo, my first memory when you entered my home was how fearless a fighter you were. Now, I also remember what a fucking scold you could be. Always criticizing the men for the most trifling things."

"Like mutilating corpses or cutting the ears off live prisoners?" the priest asked.

"Sí, exactamente."

"Did any of the barbarities you encouraged advance our cause?"

"Yes, they lit fires in the men's hearts. Showed them they could not only kill their enemies, they could also shame them. Make their families suffer as our own have suffered since the beginning of time. It was our turn to grind their faces into the dirt."

Inigo plucked the bottle of whiskey from Berto's hand.

He said, "You like to pretend you rose from the peasantry, Berto, and while your family was not as wealthy as mine your father was a university professor and you were a graduate student when you took up arms. I remember that also."

The dying man didn't care to be reminded. "Give me my whiskey."

The priest turned the bottle in his hands. There were scratches and wrinkles in the foil seal surrounding the cap. A glance at Berto's hands revealed dried blood on cracked and yellowed fingernails.

"You've tried to open this bottle, *compadre,* but you weren't able to do it."

Berto snarled, "Get out of my house, you damn priest. Look at you, dressed like some grandee. You've gone back to being a rich man's son. Or did daddy die and leave you all his money? You are a *caudillo* now, no?"

"No. I am still a priest for as long as the church will have me. I worked among the poor in New York and Washington. Until recently, my home was a space beneath a staircase. I took my vow of poverty quite seriously."

Berto gave another choking laugh. "And then what? You came home and your old closet had been left undisturbed all this time?"

Inigo nodded. "I was surprised to see it, but yes. My sister is a sentimentalist."

"Fuck you and your sister and every other damn oligarch."

The priest felt a ripple of anger, but he did not give in to it.

Instead, he asked, "Am I the only one who's come to visit you in your final hours?"

To a series of groans, Berto turned onto his side, facing away from his old compatriot.

"If you take my whiskey," he said, "you are nothing more than a thief. Like every other damn capitalist."

"I was thinking I might *open* the bottle for you, as you are clearly incapable of doing so yourself. Who knows, I might even send you *another* bottle."

Letting gravity do most of the work, Berto rolled onto his back. He turned his head to look at Inigo. "You'll bring more of the same, the good stuff?"

"If you like."

Berto asked, "You'll open that second bottle, too?"

"The person who brings it will. I could even send a glass with the bottle, unless you think drinking that way is too bourgeois."

Berto laughed, choked and finally said, "Yes, it is. The second bottle would be enough." Narrowing his eyes, he asked, "What price would I have to pay for it?"

"Tell me who gave you the first one." Inigo held up the bottle. "That and, if you can, answer a few other questions."

The dying revolutionary fell silent as he considered the proposition.

Inigo took the opportunity to ask another question. "Where would you like to be buried, Berto?"

"Nowhere! I want my body consumed by flames."

"Cremation."

"*Sí.* I want my ashes to fall on every place where we fought, you and me."

"Very well. I can have that done or …" He peeled the foil from the bottle and opened it. "I can pour this whiskey onto the ground. Leaving your thirst unquenched and your socialist righteousness intact."

"No, no, please. I have been trying to get at that whiskey for more days than I can remember. I know I am going to burn in hell. I *want* to burn forever; that will give me something to fight and rage against. Just as I fight against that damn whiskey bottle now."

Priest that he was, Inigo had to ask, "How can you believe in hell but not in God?"

Lacking the strength to laugh again, Berto only smiled. "I've seen the devil many times, God not at all."

Inigo sighed. "I have other errands to do, Berto. Answer my questions if you truly must have this whiskey."

Berto gave in and told Inigo who had given him the bottle. He answered the other questions Inigo asked, too. The priest put the bottle in Berto's hands, helped him get the first few ounces down so he wouldn't waste them. That was enough to make Berto's eyes heavy. There was little doubt they would soon close for the last time.

As Inigo turned to go, Berto cradled the bottle in his arms like a precious grandchild.

"See you in hell, priest," he said in a whisper.

Inigo looked back and replied, "If you want fire, Berto, you will surely get ice. Hell is like that. As for me, I will suffer, too."

A minute after Inigo had left, the bottle fell from Berto's embrace.

Valletta, Malta

Senator Randall Pennyman had yet to leave Malta by the time Layla Dart showed up on his doorstep. For one thing — talk about bad timing — he'd just seen on CNN International that the House of Representatives had impeached him *in absentia* that morning on a charge of bringing Congress into disrepute. Now, there was a laugh. The bastards' favorability rating had approached the vanishing point for years.

Of course, Pennyman's being exposed as a conman who'd successfully preyed on the religiously gullible hadn't helped his colleagues' standing with the public.

CNN was predicting that he'd be convicted and removed from office by a voice vote of the Senate that afternoon. Jesus, when the hell was the last time a U.S. Senator got impeached? It was 17-fucking-97, that was when. Two hundred and nineteen years ago. He'd looked it up. Way back then, the House had impeached some cluck from Tennessee named William Blount for trying to help the British steal Florida and Louisiana. The Senate acquitted Blount because at that time Florida and Louisiana had belonged to Spain, so who gave a shit?

Still, that guy got away with doing something that might have changed the future of the whole country. Fast forward to him about to get crucified for dipping into the collection baskets of fools who gave away their money on a weekly basis. There was no justice.

Now, with his picture being flashed all over Europe and probably the rest of the world, how the hell was he going to get past any country's customs inspectors? He wasn't, probably not for a good long time.

Which, in a way, was okay because he liked living in Malta. It was small, cozy and you had both the climate and diet of the Mediterranean. He'd not only gotten a nice year 'round tan, he'd also dropped 25 pounds. Up until the day that goddamn limey tabloid reporter, Giles Henry, had shown up unannounced he would have bet his heart health had improved. After that, he felt like he had palpitations about every other hour.

Not that he could do a damn thing about it other than taking a daily aspirin. He was stuck right where he was, and the country he'd come to think of as a comfortable new home — shit, he was even learning to speak Italian — had suddenly become a claustrophobic box on a rock.

Pennyman was so tightly wound he actually leaped into the air when he heard a knock at his front door. He came down without being noisy about it. That let him freeze in place. He probably shouldn't have moved an inch, but curiosity compelled him to skulk toward the door.

Maybe it was just some innocent caller. He didn't know if Malta had Girl Scouts, but maybe *someone* was selling cookies for a good cause. He'd buy a dozen boxes, if that were the case.

He listened for what he hoped would be a friendly voice announcing who had come to see him. What he got was a notebook-size sheet of paper slipped under his door. He could read the block-letter message inscribed thereon: *Senator, my name is Layla Dart. I'm here to help.*

He didn't know anyone named Layla, but he did like the Clapton song.

"I'm here to help," however reminded him of Ronald Reagan's nine most terrifying words in the English language: *I'm from the government and I'm here to help.*

He'd no sooner thought of that than a business card was slipped under the door.

Pennyman stooped silently and picked it up. It bore Ms. Dart's name and title: Campaign Manager, Oren Worth for President. A small hand-drawn arrow indicated that the card should be turned over. Pennyman complied and saw a new message: *Let's talk about a presidential pardon.*

Those words filled Pennyman's heart with joy. He felt young again …

Until he thought: It might be a trap.

One final item was pushed under the door, a California driver's license. Belonging to Ms. Dart, exhibiting a photo of a fetching young woman. Well, 36, according to the birth date on the license, but still looking very good. Nice height-to-weight ratio, too.

As a con artist, Pennyman knew everyone was a sucker for something. His weakness was attractive women. You added to that the idea of getting a free pass on his crimes and …

He picked up all of his special-delivery mail and opened the door with a smile.

"Ms. Dart, I presume," he said, handing her license and missives back to her.

Layla stepped inside and looked this way and that.

"We're here alone? No household help on hand?" she asked.

"Just you, me, and my fervent hope you're telling the truth."

Pennyman closed the door and locked it.

Layla said, "About the pardon? Absolutely. Well, assuming you can deliver the goods on Galia Mindel in such a way that my campaign can use your information to implicate both Patricia Grant and Jean Morrissey. You know, before the election."

Pennyman produced a genuine smile. Not only was this woman a looker, she was a bigger scoundrel than he was. If he wasn't careful, he'd fall in love before he even kissed her.

Layla read his eyes and knew exactly what he was thinking.

She shook her head and said, "No way that's happening, not now, not ever."

"You want me to help you steal the presidency and you won't show me a little affection?"

"I just made that clear. You want me to break your nose for emphasis?"

Pennyman made a quick appraisal. He had a good six inches in height on her and even slimmed down he had to outweigh her by fifty pounds. But she was 12 years younger and he wouldn't be surprised if she had quicker reflexes. Throw in some martial arts training and …

He turned sideways, gestured to his living room. "Ms. Dart, we are on the same page. Strictly business. Please have a seat."

She was not about to let this guy get behind her. "After you."

They were at a momentary impasse when another sheet of paper was slipped under the door. On it were the words: *Peek-a-boo, I see you.*

Pennyman scurried to a window, eased a curtain aside by an eighth of an inch.

That was enough to make his knees wobble. "It's the police."

To confirm that point a hand pounded the front door hard enough to make it wobble in its frame. Layla, wanting to distance herself from trouble, did the only thing she could. She opened the door and pointed to Pennyman. "He's right over there, officers. Randall Pennyman. He's the man you want."

Three Maltese cops pushed by doing speed-reads on Layla's various points of interest. A fourth stood guard at the door. But what interested Layla most was the guy standing next to a car parked at the curb out front just behind the police wagon. He opened the passenger side door, walked around the front of the car and got in on the driver's side.

Layla understood she wasn't being offered a ride; she was being told to get in.

Having arrived in a taxi, needing a ride back to the airport, and not wanting the cops to haul her off with Pennyman, she slipped past the cop at the door, who didn't try to stop her.

The man behind the wheel started the engine.

Then he extended a hand to introduce himself. "Frank Morrissey."

"I know who you are." Layla shook his hand. "Giles Henry sold me out to you?"

"Just like he sold Pennyman to you."

Frank pulled out, after signaling first. He never took an unnecessary chance.

"So you've been watching me the whole time I've worked for Oren Worth."

"Long before that. Check the glove box."

She did, and found a shockingly detailed photographic history of the last three years of her life. She hadn't always been as discreet about her sex life as she should have. Still, she almost asked how the hell he'd gotten the pictures, but she knew he'd never tell.

There wasn't any need to ask, now that she thought about it. Jean Morrissey had been Patricia Grant's vice president for going on four years. Galia Mindel had to be tutoring Frank Morrissey for at least that long, and he'd probably had a running start.

"You scouted me," Layla said.

"Yeah."

"You didn't care if you'd ever get to use this stuff. You did it on spec, just in case."

"Yeah."

"So the fact that I slept with the governors of both Texas and Florida while I ran their campaigns …"

"Wouldn't look good for Oren Worth's campaign."

"So, I'm going to resign."

"Yeah."

"Making it tough for the senator to hold his presidential campaign together."

"Yeah. Poor Oren."

"I don't suppose, after the election, you might have a job for me."

"Not in the administration. Outside, maybe. You show promise. We can talk on the flight home."

"One last thing," Layla said.

"What?"

"You wrote that last note that got slipped under the door."

"I wrote it, but one of the cops pushed it inside. I told them that should do the trick."

"And I proved you right."

"Yeah."

Frank had a Gulfstream G650 waiting for him at the airport.

Courtesy of the same movie studio that had provided Dorie McBride with her ride.

Hollywood having a distinct liberal bias.

The White House — Washington, DC

McGill and Patti idly played footsie in a bubble bath. The President, at the beginning of her second term, had sprung for the cost of a bathtub built for two to be installed in the White House. She'd thought there would be times when she and her mate could use a good, hot bath together. If they were feeling playful, they might even fill the tub with bubbles as well as water.

Wonder of wonders, none of the people who'd installed, maintained or cleaned the tub had ever blabbed about it to the media. *Adventures in Erotic Hygiene for the First Couple* had never become a headline for either celebrity magazines or supermarket tabloids.

Over the following years, there had been trying times aplenty, but conjugal bathing hadn't happened nearly as often as either of them had hoped. While they weren't feeling particularly amorous at the moment, they'd decided to go all out and add bubbles anyway. Who knew, maybe the mood would come upon them in mid-soak. Stranger things had been known to happen.

McGill said, "You think we could uproot this fixture and move it into our new house? I like it every time we manage to do this."

"You know what they say," Patti told him.

"Cleanliness is next to godliness?"

"Money can buy almost anything. We could leave this one here and get a new one."

"You're right. I'm still stuck in a middle-class recycling mindset. But now that I'm a budding business mogul I'll have to think bigger."

Patti smiled. "Shall I ring for champagne? We can toast your upward mobility."

"I'm tempted to say yes, but I'm not quite ready to have the butler attend me in my bath."

With a smirk, Patti said, "That day will come."

"Until it does, tell me, do you think we can get Blessing to come with us after you leave government work?"

"Already arranged."

"Oh, really? Anything else I should know about?"

"I was thinking about pink shag carpeting for our new bedroom, but Galia talked me out of it."

McGill grinned. "Galia the interior decorator, I love it. But you are taking her to Committed Capital with you, right?"

"Maybe. She wants to live in Manhattan most of the year. We'll see how things work out."

McGill nodded.

After a moment of silence, Patti added, "Sorry I beat you to Edwina."

He was unsurprised that she had heard about his offer to her secretary. "It's only fair. She was your hire. I managed to find someone else." He told her about Esme Thrice.

She nodded. "I've seen a picture of her. I'm glad she's gay."

McGill replied, "I'm glad you're not."

He reached out and gently pulled her to him. The mood was changing. Cue the violins. But in the time-honored fashion of such moments both of their cell phones interrupted. McGill picked his up, accepted the call and stuck a finger in his opposite ear. Patti moved to the far end of the tub and did the same.

"Boss, it's Gene Beck."

"Yeah, Gene. What's the word?"

"I just finished a long interview with Kim Welles out here in L.A. I spoiled a job she was about to do — voice-over for a movie. I felt bad about that so I took her out to dinner and got her an interview tomorrow with Dorie McBride. I put the meal on my new business credit card. Is that all right?"

"It's fine, Gene. Did you learn anything?"

"Quite a bit. Before I get to that, though, I have to say that on the flight west I signed an agreement to have Dorie be my agent."

That one caught McGill off guard. "You're going to become an actor?"

"No."

"So, you're going to stay with McGill Investigations?"

"Yeah."

That was a relief. McGill didn't want to have personnel problems before he even opened the doors on the new operation. "So how will Dorie be representing you?"

"She's going to manage my songwriting. I whistled a few of my tunes for her and she signed me up. Since I always record my songs on my own time, it won't interfere with my work for you. I just thought I should let you know."

"I appreciate that, Gene, and I agree there shouldn't be any conflicts. So what did Ms. Welles have to say?"

"Well, we're looking at one real unusual family situation here. Real unusual."

Gene outlined the story he'd heard from Kim Welles.

McGill listened closely without interrupting.

Gene finished by asking McGill, "You ever hear about this intersex thing before?"

"Only recently. It's not a common topic of discussion and back in my day these people were called hermaphrodites, but the President has told me that term is considered offensive these days."

"She knows about it, too?"

McGill said, "There's very little that surprises her."

"I supposed that'd be a job requirement, if you want to do it right. Anyway, the more I heard about it and thought about it, I had to agree with Kim that her sister-brother, in her words, killed Mom and Dad. The autopsy said it's anybody's guess whether they died before their house got burned to the ground or were consumed alive by the flames."

"So there was no evidence of gunshots," McGill said.

"No. Kim said nobody in the house had a gun. Almost sounds

quaint these days. But Kim said that Chris Nevers did have a fascination with knives, and stab wounds aren't going to survive a big hot fire that leaves nothing but scorched bones."

"No, they won't," McGill agreed.

"Can you imagine, though, that poor kid being born that way and then Mom and Dad arguing for years which way they wanted your private parts to be remodeled. Dad wanted a third girl; Mom wanted a boy. That'd be enough to mess up anyone."

McGill felt the same way, but he chose to pursue another line of thought.

"The police didn't find any conclusive evidence Chris set the fire?"

"No, it's circumstantial. Chris was seen at home that morning. The other siblings were off at college. The family never let anyone but them inside. And Chris was gone when the fire department arrived on the scene, not to be seen by the authorities since."

"There were no mean kids in the neighborhood who made fun of Chris and might have taken things too far?" McGill asked.

Gene said, "I raised that same point. Chris was home-schooled after the first week of kindergarten. The teacher was shocked when Kim told her Chris might want to use the boys' bathroom."

"And then teacher heard the reason why," McGill said.

"Right. After that, Chris stayed home. Until she bugged out."

"Which leaves us where?" McGill asked. "Dorie said all three of them tried to make a go of it in show biz."

"They did, and I think that's where we should head next. Manhattan. Kim said Chris turned up in New York and got some small parts in way the hell off-Broadway shows. She thinks Chris might have found people there who were more sympathetic to her situation."

McGill found that idea plausible. So much for liking Canada as the killer's home base.

"You want me to head that way, boss?"

"Yes, I'll meet you there. Hey, Gene?"

"What?"

"Did you ever get the family's real name?"

"Springstone. The kids were named Doris, Cloris and Loris. Parents, huh?"

"Yeah. Which one do we want?"

"That'd be Loris."

McGill said goodbye and took his finger out of his ear.

He looked up and saw Patti ending her call, too. She looked as grim as he felt.

"Bad news?" McGill asked.

The President nodded. "The Russians have one aircraft carrier, the *Admiral Kuznetsov.* It's a smoke-belching antique that travels with an escort of tugboats, as it's known to break down regularly."

"Okay," McGill said.

"It was making a friendly visit to North Korea. The Pentagon thought Moscow was trying to showcase it for a sale, but Pyongyang apparently wasn't buying. In any case, the *Kuznetsov* is now steaming toward the South China Sea to join what appears to be every ship in the navy of the People's Liberation Army."

"We're going to war with China and Russia?" McGill asked.

"The current thinking is it's a show of force to try to intimidate us." Patti got out of the tub and wrapped a towel around herself.

McGill did the same. He asked, "We're not about to be scared off, are we?"

The President shook her head. "No, we are not. I've been reassured many times that there is no match for the United States Navy. No other country even comes close, but —"

"People, some of them ours, will die if any shooting starts," McGill said.

The President nodded. "Yes, and since August of 1945 nobody has ever been able to pinpoint the moment when a conventional war might go nuclear. I have to hurry now. The National Security Council is assembling and I don't want to be the last one to report to my duty station."

Number One Observatory Circle — Washington, DC

Vice President Jean Morrissey perched at one end of a long suede sofa in the Sitting Room of her official residence with her new husband's head resting on her lap. The average adult human's noggin weighed 10-11 pounds. That didn't seem like much, but after the first quarter-hour or so the pressure on Jean's legs seemed to increase exponentially.

Former FBI Director Byron DeWitt had been using his wife's legs as a pillow for an hour. He'd anticipated the burden he'd be placing on his beloved and told her to roll him off her and onto the floor when it got to be too much.

"Okay," she'd said. "I'll try to be gentle about it. Wouldn't want your head to bounce more than once or twice."

"Thoughtful of you."

"But as long as you're down there, I'll want you to give me 20 pushups."

"May I use both hands?"

"Heck, you're still convalescing. You can do them from your knees, if you like."

Try as he might, DeWitt couldn't think of a comeback. The fluency of his speech was improving at a pace that stunned his doctors. That pleased him, but if he'd lost a large part of his wit, the ability to find humor in even small things, that would be a real shame.

Jean saw he was stuck and changed the subject.

"I think one year, two at the most, will be all I'm going to do," she said.

"The task in question being?" He hoped she didn't mean putting up with him.

"Being president. Dick Bergin is a good man. He'll lead the country responsibly."

Bergin, a Democratic senator from Illinois, was Jean's running mate. He was smart, persistent and responsible. The country could do, and often had done, far worse than that.

"Does Senator Bergin know about this?"

"Not yet."

"The reason behind such a decision would be?"

Jean said, "You should be back on your feet and reasonably active by then. I want you to give me surfing lessons before I get too old."

DeWitt beamed at his wife. "Kiss me."

She gently cradled his head and lifted, bending to meet him halfway. She kissed him. Lowered his head but kept her hands under it to give her numb legs a respite.

DeWitt said, "This plan, it all depends on your winning the election."

"Frank called earlier. He says it's in the bag."

DeWitt considered that. "Frank's going to cut Oren Worth off at the knees?"

"Possibly a bit higher than that, but one way or another, it sounds like the situation is politically terminal for Worth. You know, I wonder …"

"What?" DeWitt asked.

"Once I turn the Oval Office over to Dick Bergin, it'll be his choice how to staff his administration, but I wonder if I could get him to retain Frank as his chief of staff. He'd be a lot more formidable that way."

"Have Frank whisper into Bergin's ear about how he did in Worth. That should help."

That suggestion earned DeWitt another kiss.

Jean said, "Your doctors told me the brain is amazingly plastic. When one part gets shorted out, the brain figures out a new way to rewire itself. That assumes that not too many of the circuits have been scorched and all that's left is the hunger for food and the yen for sex."

"Man at his most basic," DeWitt said. "Still, if he's well mannered about both things not a bad fellow."

He smiled. His sense of humor still appeared to be present, if only semi-active.

Jean liked the line, too.

She asked, "You think you'll be up to giving me advice on how best to serve the country soon? That and, you know, deal with all the assholes around the world."

DeWitt gave her an upraised thumb. "Read Sun Tzu again. Memorize it."

"All right. If I'm going to learn to surf, I might as well do that, too. So what would old Sun have to say about dealing with China? I think I'm going to get stuck with this South China Sea mess, and the Chinese always like to test new presidents."

"I've already been trying to think of that," DeWitt said. "It was really a foggy problem at first but the clouds have started to part. You'll need not to give an inch on the international waters front or do anything else to give Beijing any other strategic advantage, but you still have to allow them to save face."

Jean said, "That sounds like a really good trick. How would I manage that?"

"What you have to do first, I think, is get Seoul on board. South Korea is the key."

CHAPTER 8

Ritz-Carlton — Washington, DC
Tuesday, September 20, 2016

In their hotel suite, Odo Sacripant told Yves Pruet, "I am a fairly versatile and dexterous fellow, good with a knife, a gun or open-hand fighting, but I think my fingers are simply too large for texting on a phone. I aim for one letter and get an adjoining one. Also, the use of an English keyboard makes things more difficult."

The French, as was their way, had devised their own keyboard layout, a design more sensible to them than the QWERTY pattern Americans used. The French keyboard was known as AZERTY. Pruet reached out and relieved Odo of his company/American phone.

"I will be your secretary, *m'sieur*," he said.

"I'm not sure you have the legs for the job, Yves."

At their Paris office, clerical and administrative duties were handled by Nanna Cuvier who might have been a fashion model if only she'd chosen to starve herself. Instead, she ate sensibly, rode her bicycle at least 200 kilometers every week and took art lessons from Gabbi Casale on Sunday mornings.

She also dressed to show off her sleek arms and legs. A devoutly married man, with a wife who would gladly kill him if he ever strayed, Odo could only admire her from a respectful distance. He did, however, urge the bachelor Pruet to pursue her.

"Her mother I might woo, if the family resemblance is strong," Pruet had replied. "Possibly her grandmother if the mother is still married."

To Odo, at the moment, he said, "Do you wish to have help delivering your message or not?"

"Yes, please," Odo said, getting serious. "Ready?"

"Oui."

From memory, Odo gave Pruet the phone number of Dwayne Kilgore, the prison guard who would act as Auric Ludwig's intermediary. Then he delivered his message.

"After evaluating the business opportunity you proposed, I am confident I can execute a successful plan. That is not to say it will be easy. Research, timing and substantial resources will be required. I can provide the first two elements. The third must come from you, but any measure of underfunding would only guarantee failure. Please advise acceptance or rejection of my proposal quickly as other opportunities await."

Pruet keyed in the message, checked for typos and hit send.

He smiled at his old friend. "If I didn't know better, I'd think you'd spent a year or two at the *Grenoble Ecole de Management.*"

Odo laughed. "I once arrested someone who did. Had to listen to his blather for hours."

"I particularly liked your use of 'execute.'"

"How drab life would be without a little joke here or there."

"Painfully boring, yes. Still a future court hearing will take your point exactly. You are clearly telling *M'sieur* Ludwig you will kill someone for him. Very neatly done."

Odo took a small bow.

"Now, all we have to do is wait for a response," Pruet said.

"Let's have some room service while we do," Odo replied.

McGill Investigations International, LLP

Captain Rockelle Bullard and Detectives Meeker and Beemer

of the Metropolitan Police Department had news for McGill. So they decided to drop in on him at his new place of business. See what the working conditions were for the civilian segment of the crime-fighting community. Not that they considered most PIs to have anywhere near the status of sworn officers, but McGill and his partner Margaret Sweeney had both been real police long enough to collect *two* pensions.

Wasn't a cop in the world who couldn't admire that achievement.

What the captain and her men had to share was news of Dr. Zoë Tinker. After she'd gone into a faint at her office, Meeker and Beemer had gently pinched, tickled and even slapped her. None of the physical contact had any effect. Margaret Sweeney had found a first aid kit in the office. In it was a packet of ammonium carbonate: smelling salts. Even that hadn't worked.

So an ambulance was summoned and off she went to a secure hospital ward. The captain, Meeker and Beemer took shifts watching over her. A person suspected of both murder and conspiracy to kill the President's husband rated more than a patrol officer.

Tincture of time and an empty stomach growling to be filled restored Dr. Tinker to consciousness eighteen hours after she'd blacked out. At that point, she had an IV line in her arm to keep her hydrated, a catheter to drain her bladder and Detective Meeker to babysit her. Meeker had been reading *Tennis* magazine, a story on up-and-coming young players across the country.

It pleased him to see how the once lily-white game was integrating fast. Marvina wouldn't feel out of place once she went pro. He was also pleased by his estimation that his girl could already beat some of the mid-teen players who were featured. When he heard Zoë Tinker moan, he dog-eared the magazine page and called the captain and Beemer.

He didn't say anything to the prisoner, just put his phone on video and recorded her stirrings. Meeker hoped for some spontaneous utterances. Dr. Tinker had been read her Miranda rights after she'd first passed out. Copies of those rights had been posted on the safety rails at the sides of her bed. Another was taped at the foot of her bed.

Beemer had wanted a copy adhered to the ceiling above the bed, but the hospital wouldn't allow that. The not-so-good Dr. Tinker looked around, her eyes starting to focus.

She stopped when Meeker and his phone came into view. "Are you recording me?"

Knowing he wouldn't be able to edit the video and still use it for legal purposes, Meeker said, "Yes."

"Why?" There was a clear sense of distress in the woman's voice, but Meeker had the feeling she was more concerned about not looking her best than being in legal jeopardy.

"I'm recording you to prove I've read you your legal rights. Right off the bat."

He identified himself and her for the record, noted the time and place of the recording.

"Do you understand your rights?" Meeker asked after concluding his spiel of the protections Dr. Tinker was constitutionally afforded. "Say yes or no or just move your head whichever way you feel."

"I do. I understand."

"Okay, we're cool then. Well, I'm cool. You're in a world of hurt. You can ask for a lawyer now, like I said, but all that's gonna do is cost you a lot of money. I've seen a lot of people in bad spots but none any worse than yours. You put a lot of stuff in those records of yours … my, oh, my, you're in trouble like nobody I ever saw."

The truth was, he hadn't read her treatment records yet. Nobody had. The permission note from the mother of the late Aubrey Gadsden had gone to the district attorney for validation. But that didn't mean Meeker couldn't lie a little and play a hunch.

He could see already it was a good one. It always amazed him how white people could go even whiter when they were in bad trouble. He'd never seen a black person get blacker. Well, maybe a little if they were embarrassed.

Zoë Tinker started to say something but Meeker held up his

hand.

"Wait just a minute. You start talking, I'm still recording. You understand that? If so, you got to say so. Say you're speaking freely."

She nodded and voiced the instructions she'd been given.

Then she asked, "Can I get a deal here?"

She repeated her story for Captain Bullard and Beemer. Each of them recorded Zoë Tinker's confession, too. Then they called for another detective to come watch over Zoë and they all drove over to McGill's new office building to let him know what they'd learned. After all, he was the target of this murder plot.

Only Dikki Missirian told them McGill was still at the White House. If the captain wanted, Dikki had a number he could call to contact McGill. She said sure, go ahead, even though all three cops were disappointed they wouldn't get to see McGill's new digs.

They felt better, if a little bit intimidated, when McGill told them, "Come on over to the White House. We'll talk here."

McGill's Hideaway — The White House

McGill had never conducted any of his investigative business out of the Executive Mansion in all the time he'd lived there, almost eight years now. He didn't know if doing so might have breached some federal statute. It just didn't seem kosher to him. So he'd avoided even the appearance of impropriety.

Now that he was the target of a murder conspiracy, he felt nobody would be able to accuse him of trying to make money from the meeting he was about to hold. Well, Washington being Washington, maybe someone could. Say he was gathering gripping material for his memoirs in the hope of making it a bestseller.

McGill had the perfect defense for that. He wasn't going to write his memoirs.

When Blessing ushered the Metro cops into McGill's Hideaway they tried to play it cool, but that wasn't easy. There were many more spectacular homes in the country. People with billions of dollars to their names built such dwellings on a regular basis.

When it came to providing a sense of history, though, the feeling that you were walking in the shadows of both heroes and villains, you couldn't beat the White House.

Not in the USA, anyway.

Blessing asked the visiting cops, "May I bring you some refreshments?"

All three looked at McGill.

"Pretty much anything you'd care to eat or drink," he said.

"Ice tea, please," Rockelle Bullard said.

"Good choice," McGill told her.

"You have Vernor's ginger ale?" Meeker asked.

"We do, sir."

"I'll have one then."

Beemer said, "I'd like a chocolate eclair. Half for me, half to take home to my wife."

Blessing would have been happy to accommodate, but McGill said, "Have two, don't short your wife."

Beemer beamed and said thanks.

While waiting for Blessing to return, which wouldn't take long, McGill and his guests took seats. He was curious to hear what the cops had to tell him, but he felt sure they had questions of their own. It was the rare visitor to the White House who didn't.

Meeker got right down to it, making a sweeping gesture with his right arm. "You gonna miss all this?"

McGill shook his head. "I'm sure all three of you know how being a cop can wear you down at times."

"A *lot* of the time," Beemer said.

Captain Bullard and Meeker nodded in agreement.

"Well," McGill said, "just getting an up-close look at what a president deals with, it makes my cop days look like I was a school crossing guard."

Rockelle understood intuitively. "If it's hard on the President, it's almost as hard on you, feeling how you do about her."

"Right," McGill said. "I can't tell you how many people I've wanted to punch out since I've been in Washington. More than I ever did in Chicago."

Meeker and Beemer laughed.

Meeker said, "You've managed to smack a few people upside the head."

McGill offered a rueful grin. "I know. I'll have to be more cautious in the future." McGill looked at all three cops and said, "All of you must have your 20 years in. You have any plans, looking ahead?"

It was clear none of the cops had expected to hear that question.

Meeker and Beemer exchanged a look with each other, before looking at the captain.

Meeker said, "You go ahead, Beem."

Beemer looked at the captain again before turning to McGill.

"Me 'n' Marvin are gonna do the same thing you did: open a PI shop. Only a bit smaller than yours."

"No office in Paris," Meeker said.

"This is news to me," the captain said.

"We're waiting until the end of 2017," Beemer said. "Then we move on."

Rockelle had to concede, "You've earned it, the two of you."

"What about you, Captain?" McGill asked.

"I'm staying a cop … thinking maybe I might become chief of police before too long. I got my master's degree in public administration when nobody was looking. I've got street experience and years in a command job. I figure I'm qualified and then some."

Blessing returned with the refreshments. Everyone had a sip or a bite of their chosen treat and then they got down to business.

Rockelle said, "Dr. Tinker woke up, knew her only chance for any kind of a plea deal was to start talking, so she did. She met Corona Moe last week in Cancun, Mexico. She was staying at the J.W. Marriott in the Hotel Zone. Moe came in an armored Humvee, the civilian kind. No machine-gun sticking out of the top. She got the impression it was Moe's personal vehicle. That makes us think he lives in driving distance of Cancun. You look at a map of the Yucatan Peninsula and you've got other tourist places nearby like Playa del Carmen. You also got a whole lot of jungle down that way. Places where the Mayans used to have their temples and pyramids."

McGill thought about that. "Wouldn't be difficult to imagine he's got a place on the beach with all the modern amenities and a hide-out deep in the boonies. A place to run to if things get too hot."

"If he tries going native in the jungle," Beemer said, "man, I can think of so many bad things should happen to his ass."

McGill said, "I'd prefer something verifiable, whatever its nature. Did Dr. Tinker give you a physical description of Corona Moe?"

"She did," Rockelle said, "and we put the details through our suspect ID software."

She handed McGill a printout.

Looking at it, he said, "This guy looks more Arab than Mexican."

"Man's got a good eye," Meeker said.

Rockelle told McGill, "What we were told, his family comes from Syria. Daddy was a prominent doctor who did something to piss off the old dictator, not the one who's tearing things up now. The doctor and his family, including Moe, caught the first flight out, which was to Rome with a connection to Mexico City. The idea was they'd come to the U.S. eventually, but they liked it down there and paid off somebody to get Mexican citizenship."

Meeker said, "Moe's full name is Mohammed Ben Hassan, at least for legal documents in Mexico. That's what Dr. Tinker told us."

"Where'd the Corona come from?" McGill asked.

Beemer said, "The guy likes his beer. Not an observant Muslim at all."

Thinking about the new information, McGill said, "Even so, Moe had to get the idea of using dying people as killers from the suicide bombers, didn't he?"

Rockelle nodded. "Dr. Tinker said it was a commercial spin on a terrorist idea. Why waste perfectly healthy individuals on suicide missions when you could use people who already knew their end was near? You just had to make sure they were up to doing one more job."

"You didn't promise them 72 virgins as a reward either," Meeker said.

"Cash for surviving family members is the ticket," Beemer added.

"I bet," McGill said. "A tainted legacy's better than none at all, and who's more desperate than someone poor and dying? But with Aubrey Gadsden things were different, weren't they?"

Rockelle nodded. "Yeah. Part of the deal when you hire the walking near-dead is you have to know they'll show up for work and do the job. That's where Dr. Tinker comes in."

Meeker said, "Moe has scouts in Mexico, Central America and right here in the States looking for people who meet his criteria. Got one last misdeed in them and the desire to take care of somebody financially before they go. "

Beemer followed up. "Moe gets the info and if it's someone he thinks he can use, a follow-up approach is made."

"That's the way it went with Dr. Tinker anyway," Rockelle said. "Moe bird-dogged her in Cancun. She had a lot of personal debt to pay off. Moe decided that the crooked lawyers he used as some of his scouts also had to have their own psych evaluations. When Gadsden fell in love with Dr. Tinker and wouldn't take no for an answer —"

"The dumbass tried to blackmail her," Meeker said.

"Be my squeeze or I'll turn you in." Beemer shook his head. "Like he could do that without incriminating himself."

Rockelle summarized. "Doctor Tinker found that Gadsden's approach lacked romance. She reported him to Moe as an intolerable risk. Swears she doesn't know who killed Gadsden. Didn't even know he was going to be killed, she says. Thought he might just get a warning."

Both Meeker and Beemer laughed at that.

"Yeah, I don't find that credible either," McGill said.

Rockelle said, "I'd be shocked, too, if any judge in DC would buy that BS, but locking up Zoë Tinker for a good long time doesn't get us any closer to grabbing Corona Moe, does it?"

Meeker said, "The man's family got their start in Mexico by paying off somebody; he's gotta have government people on his payroll right now."

"Be a necessary cost of doing business," Beemer suggested.

Keeping a straight face, McGill said, "You thought that's where I might be of help."

The three Metro cops nodded.

"Maybe. But I can't make any promises."

To keep them from thinking too deeply about the lengths to which he might go, McGill changed the subject. "Auric Ludwig is trying to get one of my people to kill me. As soon as the money involved changes hands, charges will be filed. Ludwig's going to stay locked up until he dies."

Rockelle applauded that idea. Meeker and Beemer shook McGill's hand.

All of them wondered how he'd pulled off that feat. Well, he'd tell them if and when he wanted. In the meantime, they'd gotten to see a part of the White House that wasn't included in the public tour.

Better than that, McGill said, "I hope we can all work together in the future."

Before the cops left, he had Blessing make copies of Corona Moe's likeness.

McGill was about to have breakfast when Edwina Byington rang him.

"Sir, the President would like to see you at your earliest convenience. She's speaking with the Vice President and Deputy Director DeWitt in the Situation Room right now, so there's no reason to sprint. A nice five-minute walk to the West Wing should do nicely."

"Did you see the deputy director, Edwina?"

"Only briefly."

"How'd he look? Is he coming along?"

"He had a cane in one hand and held Vice President's Morrissey's hand with the other, but he gave me a nice smile. My money says he's going to be 99% fine."

"Glad to hear it. You know by now I found someone to work for me?"

"I do. I'm well connected."

"In which case you've already checked her out."

"I have. You've made a good choice."

"Your stamp of approval makes me happy, too. You care to give me any kind of heads-up on why the President wants to see me?"

"I don't think the news is bad. If it's good, I'd never spoil her surprise."

"Of course not. I'll saunter on down."

McGill stepped into the Oval Office and closed the door behind him. Patti sat behind her desk. She didn't look up from a sheet of paper she was reading. McGill didn't interrupt her, just took a seat in front of her desk and waited patiently.

When she looked up, he asked, "All's quiet on the South China Sea?"

"So far. The forces of socialist maritime might are gathering, but so are ours. The brass hats and I were just deciding how many elements of our other fleets — not just the Seventh Fleet — we'll be sending ships and submarines. We can't simply send them all because we have other areas of responsibility to maintain. We are, however, sending vessels from the Third, Fifth and Sixth Fleets."

"You'll have to refresh me on the geography involved here," McGill said.

"The Seventh Fleet is based in Japan; the Third Fleet is based in San Diego; the Fifth Fleet is based in Bahrain; the Sixth Fleet is based in Naples — Italy not Florida. Few if any of these ships and submarines would reach the South China Sea if a conflict were to start soon. But their movements will certainly be tracked by the other side's satellites. Well, the surface ships, anyway. Their inference, of course, will be that we're sending submarines, too."

McGill pondered that a moment. "Won't they also think that if any shooting starts we'll send all the vessels that have been held back?"

"That's our hope. If they're going to put on a show of force, we'll show them overwhelming force. If worse comes to worst … well, let's pray that it doesn't."

"I certainly will," McGill said. "How's Byron DeWitt?"

The President smiled. "He's mending exceptionally well. He came up with an intriguing idea that I can't go into right now, but it's being discussed by all the people immediately concerned."

"You're all trying to tear his idea down, right?"

"Yes, of course. That's always the first step. If an idea survives the initial assault, then we see if we can improve on it or just let it be and put it to use."

"Okay, but DeWitt is still your top China guy, right?"

"There are others, but I find his insights more compelling than other views. He understands both mindsets, ours and theirs. He's checking his idea with his Chinese mentor, Hiram Chen, in Santa Barbara. When he gets that feedback, we'll see what we want to do."

"Chen is trusted?" McGill asked.

"Trusted and monitored. Has been for some time."

"Good. Can't be too careful at a time like this."

"You're right about that." The President stood, came around the desk, took his hand, pulled him over to one of the two facing sofas in the room and sat next to him.

McGill said, "You're not leaving me for some movie star that Dorie set you up with, are you?"

The President laughed and kissed him. "No, I'm not leaving you period. You are so good for me. I want us to grow old together. Like the couple in that John Lennon song."

"Grow Old with Me," McGill said. "I've always liked the Mary Chapin Carpenter cover the best."

"Me, too. So you're stuck with me, my dear henchman. What I want to tell you now is my deepest, darkest secret."

McGill thought uh-oh. If there was anyone who could take depth and darkness to extremes, it would be POTUS. Nonetheless, he quietly said, "Okay."

"In a matter of months, I will no longer be the most powerful person in the world, but I will still be a woman of extraordinary means. More than that, I will still be someone with connections to people possessing exceptionally deadly skills. Think Gene Beck, only they don't whistle."

Clearly, she meant assassins. McGill felt the hair on the back of his neck rise. Even so, he didn't think of interrupting. The kicker, he knew, had to lie just ahead.

"All that being the case, I've taken out insurance policies on you, me, our children, Carolyn and Lars. In the event, any of us comes to harm or death by violent means, the perpetrators of such crimes will face more than legal jeopardy. He, she or they will die, and very badly, for their misdeeds."

McGill was struck dumb. The only thought that came to mind was the old saw about the female of the species being deadlier than the male. If he remembered right, that notion came from a Rudyard Kipling poem. The first verse pointed out that a "peasant" could scare off a male bear by shouting at it. But when the poor sap tried the same trick with a she-bear the creature ate his ass for lunch.

Not that Kipling expressed himself quite that way.

"I don't know what to say," McGill told Patti.

"I hope you'll say nothing of this to literally anyone."

"Right."

"I'm doing this because people like Auric Ludwig, the militia crazies and others will have to learn the horrible reprisal they'll suffer if they come after anyone I love. I simply will not have it, and I have the wherewithal both to spread a warning quietly to knaves worldwide and to make good on my threat."

McGill was still working at absorbing this news when Patti smiled.

"What?" he asked.

"I just saw myself in the image of an old-time mob boss: cigar, fedora, snarl and all."

"You raise a good point," McGill said. "The mafia scares people with a hard-earned history of violence. How are you going to communicate that you mean business?"

The President smiled and then she said, "I'm going to face down China and Russia. Even Al Capone couldn't do that."

USP Hazelton — West Virginia

After having had a sit down with Jerry in his cell, mob boss Peter Mancuso came through for Jerry big time. Mancuso got right down to business, telling Jerry, "What I hear is, you're in here for killing some big shot at the Pentagon. Also, you're suspected of killing some shit-bird who gunned down a bunch of kids out playing football, which would be a good thing. Besides all that, rumors are you did independent hits when you weren't busy making your suits. I have mixed feelings about that. I admire a guy with skills, but first and foremost what's important to me is organized labor."

Meaning killers worked for bosses not themselves, Jerry understood.

Jerry said, "You know how things are, Mr. Mancuso. Cops arrest whoever's handy, not necessarily the right guy. I'll concede it might have *looked* like I killed Jordan Gilford, but you know how appearances can be deceiving. I'm sure that's why you're in here, too. I'm just a guy who does fine tailoring and you're a businessman."

Jerry doubted that Mancuso was wearing a wire, but he wasn't going to take any chances of incriminating himself. Besides, the mob boss wouldn't respect anyone who spilled his guts to a stranger. Playing the innocent was the right approach.

Mancuso smiled thinly. "Yeah, sure, you got all that right. So what I'm told is you'll make a custom suit for someone of my choice in return for my help seeing if there's a con in here who might have some information you need. Well, not you but whoever you cut a deal with."

That was a detail Jerry needed to reveal. "James J. McGill."

The mob boss first thought that was a joke and laughed.

Jerry simply shook his head, telling Mancuso he was playing it straight.

"What? You expect me to believe the President's husband needs something from you? And then what, you get sprung?"

"No, there's no chance of that. What I get to do is to keep making suits."

Mancuso leaned forward, staring hard at Jerry. "And you like sewing that much, huh?"

"I won't say I'm Michelangelo, but I'm pretty close when it comes to tailoring. It gives me joy. Makes other guys happy, too, when they put one of my suits on. Chances are they never looked that good before."

The mob boss sat back and studied Jerry. He didn't see one bit of bullshit in Jerry's estimation of his talent. On the other hand, he took it for granted Jerry had lied about not killing anyone. Both things were okay by him.

He told Jerry, "I'm old school. I got all my suits from Armani. Never heard of you on the outside. But I got a grandson who's getting married next spring. I'll ask if he knows you and would like a tux made by you. If you hear back from me, we'll talk some more."

Jerry heard back two days later. Meeting Mancuso in his cell again, the mob boss told him, "My grandson, Gianni, knows your work. His mother, my daughter, said Gianni jumped in the air when he heard you could make his wedding tuxedo. So I'm going to help you, and you'd better not fuck up your end of the deal. The tuxedo you make for Gianni better be perfect."

Mancuso didn't have to specify an "or else."

Jerry knew what the consequences of failure would be. He asked to have photographs of the young man, front, back and both sides. He'd need accurate reports of his height and weight, and Jerry would need someone to take precise measurements for him. Then there would be discussions of fabric and other details. Jerry would need the cloth and his tools two months before the wedding date.

"So what is it you want from me, and at this point it damn well better be something I can do," Mancuso said.

Jerry said, "I want to know if there's a con in this prison who can tell me where to find a guy called Corona Moe."

"You're really doing this for McGill?"

"Yes."

"What's he got against this guy?"

"Moe took a contract to kill him."

"The President's husband? The guy didn't think *that* would come back at him?" Mancuso laughed. "What a fool. People who take risks like that are bad for everyone's business. If no one in this joint knows this Moe asshole, I'll see what else I can do."

Turned out, he didn't have to do more.

A short, heavily muscled guy with a square face and features that looked like they belonged on a Meso-American temple found his way to Jerry. Didn't say a word to him. Just discreetly slipped him a small piece of paper with a few scribbled words and numbers on it.

The words were La Playa Perfecta. The numbers, once Jerry punched them into the warden's computer, proved to be the latitude and longitude of a spot between Playa del Carmen and Coba on the Yucatan Peninsula in Mexico. The view from Google Earth showed what looked like an undifferentiated green mass of jungle. Jerry didn't see any sign of a highway or even a two-lane road.

For a moment, Jerry felt he'd been jerked around. Then he thought, hell, if you wanted to hide out, what better place than somewhere even satellites couldn't find you? Under all that tree cover, there could be unpaved roads. Maybe something you could manage with four-wheel drive vehicles. Or just dirt-bikes if they were really narrow.

He sure as hell wouldn't want to live in such a place, but maybe it was meant only to be a temporary shelter before Corona Moe lit out for somewhere else. He punched La Playa Perfecta into the computer. It was the name of both a beach and a resort, each rated at five stars. Okay, so Moe liked his comfort and an ocean view when things were calm.

Jerry went to see the warden, who was also expecting a suit from him.

"You mind if I use your phone again? I think I got just what Mr. McGill wanted."

The White House — Washington, DC

Shortly before sitting down to breakfast with Patti, McGill heard from Jerry Nerón. He learned where Corona Moe lived, thanked Jerry and promised to live up to his end of the bargain.

"You'd better or I'm dead," Jerry replied.

McGill's breakfast was waiting for him when he joined Patti. "I need to take a road trip."

Looking up from her pink grapefruit lightly sweetened with brown sugar, she asked, "Am I invited?"

"Absolutely. Table that little problem in the South China Sea and come travel with me. We'll have the kitchen staff whip up a picnic basket for us."

"Well," Patti said in her presidential voice, "if you're going to be rude enough to bring up world affairs, I'll just stay home."

"Or," McGill said, "we could switch roles and do each other's job."

"No, I don't think that would work well for either of us. Or the country, for that matter. You go and have a good time, but you might let me know your destination so I don't worry too much."

"Manhattan. I'm going to see my old girlfriend, if she has time for me."

Patti smiled. "You're going to see Clare? Tell her hello for me. Oh, you can also say if she's tired of working as a fundraiser, I might have something for her with Committed Capital."

"Really?" McGill asked.

"Really. So is there a reason you need to see Clare other than the bonds of affection?"

McGill gave her a capsule rundown of what Gene Beck had learned in L.A.

"That's very good," Patti said.

Then he told her about Auric Ludwig soliciting Odo Sacripant to murder him.

"That's wonderful, assuming *M'sieur* Sacripant doesn't intend to carry out his commission."

"He doesn't. Our *entente* is still *cordiale*."

"Bon. So what about this Corona Moe person?"

"I just heard from Jerry Nerón. I have to work on holding up my end of the deal on the drive to New York."

"Why are you driving?"

"Leo can get us there quickly, and once we're in the city, I don't want to depend on someone else to get around."

"Feel free to drop my name if you need any official help," Patti said, again sounding presidential.

"Thanks. I'm thinking of seeing if Detective Louis Marra of the NYPD might help me."

"He's Clare's friend, yes?"

"He is, the last I heard."

Patti said, "Always good to have the local police on your side. I've learned that from you over the years. You think that the person behind the Georgetown attempt on your life is in New York because she once was a theater person there?"

"That and her sister suggesting it was a more sympathetic place for someone like her."

"And being an empathetic fellow yourself, it has occurred to you that you might look to someone in the local LGBTQ community for help?"

"Maybe. If I do, I'm hoping your record on advocating equality for all Americans might help me there. If I don't go that way, I'll work whatever avenues I can."

Patti said, "I'd feel better if you had more help than Deke and Leo close at hand."

"Gene Beck should be in Manhattan already. We'll meet up

with him. I bet the four of us could charm King Kong off the Empire State Building."

"Yes, well, make sure the big primate doesn't drop Fay Wray on the way down. I don't want any collateral damage, especially to you."

McGill saluted. "Yes, ma'am. I believe you made that abundantly clear quite recently."

"I was entirely serious about that, Jim. It's our little secret, but it's no joke. There's one more thing for you to keep in mind."

"What's that?"

"This person you're looking for … what's her birth name again?"

"Loris Springstone."

"Yes, Loris. The Interpol records on the killings attributed to her suggest that she'd never failed to take out a target until she missed you in Georgetown. Most obsessive people feel compelled to correct their mistakes. They can't rest until they do."

"I'm a bit like that myself," McGill reminded Patti.

New York City — Manhattan

Taps knew the morning traffic pattern in her apartment building. She knew when the rush of people hurrying off to work occurred, when mothers and the occasional father took their children to school, when the idly affluent women went out to yoga or their hairdressers. She knew just when Kostas the doorman was least likely to have anybody placing demands upon him.

Taps found him alone, not listening to music through earbuds, not reading a newspaper or a magazine, just sitting on his perch behind the small lectern where he took deliveries from the outside world. His eyes were closed and his lips moved minimally as if he was praying, whispering to the Almighty in words no one else could hear.

From force of habit, Taps moved stealthily, the loudest sound she made was a soft rustle of the Chanel linen skirt suit she wore.

That was enough to make Kostas open his eyes and turn to look at her. Maybe he hadn't heard her, though. She was wearing just a touch of Dior Amber. Perhaps he caught her scent.

A possibility she would have avoided had she been working.

Kostas got to his feet and smiled. "Ah, Ms. Springer, may I be of help?"

"I hope so. It's possible I may be leaving on an extended business trip. I wanted to thank you for how helpful you've been to me, and ask you to keep a close eye on my apartment while I'm away."

She handed him a sealed envelope.

He took it with a nod of gratitude.

"You do expect to be here for some time, don't you?" she said.

"God and the building management willing, yes."

"I'm sorry but I don't know your family name. I just put Kostas on the check."

"I will be happy to do the rest."

"May I ask you something?"

"Yes, of course."

"The assignment I might be taking on could be very demanding, tiring, possibly even risky. Would you know of any private, peaceful, out of the way place where I might go to … regain a sense of well-being?"

A new light flickered in Kostas' eyes, unlike anything she'd ever seen from him before. It didn't last a heartbeat, but it was long enough for Taps to see a keen and calculating intelligence. That and the merciless appraisal of someone who knew what it meant to spill blood.

She had no doubt he could recognize the same qualities in her.

"I do know such a place," he said. "Very isolated. Sunny with a blue sea. But you don't pay for luxury there. You *work* for the bare necessities."

Taps thought about that. "Would I have my own room?"

"A private space, yes. Big enough for you and your thoughts, little else."

"A bed?"

"Narrow and hard."

"Food?"

"Enough to live and work." Kostas looked her over in a way he never had before. "Maybe a little extra for you. You are thin already."

"Thin but strong," Taps said.

Kostas smiled. "That will help with the work."

"Nobody will try to stop me from leaving?"

"No, you may leave whenever you want, as soon as a boat is available, but there is no returning."

"Are there any obligations other than working?"

"No. You will have time to walk, think and pray."

Taps said, "I'm not looking to find God."

"That is all right," Kostas said. "This is a place where God finds you."

Interstate 95, Northbound

Keeping his word to Jerry Nerón, McGill called Attorney General Michael Jaworsky from his Chevy and told him that Nerón had kept his end of the bargain. Now, McGill's half of the agreement had to be honored. The AG said he'd contact the warden at Hazelton and the director of the Bureau of Prisons to make sure everything went smoothly.

McGill thanked the AG for his help and sent his regards to the elder Mrs. Jaworsky.

With McGill, Leo and Deke in the Chevy, they were entitled to cruise in the HOV — high occupancy vehicle — lanes of I-95 northbound from Washington, DC. With an E-Z Pass Flex transponder, they didn't have to stop for toll booths. With the military grade radar detector in the car, Leo knew well in advance where all the police speed traps were and was able to adjust accordingly.

Thus equipped and with Leo behind the wheel, they were eating up the distance between DC and NYC at a little better than a 100 miles per hour average. Or as Leo put it coasting speed. Still, it was fast enough for McGill and Deke. The only problem arose when a handful of "amateurs," to use Leo's word, passed them and the former NASCAR driver had to restrain his competitive impulses.

His ire was cooled when each of the drivers who had passed him was soon pulled over by highway cops.

"You never catch up after that kind of pit-stop," Leo said, happily.

The Vice President's Office — The White House

Jean Morrissey told her brother Frank, "I want to run this by Byron first."

Frank nodded. "Okay."

He might have argued against waiting for anyone else's approval, even Patti Grant's, but Frank had checked Byron DeWitt out back to the day his father had first winked at his mother on their college campus. That particular family story was mentioned in their wedding invitation. Frank had managed to find a copy. Ever since, the elder DeWitts had been so true to each other they could have starred in a '50s television show. Well, maybe the photos of the newlywed Mrs. DeWitt learning to surf in her bikini would have called for a costume change.

A generation later, Jean had told Frank that Byron was going to teach her to surf. Knowing Jean was a natural athlete, that shouldn't have come as a big surprise. What caught Frank off guard was the cultural and geographical shift. If Jean had said she and DeWitt were going to Aspen so she could learn to ski downhill, that wouldn't have been a shocker. At least Minnesota had cold and snow in common with the Rocky Mountains.

Coastal California, though, was warm almost all the time, had sun, sand and palm trees. It was like a whole 'nother world. Sure, it was just the far side of the country, but it felt to Frank like his sister was moving to Australia. How often would he even see her? Would he recognize her when he did? It gave him an idea of how the relatives who'd stayed behind in Ireland, back in the day, must have felt when they saw others in the family sailing off to America.

Frank Morrissey had always been smart and able to spot other people's weaknesses at a glance, but he was as tough as forged steel only because his sister had made him that way. She'd been the first to see he was gay, had asked him privately when he was going to tell Mom and Dad. This was before Frank had even had the courage to admit to himself who he was.

Jean, God bless her, had told him he would be okay. When he felt the time was right, she would ease the way with their parents for him. The other thing she told him was he'd better learn to fight because there were a lot of assholes in the world who wouldn't be nearly as nice to him as she was. To further that advice, she took boxing lessons, over their mother's objections, and passed the knowledge on to Frank. The two of them had sparred like dervishes.

The only person ever to give Frank a black eye was Jean.

Of course, the boxing practice also came in handy when Jean got into a hockey fight.

No Jewish mother ever loved a son more than Frank Morrissey loved his sister.

That was why he was both pleased and suspicious when he couldn't find out anything bad about Byron. Yes, DeWitt and an underling at the FBI, Special Agent Abra Benjamin, had conceived a child out of wedlock, but neither the mother nor the baby boy had suffered in any way. Benjamin kept her job, even continued to be mentored by DeWitt, and the child had been adopted by loving parents, Ron Ketchum and Keely Powell.

Frank had a suspicion that giving up the kid did bother Byron DeWitt, probably caused him real pain. But he didn't take it out on anyone else. What he did was learn from it. Frank couldn't find another woman DeWitt had taken as a lover between Benjamin and Jean. More than that, he hadn't gone back to banging Benjamin. The guy seemed to learn from his mistakes.

That was a sterling quality in a man married to a female candidate for president.

All things considered, Frank was starting to consider Byron

DeWitt an ally, insofar as he allowed himself to trust anyone other than Jean … and now Galia Mindel. So he sat quietly as Jean and DeWitt watched the commercial he'd commissioned to run against Senator Oren Worth. Jean would have the final word on whether it was televised and streamed online.

Frank was sure, though, she'd ask for DeWitt's opinion.

The commercial opened on a still photograph of Oren Worth as a young teen, gawky and thin with a bad haircut. In the background, an offscreen chorus of voices sang a high school fight song.

Announcer (voice over as group singing diminished): "When Oren Worth entered high school, he tried out for the glee club."

An adolescent male voice strained for a high note of the fight song and cracked.

Announcer: "He didn't make it."

An image of Worth as a young man appeared. He wore a hard hat, a denim shirt with the sleeves rolled up, twill pants and work boots. He stood on an outcropping of rock as a group of miners looked up at him.

Announcer: "Though his singing career was a bust, Oren Worth made billions as a mining magnate."

Worth (to his miners): "We're gonna make this the most profitable mine on earth and …"

The image froze on Worth's open mouth.

Announcer: "Oren Worth's twang was his natural way of speaking. Linguists say it's part of the Central West dialect."

A new video clip showed a middle-aged Worth standing at the lectern in the well of the United States Senate.

Worth: "Over-regulation is killing American business."

Announcer: "No twang now, but it's not unusual for people to polish their speaking voices. What is strange though …"

An older Worth now stood on the West Front of the Capitol.

Announcer: "Is when the highest ranking member of the United States Senate does a bad impression of the late actor Cary Grant while speaking of national unity. Listen."

Worth: "We stand together, shoulder to shoulder, every man,

woman and child …"

Announcer: "Really, Senator? This is a time to do a Cary Grant shtick? Who's next: John Wayne, Carol Channing, Daffy Duck?"

A face-on Worth moved his lips as a Wayne-like voice said, "That's right, pilgrim."

Worth continued as a knock-off Channing adding, "Hello, Dolly."

Worth summed it all up as Daffy Duck, "Ha-ha, it is to laugh."

Announcer: "We'll all be laughing, all right, Senator — when you *don't* wind up in the Oval Office. Because the closer we listen, the phonier you sound."

A superimposed graphic repeated the announcer's final line.

The closer we listen, the phonier you sound.

Frank clicked off the television. He handed Jean and DeWitt campaign buttons, elegant in simplicity and design, four words in white letters on a blue background: *The closer we listen.*

DeWitt smiled. "An implicit call to action: listen closely."

"And the implication is anything Worth says will be phony," Jean added. "You haven't lost your touch, Frank."

Before going to work for Jean full time, Frank had been a partner at the best ad agency in Minneapolis. He had a shelf full of Clio awards. A few from Cannes, too.

Still, Jean felt she had to play the role of the cautious account executive.

"Do you think the other celebrity voices, aside from the reference to Cary Grant, are over the top?"

Frank said, "Leave 'em laughing and the ad will go viral. More important, Worth won't know what the hell voice he should use at the presidential debates."

Jean looked to Byron for his opinion.

He nodded and said, "Sun Tzu would be proud of Frank."

That was the moment Frank decided to accept his new brother-in-law unconditionally.

And Jean said, "Okay, the Duke, Dolly and Daffy all make the cut."

I-95, Approaching New York City

"Hello, Clare. It's Jim."

For all the advantages Leo possessed and used in making great time heading up I-95, there was nothing he could do about grid-locked highway traffic. A news radio report said there had been an accident involving two jack-knifed semis a mile ahead of their present position. The nearest exit ramp lay a half-mile beyond the scene of the accident. They were stuck right where they were, just like everybody else on that stretch of road.

McGill had decided to make the best use of his time by calling ahead.

"Jim who?" Clare Tracy asked.

"The one with the famous wife."

"Which famous wife?"

"The one who might have a job for you, if you're tired of the old one."

"Tired of the old Jim?"

"If you're working up a comedy routine, that might be helpful."

"To your wife?"

"To me. Should I call back later? When you're not in the moment of whatever it is you're doing now."

"What?" Clare asked. "I can't bust your chops when you call me out of the blue after letting who knows how long a time go by, James J. McGill?"

"Too long," McGill admitted. "How can I make it up to you?"

"Tell me it's good to hear my voice again."

"Always, Clare. I could say I've been crazy busy, and that would be the truth, but it's no excuse. I'm sorry I haven't been properly attentive to our friendship."

"Well ... I did read in the *Times* about your recent perils in Georgetown. That scared the hell out of me, Jim. I can only imagine how Patti must have felt. I'm sorry about giving you a hard time just now. I guess I didn't want to sound overly concerned. You know what I mean."

McGill did. Clare had been one of the three significant loves of his life.

"Sure," he said. "Listen, I'm stuck in traffic about 20 miles outside of town."

"This town? Manhattan?"

"Yeah. How about we have dinner in some homey place where no one could read anything improper about seeing us together? Say, Marie Callender's."

"There are over 24,000 restaurants in Manhattan, Jim, but Marie has yet to put in an appearance. How about Lombardi's? It's supposed to be the first pizzeria in America."

"It's not connected to Vince Lombardi, is it?" McGill, after all, was a die-hard Chicago Bears fan. Clare, also from Chicago, understood his concern.

"Gennaro Lombardi was the founder; I haven't heard Vince's name mentioned."

"Okay, it's a date."

"When? As soon as traffic clears up, you'll let me know?"

"Yes."

"You want to tell me what this is all about? Wait a minute. Does this have something to do with what happened in Georgetown?"

"It does. I need to plead for your help."

"You think somebody involved in all that mayhem is here in New York?"

"It's a possibility. I was thinking you might be able to help me get a lead."

"Absolutely. Anything I can do."

"Are you still seeing Detective Louis Marra?"

After a moment's pause, Clare said, "No. He was assigned to an anti-terrorist intelligence unit in Europe. He asked me to come with, but I declined. I wanted to stay at my job. Are you thinking you'll need NYPD help?"

"I might. It's always good to get the local cops on your side before anything dramatic happens."

"I know someone else. I can give you a phone number or she

can join us for dinner."

"Let's keep dinner just between us. I'll call your friend."

"Okay." She gave McGill a name and a phone number. Clare said to use her name when he called. You know, in case the cop didn't know he was married to the President.

McGill laughed, and he could almost feel Clare's mood brighten.

"Is there anything else I can do now?" she asked.

"How much do you know about the local theater scene? Not the Broadway shows. The way out on the fringe stuff."

"Not much. I court the big money donors. They tend to frequent the big name productions. But I know some people who know some people. Tell me what you want."

McGill told her all he knew about Loris Springstone, aka Chris Nevers.

He texted her copies of the images of the person using those names.

"I'll do everything I can to help you, Jim," Clare said. "Sorry about the rude reception."

McGill said, "I deserved it. I look forward to seeing you, Clare."

Still stuck on I-95

Having grown up in a house with a rotary-dial phone that weighed ten pounds and was wired to a wall — Ma and Pa McGill being late adapters to all sorts of changes — McGill continued to be amazed at what modern cell phones could do. This amused his children no end. He described his gee-whiz attitude toward high tech as part of his charm.

He didn't take it for granted that his next call, this one to Father Inigo de Loyola in Costa Rica, would go through without a hitch. Who knew if the satellites were aligned or whatever? Maybe Central America was still a stranger to the visual blight of cell towers. Heck, maybe a Jesuit who took his vow of poverty seriously had forgotten to recharge his cell phone's battery.

None of that stood in the way. The call went through and was answered clear as a bell immediately after the first ring. God, clearly, was on his side. For the moment, anyway.

"*¿Sí?*" Yes?

"Father de Loyola?" McGill asked.

"*Sí.* I mean, yes. Mr. McGill?"

"Yes, Father. I'm calling to follow up on the conversation Margaret Sweeney had with you."

"A wonderful woman. I was most pleased to see her, and to meet General Yates. Whenever I hear voices in my part of the world that are critical of America, I always say, 'I know someone you should meet.' I would include you in that number, Mr. McGill."

"Thank you, Father."

"Of course, when I speak to some of my American friends, I tell them I know people in other countries they should meet."

"No doubt. Father, were you able to find any of your former comrades in arms who had been contacted by Corona Moe?"

McGill thought the connection of the call had suddenly dropped out. Then he realized the priest must have turned away from his phone. He heard de Loyola mutter, in Latin not English or Spanish. McGill understood what the priest had to say.

Deus, dimitte pecatta mea. God, forgive my sins.

It wasn't McGill's business to ask for specificity. So he didn't.

De Loyola rejoined the conversation on a secular plane.

"I learned of three former friends in the liberation effort who had been contacted by agents of this man. One of them, I visited. He was too infirm to murder anyone, much to his great regret. The other two did carry out the crimes for which they'd been hired. One of them died in the process; the other couldn't live with the shame. After he had given his family the blood money he'd earned, he committed suicide."

"I'm sorry for all three men and their misfortunes, Father."

"As am I. More than that, I am also very angry. I try to tell myself that being vengeful is a great sin. Awareness, however, is not always persuasive. At least in my case. Many of my old comrades are also very angry, none of them inclined to be merciful."

McGill pondered the situation for a moment.

Corona Moe had acted as one of the intermediaries in the attempt to kill him. To take McGill from his wife, children and others who would grieve upon hearing of his violent death. Yes, he had felt remorse for killing Paulette Lacroix. Even so, he doubted he'd feel the same regret for playing a role in Corona Moe's demise, but would his indifference make it any less wrong? Or was it wrong at all?

Moe was manipulating the most vulnerable people McGill could imagine, having them go out and kill other people. Just so he could make a buck. What could be more despicable than that? Sure, the Bible said, "Judge not lest ye be judged," but were there *never* any mitigating circumstances?

Civil law allowed the taking of a life without penalty if you did it in defense of your own life or that of an innocent third party. Did the writ of heaven really not cut anybody any slack, ever?

Well, hell, McGill thought, he had a priest on the phone. Why not ask him?

That was just what he did, explaining his moral dilemma and asking for guidance.

Father de Loyola listened closely and asked only one question.

"As you say you have this information, will you please give me the locations where I might find this Corona Moe person? My friends and I will go have a talk with him."

The friends not inclined to mercy, McGill thought.

Who certainly had more in mind than just conversation.

Even so, McGill provided the details to de Loyola. He was sure he'd have to answer for his choice in the end. And if he had to pay for it, at least he'd be in good company.

New York City — Manhattan

Counting the members of the two largest organized labor unions for actors, Actors Equity and the Screen Actors Guild, an estimated 30,000 actors lived in New York City. A much smaller, ever fluctuating number of actors actually made a living from their art. The count of those who achieved even relative fame and fortune was likely outnumbered by the guests at any high society wedding.

Taps had once been among the multitude of acting hopefuls who worked as bicycle messengers, slept on the couches in friends' apartments in the Outer Boroughs or communally scrabbled together the funds to do a showcase performance, hoping that someone who mattered would come and discover a gem in the rough.

The problem with that was most big-time agents and big-name producers wanted gems that were already cut, polished and placed in platinum settings. Developing talent took time and their time was too valuable to spend on up-and-comers whose upside was anybody's guess. In most cases, pursuing a career in acting was a merciless and thankless business.

Pretty much like working in any of the other arts.

Taps came to realize that after a relatively short grind of five years. She came oh so close in terms of acting talent. Absolutely nailed it when it came to portraying tragedy. In fact, she'd probably been *too* good at making people feel her pain. But she had no emotional range. Couldn't do humor — even the snarky kind — to save her life.

Things got to the point where casting directors refused to let Taps read for parts because she was so good at making them feel bad they began to feel suicidal. If she did the same thing to theater audiences six times a week, there'd be a public health crisis. That was their joke anyway.

Predictably, Taps was not amused.

Nor was she pleased by the fact that her artistic limits weren't her only drawback. Her androgynous appearance made it difficult to reach for either well-defined male or female roles. Telling the casting director she could go either way only drew snide chuckles.

Except for the time a bisexual casting director invited Taps to join him and an aspiring actress to go *both* ways in a *ménage à trois.* Taps broke the guy's nose and might have done the same to his neck only three stagehands jumped on her. To spare himself the notoriety of getting his ass kicked by a "freak of nature," in his words, the guy didn't press charges.

That was the end of Taps' acting career. Show biz couldn't tolerate physical assaults by actors. If punching out the decision makers ever caught on, the whole structure of the business would collapse. That or sensitivity to other people's feelings might become required. Neither alternative was considered acceptable by the powers that be.

The irony of the matter was that the casting director never worked in live theater again. The LGBTQ community had become a force in the arts by then, and it didn't like the way Taps had been treated. Demeaned was its word. The fact that the director was bisexual himself was no defense. It worked against him, people saying he, especially, should have known better.

The guy moved to L.A. and found work in porn flicks, gay and straight.

Ironically, Taps also had a fleeting impulse to go to California. Only that was where she'd finally lost it with Mom and Dad, and there was no statute of limitations on what she'd done to them. She might have found stunt work in films — whatever else she was, she'd always been athletic — but she didn't think she dared to take the chance.

Nobody in the NYPD was looking for her, but back home she couldn't be sure some hard-case old cop wasn't pursuing her. With one dream having crashed down on her head, she needed a means to go on living in the country's most expensive city. Do it in a way that didn't … demean — yeah, that — her every waking moment.

The question was how?

The answer came quickly. She'd really wanted to kill that bastard casting director, probably would have succeeded — and been locked up for the rest of her life — if the stagehands hadn't intervened. The lesson there was not to be impulsive. Plan before you act and get away clean.

Just as she had with Mom and Dad.

Only now, she would do it for money. Big money. It would take study, preparation, finding the right contacts without getting arrested and a complete indifference to the value of other people's lives. She figured she was already there on the last requirement.

As with her attempt at an acting career, she gave herself five years to succeed.

She'd needed only two. Her first rule was don't work in the country where you live. The second was don't fish for minnows. Go big and charge accordingly. The third step was don't forget the first two.

She'd done well by keeping things just that simple. Well, following the rules was also supplemented by training with guns, knives, explosives, toxic agents and close-quarters combat. With a relatively small amount of money and an internet connection there was precious little in the way of modern mayhem that couldn't be learned and mastered. Of course, it helped to be mad at the world and indifferent to the continued survival of just about everyone.

The two exceptions were her nearly identical siblings: Kim and Pat. As little kids, adolescents and even teenagers, Kim and Pat had tried hard to shield her from Mom, Dad and the rest of the world. But then it came time for the sisters to go to college and off they went. Taps didn't blame them for that, but she'd envied them fiercely.

Taps made a real effort to tell herself Kim and Pat didn't matter more than anyone else, but she couldn't quite convince herself. Then, out of the blue, that very day, Kim called her. That was a damn fine trick as Taps hadn't given her personal phone number to anyone.

Except, in a way she had, as Kim reminded her.

"You used to tell any creep who bothered you that he should call 1-800-FUCKYOU. I just substituted New York City area codes for the 800. Got you with the 212 prefix."

Taps laughed and then came the hard part: What did you say to a sister you hadn't talked to for 18 years?

"Lo, you still there?" Kim asked using her sister's childhood nickname.

"Yeah, I'm just stuck for what to say."

"Let me break the ice. I still love you. Pat does, too. We talk about you regularly."

"How do you do that? Do you have any idea of…" She was going to say: what I do. She changed that to: "Who I am now."

"I was visited by a man named Eugene Beck."

"Never heard of him."

"He works for James J. McGill."

"Jesus." The word got out before Taps could stop it.

"Oh, damn, Lo, did you really do it? Try to kill the President's husband?"

It was the first time Taps had broken the rule about not working where you live. The money was astronomical and the target was compelling. Doing in a figure of McGill's stature would do wonders for business. Or let her retire reasonably well if she started to feel lazy.

"Are you recording this call, Kim. Is someone listening in?"

"What? No! I'm calling to try to help you, to warn you. Mr. Beck didn't say so, but it seemed obvious he's looking for you. Mr. McGill has his own private investigations agency. He might have a lot of people looking for you. I wanted to get in touch with you first so you could get a lawyer and turn yourself in. If you don't have the money for someone good, Pat and I will help."

Taps couldn't help but laugh. "Unless one of you won the lottery, I have more money than either of you. More than the two of you put together."

"Then do the smart thing: Get a lawyer and go to the police."

It was way too late for that. "Kim, tell me one thing. Did you call me as soon as you could, right after you talked to this Beck guy?"

"Damnit, Lo, how the hell could I? You didn't exactly leave forwarding information. Pat and I talked for hours and hours before we came up with that old insulting phone number and neither of us knew if that was going to work."

"Well, I'm glad you figured things out. Thanks. Say hello to Pat for me."

Taps broke the connection and turned her phone off. She had thought she'd have to go looking for McGill. Now, it was obvious he'd come looking for her. Washington wasn't that far from New York. Kim must've told that Beck guy that the person he was looking for had a history in New York. Beck, or even McGill, might be in town already. She should have thought to ask Kim if either of them was headed this way.

Maybe she'd call back later.

Right now, though, Taps still had to do the two things that she'd planned to do earlier.

Hire an actor and buy a Chevy.

New York City — Manhattan

McGill met Clare outside of Lombardi's on Spring Street in Lower Manhattan. Gene Beck had caught up with him. Gene and Deke were talking to two NYPD patrol officers about where McGill's Chevy might park close to the restaurant, illegally if necessary. Leo was at the wheel of the car as it idled quietly.

The negotiations were beginning to look worthy of the U.N. trying to work out peace in the Middle East when a taxi pulled up behind the Chevy and the police patrol unit. Clare Tracy got out of the taxi looking like a million dollars — back in the day when that was still serious money.

All eyes turned to her as she walked up to McGill, took his hands in hers and kissed him on both cheeks. The signs of affection between them couldn't have been more obvious if they'd been displayed in neon lights. McGill whispered something into Clare's ear and she walked over to the two patrol cops. She took a business card from her handbag and showed it to the cops.

Both of them saluted, nodded and smiled.

Barring an emergency that required fire engines or bomb

disposal trucks, McGill's Chevy could stay right where it was, just outside the restaurant. McGill sauntered over and asked if he might buy the cops something from the restaurant. They declined, contenting themselves with shaking McGill's hand and saying it was a pleasure to meet him.

Clare moved to McGill's side and he introduced her to Gene, and she renewed her acquaintance with Deke and Leo. McGill asked what kind of pizza the guys would like him to have sent out. Then he and Clare went inside. She was greeted like an old friend. The host showed them to a relatively quiet corner in the front room of the establishment.

They gave their order and the one for the guys outside. Pizza all around, of course, but McGill and Clare both went with San Pellegrino to drink instead of a pitcher of beer like the old days.

Clare asked, "Are we showing our age or just good sense in avoiding alcohol?"

"Maybe a little of both." McGill said, "I'm not supposed to know it, but Patti has a farewell party at the White House planned for the night of January 19th. There will be champagne, dancing, laughter and promises to stay in touch. I intend to partake in all of the above. I hope you can make it, and bring a guest if you like."

Clare said, "I think I can make it. Would it be all right if I come alone? I might stand a better chance of meeting a nice guy if I do."

"There hasn't been anyone since Detective Marra?" McGill asked.

Clare shook her head. "All the men in this town and … I had a terrible impulse to plant a good kiss on a more meaningful spot than your cheeks. Only I didn't want to spoil my friendships with both halves of the First Couple."

McGill gave Clare's hands a gentle squeeze. "Good choice. I might have reacted improperly. You know, even though you've become such a Plain Jane after all these years."

Clare pulled her hands free, but they both laughed. "You don't know how much money I had to spend and what I had to go through in a very short time to look this good."

"So you do look ordinary most of the time?"

"Enough about me, Jim McGill. Is that gray I see in your receding hairline?"

"No, it's just an artfully done toupee. You should see me when I take it off."

"And spoil many a fond memory? No, thank you."

The waiter came with their sparkling Italian water, forestalling more laughter, and setting the tone for a more serious discussion. When they were alone again, Clare asked, "Were you scared when your car was attacked in Georgetown?"

McGill replied in a quiet voice. "I know intellectually how well armored my car is, but when somebody starts shooting at you, especially with automatic weapons, you can't help but flinch, feel cold and tense. In my case, I also wanted to retaliate somehow."

He paused as if coming to understand something for the first time.

"What is it, Jim."

"Leo saved the day and my life most likely. He got us out of the immediate danger zone in little more than the blink of an eye. But, emotionally, I must have still been gearing up for a fight because when that little old lady came around the corner and tried to pull a gun on me —"

Clare said, "What? I didn't read that in the *Times*."

McGill gave her the story of Paulette Lacroix. "I told myself that I shot her first because either Deke or Leo would have killed her for sure if they opened up. But looking at it now, I think taking that shot was probably more of a reflex than the product of reason."

Now, Clare took McGill's hand. "Whatever it was, the woman brought the outcome upon herself, and think of how many people are still weak in the knees with relief and joy that you're still alive. Starting with Patti and your children, but I'm not far behind."

McGill nodded. "I'm glad, too." He sighed and changed the subject. "Were you able to find out anything about Chris Nevers, née Loris Springstone?"

"I think so." She reached into her handbag and brought out

a square of folded paper. She handed it to McGill. "This is a copy of a clipping from a small publication called *The Gay City Times.* It describes how a gender-fluid actor beat up a bisexual casting director. The incident happened quite a while ago, but look at the actor's name."

"Nevers or Springstone?" McGill asked.

"Read."

He did. "Chris Springer."

"Don't aliases usually work that way?" Clare asked. "Variations on a theme."

McGill said, "Not always but often."

"A friend of mine looked for any acting credits in the name of Chris Springer, but couldn't find any. Neither here or in Boston. I'm still waiting to hear about L.A."

McGill told her, "We've got Dorie McBride working for us out there, but let's see if your friend turns up something Dorie didn't."

Clare knew of Dorie by reputation. "I'd be surprised, but I have one other item for you, a copy of a not very good photo."

She handed McGill a square of folded paper.

He opened it and nodded immediately. "That's her. Or him, as the case may be."

Clare explained, "*The Gay City Times* had the photo, source unknown, but decided not to run it with the story. The friend who helped me with this search couldn't find any kind of production, professional or amateur, that included a Chris Springer in the cast. Not post-punch-out of the casting director."

McGill said, "Maybe Chris has a police record for some other dust-up that didn't attract any media attention. If I'm not being too nosy, may I ask whose card you flashed to the cops outside the restaurant?"

"The commissioner's. I raise funds for some police charities when I'm not working on politics."

"Do you think —" McGill began.

"Sure, I can ask if the police have a file on Chris Springer. There are other ways besides the theater to make a living in the Big

Apple. Quite a few of them illegal."

The Bent Bobbie — Lower Manhattan

Taps tipped the bartender at The Bent Bobbie a hundred dollars to keep other customers at least three tables away from the corner two-top she'd snagged when she entered the premises. The tavern was owned by a former member of the City of London Police who was forced to resign under a cloud of suspicion. He was suspected of — but not charged with — being complicit in a computer hack of Transport for London, the city's gigantic public transit system.

When the breach was discovered, some 18 months after it first occurred, the immediate thought on everyone's mind was that terrorists were planning some immense attack at the height of the morning or evening rush hours. It was only after several more months of investigation that the motive for the crime was discovered to be money not militancy. Somebody had produced more than a million fake Oyster Travelcards.

In legitimate use, the pre-paid cards allowed riders to board all of the London Underground routes, buses and above-ground trains. The cards were billed as the cheapest, most flexible means of paying for travel in the city. They were even more affordable when perfectly usable knockoffs were sold at a steep discount.

Circumstantial evidence from the ensuing investigation pointed to Cedric Day and his nephew Gerard Day as the culprits. Cedric was one of the police department's liaisons to Transport for London. Gerard was Cedric's nephew, a student in computer science at University College London. The problem for the authorities was that the Days, elder and younger, left no tangible, i.e. legally conclusive, evidence that might allow them to be locked up. They also declined to rat each other out despite extensive and harsh questioning.

The best that could be done was to sack Cedric from his job and expel Gerard from his school. That offered the smallest of comforts. Including both international and domestic tourists, London had been known to host as many as 30 million visitors in a year. Over an eighteen month period, 45 million was not an unreasonable estimate.

So it was thought to be conceivable that the Days had made off with tens of millions of pounds — money that the police had been unable to find. Cinema and television producers rushed in to turn the Days' thievery into entertainment. The suspects themselves thought it best to leave England behind — in case the scriptwriters turned out to be more astute than the police in determining where they'd hidden their swag.

Gerard opted for distance, using a zigzag route and several aliases to land in New Zealand.

Cedric went to the closest place he knew, in terms of size, language and urban energy, to London — New York City. To lessen the chances that he might eventually be extradited to the UK, Cedric directed a shell company he'd set up to make a sizable contribution to the re-election campaign of a Congressman from Long Island. In return, the pol introduced a so-called private bill in his legislative chamber. Among other things, such legislation was executed to provide grants of citizenship to individuals who would otherwise be ineligible for normal visa processing.

Private bills were also known as slip bills, and Cedric Day quietly slipped into the status of a full-fledged United States citizen.

He soon opened a bar in Manhattan and gave it a name that thumbed his nose at the police back home — The Bent Bobbie. Rendered in American usage: The Crooked Cop.

The New York tabloids soon learned of Day's story and ran it under banner headlines. In a matter of hours his joint was packed and did a turn-away business for months. It didn't take much longer than that, of course, for the trendies to move on. But TBB, as the bar came to be called, maintained a solid base of patronage among artists, actors, and people with minor criminal tendencies who liked the idea of scheming in a place whose owner had gotten away with a historic heist.

If nothing else, many of them thought Cedric Day's luck might rub off on them.

Inevitably, they were the ones who got locked up or gunned down.

Taps wasn't aware of this trend, and wouldn't have let it stop her if she had. What she did know was the joint wasn't going to be around much longer, and the NYPD would be at a dead-end trying to investigate any plots that had been hatched there.

The buildings to either side of The Bent Bobbie had already been purchased by British banks and knocked down to make room for yet another mega high-rise. In a few months, the structure housing TBB would come down, too. Cedric Day's lease had been bought out and he would have to move on, newly aware that there were people who held grudges against him and could put in even bigger fixes than he had done.

A visiting reporter from a London tabloid, learning of TBB's imminent demise, had dropped in to have a pint and twit Cedric. "The coppers back home mightn't have gotten you, but nobody outruns big money."

In appreciation for receiving this bit of wisdom, Cedric brought the newsie a pint on the house. After discreetly spitting in the glass first.

Taps had passed the evening and the better part of the night at TBB interviewing actors. She was looking for someone who bore a close resemblance to James J. McGill. Whoever that guy turned out to be, he also had to be able to run like hell for a quarter-mile, turning at least one street corner in the process.

As part of her casting call, she'd put out a physical description of McGill without naming him: mid-40s, a bit over six feet tall, 180 pounds, dark wavy hair with touches of gray, symmetrical features, ruddy complexion, good but not stiff posture, a spring in his step. To sum it all up, she used a baseline likeness that she'd read McGill had often applied to himself: Rory Calhoun, an old-time movie actor whose work she'd never seen.

She had managed, though, to find an autographed black-and-white 8x10 glossy of Calhoun at a shop in Chelsea called Forever Hollywood. She kept the photo face down on the table in front of her. In cases where the local talent came anywhere close to what she wanted, she'd take a peek at the photo, like a gambler checking a hole card.

With more than half of the hopefuls, that wasn't necessary. She simply said, "Thank you," and forked over the $100 she'd promised for making the attempt. As someone who'd known the pain of curt audition rejections, she thought it was fair compensation for getting people's hopes up only to knock them down. With anyone else, there would have been no recompense at all.

In the normal way of things, just as Taps was about to give up, in walked a guy who looked enough like McGill to scare her into thinking he was the real thing. She was reaching for her gun when she realized this guy was too young to be McGill. Still … maybe he was the man's kid brother.

Only her research on McGill hadn't mentioned any brother.

He spotted Taps and guessed correctly that she was the person he wanted. He extended his hand and smiled. "Jack McCown. I was afraid I might miss the opportunity here. I was working late, but I got here as fast as I could."

Taps remained seated as she shook his hand and kept on looking at him. The resemblance was striking. To Rory Calhoun even more than McGill. She didn't even need to look at the photo.

"Is it okay if I sit down?"

"Yes, please. So where do you work?"

He sat and said, "I'm a 'resident' at The Tenement Museum. You know it?"

Taps nodded. The Lower East Side building at 97 Orchard Street had been home to thousands of 19th-century immigrant workers. The museum there recreated what their lives had been like. It offered a three-dimensional look at a part of the city's history, including the "people" who lived there in the form of actors wearing period clothing.

McCown leaned forward, rested his strong chin on an upraised hand and flashed his smile again. "So what do you think? Do I fit the bill?"

Taps nodded. "Standing and sitting, you do. Now, tell me if you can run."

"Oh, yeah. I ran track in high school and college: 1500 meters. Won't ever outrun an elite Ethiopian, but I can still leave most people in my dust."

Having had a moment to study McCown now, Taps thought he was slimmer, maybe by 10 pounds or so, than McGill, but so small a difference was unlikely to be noticed when someone was running away quickly.

While she was still thinking, McCown pointed a finger at the face-down photo.

"If that's who I think it is, there's no relation even though we share the same family name."

Taps sat back. "Who do you think it is?"

"Rory Calhoun. I get that a lot, how we look alike. Sometimes, I wonder if it keeps me from getting parts. Makes me seem dated somehow."

"You changed your name from Calhoun?"

"No, he changed his name from Francis Timothy McCown."

Taps turned the print over, and McCown nodded.

"Not hard to see the resemblance, but I don't think he ever ran track, and Mom and Dad swear he wasn't my real father. We all get a lot of laughs from that."

Taps kept her focus despite the irritating mention of a functional family.

She said, "I don't know exactly when I might need you. It could conflict with your job."

"I'm off for the next week. I hope that'll work for you."

"It should, yeah."

"If you think I'm right, would it be okay to talk about pay? Your post online said 'good money.' Just how good is it?"

"Ten thousand dollars."

Jack McCown sat back and blinked. "You know what? An old line just popped into my head."

"Who do you have to kill? Nobody. All you have to do is run."

"From somebody who'll be chasing me?"

Taps nodded.

"Do I let myself get caught?"

"Up to you."

"But if I am caught?"

"They won't be Ethiopians, but even if they were, you won't be doing anything wrong."

McCown said, "Ten grand would go a long way to putting on a showcase performance for me and several friends. You're really going to pay that much money for what, a prank?"

"I am."

Taps had been handing out money all night long. She took a stack of hundred-dollar bills from a courier bag and counted out fifty of them. "Half down, half upon completion."

McCown stared at the money. He felt certain there were things he wasn't being told, but what the hell, if all he had to do was show his face and run …

"I'm not going to get shot, am I?" he asked.

Taps gave the question honest consideration. "Maybe there's a … one in 10,000 chance."

McCown decided the risk was worth the reward.

He gave Taps his phone number and took the money.

She told him he'd have to be ready at no more than an hour's notice.

So if he lived in Jersey or somewhere, he'd have to find a place to crash in Manhattan.

"No problem," he said. "I'll try to get in a tune-up run or two before you call."

CHAPTER 9

The White House — Washington, DC
Wednesday, September 21, 2016

Park Jin-Soon, the Republic of Korea's ambassador to the United States, felt a sense of great unease the moment he stepped into the Oval Office. Not only was the President waiting for him, so were Vice President Morrissey, Secretary of State Helen Hargitay, Secretary of Defense Martin Dempsey, Chairman of the Joint Chiefs of Staff General Nicholas Mills and Director of National Intelligence Gregory Ishida.

Despite knowing the White House had a strict no-smoking policy, Ambassador Park asked the President, "May I have a last cigarette before I'm taken out and shot?"

His request drew smiles and a couple of chuckles.

"I'm not to be shot? Then are our countries about to go to war with China?"

The President said, "Please have a seat, Mr. Ambassador. We're here to see if we can avoid going to war with China."

Park took a seat in front of the President's desk, not far from the one on which Jean Morrissey sat. She gave him a polite nod of recognition but maintained a serious expression. The ambassador felt certain he was going to receive news his government would not like.

Quite possibly hate.

"Do you wish my country to send naval vessels to join your forces in the South China Sea, Madam President? If so, that request should be addressed directly to Seoul."

He could only hope that was the situation. Sending even a token warship to join the Americans would be a delicate matter but it could still be managed. Pyongyang had already threatened to turn his country into a sea of fire. What more could they do?

President Grant offered a chill smile. "No, that's not what we have in mind, Mr. Ambassador. We're thinking more comprehensively about the relationship between the United States and the Republic of Korea. Before we get to that, though, let's take a moment to review how well your country has done while being protected by the United States for more than half-a-century now. Helen, why don't you start?"

Secretary of State Hargitay put on her reading glasses and looked at a sheaf of paper on her lap. "The Republic of Korea's population is twice as large as the North's; the civilian economy is 40 times larger than the North's; the infant mortality rate is less than one-sixth of the North's; the average life expectancy is ten years longer than in North Korea."

In a stiff tone, Park said, "We have worked very hard to achieve all these things."

"For which your country is to be commended, Mr. Ambassador," the President said. "Martin, will you please continue our evaluation?"

Secretary of Defense Dempsey said, "The Republic of Korea has nearly 11,000,000 males ages 16-49 who are considered fit for military service; the North has just under 5,000,000. The North does have almost twice as many men on active military duty as the Republic, but the Ambassador's country has seven times as many men in reserve as the North."

Park did not like the direction of this discussion and his fear was turning to anger.

"We do not have a nuclear program like the North's."

The President gestured to General Mills. He said, "No, sir,

Mr. Ambassador, you do not have a nuclear program. You have a nuclear umbrella, provided by the United States. With your country's agreement, we propose to continue that protection indefinitely."

Turning to the President, Park said, "Madam President, please tell me the ultimate purpose of this meeting. I am becoming very concerned. If what I suspect you are about to tell me is … I think this discussion should take place at a level far higher than my humble office."

The President nodded to the Director of National Intelligence.

Gregory Ishida said, "We apologize for burdening you with this situation, Mr. Ambassador, but what we're doing here must be done without attracting any undue notice. A formal meeting between heads-of-state would take too long to arrange and would not serve either of our countries well. Speed and a veil of secrecy here are a must."

Park's burgeoning anger was shoved aside by a renewed wave of fear.

He thought his country's future was about to change in a way it would never choose for itself. Were the Americans actually thinking about leaving the Republic of Korea? Didn't they remember how horrific the situation had been before they arrived?

He found the courage to be blunt. "Madam President, do you intend to surrender us to the Communists?"

Unfazed, Patricia Grant asked, "Would you surrender to them?"

Park bristled. "Of course not. We would fight with all our strength."

Jean Morrissey leaned forward to join the conversation. "Your strength, objectively speaking, is considerable, Mr. Ambassador. You have a modern, economically strong, well-educated country. The only question is does the Republic of Korea have the *will* to stand up to a dysfunctional neighbor that can't even feed its people adequately?"

Anger made an immediate comeback. Park ground his teeth.

He looked as if he might bolt from the room. He made a heroic effort to master his temper and said, "With an explicit guarantee from the United States that your nuclear deterrent will stand against the North's use of their weapons of mass destruction, it is my personal view that we could not only withstand an attack by Pyongyang, but also …" He stopped to think and wound up laughing, without humor. "I was about to say we could drive the Communists all the way to China, but we wouldn't want their intervention again, would we?"

The President shook her head. "We have enough tension with China already."

That was when the ambassador caught on. "This is … not *all* about China, but it starts with Beijing. You need Seoul to tell the world that the time has come when we can stand on our own. Then the United States can graciously withdraw — in a measured way, of course — and show the world and China how reasonable it is. Making your defense of the free navigation of the South China Sea seem much more reasonable."

Jean Morrissey said, "It would be better for our visible armed forces to leave the Republic with the thanks of the South Korean people for all of America's sacrifices on their behalf."

Feeling an urge not to be totally steamrolled, the ambassador asked the President, "And what if my country chooses not to follow the script you've written for us?"

With the gesture of a hand, Patricia Grant passed the baton back to the Vice President.

Jean Morrissey said, "Then we'll leave anyway, and we'll take our umbrella with us. No nuclear missile submarines patrolling just off your coast. I'll make sure of that when I become president."

Playing the good cop, the President said, "Ambassador Park, this will work out better for everyone if Seoul initiates these changes quickly. Please contact your government as soon as you return to your embassy. I'll need an answer within a matter of hours not days. Things in the South China Sea are getting quite tense."

Ambassador Park got to his feet. He almost bowed but held

himself back. The Americans had to make do with the slightest of nods.

New York City — Manhattan

McGill arrived at Clare Tracy's Park Avenue offices at 9:00 a.m. Deke and Gene waited in the outer office with Clare's mountainous assistant Gorgeous George. McGill felt the three of them might have an interesting chat.

George told McGill, "Ms. Tracy said you go right on in, sir."

McGill did just that.

In his days as a humble cop or even as the chief of police in a posh North Shore suburb, he would have been knocked out by his old girlfriend's professional digs. Having lived in the White House for eight years and visited the palaces of foreign heads of state with the President, he managed to take it all in with aplomb.

Adding to his acquired sophistication, there was a far more intriguing point of interest to observe. The trick was to do so without actually staring. He must have overstepped just a little because he heard Clare laugh. He turned to look at her.

"What's the matter, Jim? Never seen a good-looking woman before?"

He said, "It's a privilege I have far more than I deserve. Every day with the President. Last night eating pizza with you. And now …"

He turned back to the other woman in the room and extended a hand, "Jim McGill."

She took his hand and said, "Detective First Grade Lily Kealoha, NYPD."

McGill released her hand and was about to turn back to Clare when the detective added, *"Hapa-haole."*

He said, "Sorry?"

"You don't know the term?"

"I do. I just hoped my curiosity wasn't that obvious."

"That's all right. I get it a lot, people trying to figure out my ethnicity. It's a hundred percent American, from Norwegian and Polynesian ancestors."

"Vikings and *ali'i nui?*" McGill asked. The *ali'i nui* were the olden days high chiefs of the Hawaiian Islands.

Lily laughed and looked at Clare. "You're right. This guy's one sharp copper."

"He used to get on me in college when I fell behind in my assigned reading," Clare said.

"Only so we could have the time to fool around with clear consciences," McGill replied.

Clare was the one who blushed now. She asked her guests to be seated and changed the subject. "Lily did a bit of legwork for us, Jim. She ran the names Loris Springstone and Chris Nevers through the NYPD database."

"I also ran the photo of the person you texted to Clare through our facial recognition system, in case she's a terrorism suspect or something, somebody who hasn't been arrested yet," Lily said.

"And?" McGill asked.

"This person you want has no criminal record or even a reason for the city's cops to worry about her," Lily said.

"Damn. I really hoped we could find her here."

"Didn't say you couldn't do that," Lily said. "I got to where I am by being thorough. Clare told me this person might have a theater background. I can't tell you how many people in this town have told me I should be in show biz. Man, I just came here on a scholarship to study urban planning. How I became a cop is another story, but lots of people wanted to see me in movies or on stage. So I have some connections in that area."

"And you worked your sources with the results being?" McGill asked.

Clare was the one who handed him a photocopy of a black and white shot.

She said, "Lily came up with this. Looks like a match to me. How about you?"

McGill studied the image. It was softly focused, but he felt sure it was the same person who'd been scouting him on Wisconsin Avenue in Georgetown. He asked Lily, "Did you get a name of who this is, even a stage name?"

Lily nodded. "Chris Springer. Did some small non-union productions and disappeared. From the acting profession anyway. Made me glad I didn't fall for trying to get into show biz."

"So she was here," McGill said, "but is there anything to say she still is?"

"That remains to be seen. Phone records show 26 people named Chris Springer in the city's five boroughs. By the numbers, there are two in The Bronx, four in Brooklyn, seven in Queens, seven again in Staten Island and six here in Manhattan."

"Do the addresses tell you anything about social standing?" McGill asked.

Lily said, "Well, going by their neighborhoods, our Chris Springers span the depths and heights of American society, from three in the pits to two not far from here on Park Avenue. The others are either climbing into or sliding out of the middle class. You think annual income is relevant here?"

McGill nodded. "Starving former actors probably live in fairly desperate places."

Both women nodded.

"On the other hand, a hired killer with a number of big-time assassinations behind her is likely to command top dollar," McGill said. "The effort to get me certainly wasn't done on a budget."

"Yeah," Lily said. "I read about that. There had to be real money behind that attempt. You did an amazing job getting out of that one without a scratch."

"My driver did the hard part," McGill said. "What I'm thinking now is we start looking at the high and low ends of the economic scale and work toward the middle."

Lily nodded. "Let me suggest something else. Might be a good idea to narrow things down by age. Make anyone under 20 or over 50 a secondary consideration. Your would-be killer should be somewhere in between, right?"

"I think so, yes," McGill said.

"Good, because I'm going to need some help getting my bosses to provide the manpower. The fewer cops we need the better. You know what I mean?"

McGill said, "I do." He turned to Clare. "Would it be all right if we put this on your card, for old times' sake?"

She nodded. "Okay, but this is going to cost you more than a pizza."

Clare handed her card from the NYPD commissioner to Lily.

She said, "Damn, I've heard about these things, but this is the first time I ever saw one."

Lily started to make the necessary calls.

United States Capitol — Washington, DC

Sitting in his elaborate office in the United States Capitol, Senator Oren Worth could not believe his eyes. His campaign manager, Layla Dart, who'd missed work for the past two days with an unspecified illness, had just quit on him. Telling him so with a text. A goddamn text. He was flabbergasted, that musty old word being the best he could summon to describe his feelings.

Goddamnit, he *fired* people. They didn't quit on him. That was the way of his world.

Thinking in those terms brought Worth up short. Was it even remotely possible that his well-ordered life had changed for the worse? How could it? He had both massive amounts of money and political power. He was third in line to succeed to the presidency right now and …

He remembered that in Layla Dart's message the evil, treacherous bitch had also told him to be sure to turn on his TV at 10:00 a.m. and tune it to MSNBC. He confirmed that point by rereading the text: MSNBC. That couldn't mean anything good for a Republican. It would be almost as farfetched for a Democrat to hope to hear a "well done" from Fox.

Worse still, his review of the text showed him a part of the message he must have overlooked entirely: an expression of Layla's personal regret. *"I'm truly sorry. I never meant for things to work out like this. I underestimated the other side badly."*

That all but made Worth's heart stop. What had the damned woman done?

He tried to rally himself. The memory of the only other person who'd quit precipitously on him came back with a rush of pleasure. The man's name was Daniel Anders. He'd been an executive vice president who'd left Worth for a position with a start-up that had offered an equity position. Worth might have given his blessing to Anders if he'd come to him and asked his opinion on making the move. Only the bastard hadn't. He'd simply felt his fate was his own to determine and made the move unilaterally.

Worth bought the start-up before Anders could even move into his office. The promised job disappeared, and for years Worth had made sure Anders never again got a position of any real significance. Only when Anders became too old ever to climb above middle management did Worth stop subverting him.

Now, he couldn't help but wonder if some kind of karmic bullshit was coming back at him. He refused to believe that. Victory belonged to the smartest, richest, least principled bastard who had the greatest reach. *That* was the way the world worked.

So why did he have the sinking feeling that he'd never be able to get even with Layla Dart? Far more painful than that, why did he have the unshakeable feeling he was never going to become the President of the United States?

He tried to tell himself that he was being foolish. He'd take up some kind of physical fitness regimen that would amount to self-flagellation. He'd beat the shit out of himself, and the uncharacteristic self-doubt would vanish.

The first step in the right direction would be to leave his office television off. MSNBC? Bullshit. Those liberal bastards could go …

Fuck me, he thought, as he clicked on the television at 9:58.

I can't help myself.

I've got to see what Layla Goddamn Dart has done to me.

He sat watching two pharmaceutical company commercials, trying to tell himself his heart wasn't racing and with his lean frame he certainly didn't have any damn diabetes. After the pitches for prescription medications came a promo for an evening show on the network.

Like he gave a shit about watching that.

For just a moment, Worth began to relax. He knew the sequence of advertising on these networks. They paid the bills with other people's products and services. Then they gave themselves a free push. Finally, there was the reporting, analysis and propaganda.

There shouldn't be another commercial, especially about him, until the next break.

Unless … Christ Almighty, the talking head just mentioned his name.

"Senator Oren Worth is the subject of a new attack ad from the Morrissey for President campaign. At the risk of sounding partisan —"

Oh, yeah, Worth thought bitterly, like you bastards are ever impartial.

"This may be the funniest political spot I've seen in many years," the show's host said.

And then the damn thing ran, showing him as a child and a young man. How the hell had they gotten those clips? Worth barely remembered sounding like either of his earlier selves. But then, oh God, there he was trying to sound like Cary Grant. He was *awful.* Why had he ever listened to that evil bitch? Why hadn't he shit-canned the whole mad idea immediately?

Then things got far worse: the voices of John Wayne, Carol Channing and Daffy Duck came out of his mouth. He started to retract into a fetal position, and then the tagline from hell came from an announcer: *Senator Worth, the closer we listen, the phonier you sound.*

Worth knew the commercial would devastate his chances of ever becoming president.

Then the show's host delivered the news that kicked him while he was down.

"What you just saw was the official unveiling of the Morrissey for President campaign's new television ad. But a bootleg copy hit the Internet a few hours ago. The spot has already gone viral with people adding new voices of their choice to replace those of John Wayne, Carol Channing and Daffy Duck. This shows every sign of becoming a national craze. Good luck holding back this tidal wave, Senator Worth."

The senator snapped off the television and snarled, "Evil bastards."

How the hell could he fight back? He didn't even have a campaign manager.

He slumped low in his desk chair. It had to be his imagination, but …

He felt sure he heard Daniel Anders laughing at him.

Ritz-Carlton Hotel — Washington, DC

Odo Sacripant also received a life-changing text that morning. Not that it would affect him personally. Auric Ludwig was the one who'd just hung himself, metaphorically at least. He'd agreed to hire Odo to kill James J. McGill.

Odo woke a late-sleeping Yves Pruet with a gentle nudge to give him the news.

Wearing a sour expression, Pruet informed his colleague, "I was dreaming."

"Pleasantly?"

A curt nod was Pruet's response.

"Catherine Deneuve again?"

"*Oui.*"

"She is still a truly beautiful woman, Yves. But she is older than you."

"I see that as an advantage. I would be the dashing younger man."

Odo nodded. "Someone seeking to take advantage of her connections to promote your career?"

A look of disgust preceded Pruet turning his head away from his friend.

"I'm sorry, Yves. I shouldn't have mocked your fantasies."

Pruet only grunted.

"You know what she says, don't you? Catherine Deneuve, I mean."

Pruet slowly turned his face back to Odo. "What?"

"She says: 'Love is suffering. One side always loves more.' Is this what you really want, *mon ami?* A life out of balance in which someone is always miserable. Isn't that what you had with Nicolette?"

Nicolette was Pruet's ex-wife. Someone who had tried to wound him deeply and had succeeded. She'd smashed his cherished classical guitar.

"No, I do not want that, but how is it you know what Catherine Deneuve says?"

"Marie told me. To my dismay, she reads magazines about cinema stars."

Pruet swung his legs off the bed and looking up at Odo said, "Nothing about your wife dismays you, but now I will have to think up someone new to fill my dreams."

"I'm sure you will, but I will cheer you up with good news in the meantime."

Pruet gave Odo a doubtful look but he said, "Tell me."

"Dwayne Kilgore sent me money."

Pruet blinked. That was all the time he needed to recall the name. "Auric Ludwig's corrupt prison guard."

"Oui."

"How much money?"

"One hundred thousand dollars, the amount promised by Auric Ludwig as an initial payment."

Pruet stood and shook his friend's hand. "You've succeeded Odo. Dwayne Kilgore will never be able to claim he could pay such a sum from his own resources."

"And he has no personal motive to kill *M'sieur* McGill."

"So he will turn on Ludwig, hoping for some degree of leniency. Kilgore's testimony and yours will guarantee Ludwig dies in prison. We have done our part of this exercise."

Odo nodded. "I will order breakfast for us while you attend to your necessities and get dressed. Then we will share our news with the boss and our new colleagues, yes?"

"D'accord," Pruet said. "While I shower, I will consider the merits of making Isabelle Adjani my new dream girl."

Another actress, Odo thought, as he watched Yves enter his bathroom.

There was only one thing left for Odo to do. Talk with Marie and see about setting Yves up with her older sister, Sophie. He'd long felt they would make a good match. He and Yves had been the best of friends for years. They might as well become family, too.

New York City — Manhattan

Taps had costumed herself in what she thought of as a don't-fuck-with-me bohemian look: a sleekly tailored black leather sport coat over a platinum silk T-shirt, tight, faded blue jeans and matte black work boots. Her blonde wig was pulled back into a tight, high ponytail. She strode into the car dealership on 11th Avenue and caught the eyes of all four salespersons in the place. Rather than rush her en masse or by virtue of a pecking order, they took a moment to sort out what she might want.

The dealership sold Cadillacs, Buicks, Chevys and GMC trucks. The man who sold Caddies and the woman who pushed Buicks eliminated themselves from contention quickly. The woman who sold Chevys and the guy who sold the trucks each took a small step forward.

Taps made a guess and pointed to the woman. The truck guy took her choice with good grace. He offered a polite smile and a slight bow of his head. If Taps ever wanted to move up to something with more space and muscle, he'd be happy to help. For the moment, he simply turned and walked away.

He felt he'd won a minor victory anyway.

The Chevy woman told Taps, "Paul has good manners, doesn't he? Five years of marriage to me has worked wonders for him. Plus, we share commissions on all our sales."

Taps thought you couldn't ask for more in a relationship than mutual respect and shared loot, but she wasn't there for a heterosexual happiness seminar.

She said, "My name's Blair. I called about the black Chevy sedan. You still have it, right?"

"We certainly do. After you called, I made sure everyone knew it was spoken for. Thanks for being punctual. It doesn't look good for me when somebody stakes a claim to a vehicle and then doesn't show. My name, in case you forgot, is Myra."

The woman extended her hand and Taps shook it.

"I didn't forget. I don't like people wasting my time so I don't waste theirs."

Myra read the subtext clearly: Let's get down to business. She walked Taps over to the corner of the showroom where the car waited, a new gleaming black Chevy Impala. Taps started at the front of the car and circumnavigated it, paying close attention to every visible detail.

Myra had the wits not to tail behind or offer any comments.

The only visual shortcoming that Taps could see was the car's tires looked less substantial than the bulletproof models on James J. McGill's car. Being showroom new, they also gleamed a bit more than McGill's car. But the two cars shared the same wheel design, and every other detail that met Taps' critical eye seemed to be identical.

Returning to her starting point, Taps nodded. Things looked good so far. Now, she needed to check the interior. She got behind the wheel and examined the dashboard. It looked entirely standard for a vehicle of its type. That had to make it different from McGill's car. Without being able to confirm it, Taps felt that McGill's car had to have special controls for emergency lights, communicating with federal and local cops, and defending its primary passenger.

There was nothing Taps could do about that discrepancy.

Then again, she intended for McGill to be in this car for a very short time.

In the previous attempt on his life, she'd wanted to get him out of his car.

This time, she wanted to get him into what looked like his car.

Taps stepped out of the vehicle and told Myra, "I'll take it."

The saleswoman smiled and nodded. No haggling meant full sticker price. A hallelujah sale. She didn't say a word about the car being the same model the President's husband used.

You never knew what people's politics might be.

Kostas answered the phone at his perch in the lobby of the Park Avenue building where Chris Springer lived. He saw it was a call from an unfamiliar outside number, one that didn't include a name.

He answered by giving the address of the building and saying, "This is Kostas. How may I help you?"

"Kostas, this is Chris Springer. I'm out running some errands. I just wanted to ask if I missed anyone stopping by to see me or if any package has been delivered for me."

In his two years on the job at the building, Kostas had never encountered a visitor for Ms. Springer. Nor had she ever been concerned about missing a delivery. He was about to respond with a simple no when he saw an unmarked sedan pull to the curb out front.

Even before the two men got out of the car, Kostas could tell it was a police vehicle. There was an arrogance to the way it arrived. Speed followed by sharp braking. His experience with cops in the old country had left him with the ability to almost smell their kind. Once he saw them, he had no doubt who they were, NYPD detectives.

Speaking into the phone, he asked, "Ms. Springer, have you

ever made any donations to a police charity?"

"No."

A direct answer but one filled with a sudden tension nonetheless, Kostas felt.

He said, "Then the gentleman who just arrived outside must be here for someone else."

"Must be," Taps agreed. "When do you get off tonight, Kostas?"

"Six this evening."

"I'll call back to check on that package before you leave."

Kostas put the phone down before the cops entered the building.

Then a thought occurred, and he picked it up and started tapping out numbers.

The cops arrived before he could finish. The older one displayed his badge and said, "You can make your call later. We have some questions for you."

Kostas nodded and put the phone down.

The younger cop had the wits to ask, "Who were you trying to call?"

"A friend in the old country," Kostas said, thickening his accent.

"That'll have to wait," the senior cop said. "You have a person named Chris Springer living here?"

"I do not have her," Kostas said, "but, yes, she lives here."

For a long time, and up to the present moment, Taps had and did consider herself a freak. How else would any gender-typical person — most of the world — look at someone who had both male and female genitals? Her mother and father each had wanted Taps to have surgery, Dad pulling to get rid of the undescended testicles, Mom wanting the ovaries to go and a penis to be crafted.

Just the *idea* of surgery had scared the hell out of Taps once she was old enough to comprehend what it meant. Somebody would cut off a part of her body, a part of her identity. The fact that her parents disagreed vehemently on which part should go only made things harder to understand or accept. As she approached puberty, both parents wanted her to cast the tie-breaking vote.

The impossibility of that situation almost drove Taps crazy. Especially given that her two sisters seemed relatively normal and happy. Recognizing their child's deteriorating mental health, her parents agreed to take her to a psychiatrist. The meds that quack had prescribed had made her a near-zombie.

When Taps finally found the will to covertly discard her psychoactive pharmaceuticals, her mental acuity returned and so did her self-loathing. A new element also made its debut, a burning sense of rage. Taps frequently felt as if her body was literally ablaze. It became a puzzle to her that her skin didn't blister, suppurate and fall from her body.

Her only reliable source of relief was to do something entirely cliché: get in the family car and go for a drive that had no set destination. Behind the wheel with all the windows down and a steady rush of air washing over her, she not only felt cool, she came within shouting distance of feeling what she imagined to be normal. When she returned home, the pain came back.

When her sisters left for college, taking their gentle encouragement and unquestioning love with them, there was no way Taps could have survived under her parents' roof. They were still trying to have their respective ways with her. So she poisoned them for making her life so toxic … and for having created the freak that she was in the first place. Once she was sure they were dead, she burned the house down around them, got in their car and drove.

This time she had an end point in mind, New York City.

The farther away from home she got, the less she felt the pain.

But it never went away entirely.

Arriving in New York, she decided to see if she could pursue acting the way her sisters had said they intended to do. Pretending to be somebody else seemed like a fine idea. If she could inhabit a role the way she'd heard you were supposed to do, she could stop being herself for a little while. Just the idea of doing that was a relief.

She never got close to making it as an actor, but along the way she met a closeted organized crime guy who gave her a new direction in life. She became an apprentice to one very smart, inventive hired killer. To a degree, *he* was the one who'd made her what she was today.

He'd also put her in touch with the company over in Jersey where she was heading right now. It was a place called Top Props. Its legitimate side — used for money laundering — provided any kind of facsimile or gewgaw a movie or TV production might want. One of her mentor's favorite, if cruel, tricks was to provide a target with the opportunity to reach for a prop gun, only to find out in his last moment of life he'd proved just what a chump he was.

Taps was greeted warmly when she entered the front office of Top Props. The people there understood she was somebody who got privileged treatment for a very good reason: You didn't want to be on the wrong side of her mentor, even if he was pushing 80 these days.

What Taps asked for on an expedited basis — as in right this very minute — were two counterfeit District of Columbia license plates reading: PHOTUS.

President's Henchman of the United States. McGill's plates.

She'd seen more than one set of plates on his car, but PHOTUS was displayed more than the others. So that was what she chose. It paid to get as many details right as you could.

That's why her next stop would be a costume shop.

The people there knew her patron, too.

She'd get first class service and nobody would ever say a word.

Yucatan Peninsula, Mexico

Father Inigo de Loyola gathered a force of 20 *soldados viejos*, old soldiers, to accompany him to Mexico. A larger number of his *compañeros* had been thrilled by the prospect of taking vengeance against Corona Moe once they'd heard how he'd been exploiting those of their comrades who were at death's door. To a man, everyone the priest had spoken with voted to kill the *cabrón.*

Not all of them, however, were up to the physical demands.

De Loyola had required them to cover five kilometers carrying five kilograms of weight in thirty minutes or less. Besides showing evidence of strength and endurance, they were required to prove their marksmanship still met a minimum standard. They had to put three consecutive rifle rounds into a target the size of a man's head from 25 meters.

Hardest of all, they had to cross a half-kilometer of jungle undetected. Those watching for them weren't half-blind, half-deaf old people like themselves but young boys and girls with keen eyes and ears. The children loved the game and showed absolutely no mercy to anyone, including family members.

Twice as many volunteers failed the test as passed them, but everyone contributed to the effort. As de Loyola had suspected, almost every man he contacted had hidden the weapons with which he had once fought. Ammunition also had been stashed, taking care to protect the rounds from deterioration.

None of the men had ever expected to fire a shot in anger again, certainly not as part of a military unit, but the devil always seemed closer at hand than salvation. A prudent man readied himself for whatever evil might come his way.

Other than those whom de Loyola called regular forces, two specialists had been conscripted, Diego Mendez and his granddaughter, Ofelia. Mendez was a hunter and trapper; Ofelia was the only family member who cared to follow in her grandfather's footsteps.

De Loyola felt compelled to ask if Ofelia, only 17 years old, would feel comfortable as the only female in the cohort. Mendez shrugged and looked at the girl for her answer. She told the priest, "If anyone should be afraid, it's them not me."

De Loyola liked her attitude and felt it likely she could back it up.

He said, *"Bienvenido, señorita."*

Before leaving Costa Rica in a convoy of three passenger vans and a truck, de Loyola made a phone call to a fellow Jesuit in Mexico. He explained he was on a very important mission, without offering specifics, and asked what the price might be to bring his people, their vehicles and tools into Mexico without hindrance and then leave in the same fashion. His brother in Christ said he would discuss the matter with the pertinent officials and get the best price possible.

He did ask, "You don't mean to overthrow the Mexican government?"

"This is not political. It is simply a matter of setting something right."

"An evil requiring that many men to remedy must be truly terrible."

After a moment of pondering, de Loyola decided to share what he knew, including the fact that Corona Moe had set up a facility for his so-called *muertos* in Baja California. Perhaps the government in Mexico City would like to look into that — the politicians who weren't already on Moe's payroll.

The Mexican Jesuit said this was indeed a terrible situation and it would be best if de Loyola and his men spent as brief a time as possible in Mexico. He arranged for their unmolested entrance to and exit from the country for $10,000. A bargain considering that smuggling a single person from Mexico into the United States could cost from $4,000 to $9,000.

In this instance, de Loyola was glad that he came from a wealthy family, and they were generous with their money. They gave him the sum for the bribe and an equal amount for incidental expenses.

The trip went smoothly, the Mexican border officials honoring their deal. De Loyola and three of his men took adjoining suites at the Playa Perfecta resort; the others consulted locals to find the best way to the map coordinates where Corona Moe had his hideout deep in the Yucatán jungle.

Within an hour of his arrival, wearing swim trunks, a black shirt with a Roman collar, sunglasses and a straw hat, de Loyola plopped down on a beach chair under an umbrella. He brought with him a hand-made sign rendered in both Spanish and English: *Repent any sin under the sun. The confessional is open.*

A second beach chair sat open on the sand next to de Loyola.

People wearing the skimpiest of bathing suits passed by, some of the women not even bothering with tops for their bikinis, without noticing his sign. The first couple who did take heed of it broke into laughter.

The young woman said, "Ay, padre, after what we did last night, I would need all day with you."

The young man frowned and told her, "That is no one's business but our own."

Ignoring him, de Loyola said to the young woman, "It is acceptable to summarize."

"No!" the young man insisted.

She told him to go take a swim, and gave him such a look he had no choice but to stalk off. She covered herself with a T-shirt and sat next to de Loyola, saying, "I don't know if it is really so terrible, padre. We are engaged to be married." She showed him the ring she wore. Then she, too, frowned and asked, "You truly are a priest?"

"I am. I spent some years in Rome. In fact, I met our Pope there. I am supposed to call His Holiness on the phone, but I am waiting for the right time."

The young woman's facial expressions cycled from awe to skepticism to curiosity.

"*¿Verdaderamente?* Truly?

"*Sí.*"

She began to whisper her story to de Loyola, in detail not overview.

Other beach-goers began to notice the white-haired man with the young woman who now had tears streaming down her cheeks — she'd stolen the affections of her fiancé from her best friend. It turned out she wasn't alone in seeking atonement while on holiday. Other women of all ages began to line up at a discreet distance. A few men joined the queue as well.

Soon, the resort staff began providing more beach chairs, umbrellas and drinks for those waiting in line. It took an hour or so, but the man de Loyola had come to find, Corona Moe, finally made his appearance to see the curious event on the beach: a priest hearing open-air whispered confessions in a place made for fun, drinking and plans for a libidinous night.

De Loyola recognized Moe from a photo the young General Yates had texted to him.

The mastermind of the scheme to enlist the dying to kill the healthy stared at de Loyola for a good ten minutes. The priest never directly returned the rude gaze. He saw enough peripherally to assess the man's growing unease. Something like the appearance of a priest on the beach was not only an anomaly, it was a sign something was seriously amiss in what should have been a secure corner of a tropical paradise.

It robbed Corona Moe of a much cherished sense that he was one of life's winners.

The man who casually profited off the deaths of others suddenly came to a shocking sense of his own mortality. He turned away from the priest and the line of scantily clad penitents and made for the hotel at a brisk walk. De Loyola's men at the resort would be watching. So, too, would the others waiting in the jungle.

Corona Moe would try to outrun his fate, but he would not succeed.

He had even failed to realize that he might have saved himself. The sign was right there in front of him. *Repent any sin under the sun. The confessional is open.* De Loyola would have heard his confession like anyone else's, and through the grace of God Corona Moe's sins would have been forgiven … had he also sworn never to commit such sins again.

Instead, the villain thought he could escape the responsibility for his heinous acts, and in doing so sealed his fate, one that would horrify even him.

De Loyola pleaded to those in line for a moment's respite.

He took out his cell phone and made a brief, whispered call to his men in the jungle.

Beijing, China

Chinese President Li Ho sat at the polished but spartan desk in his government office. Behind him were his country's flag and a painting of a segment of the Great Wall dramatically climbing a mountainside. Prominently positioned in a bookcase to his right was a framed photo of him addressing the National People's Congress.

A rank of vice minister or higher was required to have a red phone on your desk; Li had two such phones, a mark of distinction possessed by no one else in the government. The red phones were part of a secure and encrypted system of communication. No foreign country's spy service had ever penetrated the system … as far as Beijing knew.

The cursed Americans, however, were perpetually inventive. It was possible they might have found a weakness. That was why even on the red phones, the elite of China's government knew they had to speak in archaic circumlocutions. The Americans were much better at computer science than cultural anthropology.

To native Chinese, though, the meanings were as clear as newspaper headlines.

So when President Li's closer-to-hand red phone sounded he had no problem understanding either of the earthshaking messages delivered by his spy chief, Kuo Fang.

"Sir, we have confirmation from our assets in South Korea: Seoul will announce within a matter of days that the government will thank the United States for its many years of military and economic aid, and inform them that their military presence in the country will no longer be required."

Li paused before saying, "But their *alliance* will continue, and the Americans will protect their country with its nuclear missiles."

"Yes."

"Do you suspect this is all an American scheme?" Li asked.

"It is frightening to think of them as this subtle or devious, but I must consider it as a strong possibility."

"By withdrawing their visible military forces from the Korean Peninsula, they are showing the world how reasonable and selfless they are," Li said. "Making us look all the worse for expanding our hold on the South China Sea."

"But, sir, they are building an island there also."

"Only one, and only to make the statement that they can do so if they choose. If we were to drive them out now, after they've voluntarily left Korea, that would make us look even more of a warmonger."

"Or make the Americans look weak."

"Do you ever think it's a good idea to underestimate an enemy, Kuo?"

"No, sir. It's almost like one of us is advising the Americans, allowing them to sow doubt and confusion in our ranks."

"Yes, our next move will take time and careful consideration. Wisdom and patience will be our guiding principles."

That brought the spy chief to his next bulletin.

"Sir, General Hu Dai has died of sudden heart failure."

Hu Dai was — had been — someone who knew nothing of either wisdom or patience, Li thought. He would have perceived of the Americans leaving Korea as the moment to press forward militarily. Likely falling into a trap. Setting back China's relations with the rest of the world for a hundred years.

To Kuo he only said, "I will extend my personal condolences to his family. My staff will arrange a proper memorial service for the public. I assume the general wished to have his remains cremated."

"That has already been done, sir."

Only two men in the world knew that Hu Dai had been poisoned, Li Ho and one other; that person also would soon be gone — more prosaically in a traffic accident. The Chinese had been masters of the toxic arts when those bunglers next door in Russia still wore animal skins. The poison used on Hu left no traces for an autopsy to reveal, but the cremation had left no body for an autopsy.

Always best to be as careful as possible when you were the

emperor in everything but name. A point Li would keep at the front of his mind in dealing with the Americans.

Yucatan Peninsula, Mexico

Corona Moe didn't know exactly what he was running from or even if it was necessary to run at all. Still, seeing a Catholic priest on the beach at the resort where he lived most of the year was an oddity that set his teeth on edge. A nominal Muslim who hadn't practiced his beliefs in all his years in Mexico, he'd come to be aware of many of the practices of the major faith in his adopted homeland.

He'd learned of its baptisms, masses, weddings and funerals.

He knew of confessions, too, and that practice had made him wonder if Catholics were insane: telling your sins — even your crimes — to another person. Yielding such knowledge was the surest way to give someone else power over you. Blackmail would become inevitable in Moe's view. Yes, he knew of the so-called *seal* of the confessional. A priest was expected to take the secrets he'd learned to his grave with him. No force on earth could compel him to reveal what he'd learned.

In Moe's eyes, that story was less plausible than the tale of Ali Baba.

If someone wanted to learn what a priest knew, he could use torture to force a revelation. Moe would not have hesitated to do this himself if the circumstance ever arose. "You can not tell me what I want to know, Señor Priest? Let me invite you to recline on this bed of glowing coals."

Moe had heard tales of Christian martyrs, too. The thing he found most interesting about them was they were all set in distant ages. None of them was contemporary; no living witness existed to say, "Yes, this is exactly what happened. I have never seen such courage before. And then angels carried the poor fellow off to heaven."

In other words, they were folk tales.

But the priest on the beach, he was real. Moe hadn't been able to see his eyes behind the sunglasses, but he'd bet every last dollar he had that they were merciless. Moe had heard stories from men who'd slipped into Mexico from Central America. Priests there had been willing — sometimes eager — to take up the gun in their countries' rebellions. Much of it was just bar talk but … damn, if he couldn't see that white-haired priest on the beach as being the real thing.

On a good day, he would kindly forgive your sins.

Get him angry, though, and he might slit your throat.

Without even knowing why such a priest would target him, he scared Moe. Maybe, Moe thought, he was already on edge because of his talk with Taps. He knew that creature was angry at him for not giving her another chance to kill James J. McGill. As a matter of professional pride, she hadn't wanted her reputation as a killer who never missed to be blemished.

Moe didn't think she'd sent the priest. He felt if she wanted to kill him it would be done by her own hand so she might have the personal satisfaction. Still, he simply couldn't accept the priest's appearance was anything but a sign to run and hide.

Not that he could let any of his bodyguards know of his fears. None of those bastards had the brains to take over his operation, but if any of them saw his fear they might make a mistaken appraisal of their own abilities and gun him down.

So he simply left word that he wanted some time alone and set off on his motorcycle by himself headed to his jungle hideaway. He covered the first half of the distance at high speed, his anxiety urging him on. Past that point, though, his fear began to diminish as he came closer to his destination. Once he was almost there, he began to castigate himself.

He'd been foolish, cowardly even, to let a mere priest panic him.

He would spend a night at his jungle refuge, refuel his motorcycle and head back to the beach. If the damn priest was still there, hearing confessions or not, Moe would plant a foot in his ass and send him on his way. Show the bastard who the *jefe* of Playa Perfecta was.

Corona Moe was smiling as he rounded the last bend in the narrow jungle road to his sanctuary. His good humor vanished immediately when he saw a truck and two vans blocking his way. Clustered around the vehicles were more than a dozen ragtag old men. Unarmed, they wouldn't have frightened him, but each one held an assault rifle at the ready.

Moe had no doubt they would use them if provoked.

Maybe his simple appearance was provocation enough.

He opened his mouth to offer them a bribe, a ransom, anything they wanted.

Before he could get a word out, though, he was saturated from above by a shower of what smelled like liquid bacon fat. He had to stop the motorcycle and put his feet down to keep from falling over. As he strived to wipe the grease from his eyes, he heard a growl that made his blood freeze.

His vision cleared just in time to see the rear doors of the truck open. Inside the cargo box was a cage. Inside the cage was a jaguar pacing side to side but keeping its eyes pinned on Corona Moe. The animal raised its nose to catch his scent. As it did, the big cat bared its fangs, and even more menacingly licked its chops.

Whimpering, Moe tried to turn his bike. The task was made difficult because his feet were now slick from the grease that had drenched him. He reverted to his native tongue as he struggled, begging Allah to deliver him from this horror. He managed to get the motorcycle pointed back in the direction from which he'd come.

The animal, if released, would be on him in seconds, but if he could get the machine in gear and off to a good start …

Moe heard the cage door open and the animal roar.

He revved his engine. It roared louder than the jaguar, but then it died and went silent.

He was out of gas and out of luck. He turned just in time to see the predator leap at him, and he screamed.

Watching from a tree branch fifteen feet above, Ofelia saw the jaguar seize the man's neck in its jaws. She'd been the one to pour the liquified pig fat on the man below. Her grandfather had taught her that a big jungle cat would eat anything it could catch, from crocodiles to monkeys, but its favorite food was feral pigs. Pork was the food they'd been feeding it on the trip to Mexico, just enough to keep it alive and alert, never enough to fill its belly.

So when the beast smelled the grease covering the fellow below and then was released … Grandfather thought the animal would kill the man quickly, severing his spine at the neck with one massive bite, but as the jaguar dragged the man into the jungle, his arms and legs were still twitching.

Grandfather had offered to be the one in the tree, spare Ofelia the gruesome sight of what would happen. She said no. He was getting too old to go up a tree, and she wanted a greater appreciation of the danger of an animal she would one day have to hunt on her own.

Four of the men who had pointed their weapons at Corona Moe lifted his motorcycle into the truck and secured the cage door behind it. They would sell the machine on the way home and split the money. As for the bastard who had ridden it, perhaps his bones would be found, perhaps not.

Diego Mendez watched his granddaughter safely climb down from the tree.

He would have been the man to shoot the jaguar had it gone up the tree after her.

As it was, he called Father de Loyola and told him their mission was accomplished as planned. The rebels had their final victory. *¡Viva la Revolución!*

New York City — Manhattan

"Can you speak freely?" Taps asked.

She'd just called Kostas, the doorman at her building, using a disposable phone.

"Yes."

"You're off work; you've left the building?"

"I am, yes, and I have left the building."

"Did you think to look around and see if you're being followed."

She heard the man laugh quietly. "Wouldn't you know, the laces of each of my shoes came undone within the space of a few blocks. I paused to retie them and to notice who might be watching. No one was. How did you get my mobile number?"

"I called your boss and asked. I tip him very well each Christmas."

A moment of silence followed. "You've connected me to you. The police will be sure to question me further now."

Taps understood. The police had already visited her building during Kostas' working hours. She wasn't surprised about that. James J. McGill was a detective, after all, and from what she'd seen he had a lot of highly competent investigators working for him. With one of those people already having talked to her sister, Kim, she wasn't surprised they found out where she lived.

Now that McGill's people were working with the NYPD, her jeopardy had doubled.

"I'm sorry to have caused you trouble," Taps said. "Would $100,000 be sufficient to help you relocate?"

Kostas was silent for a moment and then said, "Yes, that is a fair offer."

The fact that Kostas hadn't haggled earned Taps' respect. She'd caused him a problem and offered to make things right. Restoring a sense of balance was enough for him. He didn't need to try to gouge her.

"Where should I wire the money? I'll do it right away."

She wasn't surprised that he could give her a bank routing number off the top of his head.

"Is that overseas?"

"Yes."

"Good, it'll be harder for the feds to get at it that way." She was sure her former doorman already knew that. "How far did the police go in looking for me?"

"They questioned me, searched your apartment and spoke with everyone who passed through the lobby. It seems none of your neighbors know you. Many of them were uncertain they'd ever seen you in the building. Of course, that is the way you want things. Still, the police were both impressed and suspicious that you could … keep such a low profile, they called it."

Taps paused to think for a moment. Was Kostas playing her? Was he working with the cops? Might he get a reward from either a private or public source for helping the cops or McGill capture her? After he took a hundred grand from her.

The only thing she had to rely on was her ability to read people. She didn't think Kostas would betray her because she felt sure he'd been on the wrong side of the law himself. At least at one time and likely more than that. She asked Kostas to hold for a moment and sent the money she'd promised.

Once she completed the task, she said."I just made the money transfer. If what I've paid you is sufficient, I'd like to ask you to do one more favor for me."

Kostas was quiet for a moment. "If it does not increase my danger."

"I'd like you to get a message to James J. McGill."

"How would I do that?"

"Buy a disposable phone and call the White House. You can get the number online." She told him what he should say. "Just leave that message with the operator and hang up."

"Real people answer the phones there, not machines?"

"Yes."

Kostas laughed at the quaintness of such a system and said okay. Then he asked Taps a question. "Will you be visiting my monastery?"

"I just might."

"Good. Tell the abbot I sent you."

"Will that get me a mint on my pillow?"

Kostas laughed again. "You will have to bring your own mint and the pillow, too."

McGill took Clare Tracy and Lily Kealoha to dinner at a Mid-town steakhouse called Del Frisco's, an outpost of a Texas-based chain — Clare's recommendation, twitting him about his earlier suggestion of Marie Callender's. Nonetheless, the place had the sophistication and the kitchen to be successful in Manhattan.

Flying in the face of the restaurant's primary dish, Clare had salmon, Lily went with tuna, and McGill had the roasted chicken. The White House physician, Dr. Artemus Nicolaides, had advised McGill it was time to wean himself off red meat. Nick said the regular consumption of animal fat could kill you as surely, if not as quickly, as a gun shot.

Deke and Gene, being both younger than McGill and having the benefit of other medical opinions, went with the 16-ounce filet mignon, the two of them dining at a nearby table. Waiting in the Chevy at an adjacent parking structure, Leo was having fried chicken takeout, an off-menu selection provided only to certain people, McGill apparently being one of them.

McGill was tempted to have a beer, but he thought better of it. If you were looking for a professional killer who might still be targeting you, dulling your perceptions and slowing your reaction time even slightly wouldn't be a good idea. Being a gracious host, however, he invited both Clare and Lily to indulge.

Clare had an Old Fashioned; Lily ordered a Coke.

"Going to work another shift?" McGill asked.

"Not planning to, but I know my limitations, and tolerating alcohol well isn't one of them."

"No?" Clare asked. "That sort of plays against stereotype for an NYPD detective, doesn't it?"

"Not for this one. I haven't had a drink since I left Hawaii."

McGill said, "You don't have to share if you don't want to, but I have the feeling you did something you came to regret the last time you did imbibe."

Lily said, "The *only* time I drank booze, and it was a near regret."

McGill, as good as his word, didn't pry, but Clare did. "Come on, Lily, tell us what happened."

She took a hit of her freshly delivered Coke and said, "You won't tell anyone else?"

Both of her dinner companions shook their heads.

"It was right before I came to college here. This guy and I went out on a date in a real remote place. I'd seen him exactly one time before that. If I'd stayed home maybe things would have turned out better, but he knew I was leaving and he brought some wine in a screw-top bottle. The only reason I drank any was to see what I might have to deal with here on the Mainland."

McGill nodded. He knew right then what had happened.

Lily saw his knowing expression and said, "Don't tell me you ever did that, please."

"Not me, but other guys I knew. They made presumptions and tried to take liberties they shouldn't have."

Lily looked at Clare. "You told me the two of you used to go out. He never got too cute?"

Clare shook her head. "Always the gentleman and, besides, I was easy."

McGill almost choked on his sparkling water.

Clearing his airway, he told Lily, "She brought a copy of the Baltimore Catechism on our first ten dates."

Clare put a hand over one of McGill's and leaned forward to stage-whisper to Lily. "After that, I brought other manuals."

For the first time in decades, McGill felt himself blush. Both women laughed at him. Deke and Gene turned their heads in his direction and gave him strange looks.

As things calmed down, McGill said, "I hope none of the New York tabloids had any cameras pointed at me."

"Forget about the newspapers," Lily said, "think about tourists and videos they might post online."

McGill sighed and slumped in his seat. "Getting back to our

original discussion, what happened to you and the guy who gave you the wine?"

"Oh, him. I almost threw him off the rim of a volcano. It hasn't erupted in maybe 30,000 years, but the 600-foot fall into Hanauma Bay wouldn't have done him any good. So, I thought if alcohol made guys horny and me homicidal, I'd better swear off. Alcohol, not guys. Which I did. That was a wise choice for a *wahine* who carries a badge and a gun."

"As long as we're almost back on the track of police work," McGill said, "can we review the NYPD's efforts to find the person trying to kill me?"

Clare took her hand off McGill's, and Lily said, "Sure. We checked out all the Chris Springers in town between the ages of 20 and 50. Found them all except for the one we probably want. She's one of two people with that name who lives on Park Avenue. The other tore up her right leg doing some late-season snow skiing this past spring in one of those fancy Colorado resort towns. She hit a bare patch, I heard. We checked with her doctor and with the woman's permission he showed us x-rays and surgical reports. She wasn't the one walking down the street in DC checking you out. That left us with one candidate. Normally a good situation."

"But you didn't find her or anything in her apartment, assuming you got a search warrant."

Lily smiled. "Fastest warrant ever. Judge is a big fan of the President. We didn't find a single piece of paper in the place with the name Chris Springer on it. Not even a utility bill. I know rich people have underlings to take care of that stuff but it still was weird."

"No calendar on the fridge marked 'Kill Jim McGill today,'" McGill asked.

Lily grinned. "Would've been a great clue, but no."

"The manager and staff in the building were cooperative?"

"Right-away-officer cooperative. The only thing that stuck out at all was the two detectives who were the first on hand said the doorman was about to make a call when they entered the building's lobby. The doorman is an immigrant, and he said he was about to call the old country."

McGill frowned.

"Yeah," Lily said. "It struck me and the other detectives the same way."

"What did?" Clare asked.

McGill said, "How much time does the doorman at your building have to himself when he's on duty?"

"Patrick? The poor guy barely has time to take a potty break."

"Exactly. So how likely is it he'd make an international call on duty?"

"I can't imagine him doing that. He might be interrupted just waiting for the connection to be made."

"Exactly," McGill said.

Lily added, "So we think the guy lied. When the first detectives asked him who he was calling, the doorman made up a not very good answer as fast as he could. At the time, they had no reason to be suspicious, but now … I'm going to have a talk with him in the morning."

Taking it all in, McGill wore a pensive look.

"You're welcome to come along, if you want," Lily told him.

"Thanks, I will, but I was thinking of something else. If the doorman had some kind of warning system worked out with Chris Springer, maybe all he had to do was make a call, let it ring once and hang up. That might be enough to say, 'Run for your life.'"

Lily nodded. "I thought of that, too. I even sent a car to the residence of Mr. Kostas Rokos in Queens. He wasn't in. Neighbors say he's usually home by seven at the latest. Not tonight, though. He could be eating out like us or going to some cultural event, but I don't like either of those ideas. I'm supposed to get a call when he comes home."

McGill nodded. "I don't like it either. Two people vanishing when we want to find them."

Clare said, "That could be good, couldn't it? Someone can't kill you if she's on the run."

"No," McGill said, "but we don't know that escape is the foremost priority here. It might be simple evasion."

Lily told Clare, "You've got to assume if somebody's gunning for you, they're not going to give up. Any other point of view could get you killed."

McGill agreed.

Dinner was finished with bits of small talk and moments of silence. Nobody wanted dessert. McGill and his dining companions, along with Deke and Gene, exited the restaurant. After receiving a peck on the cheek, McGill put Clare in a taxi for home, saying he'd be in touch. He shook hands with Lily, and she told him she would pick him up at his hotel at 7:00 a.m.

She'd no sooner departed than Leo pulled up in the Chevy. Deke rode shotgun as usual; McGill and Gene got in the back seat. The Chevy had just pulled away from the curb when McGill's phone rang.

Patti was calling.

Her first words were: "Tell me you're safe."

"Safe, fed and in the company of armed friends. Does the Republic still stand?"

McGill heard a short, humorless laugh. "Funny you should ask. The NSA picked up a conversation in Beijing, one we're not supposed to be able to hear, that General Hu Dai, the uniformed head of China's military and an aggressive SOB, has died of heart failure."

"I take it we won't be sending a condolence card," McGill said.

"No, we won't."

"Is there any suspicion of what we gumshoes call foul play?"

"There always is with something like this. I'm likely to be up all night sorting this out with the gang in the Situation Room."

Having almost two full terms of spousal experience in the White House, McGill didn't have any trouble reading between the lines. "All that stuff is happening and you still took the time to call me? Something more than adoration of your husband is going on here."

Despite the geopolitical uproar, Patti managed to laugh.

It always made McGill feel good to lighten her load.

"Actually, my dear," she said, "that does explain a good deal of my reason to call you. A few minutes ago, the White House switchboard received a call saying the person you're looking for, the would-be assassin, can be found in a Lower Manhattan bar called The Bent Bobbie. That message was forwarded to Frank Morrissey, and he brought it to me just before I was to go to the Situation Room."

"I don't suppose this civic-minded soul left a name," McGill said.

"No."

McGill asked, "Is there any reason to think the call was credible?"

"It originated in Manhattan and the number belongs to a throw-away phone."

"Two steps in the right direction, but ..." An idea struck McGill. "Did anyone notice if the caller had a foreign accent?"

"I listened to the recording and, yes, the man sounded Greek by birth to me. Why is that important?"

"You know this by talking with Greek presidents from time to time?"

"Among other things, yes. Now, dear husband, answer my question."

"That particular nationality matches someone connected with the larger scheme."

"Jim, you know your job better than I do, but promise me that when I get out of my meeting on China I won't hear any tragic news about you. I don't think I could take that. Not when we're getting so close to the end of ... this part of our lives."

"I promise," McGill said. "We'll leave the White House hand in hand while whistling a merry tune."

"Good. We'll also have our going-away party the night before we do."

McGill said goodbye and clicked off.

Leo, glancing in his rear-view mirror, asked, "Where to, Boss?"

Looking back at Leo's reflected eyes, he said, "Lower Manhattan. Somebody find the address of a bar called The Bent Bobbie. I think that ends with an 'ie' not a 'y.'"

Then McGill called Lily Kealoha.

The NYPD detective didn't answer. McGill's call went to voicemail. He asked Lily to meet him at The Bent Bobbie and bring along a few carfuls of uniformed friends. Next, he called Clare Tracy to ask who else among New York's Finest he might reach out to for a bit of help, but again he was asked to leave a message.

McGill was left to ponder the limitations of modern communications. Sure, you could make a phone call from any point on the planet to any point on the planet — barring the increasingly rare places where there wasn't a cell tower. That certainly wasn't a problem in Manhattan. So there were only two things he could think of: In the press of searching for Chris Springer throughout all five boroughs, Lily had forgotten to recharge her phone and the battery died on her. And Clare, being someone else who wouldn't care to learn of his demise, had turned her phone off.

All that left McGill to do was flag down a passing NYPD patrol car.

Only the hoary cliché proved true: Never a cop around when you need one.

The lack of finding any official help was abetted by Leo's ultra-efficient driving. He made weaving through post-rush-hour traffic in the most densely populated urban area in the country seem like child's play. When McGill made that observation aloud, Leo flicked another glance at him in the mirror.

"Boss, when you're driving in a knot of 20 or more cars doing better than 200 MPH bumper to bumper and hitting a curve every few seconds, that's when it's tricky to find an opening. But I managed to do that for nearly ten years. I could do this with one eye closed and the other eye checking out the girls on the sidewalk."

Gene did a wolf whistle for musical accompaniment and even Deke cracked a smile.

Then they were there, on the block where the structure housing The Bent Bobbie stood, and Leo intuitively slowed the Chevy to idle speed, the better to take in all the surroundings. New York may have been the city that never slept, but this street was definitely nodding off. The lights in the bar windows were the only ones on the block that shone with electrical brightness.

Even the street lamps seemed to have been dialed down by a rheostat. Maybe the city power company was just trying to save a buck. There certainly weren't any pedestrians nearby to call for better illumination.

The four men in the car saw the two vacant lots, one on either side of the sole remaining building on the bar's side of the street. The buildings across the avenue were dark and looked like they'd soon have a date with a wrecking ball, too.

Gene said, "I don't like the feeling of this one, Sheriff."

Leo pulled the Chevy to the curb short of the bar. He scanned the road and sidewalks ahead through the lens of his windshield. He checked all his mirrors and said, "I don't see a soul, but I don't like this set-up either, Boss."

"Deke?" McGill asked.

"Cocked and locked."

A technically inaccurate description for someone using an Uzi, McGill knew. That weapon didn't work the same way as a 1911 Colt Commander, the handgun that had inspired the phrase. But Deke would never use the more accurate description that he was ready to rock 'n' roll.

"Anybody think we should just call 911?" McGill asked.

All three of the other men gave McGill scornful looks.

"Me neither," McGill replied to their silent message. "But let's make sure we all stick around to tell tall tales about whatever we do here tonight, okay?"

Deke said, "Yeah, but this time I call the play. Gene, you go around back in case anyone tries to escape that way. I'll go in the front door. Anybody hostile pops up, he's mine. Leo, you stay out here ready to make a hospital run in case anybody needs it. Everybody agree?"

Leo and Gene nodded.

"Two questions," McGill said. "What do I do and when did this become a democracy?"

"Can't have a McGill Investigations International if we lose McGill," Deke said. "What's democratic is all the hired help can all quit the company if we want, and I will."

Leo and Gene made it unanimous.

Feeling disgruntled and thwarted, McGill said, "There has to be *something* for me to do."

"Rear guard," Deke said with a straight face.

He and Gene got out of the car and carefully approached the front and back of the building.

Leaving McGill to fume in the Chevy.

Trying to ignore the voice in his head reminding him of his promise to Patti.

Jack McCown, the McGill lookalike, waited in a crawlspace above the bar's ceiling to make his move. A vent provided air to the claustrophobic niche and gave him a view of the front door and the place's floor below to the outer rim of the bar. As usual for anyone who worked in the arts, the money person had imposed an onerous condition on him that hadn't been mentioned up front.

He'd thought he might have had to hide in a closet or even a toilet stall in the men's room before he stepped out and made his dash down the block. Either of those possibilities would have been okay with him. But, no, he'd had to stand on the bar and lever himself up to the crawlspace, praying there weren't any roaches or rats in residence.

He'd lucked out on that count, but the dust of the ages up there was inches thick. The joint's janitorial service obviously didn't do crawl spaces. Lying in the filth produced urges to both cough and sneeze. Doing either, though, would have been a dead giveaway. As that thought passed through his mind it seized on the word dead.

Things weren't nearly as simple or harmless as he'd told himself they would be. "Schmuck," he muttered, "why do you think you got paid $10,000? To play some harmless joke?" Then he realized he'd better stop speaking aloud or he'd really be in trouble.

He comforted himself with the fact he'd been given the second half of his fee. He now possessed a minor windfall. Maybe he'd stage a showcase performance or maybe he could figure out a better way to raise his acting profile. Or he could just take his girlfriend Carlie on a vacation the two of them would never forget.

While lost in thought of what kind of sexual escapades might accompany such a trip, he was jolted back to reality as he saw a man openly holding a gun walk into the bar. When Jack had arrived, the bartender had shooed every drinker in the place out into the night. He pointed out where Jack was supposed to hide and told him how to get up there. Then he said, "The place is all yours buddy."

Jack had wondered if the bartender had been paid more or less than he'd receive

Now, though, he was fixated on the new arrival. The guy looked sort of Asian with maybe some African heritage mixed in. What became certain to Jack was the weapon he held was no six-shooter. It had a magazine that had to hold dozens of rounds. In Jack's mind — and in reality — that meant it was an automatic weapon.

If the guy opened fire on him, it would be like a rip saw tearing through lumber.

The thought of dying that way made Jack dizzy.

And then the urge to sneeze returned with a vengeance.

Deke stepped into The Bent Bobbie with every nerve ending in his body humming like a tuning fork. He'd been 100% correct in making Holmes — McGill's Secret Service code name — stay in the car with Leo. He had no doubt about that because the President had called him and said succinctly, “Do not let my husband die.”

That edict had been delivered shortly after the attempt to kill McGill in Georgetown.

Patricia Grant’s words fit precisely with what his mother had instructed him almost eight years ago. “You will die before you let the President’s husband die.” After all, it was a matter of preserving family honor. Deke had become alienated from his mother for other reasons, but her words still resonated with him. They were basically the same call to duty and self-sacrifice that the Secret Service had laid down for him.

He’d never doubted that he would do exactly what all the imperious voices in his life demanded: If necessary, he would give his all to save Holmes. Still, in the present moment, there was the matter of a new context to consider. Deke’s role had always been protective.

Now, he was about to step into the *investigative* arena, taking his new job with Holmes’ detective agency, and he felt, if not scared, at least ill at ease. The knowledge that he’d been assigned to manage cases in the Northeastern United States had left him wondering if his Secret Service skills were truly transferable. If he fell short, his failure would be made worse by the fact that he’d asked for the job.

Shortly after arriving in New York, though, he’d had an idea that might be wonderfully helpful: Hire someone with a successful record of being a big-city detective as his number two, and who’d know better about something like that than a detective first grade of the NYPD? Sure, it didn’t have to be Lily Kealoha but, damn, she was a fine looking woman. If she’d qualified for her pension, she’d be perfect. She could collect that money and make a good salary with him.

The life Deke had lived while working as Holmes’ personal bodyguard had been all but monastic. He’d half-*expected* to die in the line of duty, the way McGill freelanced and took risks. With the expectation that he might die any damn day, it would have been unfair to ask a woman to make a commitment to him. What could he say? "No big deal, honey, you look good in black."

Stepping *out* of the line of fire, though, he thought he might be a suitable match for the right woman. Someone who could identify with his line of work and respect what he'd been doing all these years. Appreciate that he'd also be collecting a pension on top of a good salary.

He'd probably have to work on developing a sense of humor though.

In the meantime, he'd do what was needed to stay alive. Like pay attention to his surroundings. He saw half-finished drink glasses on most of the tables in the place, and a gap-toothed row of the same sat on the bar. Somebody had cleared the place abruptly. There was no sign of blood anywhere, so the use of force had been effective but not brutal.

What could the reason be for such an exodus?

Create elbow room for setting a better trap?

The hair on the back of Deke's neck rose. He screened out all extraneous thoughts and focused on the task at hand. He made sure nobody was lying in wait behind the bar and started down a narrow hallway toward two doors marked "Blokes" and "Birds." Beyond that stood two more doors, one the rear exit, as a sign indicated and an unmarked door that might have been an office, storage room or both.

Leaving the barroom, Deke missed the trickle of dust falling from the ceiling vent.

"Leo," McGill said from the back seat of his Chevy, "am I going to have any trouble with you?"

"Not me, boss."

"You're not going to signal Deke or Gene that I'm going in?"

"I'm sure they figured you would. It was only a question of how long you'd wait."

McGill paused to think a moment. "Did the President talk to Deke? Is that why he's doing the take-charge bit?"

"Yeah."

"Did she call you, too?"

"Yeah."

"But you refused to help?"

"I told her the single way I could stop you would be to wing you with my gun. Only with the gun I use even a flesh wound might be fatal. She said never mind then."

"Practical woman." McGill reached for the door release.

"Don't get mad at anybody, Boss. I mean, how would it look letting you get killed at this point in the game? Even if you just wound up a cripple, we'd all feel real bad. The President, your kids and all the rest of us."

McGill grunted. "Nice psychological ploy for a former race car driver."

"I was thinking of saying I saved your life once already. Hate to find out that was a wasted effort."

"Sonofabitch. You got anything else?"

"Yeah. If anything bad happens to you, do I get to keep this car?"

McGill cursed again and got out of the Chevy.

Deke stepped out the back door and didn't see Gene. There was detritus aplenty behind the building left from the demolition of its former neighboring structures. The developers must have planned to tidy up only after the last of the deconstruction was finished. Even so, there was no pile of rubble big enough for a standing man to hide behind. So where the hell was —

A soft whistle, sounding remarkably bird-like, made Deke crane his neck.

Gene was three stories up, looking down over the building's parapet.

"Nothing up here," he said in a soft voice.

Gene came down a drain pipe like a simian, explanation enough of how he'd gotten to the roof in the first place.

Keeping his voice down, he told Deke, "Once I saw there was nobody on the ground back here, I thought I should check out the rest of the place. Shined the flashlight in my phone through the second and third-floor windows and —"

The two men heard the front door of the bar open. They couldn't see who had stepped inside, but they shared the same thought: McGill. If it had been anyone else, Leo would have alerted them.

"Anyway," Gene continued, "I didn't see any personnel or explosives in the building or on the roof."

Deke said, "Nobody in the bar, the bathrooms or the office in back either."

They both shrugged. Someone had jerked their chain. Maybe to see who would respond. Maybe to buy time to set up something else. In any case, there was no point wasting time hanging around.

Deke and Gene walked around the building and back to the Chevy and climbed in. McGill would discover the same dead end they had and join them shortly. He'd feel a little better about that if he was allowed to come to the same conclusion himself.

Just as Deke had, McGill thought there had been several patrons in the bar who'd been hurried out not all that long ago. Putting a hand on a glass, he'd felt the beer inside was still cool. Hardly a good business practice to chase the paying public away, but if the place was condemned maybe the poor soul who had the mournful job of closing it down for the last time had decided he'd had enough and had given everyone an early bum's rush.

Or maybe he'd decided to keep the take in the till for himself before the big boss arrived.

McGill had seen such things happen in his days as a Chicago cop.

Venal opportunism was probably the same in New York.

He checked the room and the area behind the bar. Knowing Deke had already cleared the area for assassins, and must be out back with Gene by now, he stopped and opened the cash register. As he suspected, it was empty, except for the penny tray.

He went down the hall to check out the other rooms in the place and see if his guys had missed anything he might find.

It would serve them right if he could rub their noses in an oversight.

Jack McCown had to bite back a "Holy shit!" when he saw who entered the tavern next. If there was one guy in the world besides Rory Calhoun to whom he was regularly compared, it was James J. McGill. The freaking President's husband. If the weirdo who'd given him the ten grand had …

Oh shit, he prayed he hadn't been set up by a terrorist to do something awful.

Maybe even play the part of some kind of Lee Harvey Oswald-type patsy.

He had to get the hell out of there as soon as he could.

That damn weirdo had wanted him to run fast?

Man, he'd be setting new world records.

McGill went through every room in the place and out the back door.

It became immediately apparent that Deke and Gene had left him behind.

To his regret, he'd hadn't found anything his guys had missed.

Then, at the front of the bar, he heard someone sneeze.

A moment later a car engine roared.

"Jesus, was that the boss?" Leo asked, turning to Deke. A guy had just burst from the bar's front door and veered right. "He's running like his ass is on fire and he needs to find a river fast."

Deke said, "I only caught a glimpse, but I think it was."

Leaning over the seat back, Gene made it unanimous, "Me, too."

That was good enough for Leo. He floored the gas pedal. The engine roared its approval. They'd catch up with the runner fast, but, damn, the guy had already turned a corner of the block.

Being guys, none of them had noticed the fleeing figure wasn't wearing the same clothes McGill had worn and he was covered in dust.

Leo said, "Hope he doesn't duck into some building. It'd look real bad if we lost him."

As McGill reached the front door of the bar, a black Chevy screeched to a stop in front of him. Understandably, he thought it was his. He yanked the rear door open, piled inside and pulled the door closed. The moment it shut, he realized something wasn't right.

His car was armored. That meant the doors felt a *lot* heavier than those of a normal vehicle. You could get a decent upper-body workout just opening and closing one of his car's doors several times a day. The person behind the wheel looked like Leo — right down to the curly brown hair and early Elvis sideburns — from behind. But when McGill looked in the rear view mirror, he didn't see Leo's eyes looking back.

He saw Chris Springer — and he knew what was coming next. A Beretta M9 poked its nose over her seat back. She might have had him if she'd fired straight through the seat's upholstery, but McGill, getting older or not, still had cat-quick reflexes.

He thrust himself forward, grabbed Springer's right wrist with his left hand and seized the weapon's barrel in his right hand. He put his shoulder and hip into twisting the weapon upward while turning his head to the right. A shot went off and took a slice from McGill's right ear lobe. Springer was the one who shrieked in pain, though. The gun disarm McGill had executed broke her trigger finger and now he had the weapon.

Not for long, though. Springer stomped the gas pedal and the Chevy shot forward. Then she slammed on the brakes. Her three-point seat belt held her in place. The unsecured McGill, meanwhile, shot forward into the front seat area, his head and left shoulder colliding with the dashboard. He lost his grip on the gun and saw stars.

He had little time to gather his wits. Springer didn't make any effort to reclaim the gun; she now held a black-bladed combat knife with a razor sharp cutting edge. One swipe of the major blood vessels in McGill's neck with that weapon and death would be swift. McGill did the only thing he could in that moment.

He pressed his chin to his chest, sacrificing his jaw line. The pain of the blade slicing skin and grating on bone seared his mind, but the adrenaline the wound produced cleared his mind. He grabbed Springer's forearm with both hands and got back to basics. He bit her arm as hard as he could. Even through the thin material of the jacket she was wearing, he could feel flesh split.

Springer shrieked in agony, but to McGill's dismay she didn't pass out from the pain. McGill anticipated her next move, having seen it once already. She hit the gas, even though she didn't have either hand on the steering wheel. She'd try to brace herself before hitting the brakes, but McGill threw a wrench in her plans when he popped her seatbelt from its anchor.

She felt the seatbelt's tension slacken a heartbeat before she brought the car to a screeching halt, too late to brace herself with her free arm. She shot forward, slamming her chest into the steering wheel. The collision set off the airbag which slammed her back in the seat.

McGill had braced himself against the seat back. His neck, shoulders and back absorbed the pressure of the sudden stop. With this jolt added to his already traumatized body, it felt like the muscles involved had been set ablaze. Still, as the car crept forward at idle speed, he was able to lean forward, shift the transmission into neutral and turn the engine off.

He sat back in the rear seat and took a deep breath as the car rolled to a stop.

That was when he heard a low angry growl. For a second, he feared there was an animal in the car and an inter-species struggle was about to begin. Then he realized the sound was coming from Springer. He'd thought the air-bag had knocked her unconscious but …

Who the hell knew if she had yet another weapon?

McGill leaned forward and wrapped his left arm around her throat. He locked it in place by putting his right hand around his left wrist. He knew the human throat had the tensile strength of a Dixie cup. He could have ended Chris Springer's life that very moment.

Instead, he whispered into her ear, "What the hell is wrong with you?"

Springer understood her jeopardy. Still, she hissed, "Go ahead, kill me."

For one sickening instant, McGill felt he should do exactly that. Snuff this creature out like the toxic candle she was. Only his conversation with Cardinal Fitzroy chose that moment to come to mind. If McGill took Springer's life, he didn't think either he or his Maker would be smiling when they met.

Even so, he felt it was more likely than not that if he didn't kill her she'd come back at him yet again. She might be serving a life sentence without parole and try to plan a hit from her prison cell the way Auric Ludwig had. The cycle had to stop. If he gave the madmen, women and those in between enough chances to kill him, one of them would eventually succeed.

McGill's arm began to tighten. It would be *so* easy to finish Springer now.

Then Patti's words saved him.

He recalled the vengeance she'd promised to wreak if somebody managed to kill him. With his arm still tight against Springer's throat he leaned close and said in a flat voice, "My wife told me just the other day that if someone killed me, she would even the score and then some. She won't be President much longer but she'll still have the means and the will. Nothing else will matter to her until her retribution is complete.

"I was shocked to hear this, but now I find it a comfort. Here's how I can see things working if you were her target. She wouldn't only have you killed, she'd have both of your sisters killed, first one and then the other, so you could suffer from their deaths before you met your own, and believe me ,your death wouldn't be easy."

Springer gave McGill the response he'd hoped for: She tried to pull free. She believed him. But there was no escape. Her exertion only increased the pressure on her throat and made her gag. She settled back and McGill felt tears that fell from her eyes.

He loosened his hold on her ever so slightly. "Tell me you know I'm telling you the truth."

She managed a tiny nod.

He said, "You know, if it was only me you'd tried to kill, I just might be crazy enough to let you go. But the way I see things now, you're as responsible as I am for Paulette Lacroix's death."

McGill had to maintain his choke hold on her for only another minute.

Then, Leo, Deke and Gene returned.

Bringing two NYPD patrol cars with them.

CHAPTER 10

McGill Investigations International, LLP
Washington, DC, Friday, September 23, 2016

McGill's ear and jawline were bandaged as he took his place at the head of the table in the conference room. All of the partners entered the room after him. All of them eyed the damage he'd suffered in his fight with Chris Springer. Nobody commented as they took their seats, except for Odo Sacripant.

The Corsican shook McGill's hand and nodded in approval.

"You have always been a handsome man. Now, you have added a bit of character to your face. I'm sure *Madame la Présidente* will love you all the more for it."

The truth was, Patti had gone ghostly white when she first saw McGill, via FaceTime, after he'd been treated in the emergency room at New York-Presbyterian Hospital. After McGill had told her he'd ducked both a gunshot and a knife, she began to weep.

"Goddamnit, Jim, that's going to give me nightmares."

McGill promised to hold and comfort her anytime she needed.

He said he'd be home soon, and told Patti to concentrate on saving the world.

Now, with everyone in his new company seated at the table and looking his way, he said, "Thank you, all of you, for helping me to get through this. It was a near thing, but I made it. We all did."

Smiles, raised fists, a whistle from Gene Beck and a round of applause answered him.

Tough guy McGill had to fight back tears.

Something he'd been unable to do when Patti and his kids had swarmed him the day before.

"Okay, okay," he said when he felt things had gone on long enough. "We've got a business to get off the ground here. The publicity the firm has garnered the past couple of days from what happened in New York should give us a running start. But there's one more item of business we need to settle first."

The partners gave McGill their full attention.

"If something unfortunate were to happen to me," he said, "I propose here and now that we all agree the company's next managing partner will be Margaret Sweeney."

Sweetie started to speak but McGill cut her off with an upraised hand.

"Margaret saved the company from going under when it was a one-man shop. I'd probably have spent the past eight years cutting ribbons and running the White House Easter Egg Roll without her."

Everyone laughed politely, not believing McGill for a minute, but getting his point.

"All in favor of having Margaret Sweeney as my successor to be managing partner in the event of my demise, incapacitation or simple job fatigue, say aye," McGill said.

The vote was unanimous.

Sweetie bowed her head in humility and then asked McGill, "If I take over, can I change the company name to Sweeney Investigations International?"

McGill said, "No."

CHAPTER 11

La Cruz, Costa Rica, Friday, September 30, 2016

After a week of prayer, contemplation and working his family's fields until he was ready to drop, Father Inigo de Loyola finally found the will to phone the Vatican. His call was put through immediately. It seemed his old friend truly was anxious to hear from him.

"Francesco, it is me your grievously flawed servant, Inigo."

"Flawed or not, Inigo, you are my brother and I love you. After all, how many Costa Ricans are enlightened enough to root for San Lorenzo?"

The Pope's favorite football, a.k.a. soccer, team in Argentina.

Father de Loyola said, "Maybe I was only trying to curry favor, Francesco."

The Pope laughed. "I would not put that past a Jesuit, being one myself. But I know better, Inigo. You wear your true feelings like a calling card. At this moment, I have no trouble hearing how heavy your heart is. How may I help you, my brother?"

"Francesco, I set one predator upon another. I have sinned."

After a moment's silence, the Pope said, "Is anyone else on this line?"

"No."

"Very well. I will hear your confession, and then I will ask you my favor."

"Anything you wish, Francesco, I will do."

"*Gracias.* Father Inigo de Loyola, I would like you to become my confessor."

Trying to hide his surprise, de Loyola asked, "You will be moving your papacy to Costa Rica?"

"No, Inigo, you will be coming to Rome."

"Will you teach me to fight evil without becoming evil?"

"I will do my best. So you will come?"

"Of course. We will talk football and keep each other honest. But now I must explain what I have done and beg forgiveness."

CHAPTER 12

USP Hazelton — West Virginia, Saturday, October 1, 2016

Jerry Nerón got his tailoring workspace, a 10x15 room just off the prison laundry. It lacked any semblance of charm, but it was clean and had two windows, one to the east, one to the south, to provide natural light. *Mami y Papi* had supplied Jerry with all of his old tailoring tools, several of which had sharp edges and points. That meant Jerry had to be constantly watched by some of the smartest and toughest members of the corrections staff. The warden had warned Jerry if he ever tried to smuggle any cutting or stabbing implement out of the workroom, his tailoring days would be over, permanently.

Jerry accepted that and all the other conditions imposed upon him. The only concession he asked for was some type of music player so he wouldn't have to listen to laundry machines while he went about his art. The warden found an old boom-box at a neighbor's garage sale for him. Jerry had to reimburse the warden $12 for it and 50¢ for every CD the warden had been able to find from a list Jerry had provided.

Jerry could afford the toll because he was now earning $1.15 per hour, top of the federal prisoner pay scale.

When he felt the worsted Italian wool that he would transform into Gianni Mancuso's wedding tuxedo, he sighed in pleasure. Even if he never again knew the pleasure of a woman's touch, he would find tactile comfort in holding, cutting and sewing fine fabric.

After the Mancuso tux was finished, the warden's suit would come next.

Inmates laboring in the laundry frequently peeked in to watch Jerry do his thing.

After all, how often did you get to see someone work magic in a prison?

CHAPTER 13

Washington, DC, Monday, October 17, 2016

Two further confessions became the October Surprises that rocked the American presidential election. Trying desperately to come back from cratering poll numbers in the wake of Frank Morrissey's "The closer we listen, the phonier you sound" campaign against Oren Worth, the Senate Majority Leader claimed that Vice President Jean Morrissey's marriage to Byron DeWitt was a union of political convenience and nothing more.

Worth asserted that the Vice President had to find a husband fast because nobody in his right mind would ever elect a single woman to be president. He'd even considered making the same marriage of convenience claim against Patricia Grant, but he decided not to risk incurring a public beating from James J. McGill.

As it was, Byron DeWitt, though still recovering from his stroke, promised to thrash Worth once he returned to fighting form. Jean Morrissey said she would do the honors on national television if Worth repeated the claim in her presence. Worth used the threat as his reason to steer clear of the Vice President, badly misreading what that would do to his image of manliness or lack thereof.

A campaign manager might have advised against making the baseless claim Worth had made, but after Layla Dart had bailed out on him, Worth had decided to run his own campaign.

The decisive campaign moment, though, came on the October Monday when Ellie Booker and Didi DiMarco, back from their respective sabbaticals, tag-teamed to do TV interviews with Worth's two ex-wives. Both of them claimed that the Majority Leader was bisexual with a decidedly smaller emphasis on the feminine half of the equation.

That sexual orientation might have passed muster on the Democratic side of the electorate if it had been evinced publicly from the start, but it didn't work at all for the Republican voters. Their turnout on Election Day was the lowest in 100 years when the country's population had been less than one-third of its current number.

Jean Morrissey, running on the Cool Blue ticket, became the nation's second female president. Neither Ellie Booker nor Didi DiMarco ever revealed that they had gotten their interviews with Oren Worth's reclusive former wives through the machinations of …

Galia Mindel, who may have been out of the White House but hadn't lost a step.

CHAPTER 14

The White House — Washington, DC
Thursday, January 19, 2017

The gang at the White House didn't party all night, but they came close. Few bars in town could match the selections of wine, whiskey, brandy and beer that were on hand. Despite all the alcohol, nobody got nasty, maudlin or falling-down drunk. They were too busy having a good time: talking, laughing, dancing and promising to stay in touch, work together and confound their political enemies.

All the senior White House staff and members of the President's Cabinet and their spouses were there. Pausing the music, the President called for everyone's attention and then introduced SAC Elspeth Kendry. Patricia Grant asked for and received an ovation to honor the Secret Service for keeping her and The First Family safe for the past eight years.

She followed that by honoring Dr. Artemis Nicolaides for keeping a close eye on her daily health, and more especially for getting a certain henchman to understand that he was not, in fact, immortal and needed regular check-ups. Everyone laughed at McGill's expense, which he took in good humor.

The president next presented Edwina Byington and Gawayne Blessing.

She told the President-elect, "Jean, you're going to need a great personal secretary and a splendid head butler to keep things running smoothly around here, but you can't have mine. Edwina and Blessing are coming with me."

She kissed each of them on a cheek. Edwina beamed. Blessing blushed deeply.

Galia had asked to remain out of the spotlight, and that request was granted.

McGill had no such luck. The President extended a hand and said, "James J. McGill, would you be so kind to as to join me?"

McGill got up from the table where he'd been sitting with his children, Carolyn, Lars, Sweetie, Putnam and Maxi. As soon as the President's Henchman was upright, a round of applause began. McGill decided he couldn't have that. He went up on tiptoe, pranced forward and did a pirouette. He curtsied to his wife and stood next to her.

He had the room in stitches by then. Always better to have people laughing than to think you were somebody special. That was a notion the President completely rejected.

She kissed McGill in front of everyone, and not on the cheek.

He had the good manners and the wit not to make fun of that.

Patricia Grant took her husband's arm and said, "I wouldn't be here tonight, none of us would if it wasn't for Jim. The truth is, he and I didn't get along at all the first time we met. I was horrible to him. But he saved me from the darkest moment of my life. I was mourning the loss of my first great love, Andy Grant. I went to the cemetery soon after Andy was killed, hoping for some symbolic moment of both closeness and closure. Before I could reach the gravesite, I saw Jim was already there. He was down on his knees. He was praying. Tears streamed down his face. All this was after he'd helped to catch Andy's killer."

McGill was visibly moved by the memory.

Patti continued, "As shattered as my heart was, in that moment I felt healing begin. When I felt bold enough to visit Jim's house unannounced, I was welcomed warmly and privileged to meet his three wonderful children, Abbie, Ken and Caitie." The President choked up, "In the years since, besides finding a second soulmate, I … I received the unimaginable gift of becoming a second mother to the McGill children. Thank you, Carolyn. Thank you, Lars. Thank you, Abbie, Ken and Caitie. Thank you, Jim." She kissed him again.

McGill put an arm around his wife and this time he let the applause continue.

When it finally died down, she added, "That's all I have to say."

McGill shook his head and told Patti and the room, "Oh, no, my good woman. You don't get away that easily."

Cheers and whistles filled the air. There had to be a surprise coming, everyone felt, and they couldn't wait to find out what it was.

McGill told them. "Some time ago, I had my official portrait painted as the henchman to this beautiful woman. She was supposed to have hers done long ago, but what with one thing and another it never got done — not under her auspices anyway."

That was the only hint anyone needed. They knew what was coming now and they cheered.

McGill put up a hand to calm things down.

"Working quietly with the official White House photographer and favored news organizations, I collected and curated my favorite 20 likenesses of Patricia Darden Grant. Then I turned them over to one of the gumshoes working in my Paris office. She also just happens to be an honors graduate of the School of the Art Institute of Chicago and an amazing portraitist, and now we're all about to see what she has wrought. Ladies and gentlemen, Gabbi Casale."

Gabbi appeared to a rousing ovation. She pushed a rolling easel on which rested a draped oil painting. Everybody in the room adjusted their positions to get a good look. Gabbi kissed her patron and the President on both cheeks and then went to stand on the opposite side of the easel.

McGill said, "Any time you're ready, Ms. Casale."

She nodded and dropped the cloth.

The reaction was instantaneous. Oohs and aahs, cries of delight and then waves of applause. It was far from a glamour pose, though. The likeness was taken from a photo of a working moment: Patricia Grant's first State of the Union message to Congress and the American people. Her hair shone, her eyes were clear, bright and full of purpose, her features were crisp and unlined and her mouth was slightly opened to deliver a message of hope and unity. Her right hand was raised and her index finger pointed upward, the intended direction of her leadership.

Gabbi got a warm embrace of approval from the President and a few whispered words.

Then McGill hugged Gabbi and told her, "If Yousuf Karsh had worked in oils …"

He gestured to her painting.

Among the multitude of other perks that came with living in the White House, when you threw a party you didn't have to clean up afterward.

As they lay snuggled together in bed at the country's most famous address for a final time, McGill asked Patti, "Are you ready to let all this go?"

Patti nodded and said, "I am. What about you?"

McGill said, "Me, too."

CHAPTER 15

West Front United States Capitol — Washington, DC
Friday, January 20, 2017

Byron DeWitt stood unaided next to the President-elect. He held the Morrissey Family Bible, printed in Ireland and brought through Ellis Island by Desmond Morrissey more than a century earlier. Barely noticeable beneath the bible was a far slimmer volume wearing a plain brown wrapper. It was *two* centuries old and printed in the original Chinese. Sun Tzu's *The Art of War*. Required reading for any President who wished to be successful.

It had been a wedding gift to DeWitt from Hiram Chen, his mentor on all things Chinese. DeWitt had decided if Jim McGill could be his wife's henchman, then the former FBI Deputy Director could be Jean Morrissey's *cōngmíng rén*. Wise man. Probably wise *guy* more often than not. The President-elect placed her hand lightly on the Bible.

Following the lead of Chief Justice Craig MacLaren, and with most of the country and a good part of the world watching, Jean Morrissey spoke her oath of office. "I, Jean Marie Morrissey, do solemnly swear that I will faithfully execute the Office of President of the United States, and will to the best of my ability, preserve, protect and defend the Constitution of the United States."

Frank Morrissey had tears in his eyes. After the new President shook hands with the Chief Justice and kissed her husband, Frank stepped forward and kissed his sister. He also whispered in her ear, "You just watch, Sis, we're going to do great things, even if we have to drag the bastards to it kicking and screaming."

Jean laughed and said, "You bet."

The new President turned and embraced Patricia Grant.

"Will I be able to call on you for advice?"

"Any time," the former President said.

Standing next to her, McGill added, "Bearing in mind that we're getting old and turn in early."

He got a big presidential hug, too, and a quiet message. "If there's ever anything that needs looking into that isn't right for the government to do, I'll be calling you, too."

McGill thought about that for a second.

Then he replied softly, "Probably be good to use Galia as a cut-out."

"And Frank, too."

Jean was no fool, and now she had a wise man at home.

Moments later, McGill and Patti boarded the Marine helicopter that used to be known as Marine One. But that call sign was reserved solely for the President, not any of her predecessors.

"What do they call this bird now?" McGill asked Patti.

"Transportation."

The former First Couple watched the White House, the Capitol and the city's parade of monuments fall behind them as they made the short hop to Joint Base Andrews. In the past, the outgoing chief executive and spouse boarded their former presidential Boeing 747, also now known by an obscure call sign, and jetted off to their home state. That wasn't the case this time.

Patti Grant had decided to save the taxpayers money and make a fashion statement.

A gleaming new Gulfstream G650 ER awaited her and McGill. The plane could carry 19 and sleep ten comfortably. Besides the pilots, there were two Secret Service agents and a male cabin attendant aboard, and so was Patti's new security chief, Celsus Crogher.

He looked at his watch as if to tell Patti and McGill they were late.

Instead, he said, “The captain and the co-pilot don’t have a flight plan.”

Patti just grinned and walked forward to the cockpit.

Celsus gave McGill a critical look and said, “Don’t *you* know where we’re going?”

McGill shrugged. “No, Celsus, I don’t. Whatever happens next is a surprise.”

ABOUT THE AUTHOR

Joseph Flynn has been published both traditionally — Signet Books, Bantam Books and Variance Publishing — and through his own imprint, Stray Dog Press, Inc. Both major media reviews and reader reviews have praised his work. Booklist said, "Flynn is an excellent storyteller." The Chicago Tribune said, "Flynn [is] a master of high-octane plotting." The most repeated reader comment is: Write faster, we want more.

You may read free excerpts of Joe's books by visiting his website at: *www.josephflynn.com*.

www.ingramcontent.com/pod-product-compliance
Lightning Source LLC
Chambersburg PA
CBHW071219250626
47163CB00001B/37

9780997450026